# IN HITLER'S HOUSE

THE MEMOIR OF WILLIAM WEBER: A STORY OF ESPIONAGE AND STOLEN LOVE

JONATHAN WHITE LANE

Jonathan White Lane /Bookster, Inc.

20748 Stone Oak Parkway, Suite 107

San Antonio, TX, 78209

www.booksterbooks.com

Publisher's Note: This is a work of fiction. Except for historical figures now deceased and events and locales in the historical record, names, characters, places, and incidents are a product of the author's imagination. Ordering Information:

Quantity sales. Special discounts are available on quantity purchases. Email Booksterbooks@xemaps.com

In Hitler's House Book Two / Jonathan White Lane. 1st ed.

eBook ISBN 978-0-9742865-4-9

Paperback ISBN 978-0-9858131-7-6

❀ Created with Vellum

# BOOK TWO 1939-1945

## UNREAL

"Cracks and reforms and burst in the violet air
Falling towers
Jerusalem Athens Alexandria
Vienna London
Unreal"

T.S. Eliot, "The Waste Land"

*This book is dedicated to my beloved wife Carlotta Krause Weber, and to my friend Sir Paul Dukes. Their unparalleled courage and their work in the service of freedom is hidden from history, but not from memory, and not from my heart.*

*--William Weber*

# ACKNOWLEDGMENTS

I would like to thank the great historians of World War II and the biographers of Adolf Hitler, most especially William Shirer and Joachim C. Fest, whose work I used to freshen my memory of many of the incidents recounted in this book.

Where my memory differed from their accounts, I chose to relate events as I remembered them, not as they have entered history. If this offends or sows confusion, I can only apologize.

I would also like to thank my secretary, Linda Forbes and my editor at Grosset and Dunlap's, Charles Gottlieb, both of whom have the patience of saints.

Any errors in this text result from the fragility of memory and are exclusively my own responsibility.

# 1

Adolf Hitler's special train, the *Sonderzug Amerika*, sped through the night, penetrating deep into Poland. It was now the October 4, 1939, and he had his war at last. He had been possessed to visit the front from the moment the first reports of success came in. The *Wehrmacht* was untried and the populace of the Reich had greeted the commencement of hostilities with what Hitler considered reserve bordering on disloyalty. The fear was that the soldiers wouldn't fight well, and if they didn't the battle would become bloody and the loyalty of the *volk* might be lost.

His train was one of three official specials. The other two were the *Sonderzug Heinrich*, Himmler's train, and the *Sonderzug Goering*. They traveled together, each pulled by two fuming *Deutsches Bahn* K5E locomotives, which made them extremely fast. Even though the Polish Air Force was supposedly destroyed, all three trains carried flak batteries concealed in freight cars just behind the engines.

These trains were essentially the German government in a mobile state. When they were running, they remained in communication with Berlin via telegraph and encrypted radio. At stops, the post was brought and the telephones were connected into the OKW's communications system.

Hitler continued to be extremely careful to keep me absolutely out of the public eye and as much as possible away from his subordinates, but he also wanted me with him.

The previous day, France and England had declared war on the Reich, and now we were glued to the 700 watt shortwave radio, attempting to pick up broadcasts from the United States. Hitler was terrified that Roosevelt would join them, as I secretly hoped and trusted that he would.

I had intentionally given Hitler advice designed to encourage him to invade Poland. My expectation was that France and Britain would then attack him from the rear, but so far nothing was happening. If the United States came in, I felt sure that they would finally show some aggression. The collapse of his malignant government would be sure to follow.

It was just past midnight on the train and we were analyzing Roosevelt's Fireside Chat of the day before. Hitler, who was used to lying publicly about his motives, expected others to do the same.

He didn't understand what I knew, and certainly didn't know how very disheartening that speech had been to me. When the President of the United States speaks, he is to be taken at his word. He means what he says. So, to my shock and horror, I had realized what his words meant: he had no intention of entering the European war.

At Hitler's insistence, I had translated the speech as it was read out by the president, relying on Hitler's secretary, Frau Christian, who was a shorthand expert, to transcribe. Toward the end of the war, I also began a translation of her memoirs, but unfortunately lost track of the manuscript. I believe it was burned in the bombing of the Berghof, or perhaps stolen in the looting. It was quite long and detailed, and if it's ever found, it will be of significant historical value, I would think.

As a matter of fact, Hitler had kept a diary there, working on it regularly every few days. Toward the end of the war, it was lost in a plane crash. He was bitterly disappointed. I was, too. It would have been a remarkable indictment, and put to rest forever the lie that there was no holocaust, and the equally pernicious one that he wasn't directly involved.

He devised the plan. He chose Xyklon, an insecticide gas, as the primary means of murder because he liked to think of the Jews as insects.

"Look here," he said, "he says he's committed to keeping war from the western hemisphere. Is he really saying that he's going to support the English and the French, Willy? Is that what's behind this?"

What had happened when the Doughboys had arrived in France in 1917 was never far from Hitler's mind.

"I think his more important statement is 'This nation will remain a neutral nation.'"

"If he's lying?"

"That's not very common among presidents."

"You're a naïve fool! All politicians lie. You can't do politics without lying. If they come in, we're ruined! They'll send tanks and planes and bombs, Boy! You don't know what it's like to be up against them. I do, I lived through it, remember. Look here, 'Even a neutral cannot be asked to close his mind or close his conscience.' That's pure belligerence, Willy."

We were alone together in the *Fuhrerwagen*, which had a sitting room, an office, two bedrooms, a room for the valet, a dining room and a bath. The train itself was a buzzing hive of activity, but not this car. People entered carefully and spoke quietly in the *Fuhrerwagen*. Here, only Hitler shouted.

He stared at the drawn shade of the window beside him. After dark, the train was blacked out because of the danger of snipers in the woods through which we were racing.

"Roosevelt won't come in."

"Oh, shut up. I'm sick of you. You're the one who told me England and France wouldn't fight. You're nothing but a naïve idiot."

"They won't fight."

"They declared war! They're massing opposite the Saarland right now."

It was true enough, I couldn't deny it. I concealed my elation behind a somber mask.

"I think I told you that I saw the *poilus* when I was there last year. They're not ready."

"It's the largest army in Europe."

"And they will stay behind their fortifications. The Maginot."

"And come after us right through Belgium! Thirty divisions are moving, Willy. You said they wouldn't do it. You're a lying bastard. I forget you're an American. Shit! I should have listened to Heinrich when he said to shoot you!"

"You never told me that," I said, trying to keep the horror out of my voice. How close had I been then? How close was I now?

"Willy! Willy! Come—" He stood up despite the swaying of the train and threw his arms open. As was happening more and more often, we embraced. Good. I let myself sink into it. When I did, though, he broke away. He paced up and down the small room.

"I'm so agitated. You cannot imagine! I never thought they'd declare. And now it's like being completely at sea. What will Roosevelt do? What happens if thirty French divisions cross the border? You know what I have in opposition? Seven! Merely that!"

I might add that I'd known that there were some there. I'd found out on my way across the border. I'd intentionally misinformed Paul, hoping that the idea of a simple walk-in would encourage the French to act.

"You've got how many divisions in reserve over here—no, don't tell me. But you aren't going to need that reserve, are you?"

"There's been some heavy fighting."

"I thought we were annihilating them."

"Goebbels! That jackass! Our news is a crock of shit. Listen to the BBC."

"The BBC talks about evacuations all over Poland."

"Thirty divisions invading me in the west! Roosevelt about to get mixed up in it! Every single fucking adviser a liar! A liar! And you—you worthless little prick. Ha! Smooth as silk, you are. My Willy, just like me. We belong in top hats and tails, you and me, wicked dancing men that we are."

"The French will not come and without them the English can't. And Roosevelt said that he's going to remain neutral and he will."

"Oh, shit, I'm going crazy, my heart's going berserk."

"Now just calm down, I'm telling you the truth."

"It's overspeeding, I'm dizzy. For fuck's sake get the doctor in here!" Leaning far back in a chair, he closed his eyes. "Waves of bombers...they'll level everything, I can see it now. Oh, fuck! All I wanted was the goddamn corridor and now I'm going to have the whole miserable country on my hands. What do we do with Poland?"

"Farm it."

His eyes met mine. "You understand."

"As I told you, I've read *Mein Kampf* carefully."

"And you approve?"

"Are you going to kill the entire country? All the Poles?"

"Why would you imagine me capable of such a thing?" He grabbed the phone and shouted into it, "Get Morrell in here!" He slammed it down. "I mustn't die now, not right at the start."

"Nor at all."

"I'm sorry I burst out like that. Heinie never told me to shoot you and I would never do it." He took my hand and held it to his cheek. Tears came popping out of his eyes, the actor at work. The real man, the monster, had revealed himself to me a few moments ago, and I would never forget it.

Morrell came blustering in. He wore a black smoking jacket decorated with some sort oriental writing and carried a physician's valise. He turned to me. "What's going on, Herr Weber?"

"He's nervous."

"Yes, that's right, ask him, not me. I'm the damn patient, you ass!"

Morrell gave me the slightest of winks. "Very well, Herr Hitler, let's get you to bed then. Valet! Where is that man?" It was now after one.

I said, "He asked two hours ago if he could be relieved. He's sleeping."

"All right, then you help, Herr Weber. Come on, Wolf."

Morrell was in no condition himself to assist Hitler through to the bedroom, so I did it. I got his tunic off—he had started wearing an undecorated uniform as soon as the war began—then helped him with his shoes.

Morrell injected him with something.

After a moment he threw himself onto the bed. "Oh, my, that's better. Far better. You're a genius as always, Morrell."

I wondered what he'd given him but I thought it better not to ask. Some soporific, immediately effective. Powerful, too.

"Willy, I'm falling asleep. Where's that damned Krause! KRAUSE!"

The supposedly off-duty valet came rushing in. He was in his altogethers and looked like an agitated crane with his bobbing head and awkward, prancing step. But he got things expertly in hand and soon Hitler was wearing his favorite blue pajamas and tucked into bed.

I said to him and Morrell, *"Schnapps?"*

"Oh," Morrell said, "yes, please."

Back in the living room, Krause asked if something had gone wrong.

"He's having night fears," Morrell intoned. "Very common for one under pressure, and he is certainly that. I've given him a calmative and a soporific."

"He's got to be up at six."

"You could have thought to tell me that, Krause."

The valet spread his hands, then grabbed the bottle I was just opening and chugged a great gulp of the strong liquor. "I had no chance."

"Well, it's all right. I'll wake him up with amphetamine. He'll dash around like a lunatic, but it's Hitler, right? Nobody will be in the least surprised."

Morrell is always portrayed as a sinister incompetent, but he was actually extremely knowledgeable about his potions and had a passable sense of humor, although with a heavily ironic cast to it. But I like heavily ironic humor, being a heavily ironic German myself. Eva was right about him being dirty, though. He never washed. I would never have taken one of his "special" injections. Most of them were just ordinary dope, but the special ones were black stuff, some of them, others brown and green. They smelled awful, like the sweat of a pig or something. Someday somebody should try to find out what the hell he was shooting into Hitler's veins every day, and see if it was slow poison. I don't think Morrell cared a damn for Hitler. Hitler certainly treated him like a dog.

Morrell's early career is lost in the murk of the Weimar years. I think that he sold knockout drops and such to whores and their alphonses. Poisons, too, probably. Whatever he got up to, it had taught him a lot about the human body and how it reacts to certain chemicals and preparations, in particular ones made from animal carcasses.

I was done in myself, and covered with the thin, oily film of coal smoke that penetrated all the trains of the past, even the most elegant. I well remember my first ride in a train pulled by a diesel. Not a bit of smoke anywhere. Wonderful.

"I'm going to have a bath," I said. "Then I'm turning in."

As I left, I heard Morrell exclaim, "He's bathing in *here*?"

"Of course," Krause replied with a sneer in his voice. "He's the *Hitlerficker*, you know. He'll probably whomp one up him before he goes to sleep."

I stopped. I returned. "I have good ears, Krause."

"I don't care what you have."

"You will find that you do." With that, I walked off. Little did I know that there would be an incident a few days later that would lead to Krause being fired. Nothing to do with me, but that's certainly not what he thought, and it made the other servants far more deferential to me than they had been. Even so, I was becoming more and more aware that they thought me their boss's homosexual lover and despised me for it.

I slept a black sleep, typical of my wartime years. I've never been much of a dreamer. I did imagine, though, the dreams of others in the vast suffering that filled the nights of Europe. Ever since those years, I have always marveled at why it is that the most civilized and cultured portion of humanity, the Europeans, would also be the most violent. The continent is peaceful enough now, with the European Economic Community becoming more influential. One must hope, though, that another lunatic will never come to govern any of these intricate, overcrowded, and powerful states.

I had set my little travel clock to buzz me awake at six. When I awoke, I dragged myself into the bathroom and found Hitler already there, busy with his shaving ritual, which involved the use of two razors.

"'Morning, Son."

"'Morning."

"Still mad at me?"

"Still mad at me?"

He laughed a bit. He didn't seem particularly wired up. I asked him if Morrell had awakened him.

"Not at all. I woke as soon as light started seeping in under the shade."

He was in his drawers—we both were—and now brushing his teeth.

"Why don't you use two toothbrushes, too?"

"Did anyone ever tell you your sense of humor is sadly lacking."

"Yes, you. But only when I'm being funny."

He finished and spat. For a few minutes, his breath wouldn't be bad, but if you were in a small room with him for any length of time, you knew that nothing would quiet the gas. Morrell had prescribed some sort of pill, but all it did was make it smell like charcoal instead of sulphur.

His breath was capable of knocking a dromedary unconscious, his gas could have lit a city and his body smelt of overheated tires. Nothing he did changed any of it for long. He used to gargle with a dilution of peroxide, which only added a chemical note to the odor on his breath. The result of his soaking in scented salts made even those of us used to him quite frantic, a perfumed stench being particularly hard to bear. And as for the gas, I always wondered why he wasn't more uneasy around open flames.

"Willy, Krause has a uniform for you. Wear it whenever we are in public view, but keep out of sight as much as you can. British Intelligence will be taking photos, you may be sure. I don't want them trying to match your face."

I went into my bedroom and found laid out on the coverlet a uniform of the German University Students' League, the NSDStB. Never mind the German word, it's miles long. It was certainly innocuous enough—what intelligence service would care a tinker's damn about some student, not even a combatant?

I heard Hitler call to Krause, "Fachinger Water!" He wouldn't drink any water drawn from Polish sources out of fear that it might be poisoned.

After we were dressed, I encountered him in the living room.

"Where am I to go?"

"What's going to happen, Willy, is that a Colonel of the *Wehrmacht* is going to meet you and take you on a tour of his brigade's action area. I want you to take a close look at everything, converse with the men, then come back to me with your impressions." And also stay out of range of any cameras, I assumed. But I didn't care. It sounded far more interesting than following him around peering into bomb craters.

He picked up a sheaf of papers. "Here, an intelligence report from the west. The French are ready to move but they're simply standing pat. Not a peep out of them." He clapped me on the shoulder, then went into the dining room. I followed and we sat together for the Hitler breakfast, the zwiebacks, the marmalade, the chamomile.

"You may see some action," he said. "What do you think of that?"

"I should be a soldier."

"I know how you feel. But who would get me my minerals, my gold?"

"If I see action, I'll welcome it."

He wiped his lips and got up. "I would, too, but we must both stay well out of danger. Our lives are more important than those of the common soldier."

That is an exact quote.

"Stay back," he said as he got off the train to a sparkle of flashbulbs and a great eruption of heils.

Soon after, I followed onto the platform. It was a simple little station in an unutterably dreary rural town. The angle of the rooflines conveyed a subtly oriental feel, as if this place was the exact spot where the western world began to give way to the eastern.

I was met by the colonel and two of his staff officers. All three men wore uniforms that had seen some use. They were shaved but not very cleanly. They looked tired.

We exchanged salutes.

"Herr Weber, I am Colonel Fritz Meck," he said. His diction was precise and very Prussian. He took my hand, shaking it in the quick, hard Prussian style. He had dueling scars on both cheeks, conveying the unfortunate impression that he was grinning at all times.

We traded the salute, and then he took me to his staff car, which proved to be a *Kubelwagen* thoroughly covered with Polish mud. The *Kubelwagen* was a Volkswagen Beetle with an open body and bigger tires. This early version, a Type 62, had canvas doors and did not look to me at all safe.

In fact, though, it was a reliable machine, actually in the way it felt to ride, quite a bit like a Jeep.

As I was getting in, a military orderly came puffing up with a black leather bag. "Herr Weber, Herr Weber, here it is!"

I took it. "Ah. What is it?"

"The camera! The leader said you left it behind."

"Of course. Thank you." He'd forgotten to mention it, I supposed then, but later realized that he'd held it back on purpose, so that the men I was with would know that I came directly from him and treat me accordingly.

I put the bag on the seat between myself and the colonel. The only sort of camera I'd ever used was Maddie's Jiffy Kodak. This was a Leica III, to me an entirely mysterious contraption.

We travelled on wretched roads and dreadful tracks, but through the blushing Polish autumn, in pine forests and through fields lined by blazing trees. There was an odd sense about it that I would describe as settled wildness. It was not like Germany, so carefully trimmed.

"Might one see wolves in these forests?"

"I would think."

This man was a commanding officer summoned to take an annoyingly well connected boy on a tour. I understood his taciturnity.

"Where are we going?"

"To my brigade sector. I can't tell you exactly where we are, but it's in Western Pomerania in the operational area of Army Group North."

"Is there a battle going on?"

"You'd have been given a steel helmet, young man! Incidentally, where are you studying?"

Oh, dear, I might get tripped up. As usual Hitler had not exactly thought of everything. At different times, both Fribourg and Munich had been suggested to me. I had never been in Fribourg but I knew Munich well, so I said that I was matriculated there.

"Ah, Munich. Believed by some to be a university."

"I gather you don't approve."

"I graduated Fribourg. What do you imagine that you're studying?"

I reached for something quite vague. Hopefully uninteresting. "Philosophy." I continued the joke. "And what do you pretend to have your degree in?"

"Mathematics. That's why I ended up in infantry instead of artillery."

"I don't understand."

"I'm being sarcastic. We Friborgers can do that. You don't need mathematics to measure the depth of the mud you're traipsing through. Anybody with mathematical skills should be in artillery."

We turned sharply, then moved into a thick stand of pines. The driver pulled the vehicle up into an area where there were a number of other machines, among them a looming mechanized troop carrier with treads and a small carry-all. "We aren't in an active area, but this is war, so surprise is always possible. Bear that in mind."

As we walked toward the edge of the trees, I saw a forester's cottage ahead. No doubt we were on one of the great Polish estates.

Inside, there was a crowd of officers and subalterns pouring over a scale map of the area. When we entered, everybody immediately snapped to attention and saluted.

"At ease," Colonel Beck said. "Do I smell coffee?"

An orderly came forward with a steel mug. Beck took it and sipped, watching me over its rim.

"Where's the actual front?" I asked.

"You'll see soon enough. I'm going on inspection in fifteen minutes. Gentlemen, this you have before you the cause of my mysterious summons to the *Fuhrerzug*. This is Herr Weber, who believes, oddly enough, that he is a philosophy student. He is here to take pictures and be treated like a royal prince. He came right down off the *Fuhrerwagen* itself, so bear that in mind."

The silence that followed these remarks was not reassuring. I could detect no enthusiasm at all for a well connected young man sent here to disrupt their routine. In fact, these men were much like the people in the streets of Berlin. They were going about their tasks no more than dutifully.

"I am here to form a report that I can take back to Hitler Youth and gymnasium students to encourage them to take up officer training."

"I hope they have time," one *hauptmann* said. "The way this is going, we'll be finished by the end of the month."

"Heissler, please," Beck said. "Let him just do it. Here, Weber, take a photo of us now. Then you'll come with me on my readiness inspection." He gulped down his coffee and stared into the cup. His peculiar expression was a sourness, I realized, embedded in the enforced grin. How had he managed dueling scars on both cheeks, a mathematician? German collegiate culture was a world away from our own.

The appearance of the Leica drew some whistles of admiration. I raised it to my eye and took a photo of them, all looking entirely grim and warlike. At least, I hoped that I'd taken a photo. I'd pressed a button and heard a faint click.

We returned to the *Kubelwagen* and moved out into the field beyond the forest. Beck said, "the Poles are over there beyond that stand of trees, perhaps a kilometer back. We're ordered to move up and come in on their southern flank, which is in the air. To the north, another brigade is doing the same. They will either be encircled or withdraw. When the movement takes place, you will stay with me. We will not enter the battle zone, but you will have a good chance to take photos of the men going into action. Then you'll return to my HQ and from there go back to the *Fuhrerzug*."

"I understand." I looked toward the distant trees. All seemed quiet.

Let me just explain the terrain a little more carefully, so that you can understand exactly the horror that proceeded to unfold. The line of trees was about five hundred meters due north. Presumably, the Polish Army was some distance beyond them—as it turned out, very presumably.

In front of the trees was a scrubby area, probably the remains of forest that had been cut for wood. To the south was an old road, a continuation of the one we'd come in on, and beside it an even thicker growth of trees.

The *Kubelwagen* was equipped with a radio, which Beck now started. After it had warmed up, he got acknowledgements from his junior field officers, then ordered the attack.

At the same time, I saw men on horseback appear on the road. They had come out of the seemingly impenetrable woods, horses and all. They wore dark khaki uniforms and caps with thick red bands. They carried lances at least eight feet long. I watched them forming up along the road. What unit were they? I thought the *Wehrmacht* was entirely in field gray. So were they SA, perhaps, some sort of parade unit come out to taste a bit of the real thing?

"Ah!" Beck said. Then *"scheisse!"* He waved me back. But where was I to go? I stepped away from him.

The next thing I knew, German troops seemed to appear out of the ground. The clearing, which had been nothing but tall grass, was now filled with soldiers. Oblivious to the cavalrymen, they began moving forward toward the northern tree line. They were hunched over their rifles, keeping low.

Beck said into the radio, "What is this? Fritz, Ulans! We've got Uhlans back here!"

There were now perhaps three hundred German soldiers in the field. I finally realized that the cavalrymen were Poles. Still, they stood silently watching. On the distance, I heard a chugging noise, like a motor turning over. A couple of the soldiers disappeared into the grass.

Beck and his driver crouched behind the *Kubelwagen*. I stared stupidly at the Ulans. There was a buzz like a beetle flying past my head. "Down! Down!"

I went down on one knee. I still did not understand that we were under fire, much less that we had been surprised by the supposedly incompetent Poles.

The Uhlans lowered their lances and began trotting forward. Now some of the Germans aimed their rifles. The chugging noise got louder, and I could detect movement in the northern tree line.

"Is that a machine gun?" I asked Beck.

"*Ja,* they've got us by the fucking balls!"

But what was this? Were the Germans to be trapped between the Uhlans and the machine gun?

An entire row of German soldiers went down and this time I heard terrible cries, the forlorn wail of the dying.

"Are they being shot? What's going on?"

The *Kubelwagen* lurched forward a few meters, then stopped. Now the soldiers had gone to their knees. Some were firing at the machine guns, others at the Uhlans. The Uhlans were riding faster, some getting shot right off their horses, but not all.

A horrific scream rent the air and one of the Uhlans raised a broken lance. The end of it was buried in a soldier's stomach. He gripped it, vomiting blood as he disappeared into the grass.

Beck was shouting into the radio. "We are under attack from a squad of Ulans and two WZ-28s at least, with a platoon of infantry enfilading us from—"

An explosion drowned him out. Ahead of us, a geyser of dirt flew up. The geyser had a man in it, a bag with flopping arms.

"Also a WZ-36. Where are they coming from? Is the line broken ahead?" He listened. Then he changed frequencies. "Pull back, pull back, we've called up a tank." He turned to me. "You're seeing some action."

"I should say. Are we in danger?"

"Only of getting our heads blown off."

"Ah, good, nothing more than that."

"Well, you've got some spirit, Municher or not. I have no idea how these Poles ended up back here. Something is wrong ahead, but I won't hear about what it is until they have time to communicate with us."

An astonishing clatter started up along the road where we had come, and in another moment there was a truly enormous vehicle there, a tall stack of iron mounted by a young man in a black uniform. It had a machine gun and a small barreled cannon sticking out of it. As it moved, two furious plumes of exhaust gushed up from the rear deck. I could see behind a small glass slit the eyes of a boy.

It lurched along the road a distance, then stopped. The Ulans were about a hundred meters in front of it, no more. The commander, standing grandly in his turret, barked an order into a microphone. A moment later, the tank's machine gun began making a hellish racket, so loud that I cried out. More of the Ulans fell, and the blasting of the gun now mixed with the screams of dying horses.

This arbitrary, meaningless killing seemed so odd to me, so very strange. As, in fact, in all the years since the one thought about war that has remained with me is that it is so very strange.

On the far side of the tank, the one facing the forest, their appeared an eruption of flame. The commander lurched away from it, then at once shouted down into the hatch, "Damage control! Commence firefighting!" A wisp of smoke came out around him. He dropped down into the body of the tank.

"Oh god," Beck said.

"Has the tank got a fault?"

"Fucking gasoline bomb! Bastards!"

Another explosion occurred, causing a white flash of fire to spark out of the still-open turret. It left my ears ringing.

"Get out of the damn thing," somebody shouted on the distance. I felt heat against my back. The *Kubelwagen* in which we were now sitting had also been set alight. The gasoline tank was burning. In another moment, the driver grabbed me under the arms and pulled me out.

Just a few feet away, the tank was now completely engulfed in flames. From inside there came screams, high whoops of agony. Again and again they came, whoop after whoop, a chorus of them. I ran to the thing. It was like coming up to a hot oven. There were hatches but I couldn't touch them from the heat. They were smoking, the paint visibly blistering. The screaming went on and on and on. Why didn't they come up out of the turret?

Behind me I heard a *crump*. The *Kubelwagen* had exploded. I finally realized that not only were we were in a firefight, we were losing. So the radio reports of an easy victory had indeed been lies, just as Hitler had intimated.

A plane whooshed over, then made a long turn above the north woods where the machine gun fire was coming from. Before the tank was set alight, I suppose by partisans hiding in the woods, it had cut all the Ulans down, men and horses alike. From inside the burning tank there was now silence. The *Wehrmacht* soldiers were nowhere to be seen, all either down or once again crouching in the shelter of the grass.

Beck pointed at the plane. "Watch that."

Buzzing loudly, it gained altitude. I could see that it was a Stuka. It circled once. Both Polish machine guns continued sputtering away.

I could see the propeller aiming down at us. A horrific screaming siren started up. It was like nothing I'd ever heard before, the scream of an infuriated banshee. The Stuka sirens would become infamous as the Horns of Jericho.

"Run!" Beck shouted. I followed him and the driver as they raced wildly through the woods, which exploded with such force that we were thrown to the ground. Trees went down like bowling pins. "*Scheisse!*" He glared wildly at me. "He's got the wrong fucking woods! Keep running, Boy—oh no, Fritz!"

The driver had been crushed under a fallen tree. He was on his back, his abdomen and legs completely invisible beneath the thick trunk. His hands caressed it, fluttering back and forth along its surface as delicately as if it was the miraculous flesh of a woman. His teeth were bared. Blood was foaming out between them. His head began pitching back and forth. Each time it happened, he yelped. He began slapping the trunk.

"Run, Boy! God damn fuck!"

The siren started again, and I could see the plane above the trees, once more diving right at us. I ran as hard as I could, but it was obvious that the bomb was coming right down and we were for it.

The plane roared past so low that the treetops pitched and swayed with its passing.

The engine noise declined. Beck jumped about, looking for it through breaks in the forest cover. "There, he's got it now."

The driver lay still, his hands covering his face. Blood was coming out between his fingers. He was making gobbling noises. Then his hands dropped and he was silent.

Beck stared down at him for a moment, then ran back toward the burning tank. I followed. The air was full of the horrific stink of high explosive that the penetrating odor of burning hair. There was an enticing but also loathsome smell of roast. I tried to blow it out of my nose. Nobody was cooking any pork around here.

As we emerged from the forest, I heard a distant but quite loud explosion. The Stuka had found the correct target and the Polish machine guns were no more.

A runner came up. He had on his back a field radio. These were not the handheld radio telephones one sees in the movies nowadays, but a heavy and fragile piece of equipment that filled a large backpack. Sticking out from it was a six foot long antenna which whipped back and forth as he ran.

He thrust the headset into Beck's hands. Beck listened, then shouted, "All right, move them out, move them out. Quickly! We still have an objective to reach, yes?" He paused. "I'll have medics up." He said to the radio operator, "General frequency, medical call." He then spat map co-ordinates into the receiver and replaced it in its hook. "All right, Boy, you and I have some horses to shoot." He strode off toward the ruined heap of Ulans.

"I don't have a gun."

He stopped and glanced around. "There's one. Right there, get that."

He was pointing to the soldier who had been killed by the lance. He lay on his back, a boy younger than me, fuzzy-cheeked and as blond as sunlight. His chest was soaked with blood and the flies around him were berserk, whirring devils. His rifle was still clutched tightly in his hands.

To get it loose, I had to pull his fingers back. When his knuckles popped, I almost vomited on the poor fellow.

There were eighteen horses in all, many of them still alive, lying about with their guts between their legs or a hoof twisted skyward or a sucking hole in the chest. As we walked toward them, their eyes moved with us. Some of them would raise whinnies and strive to stand up, while others were glazed with shock or too badly injured to care.

There was a noise, strange, that at first seemed like sarcastic laughter. But when I saw Beck's face, I realized that he was crying.

We shot horses for half an hour, then returned to brigade HQ clinging to the back of an ambulance. It was dark then. Some soldiers were singing in the shadowy camp. Overhead, the vault of stars spread their light. Were they sad, I wondered, or merely part of the vast indifference? I thought of Blake's lines in contemplation of the approach of night:

"Soon, full soon
Dost thou withdraw;
then the wolf ranges wide..."

# 2

A HQ orderly explained to me, "You cannot return to Bad Polein tonight. The *sonderzug* will have moved by the time you arrive. We're also moving HQ forward so you'll come with us. We'll catch you up with the *sonderzug* in the morning. It'll be at Plietnitz."

I had no idea where any of these places were, or where we were. "Yes, very good."

The HQ staff orderlies were efficiently filling a large carrier with maps and equipment. It was hooked to a *Phenomen Granit* which had seating inside for eight in addition to the driver. Another *kubelwagen* had been brought up. Colonel Beck and his adjutant rode in it. I rode in the driver's cabin of the *Phenomen*.

I was profoundly shaken by what I had seen earlier. The Poles had seemed fierce and effective and incredibly brave. The Ulans had sacrificed their lives to draw the Germans out of their foxholes so that the machine guns could enfilade them. As we drove ahead, bouncing and slipping along the serrated road, I kept hearing the men in the tank. You hear screaming in the movies or on the stage, but it is nothing like the screaming of people who are actually dying. Once you have heard that, any attempt to simulate it sounds childish.

There is a note in it that cannot be duplicated by an actor, a tone of despair which infects your own soul. In the night I hear it still. In fact, as I write this, sitting on the Literary Walk in Central Park in the gathering evening, I hear it, but not just from that one tank crew, but from the howling vastness within me, the great unruly crowd of my dead, an ocean of lives unfinished, that I can never save.

In the last fragile light, we came to a manor, a fairly large one. I realized that we had been traveling across a great Polish estate. There was an elegance to the structure that suggested the influence of Palladio. Like the Villa Chiericati in Vancimuglio, there was a projecting portico, with the main rooms built on a *piano nobile* with, I assumed, kitchen and storage below. The upper floor was more developed that that of the Villa Chiericati, and I could well imagine some fine quarters inside. I could not tell the material the villa was constructed from, but the ivory paint that covered it gave it a distinct air of elegance, reminding one more of a London townhouse than a country estate.

The house stood on a hillock, its windows dark but its chimney issuing a substantial stream of smoke.

As we got down, Beck gathered us around him. "This is the seat of the Count Rodryg Kalinkowski. I want to warn you that his son Geog is in the $15^{th}$ Poznan Uhlans, and I believe he was lost in the skirmish with us this afternoon. They do not know it. The Kalinkowskis are related by distaff to the Von Manowardas who are my own cousins. So we should receive a good welcome. If we get it, we will act as guests. If not, we'll take charge as required. But the family must not be harmed, nor their possessions removed."

Beck proceeded up the steps to the front door. He knocked three times, then stood aside. It took courage, I thought, because a burst of gunfire could easily have come out.

A light came on in the proscenium, then the door opened and a tall man of perhaps fifty stepped out. He was dressed in tails and for all the world looked exactly like a similar servant in England or France or Germany, or anywhere in Europe, for that matter.

Amazingly, Beck produced a calling card, which he sent in. A moment later, the servant reappeared, leaned toward him and asked a question. Beck glanced down at us and I heard him say, "We are six."

Meanwhile, the rest of the unit was coming into the grounds, trucks grinding, half-tracks rattling, men marching in columns. This was only the headquarters company, of course. The brigade itself was much larger.

All of these men were part of 6$^{th}$ Army, then under General Fretter-Pico. Later, they would be under the command of General Paulus and would be encircled at Stalingrad. As I looked about at all the orderly soldiers and impressive equipment, I thought that I was in the midst of the finest military force ever established. And yet, any of these men who survived until 1943 would end up among the 400,000 trapped in Stalingrad. Of the 91,000 who survived long enough to be captured when Paulus surrendered to Zhukov, only about 5,000 would eventually return home.

I have spent some time in recent years looking at casualty lists held by the *Deutsche Dienststelle*, the German government agency that keeps records of the *Wehrmacht*, trying to find the names of soldiers I knew. Colonel Helmut Beck is there. Captured at Stalingrad, never returned, no record of his fate. There are others, but most of them men I knew only in passing. My wartime years did not often put me in the ranks of the military. I spent my time in two sorts of places, palaces and alleys.

Oh, my, though, I remember that night. As we sat awkwardly in a formal receiving room, the moon rose grandly up the tall front windows, and I could see the soldiers outside like statuary that was inexplicably moving, as if it was controlled by some hidden magician. There was none of the strange, robotic racing about that one saw in the cities. I recalled from Henry V, "from camp to camp through the foul womb of night, the hum of either army's stilly sounds," and thought that there were Poles, also, under this moon, seeking the same deliverance all soldiers seek, from the dismal end that haunts their hours.

On the wall between the two tall windows I faced there was a very nice Isaac Levitan, a landscape of a road stretching off between shining and endless fields.

"Look," I said, "it's where you're going."

Beck's adjutant Major Walther said, "This place is a forest."

"That's a painting by the Russian landscape artist Isaac Levitan," I said. "It's land east of here. The Russian *Steppe*."

"Ah, we need a *steppe*," another of them said. "A place to spread out in." He gestured toward the painting. "In fact I'll be glad to take land like that for the great farm I intend to build. They say on the radio that nothing's growing on the *steppe* now, not a stalk of wheat or anything." He made a little chortling sound in his throat, communicating condescension. "I could make a fortune in land like that."

And you wonder why they were willing to follow Hitler and attempt to steal an entire country? Britain had its larcenous thalassocracy, did it not, with colonies all over the world there to be plucked bare. The Germans looked at that and saw the logic in an empire of their own, a land empire, and Hitler told them they were the natural inheritors of the east, and deserved to own it, and they grew greedy.

As it's quite impossible for a tourist to leave established routes, I haven't yet gone into Poland to look for that old estate. But I do intend to go. I intend to find out what, if anything, is left.

I'm sure the estate a collective now, the lovely home in ruins, probably lived in by starving peasants under conditions far worse than they knew when the count managed the land. Almost all of that old *mitteleuropean* aristocracy died, the Prussians, the Poles, all of them. It was absolute carnage.

Quite suddenly, the count appeared. "Soldiers, well," he said in rather careful German. He addressed Colonel Beck. "Have you word of our cousins?"

"I last heard from Kurt a month ago. He's vacationing in New York."

"A Prussian on vacation during time of war?"

"My dear, Kurt has turned sixty."

"Ah, time! Very well. Last night the officers who stayed with us were Poles." He smiled warmly. "But never worry. I have the housekeeping staff changing the bed linens."

There was a murmur of laughter. He went across to a table. "Georg," he called, then spoke in Polish to the butler when he reappeared appeared.

"Gentlemen, cocktails are on offer. I can give you English-style gin and bitters or some very sound Polish vodka and the same bitters, or a martini. I do have a bit of vermouth and some olives."

"*Schnaaps*?" one of the officers asked.

"Alas, your opponents broke up all of my bottles before they withdrew this morning. I think that they anticipated your arrival."

"Well, for my part, I never feel I'm going wrong with a martini," Colonel Beck said. "They set my feet to dancing, though."

"Are you a married man, Sir, if you don't mind my asking?"

"Not yet. Why?"

"There are three young women hidden in this house. Hidden away in case you were brigands. But if you don't mind that they danced with uniforms of a different stripe last night, I think that they would be delighted to come and dance with you."

Beck went to his feet, followed by his officers. "Count Kolzinski, we would be honored." I also stood.

A door slid open, revealing a sitting room and three girls who looked to be between seventeen and perhaps twenty at the most. The hard electric light caused them to shimmer like apparitions. Slowly they came forward, stepping as carefully as they would crossing a stream on slippery stones.

The feeling that shot through me amazed me. It was an immediate surge of genital excitement, primitive and powerful, indeed, almost overwhelming. Since that moment, whenever I hear of soldiers committing rape, I understand. I do not condone it, certainly not, but I know well the brute emotion, emerging out of the fear of death, that drives them, and why it is that later they cannot really explain themselves.

Such emotions live in us only in time of war, retreating like an ugly fog when peace once again dawns. In war, you can shoot a man right in his terrified face. You can stand there dispassionate as his head explodes. Then, in peace, you look back and feel your own face with trembling fingers, and resolve to think of it no more.

They had an ungainly Russian Victrola which the girls cheerfully cranked up until I took over. One of them put on a record. I had expected something social, a fox-trot suitable to this small room, but instead it was Cab Calloway's "Call of the Jitterbug."

America! You found its voice everywhere, even then, the call of happiness from far away.

Well, I wasn't waiting. I went out at once with the closest of these hot-patooties and began jitterbugging her in and out. And she knew what she was doing, let me tell you. Soon Beck joined us. Then one of his braver majors took the floor, also throwing a decent jitterbug. So there we were, two *Wehrmacht* officers and me jitterbugging our hearts out in the depths of Poland while everybody else in the party clapped and laughed, and the count himself played like Calloway, mouthing the words and making as if to direct the band.

When the song ended, we couldn't stop laughing. Then the second daughter said, "One of mine. I'm a blues queen." And then I was hearing "Baby Won't you Please Come Home," and I danced with her close to me, slowly fox-trotting in the roses of her perfume. Her dark eyes gazed up at me with a silent desperation that haunts me to this day.

Given the fate that befell these men, I have imagined that the voice of Besse Smith wailing "baby won't you please come home," was really that of the angel of death calling them into the shadows.

Dinner was announced by the butler, and we went in to a table so magnificent that it would have been a credit to any great *schloss* or English country house. The room was lit by a chandelier and three candelabra. On the table was a magnificent haunch of venison, and as we sat, liveried servants set about carving and distributing plates of juicy meat, rutabagas and green beans, all exquisitely prepared.

The scent of pine, sharp and rich coming in the windows on the night wind, and an old wine—a marvelous Eschezeaux, I believe—oh, goodness, such a last moment of civilization in that place.

Beck, smiling and attempting to be merry, cut a very peculiar figure, but he had obviously been often at a proper table before, and chatted left to right with the courses. The others had no idea how to act in a social situation, and spent their time wolfing food and speaking out to the whole table any comment that crossed their minds.

I could see the contempt in the count's eyes. I feared that he might utter an insult, but Poland is a land which has many times been under foreign domination, and he held his tongue.

His countess had come in with him. She was shaking with what we used to call St. Vitus' Dance, now laughing and twitching and flouncing helplessly as she directed her food and told stories of the hunt as it had been practiced in that place.

As she spoke of their lost times, the tall drapes blew gently and the moon slipped past the tops of the windows. Her voice, thickly controlled but filled with the music of the past, sounded like something from some eerie eternity. But that 'earlier time,' on my questioning, proved not to be the decades ago that I had assumed, but actually just last week! She was describing the hunt in which this very stag had been brought down.

But they couldn't hunt now. How could they? Their guns were to be taken. I suppose in the way of people who have ruled for a long time, and those Polish names went back, some of them, a thousand years, she saw time not in terms of days and years, but as series of little eternities, and knew in her depths that last week's hunt had entered one of them, and no new hunt would ever be mounted.

Deep in the night, I was awakened by a hand coming onto my forehead. I started up, but heard the count's voice whisper, "No no, all is well. Sh!" He came down beside the bed. "You are not German."

I was surprised. "How did you know?"

"You speak like an aristocrat, but you aren't one. Who are you? Where are you from?"

"I'm an American."

"*What*! With these devils?"

"An observer."

He thought about that. "Will you return to America?"

"Yes."

"The bastard English and the bastard French have abandoned us. Tell Roosevelt to send us waves of planes! Send them quickly, quickly! Our light is being crushed out, American." He gazed into my face. "Save my family, take them with you. Please, my beautiful girls, my darlings!"

In that moment I found a new depth of hatred for Adolf Hitler and a new depth of shame for myself.

"I will tell the Americans, but I think you should prepare for the worst. You're behind German lines now. Make for Rumania before their administration arrives. Probably a couple of days. I'd leave tonight. Don't even wait for first light. Have you a car?"

"Yes. Gasoline, though, only some. Perhaps not enough for Rumania."

I went into my wallet and came up with a few hundred marks. "Take this. It might help."

He bowed his head and slipped the money into the pocket of his dinner jacket, and was gone like a wisp of night wind.

I tried hard to locate the Kozinskis. In 1960, I went to gray, sad Warsaw, ending up in the care of a minder called Henryka Wojcik, too young to remember anything much of the war.

Eventually, I was conducted to a gray block in the Praga District. We walked up five flights to a long, dark corridor where Henryka knocked on a door. A moment later, a tall man appeared from behind a curtain that divided off a sleeping area. He was pale and narrow and his hair was white, but there was no question, it was the count. I stood and formally shook his hand and inclined my head in the old way, in deference to his rank.

"No, no," he said in French, "we're past that now."

"In Polish, Sir," the minder said.

He laughed a little and repeated himself in Polish. "My daughter Galina," he said.

As I took her hand, I remembered her from that wonderful last night more than twenty years before, how she had jitterbugged, how pretty she had been. She was now quite heavy, poor woman, no doubt afflicted by the local diet which, as far as I could determine, consisted exclusively of potatoes and cabbage seasoned with gray chunks that could have been anything from horse to gopher. There was better food in the milk bars, but still none of the old Polish delights. In the PPR, food is regarded as fuel, nothing more.

I said in English, "Remember our Jitterbug?"

A smile lit her face, revealing two gleaming steel teeth."Oh, yes, yes!"

Her father shook his head sharply.

She added quickly, "We remember nothing of the old time. This is a worker's paradise now, and we are workers and very happy for it."

They both smiled mechanically.

I concluded the interview as quickly as I could, managing to leave behind fifty dollars and feeling somehow an utter heel.

Back twenty years before, I had been transported to the *sonderzug* very efficiently by the *Wehrmacht,* which was still superbly organized. I carried in my pocket copy of a description of the engagement I had been a part of, that Colonel Beck had told me he would be entering into the brigade's war diary.

I have read its words, death couched in the terminology of victor, "a flanking attempt...disrupted by quick infantry and tank action...18 Uhlans fallen...altogether nine German dead to twenty eight Poles," and so on. Looking back across the years, I can find on a map where the boys in the tank burned to death, where the innocent horses were slaughtered, where the Polish machine guns were placed and where the German infantry had their foxholes. But in the moment, that was all incomprehensible. I was not a military man able to keep a map in his mind. I heard distant, rhythmic sounds and observed a series of seemingly disconnected incidents. I witnessed a small explosion that happened to blow a human being to pieces. I heard sizzling in a machine that had been mysteriously set alight, the sizzling of roasting boys.

I arrived at Hitler's train in the sidecar of a motorcycle, tagging along with a staff messenger. As we drew up to the platform, I could see him gazing out the window. He at once stood up and began moving through the *Fuhrerwagen* toward the door where I would enter.

"Ah, Willy, thank God! I hear you were in a terrific battle!"

We went into the car. When we were alone, he embraced me, then stood back and looked me up and down, his face glowing. "The report says that you showed great courage!"

"I did?"

"Of course it's so natural to you that you aren't even aware."

"The Poles did attack us. I noticed that."

"And?"

"They didn't do very well."

As we spoke, a number of generals had come into the car. As always, he did not want my face to be seen. His arm still around my shoulder, he drew me out of his office and into the parlor.

"The valet is gone," he said. "He won't be back. We'll soon have another." In the histories, it's said that Krause was discharged because he had filled Hitler's Faschinger Water bottles with Polish tap water, but the real reason was that Hitler overheard him calling me Hitlerfucker. He was fortunate to have been sent back to the navy and not shot.

"I have meetings now," he said to me, "but I have also an idea for you that you're really going to like, I think. Quite a good one." He slapped me gently on the butt. "Wait, we'll talk later."

I had my Eliot with me, the 1920 edition of *Poems* inscribed to me by my father, "On the occasion of your own twentieth, my beloved son, from *Vati*." That had been just months before I had walked into the library to find those copies of *Der Sturmer* scattered across the floor.

By that time, I knew the poems by heart, but I read them anyway, experimenting in my mind with translation into German. I don't think, actually, that anyone who isn't an English speaker can really apprehend them, no more than can Baudelaire be adequately experienced in anything but French, or Holderlin in German.

I found lying on the table that was there between the two cane chairs that were in the room, a mock up of a proposed magazine called *Signal*. It would, of course, become the propaganda bible of the *Wehrmacht,* published bi-weekly throughout conquered Europe in at least ten languages. The type in it was all "*lorem ipsum*" but I could see by the flashy layout that if Hitler let it go on, it was going to become one of the most prominent publications on the continent, which it did.

I turned on the radio and twisted around looking for music, but couldn't find anything. It was now punishable by death to listen to foreign broadcasts, but not on the *fuhrerzug* or, in fact, in the Berghof or any Hitler lair. We listened to what we pleased, and the British and American newspapers were delivered to us from Switzerland no later than they would have been in peacetime. I used to sight-translate for him at the Berghof, choosing to read out the stories that were most likely to make him angry. When he really went off the edge, it was something to see. He never chewed a rug, but his eyes rolled around and his spit would fly like stinky dew.

Carlotta loved it, laughing right in his face, but Eva would fuss at me. "Don't tease him, Willy, it's not nice," she would say.

Eventually I was brought a tea in *Wehrmacht* monograms rather than those of the *Fuhrerzug*. Lunch had come and gone before I arrived, so I was glad of the sandwiches. The *zug* teas were, of course, heaped with the sweet cakes and chocolates Hitler had to have.

The sun was setting when he finally appeared.

"You were right, it looks as if Roosevelt will remain neutral. And the French are indeed sitting on their asses, so I can deal with them when convenient. But do you realize how uniquely situated you are, Willy?"

"We're neutral. Yes, I see that."

"You can still travel. Go to Switzerland or Sweden and from there anywhere you please. You can go to London and give me firsthand reports. Confer with Churchill, even. Could you manage that?"

"I would imagine so."

"Don't imagine! No imagination in Germany except the leader's! Tell me yes or no."

Churchill was now First Sea Lord in the Chamberlain Government. I thought it likely that he could be approached. "Yes," I said, forcing to keep any excitement out of my voice, but here was another chance! Now surely I could get those supply lines of mine interrupted. Yes, of course, he commanded the entire British Navy, he could do it with ease.

"Tell Churchill that I won't fight England. Yes! I refuse to fight my Anglo-Saxon cousins, tell him that. Tell him to let the French go it alone. If I get in there, I'll bring order to France at last. He'll appreciate that. He believes in strong government just as I do."

What an extraordinary misreading of Winston Churchill. But not a complete mistake. Hitler correctly sensed that there was a similarity between them. Both men were utterly ruthless. But what he did not understand was that their causes were fundamentally different. Churchill was ready to fight to the death for everything Hitler despised, and vice-versa. In the truest, deepest sense of the word, the two men were enemies. In '39, Churchill had already known it for years. Hitler never really understood it, not until the day he died.

"And you could perhaps find Putzi for me. I miss him. I miss his piano playing, tell him that. All the good times! War. So painful but so necessary. We'll be done by the end of the month, incidentally. Tell Churchill that we have no intention of going west. If they don't fight, neither will we. He has my word on that."

Just in time, I stopped the burst of laughter that was on its way. His "word!"

I wanted this trip. I wanted it badly.

He glanced outside. "It's night now. You can leave in the morning." He threw himself down in a chair. "I need the girls, Willy. I need Carlotta, really very badly. I'm aching."

"Come back to the Berghof. We can go together."

"Not possible, not until the campaign is over."

"You could fly. There one day, back the next."

He considered that. "No, I have a visit to a wounded transport tomorrow and who knows what after that? On forward, always closer to Warsaw."

"Have them come to you."

"Everybody sees everything around here. It's bad enough having them all staring at you and wondering who in hell you are. They don't need to see Eva. And Carlotta—good God, no."

"I can see that."

"You fuck Carlotta, don't you?"

He was very good at this sort of change of subject, designed to shock one into telling the truth. But I had nothing to hide, here. At the Berghof we were living in the same room. "I do."

"Is it pleasant?"

"Very."

"Do you love her, then?"

"I might. I could."

"Willy, don't marry Carlotta. I need her, too."

"I realize that, Alf. I never would."

He leaned forward in his chair. His entire demeanor now expressed pleasant relaxation. "Does she say much about what I need her for?"

I realized that, in this moment, I had Carlotta's life in my hands. The wrong answer to this question, and I had no doubt that she would be shot within the hour.

"Nothing whatsoever."

"Have you ever asked?"

"Of course I have. I'm fascinated and curious."

Beneath the mustache, the smile was tight. His cheeks were cherry red. "What did she say?"

"To be exact, she said 'go fuck yourself.'"

"What about her other clients? Goering? I loaned her to him for the specific purpose of finding out his tastes."

"And she won't tell you a thing."

"Exactly."

"It's her honor, Alf. This is her work and her honor."

"Her loyalty is her honor. Just like my SS boys. And you. You remember our moment?"

"I do."

"Then I know I can trust you in England and America."

"You can."

"But if you hadn't given your word?"

"It's beyond that now. Of course you can trust me."

"My boy. Of course I can." He paused for a long time. "I need something else."

"Yes?"

"No, later. I have dinner now with the General Staff. They all want to tell me their troubles. But after."

"Very well."

I took my dinner alone. My mind was racing with possibilities. He had walked into a trap. It was perfect, just perfect.

Later, I heard a film going. Every night was movie night at the Berghof and in the Chancellery, but I hadn't known that there was film equipment on the train. I went forward into the office. I didn't dare go into the dining room where it was being shown, but at least I could listen.

It was, of all things, "The Wizard of Oz." I imagined them, all of those tin men in there being led by a dreamer on a yellow brick road that led eastward all the way to China.

I believed Hitler now when he said he wouldn't go to France. Reality was unfolding differently from the way he had anticipated in *Mein Kampf*. He could make a lightning strike out of Poland and do what the western powers had hoped he would do in the first place, which was to destroy Soviet Russia.

Obviously, I was mistaken. But I believed him to be a logical man. I had no understanding of the depth of hatred that festered inside him.

Hitler was not fighting a new war. In his mind, Germany hadn't lost World War One at all, but merely been tricked into believing that she had. As far as he was concerned, that war was still going on, and he intended to win it.

The film ended and I could hear him talking and talking. I was glad that I wasn't in there. Finally I went into my bedroom, got on my nightshirt and went to sleep.

At some very late hour, I awoke to find him sitting on the edge of my narrow bed. He was in long johns. He said, "Willy, there is something I need at times. It's to balance my success, I think. I have wondered why I need it. I don't understand myself, but which of us does?" He knelt beside the bed and took my hand. I wanted to pull it away, but I was frozen, frankly, with foreboding. "I've thought of what a boy might do that would help me." He bent his head low and murmured.

What in hell was this mad creature wanting now?

"I can't hear you."

He raised his head. In the semi-darkness, I could see the pain in his face. He said, "I will lie on the floor and you will kick me."

So this was it. Masochism. Understandable, he must feel terribly guilty, the devil. I almost laughed aloud thinking of how much Carlotta must enjoy giving him pain. 'Men, they're all fuckfaced shits,' was her motto. But I could break through her anger, and when I did she melted in my arms like a sweet Madonna.

"Speak, for God's sake!"

I laid my hand on his cheek. "Come on," I said, "there's not enough room in here."

He began to weep. "Oh my God, thank you. Willy, I was so afraid to ask. Please don't despise me for it."

"Nobody can understand the pressure you're under, Alf. We just have to accept it."

"The women—they can't. Only Carlotta. Not even Eva."

"Come, we'll go in the parlor."

"It's why I fired Krause. I have to have this. But he can't know, he mustn't."

Inside, I was sick with fear. This was truly the unknown, here in this dark place with this bizarre emotional cripple.

"It's going to hurt."

"It needs to. It must."

"Is this what Carlotta does?"

"Not exactly. But I thought it was what a boy might agree to do."

"Lie on your back."

"I don't want to see you do it."

"Which is why you must."

It was all I could do not to kick him to death. But I was young and hungry for life, me and a million other kids out there in the night. I kicked him in the kidney and he squalled, then clapped his hand over his mouth. Too loud and he'd have a swarm of SS in here in a moment. I gave him a few more, in the leg, in the ribs, and when he turned away from me, a couple of nice ones in the butt.

I could see that he'd gotten a hard-on. I certainly wanted none of that, so I said, "I've seen enough of you tonight. Go in your room and shut the door. You're to remain there until you're called."

I went into my own room and lay in the bed smoking and reflecting that this train sitting on its quiet siding in the night was the capital of hell.

# 3

I felt filthy and I was acidic with hate. I could imagine him in his room masturbating while he contemplated my shoe striking his ribs.

How vile could one man be?

I stared out my window. Night clouds were rushing past. A guard stood in profile against the light shining off the nearby station platform. There were no distant flashes of guns, none of the ominous rumbles you hear in war movies.

For not the first time, there came to mind the idea of killing him. Before this, I'd been afraid for my own life and also unwilling to take that of another human being, but those feelings were changing. What did my life matter if losing it might mean relief for all the people he was hurting?

But would it? I was hardly an expert in the internal machinations of the NSDAP. Maybe Goering would take over, though, and he was horrified by the war. Or Himmler or Heydrich might. Either of them would continue it, and probably do a better job that this vile little troll.

Lying there in that railroad car, listening to the silence that filled it, I decided that nobody would be worse than Adolf Hitler, and I should kill him.

Immediately, there came an awesome thought: 'why not now?' Yes, right now. I could go into his compartment and choke him to death.

I sat up in my berth. Yes, now.

I got to my feet. I opened my door. The short corridor was empty. Across it was his compartment, its door closed.

I stepped out. I would enter quietly, steal close, put my hands around his throat and press down until his windpipe was crushed. In a couple of minutes, he'd suffocate.

The corridor was lighted, which meant that I could see only blackness through the window in the door at the end of the car. Was there a guard standing there, perhaps even now watching me?

Yes, perhaps so. Probably so. Hitler was always guarded. Always. I went down the corridor to the WC and went inside. My guts heaved and I vomited into the sink. I washed it out a little bit and then took a piss. I was just coming out when I heard voices.

It was Hitler. He was right outside the door, talking to somebody. He hadn't even been in the compartment. But why was I surprised? The man lived by night.

When the other voice answered, also speaking very low, I realized that it was Himmler. I pressed my ear against the door but couldn't hear what they were saying. I did hear a chuckle, though, as if they were sharing a quiet secret.

I went out.

"Oh!"

"My Leader! Herr Reischfuhrer!"

"Willy, I didn't take you as a night owl like us. We two are up at all hours."

"I was—" I inclined my head toward the loo.

"You go to sleep, boy. You've had a hard couple of days. He was at the front, Heinrich."

"Yes," Himmler said. He smiled at me, and I imagined that I saw reflected in it all of my supposed secrets. He stripped you, Himmler did.

I murmured a goodnight and returned to my compartment.

Once behind the closed door I concentrated on slowing my heart. I took deep breaths, I told myself that they could not know my thoughts—and immediately realized that I didn't believe that. Hitler could see deeply into a man, as I knew from hard experience. He had claimed to me that he didn't believe in the black arts, but he was a master of them.

I was young. My body was tired. Despite the turmoil in my mind and heart, I soon slept.

Just after dawn, I was awakened by soft, persistent knocking at my door. It was a steward, who told me to dress. I had movement orders in an hour. Before that, there would be breakfast for me in the dining room.

When I went in there once again was the Hitler breakfast. It was all I could do not to hurl the pot of Chamomile against the wall.

I was taken away early in a sidecar by another motorcycle messenger. Hitler had not awakened and I was tremendously relieved by that.

The morning was gray, and as I stepped down from the train, I heard the car's service motors whining. There was activity inside. Was Hitler up early, then?

"Let's go," I said to my driver.

"Yes, Sir." He started up the engine.

At that moment, I saw Hitler. He was standing back from a window, just far enough to be in shadow. But it was him. His arms were folded. He was in his shirt and braces. I sensed his gaze touching me.

As we pulled away I had the oddest thought, one that once again touched the edge of the supernatural. I thought, 'That man's soul is called by the name Death, and Death has fallen in love with me.'

At that time, *Nosferatu* was the only horror movie I had ever seen, and as the motorcycle whipped past adjutants, busy orderlies, cook staffs working field kitchens, all the chaos that must attend a mobile government, I thought of the vampire's long, questing claws, and felt their caress across my throat.

We stopped at a provisioning depot and I was issued another helmet. I'd left the one that I'd used at the front in the Kozinksi's chateau. One could not leave the rail yard without one, not even the *Hitlerficker*, I suppose. So off we went, my driver in his *feldgrau*, me in my student's uniform and *stahlhelm*.

I was damned uneasy about traveling on these lonely roads. Here, with pines lining both sides of the narrow, unpaved roadway, we were real targets. Additionally, the helmets of that period were not designed to stop bullets, only shrapnel, and only some of that. So I felt very vulnerable indeed.

We were about ten kilometers out when we went racing into the center of a *shtetl*. This village was a possession of the Kosinski estate, I felt sure, as it stretched far and wide in these parts.

The motorcycle guttering, we moved slowly ahead. A *landser* on guard waved us down.

"You cannot proceed," he said. "There's trouble here."

Ahead I could see that a makeshift gallows had been erected in the little square at the center of the community. A man was hanging on it, his legs slowly kicking back and forth. To one side, there was a line of similar looking men, typical *shtetlers* with great long beards and curls. Some of them were standing passively, others shifting about uneasily. One man pitched forward as I watched and retched loudly. Around them there were the women and children of the village, crying out, begging for the lives of fathers and husbands. I did recognize some of their Yiddish, and that majestic prayer, *Kaddish* came to mind, with its eloquent expression of dignity of the soul.

"*Yitgaddal veyitqaddash shmeh rabba,*" "May his great name be exalted and sanctified," "*Be'alma di vra khir'uteh*" "In the world that his will has made."

My hand went to my pocket, to *Judea Capta*. Tears came into my eyes. The young *landser* saw and said, "*dies verdammten Juden, der Ort kriecht mit ihnen.*"

"What did they do?"

He shrugged. "*Sie taten Judenbuben.*"

Another man was lifted into the noose and left to dangle, spitting and choking and whipping his arms about. A tall woman in a black dress strode up, embraced him by the hips and put her weight on him. His neck cracked and he was still. As she was walking away I saw her face and I will never forget it. There was no sadness there, no hate. There wasn't anything. She was empty, that woman, just simply empty.

An SS officer, tall and handsome and as blond as wheat, went to her, grabbed her shoulder and slashed her across the face with a nasty dog whip.

Her left cheek was laid open. In the sheets of blood, I could see the gleam of her clenched teeth. She continued to walk. He pulled out his pistol and shot her from behind. Now her face flew out into the air, in the form of a haze of blood and bone. By the time she was toppling, another man was on the gallows, once again spitting and gagging and flapping his arms like some sort of great, berserk bird.

"We had better go another way," my driver said.

"Yes." I was forcing myself to remain calm, but I was resolved on one thing: I would not forget this outburst of madness. I would inform Hitler. I would see these men get the punishment they so richly deserved.

In such a time and such a situation, a civilized human being may be, as I was, transformed into a blind, confused fool. One moment, I was contemplating the murder of Hitler, then next thinking to appeal to him to redress an atrocity.

We went along one narrow road after another, traveling across most of the morning. Eventually, we came into the outskirts of a city. It proved to be Stettin, which was absolutely silent, not a soul in the streets.

When we reached the railroad station, my driver got off the bike and saluted me.

"Thank you for a safe ride."

"We were lucky."

"Is it dangerous along the roads?"

He shrugged. He wasn't about to talk defeatism to a friend of Hitler's.

A flight of Stukas went over at low altitude, their engines thundering.

The driver peered up at them. "Necktie soldiers," he muttered. "Lucky bastards." No luck in war, though. Inside of a year, the Stukas would come up against the RAF. The envied "Necktie soldiers" were flying straight to hell.

There was a train in the station with the old two-wheeled steel carriages from the pre-war era. Germany was too indebted to buy decent carriages from abroad, and her entire industrial establishment was given over to arms production, so no new German models were appearing. Fortunately for this pampered little whore, though, there was a "supercar" at the end of the consist, in which I was given a private room. Hitler had made sure that I would be hidden safely away on the trip back to Berlin.

The other cars were full of SS and regular soldiers going on leave, also bureaucrats, all singing and drinking and trading war lies.

Hitler had probably worried about me being seen by agents, and my photograph ending up in the *Deuxieme Bureau* or the SIS , but he also wanted to show off his war to me. Like all demagogues, he was a fantastic narcissist, meaning that the idea that I might react with horror would never occur to him. He was proud of the mayhem he was creating, so he assumed that I would be impressed.

Contemplating this as the train sped along and a steward served me a good meal of bratwursts and red cabbage, chased with white beer, I came to think that Hitler, the genius at manipulation of others, had essentially no feelings. He was unaware of how emotions worked because he was unaware of how they felt. Eva wasn't a lover. She was no more to him than a doll, there for appearances. I wasn't a "son" at all, but only a supplier he needed for his war effort. The only one of us I thought he might have feelings for was demure little Carlotta, who could administer pain severe enough and debasement vile enough to bring to fitful life in the form of misery and humiliation the few disfigured fragments of humanity that must still exist within him.

Again and again, long trains of boxcars passed us going east. Probably at that stage most of them were supply trains. But that would not be true for long. Although I had no knowledge of this at the time, the reason that Thomas Watson of IBM had been given the Order of the German Eagle was that the company provided the punch-card technology that enabled the Nazis to identify Germans of Jewish and other unwanted ancestries, and to locate the socially unproductive for their euthanasia and forced work programs. Doctors did the gassing of the disabled, the malformed and the simple. If you think of the *volk en masse* as the body, then the murder of innocents is nothing more than clearing out infection.

The concentration camps also used IBM equipment to keep track of prisoners. I know this because Dieter Junger became an operator of these "wonder machines," He must have shared responsibility for the gassing of many thousands, but that story is for later in my text.

Hitler, of course, had instantly understood the value of IBM's technology as a tool to help him turn a chaotic democratic state into an efficient totalitarian one. To do that, and do it well, you must have deep access to the individual. You must know his whereabouts, his associations, his racial background, his income, possessions, all of it. If you have a person's data, you can control him. Fortunately, in modern America we have privacy laws that limit the ability of both government and private entities to collect data on us. The America of 1978 is a fortress of the individual. We live in a splendid privacy that is not only the foundation of our freedom, but also the border that defines the person. Blur that border by wholesale invasion of privacy as Hitler did, and the individual becomes unimportant, even—and especially—to himself. Once his privacy is taken and his individuality lost, his freedom is an easy thing to take.

Watson gave Hitler the tool that enabled him to steal the privacy of the German people, and in Willy Heidinger, the head of Dehomag and a keen Nazi, the man he needed to make sure it was done right.

Back in Berlin, I went at once to my house in Wannsee.

In my mind, I was already planning what I would say to Churchill, but first I wanted a bath and a good dinner. Above all, a bath. First, though, I telephoned the Berghof.

Carlotta answered, "Residence." Hearing her voice, so soft and yet so somehow profane—was electrifying. I immediately wanted her. Or let me be more precise, I wanted them both. I wanted to completely lose myself in the flesh, and right now.

"I'm on my way home," I said.

"You were in a battle."

"Yes."

"Eva was very worried."

"And you?"

"Oh, Willy, either come home and stay home or go fuck yourself!" She slammed down the phone. I stood looking at the humming receiver in my hand, and thinking of her, and the love I felt running between us like a deep, inner river.

The Foreign Office soon telephoned to let me know that a permanent *laissez-passér* was in place for me at the Basel customs' point. From there, with my American passport, I could go right on into France. The German officials had been instructed not to stamp an exit permit, as was the usual practice. As far as the French were concerned, I would be an American commercial traveler who had been doing business in Switzerland and now desired to do the same there.

I was delighted to next hear that Hitler's D-2600 was going down to Munich in the morning, and I was welcome to a ride. So I had my bath and a bit to eat, then sat in my smoking jacket before a good fire, read some stories of Thomas Mann and listened to the BBC.

In the quiet of my heart, though, I kept safe my decision to murder Hitler. We'd been alone together before and we would be again. In the quiet of my heart, I waited.

Freya Halter, the housekeeper I had added to the staff, came and went rather nervously. I was reading a forbidden book and listening to an illegal radio station. The former infraction could send me to a concentration camp for six months, the latter to the main police station for an appointment with its guillotine.

I finally said, "Frau Halter, as a member of the personal staff of the leader, I am required to listen to foreign broadcasts in order to better understand the mind of the enemy."

"Yes, Herr Weber."

"Do you understand English?"

"No, Herr Weber."

"Very well, then you aren't disobeying the new law any more than I am."

She went prancing out, clearly much relieved.

I was reading Mann in English—a minor but superb story that very much fitted my mood. It was called "A Weary Hour," and brought to mind many of the peculiar characteristics of war, the waiting, the sense of hopelessness and doom, the feeling of being drained of everything.

In bed, my mind returned, of course, to those poor men being made to stand in line like schoolboys in order to be strangled. Not hung—a quick snap of the neck—but made to endure the agony of suffocation at the end of the rope. And that woman who had sought to relieve her beloved's suffering by hastening his death...the sound of the blow striking her, crisp and cutting, and then the crack of the pistol and her face taking flight as an eyeless, pink haze.

At about three I finally gave up on sleep and wrote Hitler a long letter about what I had seen. Thus I joined that great crowd of Germans who, when witnessing the atrocities of the regime, would say to themselves, 'if only the Fuhrer knew.'

The *einsatzgruppe* that I had seen doing its work was an early formation of what would rapidly become an enormous task force specifically created by Hitler to kill anyone who might be a threat to the *Wehrmacht,* which, in practice meant any gypsies and Jews they could find, and any Pole that showed the slightest sign of resistance.

As I finished, dawn crept up, spreading gray light down from a dense autumn sky. I dressed myself. In a time like this, a private citizen, was not going to be able to find a valet in Germany, not even the *Hitlerficker*.

Before proceeding to Templehof, I stopped at the Chancellery and took my letter about the atrocity to Frau Schroeder, who was at that time keeping Hitler's office there. The ever so discreet Frau Wolf was with him in Poland. When he was organizing the machinery of death, it was always Frau Wolf who took the dictation, I believe. He called her "Wolfin." She-wolf. They were Wolf and She-Wolf. She is not visible in history.

She's still about and I have written her letters, but no reply. I believe that, in 1941, she took the dictation and cut the orders that led to the Wannsee Conference that initiated the Holocaust. All of that was burned in the Chancellery garden in the last days. She burned it, in my opinion.

The other secretaries were never exposed to any of that, so that in later times they could truthfully say that they'd never heard him mention it or seen anything written down about it.

I handed my letter to the affable lady and told her that it must get to him most urgently. She said it would go out with the air courier that afternoon.

Then I went on to the airfield, where his new plane stood apart, gleaming and polished. Inside, it was no longer an airliner at all, but a very swanky sort of salon consisting of two compartments. Bauer, Hitler's pilot, welcomed me and took me forward to Hitler's private room. There was a couch along one side of the cabin, and swiveling seats on the other. Behind a small table was a more elaborate chair. This was the "Leader Seat."

"You're welcome to use it," he said. "But understand that it's fitted with an automatic parachute." He indicated a lever. "Don't pull this or you'll shoot right down through the floor and out into the airstream. The parachute will then open itself and you'll float to earth in the chair."

"Good God."

"We must protect the leader."

I sat down in what must have been the first ejection seat. I believe that the first military version was deployed in night fighters by Heinkel a short time later. The seat was also armored, but despite all this was quite comfortable. As solid as the Condor felt, I really liked being in a seat that would throw me right out of the plane in the event of trouble. Of course, I also worried that it might go wrong and send me flying out without warning.

Some high-level SS came into the plane, but thankfully remained in the rear cabin. Bauer closed the door to the back and said, "You can wait until they've left before going out. There'll be a car for you from the house." He'd gotten Hitler's usual instruction: Willy is not to be seen.

The Condor pulled away with a press of energy, almost like a 707 does these days.

When, two hours and a half later, we circled the Hitler airfield near Berchtesgaden, I immediately saw my own car sitting parked near the small shed that had been built as a waiting area.

It took time for the SS officers to assemble their gear and get off the plane. They were going to discuss some sort of security system with Himmler, who had flown back for the meeting. I believe that, over the next few days at his house, the formal organization of what would become four large murder task forces was defined.

At the time, I had no idea of the scale on which they were planning to kill. I thought that the soldiers and SS I had denounced were war criminals, and that was what I had told Hitler. They were flagrantly violating not only the Geneva Convention, but even the Reich's own murder laws.

Yes, I had read *Mein Kampf*. No, I had not grasped the true meaning of *lebensraum*. The idea that making living space would require the killing of entire nations was simply beyond my imagination.

Hitler was a far more logical man than I. Also, I have to say, smarter. He was always a step ahead of me—of all of us, with the possible exception of Carlotta. But not even she understood the magnitude of the murder program, not even when it was in progress.

When I got out of the plane, I walked immediately toward my car.

The SS were still getting into three Mercedes that were pulled up nearby. As discreetly as possible, I kept my head down and my Fedora over my eyes. I didn't think it much mattered, but if Hitler asked Bauer whether or not I had been discreet, I wanted the answer to be in the affirmative.

My bad angel was behind the wheel. Seeing her, drinking her in, I almost wept. It had been terrible in that battle zone, more so than I realized until the moment that I saw before me this dear image of womanhood—not exactly of peace, but certainly of the female gender at its most appealing.

She rose out of the car like a Rhine Maiden coming up from the water.

"Hey, Willy," she said as she cuffed me on the shoulder, "you look sick. Is the food shitty out there or what?"

"I'm so glad to see you again." I tried to embrace her, but she immediately got back in and started the car. "I didn't know you'd learned to drive."

"What's to learn? I love this thing. Golly but it goes!"

"It does indeed. Would you like me to drive us home?"

"Fuck no. I've got it now and I'm not letting it go. I've been driving all over the place in it the past few days. Eva won't ride with me, the snoot." She whipped it around and accelerated onto the macadam road that led away from the aerodrome. "You know, it does a hundred and fifty klicks easily."

"I know. If you go so fast, you'll get stopped, though."

"I have been. But I just flicked open my pure and showed the little man my Hitler pass and he erected his arm and offered to escort me. I've been all over the *Oberst* and down to Munich. Fast, Willy, *fast*!"

We went shooting along the straightaways and squealing around the curves. As we sped through Berchtesgaden, SS gates flew up, cars swerved and people leaped out of the way.

"Oh, wonderful, they've become terrified of my car."

"You're such a stick, Willy."

"The Leader isn't going to like you scaring people with a car that everybody knows comes from his house. He prefers we be discreet, as you know very damn well."

"So what's he going to do?"

As we whirled up to the Berghof, I saw Eva standing at the foot of the stairs looking fresh and girlish.

Carlotta said, "I'm going to fuck your brains out tonight. Do you mind?"

"I do not mind."

"Queenie and I had a couple of cat fights over the past couple of days. We're ok now, but let me put it this way, she fights like a girl and I fight to win."

"Queenie?"

"You've never heard her called that? She's the mistress of the house, that one, and she makes sure everybody knows it. It can get pretty nasty when she's bored. Which has been always since you two left."

We drove up to where she stood.

"Willy, I've been so eager to see you!"

I got out of the car and kissed her hand.

"Oh, Willy, more than that, I've been too worried!"

We embraced and she kissed me, but chastely—except, of course, for the tip of her tongue.

Carlotta came marching around the car, grabbed me, pulled my face down to hers and plunged her own tongue practically back to my uvula. She tasted of peppermint and cigarettes.

Eva waited, watching with a rigid smile. "Tea," she said. "Shall we go up to the teahouse or have it here?"

"Oh, not the teahouse," Carlotta said. "Why go all the way up there unless we have to?"

"Well, then, my dear princess, we'll do your bidding, as we always do."

In Hitler's absence, there was no SS guard on the door, which was rather pleasant. Having those silent, staring men around was never comfortable. One knew that they saw and heard everything, and wrote detailed reports.

Inside, we took seats in the living room. One avoided the Great Hall. It was no place for anything except official meetings and movies.

Eva said, "The Reichsfuhrer SS has invited himself to dinner."

Carlotta rolled her eyes. "Oh, God, let's feed him something awful and make him go away. Is there any English food? We could feed him English food."

"He'll be given a good dinner. He particularly wants to speak to you, Willy."

That certainly was a grim prospect. I still remembered his attempt, years earlier, to convince Hitler that I was a Jew—which, under the Nuremberg Laws, I may have been. In fact, thanks to the insanity of those laws and the efficiency of the IBM card sorting machines, the number of German people considered Jews had increased from 500,000 to more than 3,000,000. Every day, more people, completely unaware of their ancestry, received one of the dreaded postcards summoning them to the local Gestapo office where they were informed that they were, in fact, Jewish. Then, just like that, they lost everything, jobs, professions, their entire place in the society. People wouldn't even sell them food.

"Let's get him to dance," Carlotta said. "Do you suppose he can Charleston?"

"You've play Alf's records too much. If you play them out, he'll be furious."

"As you say every day, and as I endlessly reply, I do not care if Alf is furious. Alf is always furious. That is the case. Anyway, a lot of people enjoy his temper. It used to turn on that enormous girl from England so much you could smell her drippings from across the room."

Eva snorted in disgust.

"It's nice to see you two enjoying each other."

"We get along very nicely," Eva said.

"No we don't." Carlotta tossed her head. "But we're here, the boss's birds locked up together in our big fat cage."

"Weren't you sisters coming up, Eva?"

"Oh, God," Carlotta said, "those corpses. Don't get me started. When they're here, the SS install a tombstone in the foyer."

"They're lovely and they're fun and I enjoy them."

"No you don't. That's why you disappeared into your room yesterday and left me to sit around not talking to them."

"I heard a lot of laughter. You seemed to have a good deal of fun, if you ask me."

"I have absolutely nothing in common with those crows."

It crossed my mind that Eva and Carlotta might be in love. That would be an interesting complication.

"You cheat them at cards and make a pile doing it. I've seen you."

"I'm extremely honest. It's pathological with me."

"And as soon as they leave, off you go to the town to get hammered with the money you've lifted off them, since you have none of your own."

"Himmler," I said.

"Where?" Eva cried.

"Not here yet. But we need to dress."

When we went up, I discovered that my things were gone from our room.

"If I may be so bold, where are my clothes?"

She gestured toward a heap on the closet floor. "They wouldn't let me hang them anywhere else, sorry." Her Paris dresses now filled the hangers.

I dug down, eventually finding my monkey suit and braces, but no boiled shirt and no drawers. "I need underwear."

"Your undies. Lemme think. Oh, yeah, they're in the bottom drawer of Alf's dresser."

"They're in Hitler's bedroom?"

"Yep."

"You don't do things like that!"

"There is no room in here and I'm not allowed to use any of the other guest rooms. Ergo."

"Don't stick my things in Hitler's dresser! He's Hitler, for God's sake."

"He's a warmongering shit. Sending all those lovely boys off to die." She spat on the floor. "If you want your underwear, you know where to find it."

I got my things from Hitler's room and piled them into the bottom of our closet along with my other stuff. I was becoming more confident with self-dressing and when I was finished felt that I looked rather well turned out.

For her part, Carlotta had become a vision of perfect beauty, her features emphasized by her skill with face-powder. Her face was framed by a bob so fetching that her appearance forced one to consider the possibility that divinity might inhabit the female form. She wore a white silk gown that clung to her with romantic desperation, yet floated about her like a cloud as she moved, revealing first the curve of a breast, then a gleaming hip.

She flipped a cigarette into her mouth, lit it with a big match from the kitchen and said around its bobbing cylinder, "All right, so now we must go face-fuck Hiene. Isn't it going to be a rattling fun evening? Whenever I see him, he makes me think of grocery lists."

"You said you wanted to get him to Charleston."

As smoke roared out of her nose she was the most beautiful dragon in the world. "Oh, he will Charleston."

We went down into the great room. At precisely nine, two of the inevitable Mercedes 770s drew up to the bottom of the steps. Eva, who had been listening to the wireless, came forward. "I'll go," she said as she swept past us. She was outraged that Carlotta was also wearing white silk.

When she went outside, I said to Carlotta, "Didn't you check with her?"

"I did."

"Then why did you wear white?"

"Because I checked. Anyway, in Asia it's the funeral color. And since it's always a funeral when Himmler comes, I thought it was appropriate."

"How do you know about Asia?"

"I'm interested. I read. If you hadn't noticed, there's an excellent library in this house."

I had noticed book backs in various shelves, that was all. I had never pulled anything down.

Himmler and Eva came in. I'd feared that he would be in uniform, but instead he was jammed into a clumsily tailored Tuxedo. He looked like big black box.

"My dear," he murmured to Carlotta as he bent over her hand.

Sunset had brought a cold dankness to the house, and we gravitated toward the roaring fire in the living room. Eva said, "Willy can mix us some drinks. He has that wonderful American touch with a martini. Very dry, yes, that's the way in New York?"

"Absolutely. Gin, a touch of Vermouth, an olive. That's it. Shaken 99 times exactly."

There were two bars in the Berghof, this one and the one in Hitler's study. They were both rudimentary, but I was able to get our waiter, a gentleman whose name I do not recall, to bring up some ice and olives from the kitchen. The olives were black, but I managed some pretty decent martinis poured into champagne *coupes*, each decorated with an olive as black as coal.

Dinner proceeded with Himmler attempting to chat to us. His efforts were at least as stupefying as what transpired during lunches in the Chancellor's Merry Restaurant. He attempted to talk dogs, but Eva detested Hitler's and Bormann's shepherds because they frightened her yappy little rugs. Next he shifted to a discussion of tires. He had seen Carlotta roaring around in my car, and thought she might be interested in racing. He chose to discuss fast tires. She watched him with the sort of morbid fascination that unfunny comedians must see.

We finally finished a really good English-style roast of beef, an unusual dish in Germany and most welcome. I'd smelled it cooking earlier and gone down to the kitchen to find *Scharfuhrer* Kreisler substituting for the dreaded Anna Doehring, who had gone to the *Fuhrerzug*. The roast had been gotten God only knows where. It was in honor of my return.

Himmler said, "Send in my compliments to Frau Doehring."

"Parsnip pudding Anna? She's gone off to the *zug*," Carlotta said. "There's a real man down there. Your fellow, Kreisler. His *schnitzel's* a love potion." She hung her tongue out and wagged it at Himmler.

"We always look for multiple skills in the SS. Which gets me to the reason for my visit, Willy. There will be a young officer here shortly. He is called Helmut Hitzinger. He also attended Harvard, but graduated."

"I will eventually. I've been busy."

"After that he was at the Sorbonne, where he studied philosophy and logic."

What in the world was the point, I wondered? But then, a short time later Hitzinger arrived and I was horrified to see that I recognized him at once. He had been the officer in charge of the murder of the Jews that I had written to Hitler about.

The three of us went to a corner of the Great Hall, Himmler and myself in evening dress, Hitzinger resplendent in a very adequately tailored SS dress uniform.

"Willy is a private hero of the Reich, as I've told you, Helmut. He has the Order of the German Eagle and also the distinction of surviving an attempt by a British agent to toss him out of the Graf Zeppelin."

So, was Edgar Waite really a British agent after all? I still had no idea, but the feeling that he had really been working for Himmler didn't change. Simply because I was an unknown quantity, Himmler might have wanted me dead. Just for that.

"I'm impressed and grateful," Hitzinger said. "On behalf of all of us soldiers."

"Why not share a bit of your own background with Willy?"

"Harvard, '34. Public Administration. Then the Sorbonne, philosophy under the utilitarian Elie Halevy. I think that his ideas on the concretizing of duty as social impulse were what brought me to this organization."

At the time, I was as impressed as I was horrified. A Sorbonne philosopher a Nazi? Hitzinger may have studied under him, but if so he had seriously distorted his ideas.

"I wanted you to understand something of Helmut's background." He drew a typed sheet out of an inner pocket of his jacket. "You say here, 'This officer was acting in complete disregard of the Geneva Convention, and not only that, executing these men in an intentionally cruel manner, apparently only because they were Jews.'"

In surprising me in this way, he'd obviously taken a page from the Hitler psychological warfare playbook.

I said nothing.

"Helmut, I would like you to explain to Willy what he was actually seeing."

"Yes. Very well. The fact that these men were Jews was not exclusively relevant. They were offering resistance in an active battle zone in a theater of war. Under the Geneva Convention, that qualified them as combatants."

I finally found my voice. "Not prisoners?"

"Not prisoners."

"They were bound with their hands behind their backs."

"It was the heat of battle. We had just captured them making gasoline bombs."

Himmler said quietly, "I think you know what a gasoline bomb can do."

"Did the boss even see my letter?"

"He wired me back, 'Willy is horrified. Please explain to him.'" He handed me the wire. Unless it was skillfully forged, it had indeed originated in the *Fuhrerzug*. "I am sure you recall the conversation you and Chancellor Hitler and I had upstairs in his study a while back."

"Yes."

"This matter of surgically cleansing the *volk* of infection is going on now, and it's going to become more and more extensive. Helmut here will soon go to a facility we are building in the Polish town of Osweicim which will be one of a number of clean, sanitary camps where we will separate out population elements our eugenicists have determined to be socially dangerous."

"And as you know," Helmut added, "Charles William Eliot was both America's leading eugenicist and president emeritus of Harvard College when he died. I have enormous respect for him and for his ideas."

"As do we all," Himmler said. "What we're doing here is trying to make a case for the rationality of our cause. Because you wouldn't have written what you did to the boss if you had really understood what you'd been told upstairs."

"It just seems unreasonable to me. Strange and too apocalyptic for comfort. Killing people who've done nothing wrong."

"Willy, calm down. You're not seeing reason. The men you saw being executed *had* done wrong. Gasoline bombs are wrong, Willy."

"You weren't killing them simply because they were Jews?"

"Not at all. We're building holding areas to separate racial and other undesirables. Good, well-managed places where they can live out their lives in peace so that those of pure German blood can fully express themselves at last in the world. You should see it as we do, as something beautiful and, ultimately, kind, since it prevents these lower orders from turning to crime and riot and being seduced by communism."

I hate to say it, but in 1939 it didn't sound all that wrong. An extreme solution, yes, but in the context of eugenics theory, a logical one. Never forget that reasonable people do not do things they believe to be unreasonable. Helmut was neither a fanatic nor a bigot. He was a rational man who was acting according to scientific principles that many people in those days accepted without question. The work of Eliot and other eugenicists was accepted in most quarters without much question.

Don't think that I mean to excuse the people who accepted such ideas, though. I mean instead to warn you. Take the negroes in this country, who have endured generations of oppression based on the idea that they're subhuman. And to this day, try to get a Jew into a club in New York. You'll find resistance almost everywhere except at the Harmonie and the Cosmo.

The thing was, I could not make myself believe that Jews deserved to be segregated, any more than I now believe that negroes do. Although, in 1939, it would not have occurred to me that the blacks deserved a place and the table of the white race, and for many people, especially in Central Europe and Russia, that extended quite naturally to Jews, too.

My Carlotta, whom I just reveled in, was, of course, a Jew. I was pretty sure Hitler was one. Otherwise, why had he blown up the town where his blood grandfather was buried? Because he was buried in the Jewish cemetery, that's why, under a Star of David.

I have tried to organize archaeologists to go to Dollersheim and piece the shattered gravestones back together, but so far the entire German university community has met my proposal with silence.

Himmler and Hitzinger were waiting for me to speak, but I didn't know what to say. Their arguments were impeccable and I was not intellectually equipped to counter them. But also I could not agree that the Jews should be sequestered. *Judea Capta* was in my pocket, Pappy in my heart. What I really wanted to do was cry.

I said, "I believe that we're keeping the ladies from dancing."

"A last thing," Himmler said. "Come here."

The two of us stepped out onto the terrace into a bright, cold night. The mountains glowed beneath riotous starlight.

"Have you a pistol, Willy?"

"I do not."

He drew a small one out of his pocket. "Take this. When you're here, the girls prefer my men to remain at the perimeter. The house needs protection."

It was a small Mauser which would in coming times bring me a chilling surprise.

"Thank you. I'll keep it with me at all times." I put it in my pocket. I thought, 'now I can kill him.' I hadn't dared to buy a pistol, which was not so simple in the Third Reich. There had to be an interview. Identification.

He looked up into the stars. "No matter how peaceful a place may seem, in wartime everywhere is dangerous."

"Still, the perimeter seems very well guarded."

"Do you know that we have found British agents within a few hundred meters of this house? You could have an intruder."

Back inside, Hitzinger had gravitated to the fireplace and was chatting to Eva and Carlotta.

"Oh, there you are," Carlotta said. "We've decided to Charleston."

"Not me," Himmler said quickly. "Too heavy footed, I'm afraid."

"Nonsense, you deserve a little fun, too, as hard as you work."

"I'll watch and clap along. I'll enjoy myself thoroughly."

"*Clap along*? This isn't a *Schuhplattler*." She put her hands on her hips. "You'll dance."

"How dare you give me an order!"

She laughed in his face, and from his expression, it was all he could do not to slap her. Seeing the friction, Hitzinger immediately stepped away and began gazing at the darkness that filled the great window. Eva went to look for a record.

I whispered to Himmler, "They have a wager."

"Ha! So that's the reason for this insolence. Who wins if I dance."

"Eva."

"Stop that whispering," Carlotta said.

Eva put on a Charleston. I don't remember the song, but it was a raw geechie Charleston, that I do remember, as black as it could be and a spectacular example of what the Nazis called *negermusik.*

"It's too bad we don't have Goebbels here, he would so enjoy this," Himmler said in a voice dripping sarcasm. With little wink toward Eva, he took off his jacket. "Now we shall see."

In those days, I loved the Charleston and so did the girls, and it turned out that Himmler could actually manage it a bit.

Carlotta did a few steps with him, then doubled over, convulsed with laughter. "You look like a penguin." She hopped from side to side, mimicking him. Hitzinger had become a statue, his back to us, apparently obsessed with the invisible view.

In those dear, dead days before arthritis and lumbago and whatever else has slowed me to my present lurching creep, I loved to dance. From the Charleston to the Twist, I was center floor all my life, and that night was no exception.

Himmler managed about five minutes of it before he lost his breath. Hitler had his bowling and his walks, but Himmler had only dinner. He was a real eel, though, and of all the inner circle who survived the capitulation, he's the one I would have thought might have escaped. He didn't, though. I've looked at the photos, read Selvester's testimony and Wells's description of the suicide.

Carlotta next dragged Hitzinger onto the floor, and he proved to be a real rug surgeon.

So there I was, dancing with the Nazis. A shameful business to have to admit. But there it is. In all that terrible time we had happy days in that house. I don't honestly know what my moral stance should have been. But I do know this: my outward complicity was an *entrée* into their secret world, which, in '39 I was just beginning to understand how to use.

When the next record went off, Himmler put his jacket back on. "We can't linger. My train is in Munich and we're scheduled to leave for the front at one. Anyway, all of you are young enough to be *swing-heinies*, and we don't need servant talk, do we?"

Hitzinger could hardly conceal his disappointment, but contented himself with saying his goodbyes to the ladies. Carlotta, of course, was an enthusiastic *swingjugend*. Not politically, but she was full of dance and joy and loved above all things to swing and party and be a happy girl. My dear, cute, fierce little Jew. I want to put my arms not only around her, but around all of them—so many—for the death camps were a killing ground primarily for the young and the old, and many more are young than old.

A toast to you, ghosts.

# 4

Sullenly, Eva dug fifty marks out of her purse. "You knew he could dance. How?"

"I've seen him do it before, with clothes and without," Carlotta said.

"Without?" I asked. "What was that like?"

Carlotta stuck out her right hand and curled her index finger up and down.

Eva glared at her. "Is that supposed to be funny? An insult to the *Reichsfuhrer SS*?"

"Am I laughing?"

"No, lying. You're lying, aren't you?"

Carlotta burst out laughing. "I never give up my little fleas, you should know that by now, Sister."

"Don't you sister me, you puke-faced *minette*!"

I guessed that Eva had been trying to find out what Carlotta did privately with her own man. Probably, they'd fought about it. Now that she was revealing something about Himmler, I thought that more about Hitler was going to be demanded.

"I'd like to take a big fat hairbrush to your bottom, you bitch."

"Would that be fun for you, then? Are you that sort, too, not just a tongue hussy? 'Oh, Carlotta, I'm so hot I can't sleep.'"

"Shut up!"

"'Be nice to me tonight. Be *nice*, Carlotta.'"

As Carlotta taunted her, Eva turned absolutely red. Her eyes, dancing toward me, were desperate. In another second, she was bound to leap at Carlotta.

"It's nothing to me," I said, which was becoming my constant phrase among these degenerates. "Everybody needs comfort. Especially in wartime."

Now Eva's eyes opened wide. "Wartime? What are you talking about?"

"Look at her," Carlotta said, "she doesn't even know. You, all you ever listen to is dance music and do flirty-flirty with Himmler's lugs. How long since you read a newspaper or listened to a radio? A year? Two? Never?"

"Just because they know you're a whore and won't touch you, you're jealous. Of course the boys like me, I'm beautiful and a real German."

"I'm a real German!"

Eva wrinkled her nose as if smelling something vile. "Paperwork! All sorts of criminality among the bureaucrats."

"What's that supposed to mean?"

Eva leaned forward. Her lips were tight, her eyes hard. Her face had become ugly, shockingly so. "Paperwork changes nothing and I know it and so do the guys."

Carlotta was now as still as a snake. I thought that she was going to strike, but that is never the snake's first choice. It wants to live, it wants to slip away. She changed the subject. "Chatter like this is unimportant. But you do need to keep up with affairs, if nothing else for your own safety."

"Here? This is heaven. There are no affairs here. The gardens, the swimming, the skiing. Those are our affairs."

"We happen to be at war with Poland, to enlighten you *Deutsche Madchen*."

"Oh, well, I'm sure there's a reason."

"No wonder he keeps you shut up. What an idiot."

"How dare you insult me! Your better!"

"I don't call a photographer's assistant anybody's better. Anyway that old drunk just did porn until he latched onto Alf. He's no different from some sleazy alphonse."

"Vicious little bitch!" Eva leaped at her.

I got between their clawing entanglement. "Easy! Hey, I want some fun tonight."

Eva broke away and immediately burst into tears. I moved to comfort her, but Carlotta was there first, and then they were in one another's arms.

"Good, this is more promising! Is there room for three?"

We danced some more, that wonderful, athletic, exhausting old dance, until at last the girls had danced their rancor away and were once again laughing and enjoying one another. They were lovers, certainly, and so they remained. Over the years, I never ceased to find their fiery affair beguiling.

After about half an hour, I stopped Eva from putting on another record. "OK, time, ladies. I want to go upstairs now and go to bed."

They both looked at me in frank horror.

"I mean with you, of course."

Eva gave me a sidelong glance. "Oh?"

"Let's go," Carlotta said.

Eva took my hand and off we went to her little suite. As soon as the door was closed, we took turns stripping one another. A sort of ceremonial grace came into it. They kissed hungrily, and I found myself touched by the passion they shared for each other. Eva was hardly a tongue-hussy, which was what the Berlin whores used to call an old maid looking for lesbian action. This was real love, simple and direct.

They kissed one another in the deep place, and long. In the light of Eva's pink shaded bedside lamp, they were beautiful to see, wound up together in a frolic of legs. They weren't strictly homosexual, far from it, but they were what were called in those days *heine schwestern,* hot sisters.

I soon made it a *menange a trois*, and thus we began a relationship that would last until the day in 1945 that a battered old 770 pulled up to the front and Eva set off for Berlin and the *Fuhrerbunker*.

I'm not ashamed of my unusual sexual life during the war. In such times you want to live as much as you can and as fast as you can, and the younger you are, the more you want to. Although when I think about it, I was already practicing for the Berghof when I lived in Malibu. My house was a hippie commune before there were hippie communes. By comparison, the Berghof was pretty staid, it being just the three of us unless Hitler was there—which, a few days later, he was.

It was a rare warm afternoon, October the 7th. We were sunning ourselves on the terrace, the three of us starkers, as had immediately become our habit once we began having sex together.

So when one of the waiters came out, which they were forbidden to do, Eva, who had learned something about cursing from being around Carlotta, yelled "Fuck a living duck," grabbed her housecoat and threw it around herself.

By contrast, Carlotta slid into a more provocative pose.

The waiter blurted, "The boss! Ten minutes!"

Eva, now on her feet and wrapped in the robe said, "Thank you, Louis" in a tightly controlled tone. She had gone in an instant from fury to bursting excitement, I could see it. Carlotta merely rolled her eyes and spread herself more openly to the sun. Louis ran off like a terrified little boy.

Carlotta said, "*Scheisse*, last sunny day until May and here comes work, wouldn't you know."

"You love him, too, bitch-face. Admit it."

"Shut up."

There was a clamor inside and we all ran for the stairs just as SS were rushing up from below to mount their guard posts. There were more than a few guffaws as Carlotta and I, still buck naked, took the back stairs three at a time. Eva walked regally up the front and disappeared into her room.

I threw on a lounge suit.

"I like you naked."

"I like you naked, too, but not now."

"You're so pretty, Willy. I know I've told you that a thousand times." She came to me and put her arms around me. She began working my member.

"I'm trying to get a collar on, hey!"

She stroked it up. "It's such a nice one. Getting it stiff is my hobby."

"But not now. Get some clothes on."

"Why? Right now all that's in his mind is naked girls, you may be sure. Which reminds me, I've to go down and eat some cabbage."

What response could there be? I couldn't imagine what she meant. But she promptly threw on a dress, a short blue one with a pinafore top. A couple of puffs of powder, a brush through her hair and she was transformed in appearance from a woman of twenty to a girl of fifteen. She could make herself look old, young, it didn't matter. Her skill at this was quite remarkable.

Although neither she nor Paul Dukes ever mentioned it, I have no doubt that she'd also been coached by the master at some point. Dukes always said that G. I. Gurdjieff, had brought the secret of "plastics" with him from Tibet. I enquired about this of both P. D. Ouspensky and Jeanne De Salzmann, but got nothing out of them.

There was also in Carlotta that actress who, as I later discovered to my cost, is the only person who is really there. Her bluster is a trick, put on to conceal the fact that she isn't real. Behind her eyes, if you look long you see something that I think is emptiness. Someone who lives and suffers as she lived and suffered dies even as they live on, a kind of furious automaton, seeking always for some signal of a love they might trust.

I have tried hard to send her such signals, but she does not believe them, not really. Still, though, I love her, more now even than in those steamy young days.

As she went down the servants' stair, a rising buzz of voices came up from the great hall. In it, I heard his voice, low and graveled, giving orders. He sounded tired. I thought to myself that he must be glad to be home.

For him, though, not even this house was a real home. Eva was his home. Eva and Carlotta. To a lesser extent, me.

I recalled a poem of Frost's, "Death of the Hired Man," which I had recited at a citywide high school speech meet when I was a boy, "Home is the place where, when you have to go there, they have to take you in."

His voice rose and dropped, rose and dropped, a torrent of words amid the surging buzz. Heel clicks and *jawohls* indicated the presence of military. I crossed the hall to where I could look out over the drive and saw a long line of cars and some resplendent officers still walking up toward the stairs. I counted twenty cars until the curve, and there were more behind.

"Where is Willy? Willy! Willy, I want you!"

I ran down at once, just like an excited child.

"Yes, yes, Wolf!"

He wore the simple uniform tunic he had adopted for the war. He was surrounded by resplendent generals who circulated amid a drifting cloud of adjutants. Voices, kept soft in the presence of power, now fell to silence. I was watched by shark's eyes in tight, cold faces.

As I went toward him he gave his head a sharp shake and gestured toward the other staircase. Gladly averting my face, I crossed and mounted it.

Eva was there. "What's going on?"

"He's *geladen* with generals."

"*Scheisse*!"

"He sent me over here, so we'll get him in the end, never worry." I went into his study and sat in my usual chair. Eva came in and took a drink of *schnaaps* from his little bar.

"Is there any whisky there?"

She brought me some of the Grant's. "Dare we smoke, Willy, do you think?"

"You, too! The second he shows up, all I want is a cigarette."

"I know, it's hilarious."

She was splendid, her eyes shining.

Carlotta came in.

"When did you grow down," Eva said.

"Shut up. I'm at work."

"Work, you call it! You're one of the luckiest women in the world."

"And I'm still at work. Oh, Willy, where's the smokes?"

"We can't smoke in here, Princess, not tonight," Eva said.

"Fag me, Willy."

I took a cigarette from my case, gave it to her and lit it. She strolled out onto the balcony. We could see the cigarette end rising and falling in the dark.

"Oh, damn, fag me, too!" I gave Eva one and she went out, too.

Not a minute later, here was Hitler. Striding in, he threw off the tunic. "Damn uniforms itch," he said. "What's that? Who's smoking?"

"I'm not."

Eva and Carlotta reappeared. Their cigarettes had gone over the edge, I supposed.

As she looked at him, Eva's face melted with love. Carlotta, too, as much as she tried to play the cold professional, watched him with eyes full of eager fire.

Silently, he walked to Eva, clicked his heels and kissed her hand. He then did the same to Carlotta, who curtsied like the schoolgirl she had made herself up to appear. "Lovely," he said softly, "lovely." He drew his hands together and gazed at them. "Later, then."

They stepped out, closing the door behind them.

"Willy, I get letters first from one of them and then the other, full of complaints and accusations. They denounce each other on a regular basis. Once I got a letter from Carlotta that was simply a list of insults she claimed Eva directed at her. Bitch, whore, pig, on and on. What do you make of it, Willy?"

"They're in love."

He laughed. "Ah, of course! Why didn't I see it? I'll put the letters in the burn box, then." Dropping into a chair, he continued, "I've been flying since noon." He held his hands over his face. "Down there, they're all plotting. They have a secret group. I know the whole story, of course. They want to kill me and negotiate with Britain and France."

I thought, 'I could do it. I could do it tonight.' I said, "But we're winning."

"That hasn't occurred to them yet. When it does they'll be heiling me like Hitler Youth."

"Will you have them shot?"

He shrugged. "Willy, I have an addition to the mission I mentioned to you in Poland. I won't lie, it's dangerous."

"All right."

"Can you live rough in a forest?"

The answer should have been a good, old-fashioned American 'are you kidding?' but I knew him well enough not to do that. Instead I told him I would manage.

"That's my Willy, it's never 'no.' Incidentally, the French did nothing in the Saarland except leave, which is as you said it would be. What I want you to do is to go to France before London and go out into the countryside. There is a forest above the Maginot called Ardennes. Go in there and take photographs, especially foresters tracks, that sort of thing. Close ups, I'm not looking for tourist photos. There will be mapmakers in there, apparently French but really ours. Stay well clear. And if any French want to take your film away, expose it. Under no circumstances should they see it. In any case, if they do see, they'll likely shoot you, , American passport or not. I want those pictures—and you—so be careful, please. Also take notes. Is the ground hard, soft, what's it like? That sort of thing."

"Is it in the military area?"

"No, that's farther south. Stay well away from the Maginot. As far as the films are concerned, go back to Paris and take them to the Swedish embassy. Be careful around there, the *Sûreté* is watching. When you go to the embassy, say you are Herr Winkler. Give them the film and your written descriptions for the bag."

"Yes."

"Willy, do you still—" He locked eyes with me. "How do you feel?"

I stood up. I opened my arms. He came to his feet and came into them. I held him for a moment, reeking breath and all, then said, "Go to the girls, Alf. They're trembling with eagerness."

Now he stepped away. "Why am I like this?"

"Never mind. We are what we are, all of us."

He took one of my hands in both of his. He looked down at it. I thought he was going to kiss it, and almost raised it to his lips for him, but he dropped it. There was that in him, too, deep. Perhaps that's why he loathed homosexuality so. He loathed himself.

This man, who when I'd decided to kill him was an abstraction, now stood before me full of life and—how to put it—reality.

This was going to be hard, but I was determined.

I'd hidden the gun at the back of a drawer. Carlotta's hands went everywhere and I didn't want her to find it. She'd go around blaring like a megaphone, 'Willy keeps a fucking pistol!'

When the right moment came, I would use it. Not tonight with the house so full and the SS everywhere. But soon it would be just the four of us and all would be quiet. I would steal into his bedroom and blow his brains out.

"There has to be a dinner, then another conference before they leave. Keitel and Rundstedt and von Bosch will be here overnight. They conquered Poland with my considerable help and now they can't believe it. Stupid pigs! It's a new world—a thousand year nation! More, Willy. That land is Germany now."

I wanted to question him about his plans for the Poles, but I thought it too dangerous. Adding such questions to the letter and my previous concerns about the Jews would cause his suspicious mind to fester. He forgot nothing, that man.

"It's a signal victory, Alf. We're all very proud of you."

"On to other matters," he replied. "Paul. He's still in France. Look him up. He should be working for us, you know. Good man. And Putzi is now definitely interned. See if you can get in to see him. Give him my very best and tell him that we can get him out if he wants to come back."

"He's in prison?"

"An enemy alien being kept in the basement of a railroad station." He laughed. "He's no political genius, poor fellow. Tell him Wolf misses his big hound face!"

As always on official evenings, Carlotta and Eva and I dined here in the study. Eva would sit hunched over her food in a state of humiliation. But she was never angry at him. Her love was too deep for that. Instead, every footfall on the stair would cause her to go alert with anticipation.

Late, he went upstairs with Carlotta, and I screwed Eva very lovingly and gently in her bed, and whispered that she was my little doe and as she came to the *petit mort,* she called out my name in a sharp, precise way, like a schoolteacher snapping at an unruly child.

When he came down all flushed with a towel around his middle, she was ready for him, dressed in a deep red gown and swimming in perfume. As always, Carlotta had transformed him into a satyr. They went into his bedroom.

I said to Carlotta, "What do you think the generals would say?"

"What they say anyway. That he's completely crazy."

We were in the study. The bedstead next door was chugging like a flivver.

"Do you enjoy him?"

"Sure." She came to me. "You fucked her. I can smell it."

"That nose! You can smell like his bitch Blondi, do you know that?"

"You'd better be ready for me, William Weber, is all I can say."

Back then of course I was ready. We didn't dare go down through the fog of generals and up to our room, so we used Eva's still warm bed. As was often the case after one of Carlotta's sessions with Hitler, I had the impression that she was screwing him in the mind, me in the flesh.

I think that a great part of his attraction to women came from the fact that he trusted them with his perversity. This intimate revelation of the hidden heart just melted them. As grotesque as it was, it was still a man giving himself in utter nakedness, which invoked the deep protective instincts of the mother to the babe.

When Carlotta punished him, however he bade her to do it, the best thing in her, protective and cherishing, came to the surface.

It was that not way with all the others--Valkyrie, I suppose, who shot herself and Geli who wanted to save him from it. But Eva played his Venus with aplomb, and Carlotta his Erinys. His personality was so extreme that even if he had been nothing more than a shopkeeper, he would have evoked these primordial currents in all who loved him —as, indeed, he did to the entire German nation, not just his women...and me.

I slept in Carlotta's arms that night, fitfully, uneasily listening to the night wind that so often howled in the eaves of the Berghof and thinking of the men at the front huddling by their fires, faceless in the tide of war but each unto himself essential beyond price.

When dawn came, cold fog and a dripping sky, I pulled on my trousers and braces and went down into the silent house. The generals who had rated a room in the Berghof were asleep. In the foyer, the SS guard sat in a hard chair, slumped forward and purring like a tomcat. I wandered over to the map table that now filled the space before the huge window. There were papers scattered about, and I recalled Churchill's request for lists of armaments, which I had so far been unable to fulfill. Almost at random, I scooped up a bound document and took it up to our room in the back, where I slipped it into the file pocket of the suitcase I intended to take with me. I didn't look at it.

Smelling coffee, I went down to the kitchen where I found a breakfast buffet being prepared. Eager to head off the Hitler breakfast, I put sausages, a couple of eggs and some toast soldiers on a plate and poured myself coffee in an SS mug, not one of the delicate Berghof coffee cups. I took my booty to the dining room and ate it in the alcove.

I sat facing the terrace view, so that anybody coming down from upstairs would see only my back. And indeed, when two of them came down, I heard one start to give me 'good morning' and the other whisper to him, "Stay away, it's the *Hitlerficker*."

Soon others arrived. They all began chatting to one another. I knew next to nothing about the military, so I couldn't really tell who was who. Little was said, but I did hear some French, *Semois*, then *Naimur.* Was the conference about an attack on France, then? If so, then Hitler was after all going west before he struck at the Russians. Along with practically everybody else, I had expected him to plunge right into Russia. The declarations of France and England had done little more than amuse the newspapers. The French were calling it the "joke war" and the Germans the "sitters' war."

I would have liked to stay a bit longer, but, as I was learning, any delay was now regarded by Hitler as the next thing to a betrayal. I'd have liked also to take my car instead of the train, but I doubted very much that an American showing up at the border in a BMW sportster was going to incline French customs to grant me an easy passage into the country. I decided that I would drive it to Munich, though, if only to keep Carlotta from wrecking it.

Later, I made Eva and Carlotta laugh by insisting that they swear they wouldn't kill each other while I was gone, and left hoping that they would actually manage this. The three of us took a private moment in Eva's suite to kiss goodbye. We came together in an embrace and it was so very, very pleasant.

I said, "I understand now what the *Muselmann* see in it."

"But we are four," Eva said. "Two wives to two husbands."

We stole into Alf's room where he lay sleeping curled up on his side in the narrow bed that had been with him for years and that he cherished.

"That thing certainly bangs and rocks," I whispered.

"Sh! You'll wake him up."

"I'm awake and Willy get the fuck out of here. You've got a mission, last I heard."

Eva was horrified and Carlotta burst out laughing.

He sat up. "What's going on? Are you here to play some joke? This isn't a house party. Those days are over." He looked from one to the other of us.

Eva raised her shoulders and tilted her head in that way that she had that was such a gesture of love.

He said to me, "Goodbye, God is with us." He winked.

Carlotta said, "Willy, if you get killed, I'll kill you."

I left quickly. As I drove through Berchtesgaden people hurried out of the way, seeing the now infamous car. Carlotta would be furious when she discovered that I'd taken it, but if she was going to drive, she was far safer in one of the lumbering 770s.

I got to Munich just in time for the afternoon express. The trains to Switzerland were still decent, as, in fact, they remained throughout the war. The traffic on that line was soon to become exclusively devoted to officialdom and privilege. Even in '45, wealthy and powerful Germans were still taking vacations in Switzerland. When the surrender took place, a large number of them simply stayed on, enjoying the wealth they had hidden there and eventually becoming Swiss citizens. If you could open all the vaults in Zurich, you would find an extraordinary treasury of art, jewels and gold, still to this day.

When I got to the station, the crowd on the platform was literally huge. Desperate Jews were offering huge sums for a space on the Swiss train. Many of them had not been Jews until the new law, and had just discovered recently that they came under its purview. Touts stood on the steps selling tickets, some doubtless stolen, others counterfeit.

These new Jews had generally been entirely German with no idea that they were Jewish under the law. In a sickening, stunning moment, as I have said, they had lost their entire social and economic validity. Plenty of them had been Nazis, some even party officials.

This is a forgotten reality of history, the fact that Jewishness was extended to so many by the law. Hitler was right when he said that he'd made it too strict, but it was too late now. In future years scenes like this would be repeated all over Europe as the Dehomag Hollerith Card Sorters ground eagerly away, dropping their harvest of lives into the hands of the Gestapo and the SS...and the wealth and property of the victims into the treasury and thus also the coffers of the Nazi elite.

Back in the fifties, I tried to see Thomas Watson. I wanted to find out how he would react to meeting another recipient of the Eagle. And what of Willy Heidinger, who had been so proud of their machines' role in enabling what he called the "corrective procedures" that were, in fact, the holocaust? I would so like to have spoken with him. And what did Wilson think of him now, who had said, "We are proud that we may assist in such a task, a task that provides our nation's Physician Adolf Hitler with the material he needs for his examination. Our Physician can then determine whether the calculated values are in harmony with the health of our people. It also means that if such is not the case, our Physician can take corrective procedures to correct the sick circumstances."

Hitler, as lead *volkisch* physician, reassured his SS doctors that they could not violate the Hippocratic Oath by killing Jews and Gypsies and all the rest any more than they could by killing microbes with insecticide.

Desperate new insects shouted along the platform, calling *Helga, Kurt, Emil, Georg, Maria* in the ocean of the crowd. And what happened to me? With my Hitler *lissez-passér*, I was ushered into the train and swept into its quiet interior full of officers and other nameless excellencies like me in their flattering suits with their chattering ladies at their sides.

We were the ones who would enter Switzerland without paying a huge exit fee, the business people and the spies and the officers enjoying a leave away in neutral territory.

When the whistle shrilled, the left-behind on the platform howled their woe and we began to move. As we slid past the them, I saw George Grosz caricatures glaring at me, their hands clutching wide-eyed Kurt Gunther children, and in the shadows a girl who reminded me at once of Carlotta when she lured me with night eyes. Hers was the yearning face of the woman in Franz Stuck's "the Sin."

The engine wailed again, and I could almost hear in the *tok tok* of the wheels the hammering hooves of the horse in "the Wild Ride."

Death was everywhere on that platform, and there were hanging pots of begonias as well.

Not long after we left the station a waiter came along ringing his gong, and we all went to the dining car just ahead of us, coupled right behind the engine so that we important ones would never have to go back into the rest of the train.

I had a lovely piece of salmon and with it a decent Dr. Loosen, not old enough to be oily, not young enough to be simple. It was the sort of wine Hitler would have loaded with sugar cubes.

There was talk, of course, the knowing chit-chat of the important. We knew more than the cattle in the back, after all, we special ones.

A dining companion: "Do you know that when Hitler found himself forced to attack those dirty Poles, he wept?"

Me: "Did he?"

"Yes. I have a friend who knows him personally and said that it's true."

"Ah. I'm impressed."

It went on like that, everybody an insider, everybody possessing secret knowledge of the genius.

There was a woman with foxes around her neck, and I thought that those dead creatures had the brightest eyes in the room. I wondered, 'do I, also, look so dead?'

After lunch, I decided to stretch my legs with a walk along the train. When I went through to the car behind us, I found myself confronted by a chaos much worse than I had imagined. The compartments closest to the door were occupied by soldiers in *feldgrau,* obviously the batmen and servants of the officers in our car. But farther along there were people everywhere, bursting out of the compartments, filling the narrow aisle, men women and children.

I could see the fear in those clutching eyes and smell it in the sour stink of cheap tobacco and sweat, and in the awkward attempts to appear presentable. There were crooked collars and soup-stained ties, dresses slack from wear and children so brown with dirt that they might as well have been Lascars or Sarawaks. But these were not the abject of war, not yet. They would come later. These were mostly middle class people unexpectedly uprooted, and that's the appearance they presented, doctors, barristers, other professionals in sagging worsteds, their terrified ladies and babies clinging to them.

They were the first among what would swell to a roiling glut of migrants going here and there, riding the rails, walking the roads, dying in their millions in this new sort of war, which was primarily about and against civilians.

I soon returned to "our" car, where I ordered *schnapps* and sat tippling and watching the countryside roll by, as the engine wailed and the carriage swayed and the sun slipped westward toward night.

# 5

The three of us had in some sense been drawn not to Adolf Hitler, but into him, like insects buzzing in a pitcher trap. We were not subject to the tirades, the drama, the doctrinaire posturing or the compulsive domination that his subordinates had to endure. With us, Hitler was alone with himself. We were living shadows, the three of us, reflections of the desires that coiled through him like greasy smoke.

Because we were part of him, we were also uniquely independent. Unless we tripped over our own feet somehow, we were above suspicion.

For this reason, this particular secret projection of Hitler found himself going through quite easily into Switzerland and then France. One went from the German *banhof* to the French railway annex, stopping first for German customs, then Swiss, then French.

At the German customs crossing all the frantic horde from the train was clamoring to be let out, screaming in anguish when they were short the exit fee. It had to be right to the *pfennig* or they were turned back, their passports stamped *Kein Ausgang.*

With my pass, I was not only waved through, the entire customs team snapped to attention and saluted me. As promised, no exit was stamped into my passport. Swiss customs was also easily accommodating. When I arrived at the French crossing, my business was asked. I fell back on Weber Electric. No customs official was going to question a purveyor of exotic electronics like vacuum tubes in time of war, so I was soon on my way to Lyon.

Just like that, in the moment of crossing a border, normal Europe reappeared like a ghost re-fleshed. There were no frantic passengers on the French train, the corridors were not jammed with refugees and the immutable sense of the ordinary conveyed confidence and contentment.

This was France, a country with regular laws and established rules. Nothing could change that, one might be tempted to imagine. But as we clipped along in the failing afternoon, I thought to myself that this world was truly poised under a sword. In the house of Adolf Hitler just a few hundred kilometers away, a great movement of troops was being organized, orders cut, logistics prepared, divisions set into motion.

I sat smoking and reflecting, attempting to make sense of it. As the angle of the sun grew long, a silver fog appeared. Another waiter came along with another gong. I went to the dining car for the last sitting at nine, and ate an entrecôte and drank a claret. Railroad fare, nothing more, but French railroad fare and so quite adequate.

As always, I stopped at the Crillon. I wished that we were together, the three of us, or in fact even the four. Why not? We were whole when we were four, three fleshly planets orbiting the dark Hitler sun.

I asked the concierge to find me an escort, one who had good conversation and who could either sing or play. I needed civilized talk and music. I had been in the land of the barbarians long enough. No more Holderlin and Bach for me. I wanted the *Follies Bergere* and the sweaty dives of Pigalle.

Her name was Vera and she was ambitious for a grand life, delighted to be with a gentleman of the Crillon, and him in a suite, no less. We went to Maxim's for a late supper, then in the wee hours to see my beloved Josephine Baker. She sang in that sweet, sad voice of hers and looked as always so very lovely. Her subsequent history in the war years is one of great heroism. What a beautiful life she led! Back in the sixties when I heard of her struggles, the loss of her castle, and I wanted to step in. But of course in Jackie O and the Monacos she had much more desirable supporters than a grotesque old spy like me.

It was nearly dawn before we returned to my suite. My monkey suit was wrecked from too much dancing and too much drink. Vera was intact, though, her professionalism never allowing her to stray too far from her responsibilities.

The hell with responsibilities, as far as I was concerned. I needed escape, to be not only physically but also psychologically outside of Hitler. Out in the world though I was, I still felt the claustrophobia of the prisoner.

So I decided on old reliable and got, after a good deal of cajolery and cash, the night manager to find us some opium. Next, I had to convert this social professional into a whore. Not too difficult, of course, as she was simply pretending not to be one. A Moroccan gent came up with a valise containing pipes and what proved to be lovely smoke, and waited politely in the parlor while we enjoyed a leisurely screw in one of the bedrooms.

When he finally brought us our pipes, he commented that he did not often have calls to such a fine hotel as this one. "But I am here," I said, "Satan's own son and I must have my dope."

As Vera and I opened ourselves to dream, she sang "L'Etranger" in a voice like a breeze. "I am a stranger, a stranger ill at ease in what was once my home..."

I thought to myself that what is lost is lost, and I was lost in another man.

The opium did its duty, carrying me into an illusion of freedom. Vera's song seemed to become an actual breeze, and the pale silk of the bed sheets a swishing fleet of clouds.

Sleep came and the dreams that opium brings, sentimental and unformed, and then the familiar sweet door opened into my private paradise, which I called then and still call "the Land of Nobody Here."

When I awoke at noon, Vera was gone. Our arrangement had been for a thousand francs, and she'd taken exactly that and a tip of a hundred from my wallet. I wrote a note to the night concierge complimenting him on his choice and including a hundred francs for him.

In the afternoon I went round to garages looking for a car to hire. There were no rental agencies then, and most of the mangers reacted to my request with a thick dose of suspicion. Hire a car? When would you stop, in the wilds of Spain or Portugal? What are you doing, running guns or dope, or perhaps both.

I finally found a serviceable Renault, and at the rising of the next dawn set out for the Ardennes.

It proved to be exactly as my *Baedeker* described it, "a densely forested wilderness, thinly populated and possessing no particular attractions for the tourist."

Nevertheless, I did exactly as requested, driving along tracks until the car was in danger of being mired, stopping frequently to take photos of the track and the ground around it, then driving on. Once when I stopped, I thought that I heard voices, but a walk off the track revealed nobody. I could not drive on, so I turned the car around and stopped it atop a small rise where the ground was drier than it was in the low place where I'd initially parked. I intended to scout around a bit and didn't want the tires to sink into the mud. I was easily ten kilometers into the forest. Although the track out was clear enough, I would not have liked to report the car mired, which would entail a need to explain why I had driven into the Ardennes in the first place. The French are a suspicious race.

As I walked ahead, I heard the voices again. This time they were distinct. Moving carefully, I went closer. A voice said in French, "*Arrete.*"

I said, also in French, "Yes, of course."

A man appeared. He was wearing the dark blue coverall of a member of the French forestry service. "Why are you here? Have you become lost?"

His French was, like mine, good, but—also like mine—not native. There was about it the edge of an accent that marked it either as the learned language of a German speaker or the natural French of an Alsatian. He was good enough that I couldn't tell.

In the next moment, a group of men, also dressed as foresters, appeared around a bend just ahead of us. Between them they carried a large wooden frame painted dark green.

They stopped. Then they slowly backed out of sight.

I said, "I'm an American botanist. I study conifers. I came in here for the pines."

His eyes went from me, then back along the path, then they returned to me. There was now a resolution in them, and one that I did not like.

A gun appeared in his hand. "I am so sorry," he said. I could see his thumb manipulating the safety.

There was no time to explain. There was no time for anything. As I threw myself to one side, he fired. I hit the ground and rolled away from him. Quite calmly, with the practiced skill of a well-trained soldier, he stepped toward me and braced the pistol.

I took the only chance I had left and said in German, "I am here for the Reich and so are you."

He continued to prepare to fire.

"We both have our work in here. Let me do mine." As I rolled, the bullet passed so close that I felt its hot wind against the back of my head

"You'll be court martialed," I shouted, "stop this!"

"Have you any document?"

As I stood and raised my hands, I said, "Have you?"

"What is your unit?"

"I can't tell you and you can't tell me, and we both know that."

He stared at me. I stared back. I said, "I'm doing terrain analysis. You?"

"Measurements."

"Want a smoke?"

"No."

"Mind if I do?"

"No."

"No no or no yes?"

He smiled slightly. "You may smoke."

I took out my cigarettes and lighter.

"Those aren't French." He sniffed. "Or German."

"American." I held out my case. He took one. I lit him.

"Good!"

"Indeed."

He slipped the pistol back into his overall. "Now we leave it. Go away from here."

I had survived, but who was he? What were these men doing here? I tried to draw him out by offering a bit of information. "I'm taking soil samples."

Solemnly, he nodded, but offered nothing in return. He walked off around the bend and I saw him no more. When I got back to my car and got inside, I found myself shaking so badly that I couldn't manage the cigarette and tossed it away. I rolled up the windows, locked the doors and leaned my head against the steering wheel. I was amazed at how much I wanted to live, the clawing desperation of it, then this wild, uncontrollable shaking.

I drove all the way back to Paris, stopping only for petrol. At the hotel, I wrote out my notes and sealed them along with six rolls of film in a heavy envelope. I then went to the Swedish Embassy. Rather than take a cab and risk being followed, I walked, window-shopping idly as I went. I stopped for a coffee, then wandered into a shop and bought a small bag in which I could carry the envelope.

The Swedish Embassy was an imposing structure, a bit more baroque than most of the embassies, and guarded by a pleasant young soldier, unarmed, who went to attention as I climbed the steps to the entrance.

Inside, I told the receptionist that I was Herr Winkler. She silently took my envelope and stepped into a side room. A moment later she reappeared with a smartly dressed man of about forty. He had a sheet of yellow paper in his hand, which he held out to me.

It was a cable from "Doctor Heer." It said simply, "Be safe, H."

I took it and left the embassy. I wanted to get away as quickly as I could. I hadn't forgotten Hitler's warning that the *Sûreté* watched this place.

During the war, the Swedes were only officially neutral. Their freedom depended entirely on Adolf Hitler, which they understood very clearly. They sold him iron ore and many other commodities. Their only demand was as it had been from the beginning, that they be paid in gold. It is my belief that Swedish embassies provided Hitler with more support of the kind I was being given than history has recorded. I do not base this on any information more than this one incident. But surely such accommodation must have been made in other cases, perhaps many of them. They were like the Swiss, neutral but compatible. However, when they realized what was happening to the Jews, they opened their doors to them. They saved many lives, the Swedes.

The next part of my mission involved locating Paul Dukes, who proved to still be at Gurdjieff's establishment in Fontainebleau. I had found the place peculiar and didn't relish a return. Too many thin, dried out English with tight, uneasy faces. It had the atmosphere of some sort of penal institution, frankly.

When I telephoned, all I could manage to do was to confirm that Paul was there, but not speak to him. I had hoped to invite him for a dinner in a quiet restaurant like l'Ami Louis, where we could really talk, but that was not to be.

I arrived at the place the next afternoon in the sort of slow rain that comes to that part of the world in autumn, sharply cold and suggestive of coming snow. It fell upon the wide, ill tended lawn before Gurdjieff's Prieuré, on the distant houses of the town and the great trees that surrounded the rather tumbledown old estate, and in my heart, for I was finding in myself a growing sadness, the origin of which was my continuing frustration and helplessness before the torrent of history I so longed to stop flowing.

I had grown up in a world ruled by law and with the belief that a human life was both a sacred possession and a sacred trust. What I had seen in Poland and what had at the same time transpired between me and Hitler had created a conflict in my interior universe. I wanted to stop him, certainly, but I kept finding myself wishing that I didn't have to despise him.

When I had seen that note from him, I felt the eternal call of the father, 'be safe, come back to my side.' I had never been needed by my cold Prussian *vati* like I was needed by this sentimental Bavarian. His sharing of intimate and abnegating truths had drawn me to want to shelter him within me. I was coming to understand Carlotta's adamant refusal to reveal his secrets, for I now shared it.

Was this love, or had he devised yet another level of *blutkitt*? Or were both things in play? I told myself, 'you are not helpless, he is still the enemy of mankind and the enemy of the world and you still have an obligation to defeat him and kill him if you can.'

As I walked up the slick brick walkway to the entrance, I let the tears that were pouring from my eyes mix with the rain. I did not feel myself weeping. The tears were coming from some place in me it had no access to the surface of my heart. I wept not only for Hitler, but for the fact that he was in the world. I wept for him both as father and as monster.

The door was opened by a cadaverous, chirpy Englishwoman who lifted a frighteningly cheerful grin, then stepped aside so that I could pass.

"I'm here to see Paul Dukes."

"We know. Mr. Gurdjieff will see you first."

Damn. That glaring oddity again. I'd hoped to avoid him. I was led into a room filled with cushions and rugs, including some rather good ones, old silks actually, hanging on the walls. Hitler had said something about him being a rug salesman, and as I lowered myself onto a cushion, I prepared for a sales pitch.

"Hitler send men to Tibet to find monastery. You go Berlin, talk monks there. They have power for you."

I had no idea what he was talking about.

"Now you asleep and awake at same time. Better than before, good! Still, you drive cart all akimbo and your horse out of control.

This is your life. Go to monks, they have power for you to wake up."

"I am awake."

He locked eyes with me, and I suddenly felt like a child. It was really very peculiar. In an instant, my whole attitude toward him changed. He had the charisma of a Hitler, but also there was a sense of what I can only call compassion there—something that Hitler, to say the least, entirely lacked.

My whole being—the whole way I was—transformed from certainty into question. Who was I? What was I doing with my life? For that matter, why had I even been born?

"Now, you see. Now you have question. Ask!"

"What do you mean by 'awake?'"

"Good, good, one day you find out." He smiled, revealing teeth that had certainly never encountered a toothbrush, the teeth of a man from ancient life. "You go on now with your spying. Try to stay alive, you have much to learn and you can learn. You *can* learn." He reached for a glass of tea and sipped from it. The interview, I gathered, was concluded.

"Hullo, old chap."

I turned to the sound of the voice and there was Paul standing behind me. "Ah, good. I was afraid I wouldn't see you."

"No, no, the office told me you were coming. Come, let's have a walk."

As I got up off the cushions, Gurdjieff said, "Mr. Dukes, are you going spying again?"

Paul nodded, his face dancing with amusement.

"Pack your things and get out."

"What?"

"Go! Now! Pack up and go!"

"Mr. Gurdjieff?"

He waved us away.

In the corridor, Paul said, "He's a master at delivering shocks, and I have to say, that was a shock."

"You like it here?""

"I'm becoming a new man here. Mr. Gurdjieff is a master of the first order."

He lived in a little sort of dormitory room with two other beds in it. While he packed his valise, I said, "I'm at the Crillon. You can stay there as long as you like."

"I have a flat in Montparnasse. Not much, but a roof over my head at least."

In the car I said to him, "Hitler wants you back."

"Back? I never worked for him."

"'Back' is what he said. Perhaps he imagined that you worked for him."

"Am I going to end up on the disappointing end of a firing squad?"

"Dunno."

"Because re-establishing my link with Hitler would enable me to return to duty."

"With us?"

"And who would that be?"

"Ah, Paul, that's the question."

"Surely you haven't become a Nazi, Willy!"

"Hardly. I am loyal only to his defeat, but I think I am also in love with him. I guess that makes me one of the good angels you never see."

"That's as cryptic an answer as I've heard."

"Not really. It means that I'm loyal to civilization but lost as to how to proceed."

We drove along, him thinking his thoughts, me tormenting myself by not wanting to feel as I did toward Hitler.

"Have you done any good?"

"In what sense?"

"You give him advice, Willy. I know you do. I also know that he trusts you."

I did not answer at once. Right now, I was a spy without a country. If I explained myself to Paul Dukes, I would become his asset and fall under his command, and I wasn't at all sure about that.

"I could kill him, I said. "That's something I think about."

"Nobody will thank you."

"The Jews."

"Not at all. If Hitler goes now, then somebody competent is going to replace him. Himmler, probably. He is a passionless, logical man. We want Hitler's passion and fury and the mistakes that are apt to go with them."

I drew the car up to the hotel and we alighted. As we went in, I found myself hoping that Paul had evening togs, as I wanted to fulfill his desire to enjoy Paris at its most decadent. I was hoping that the concierge could conjure up two Veras and, this time, a substantial amount of hashish. I didn't want an opium headache, which would certainly come on me if I smoked too frequently.

"Maybe the Nazis would fall altogether," I commented as the maid unpacked him. He'd said nothing more about his flat, so I assumed that he was spending the night here. I was happy to see her bringing out a set of togs.

He said to her, "Pressing on those, please." Then, to me, "A hell of a gamble that would be. We'll more likely end up with competent Nazi leadership."

It was an unsettling thought, indeed. But it wasn't enough to lessen my growing desire to kill Hitler. He was a monster in the true and ancient sense of that word, with abilities arising with his perverted self-obsession that almost defied understanding. I wanted to kill what he was doing to the world, and also what he was making me feel about him. The tenderness toward his needs that was emerging in me was like some parasite consuming all within me that I had grown up expecting to value.

I would kill him.

"Look, let's enjoy Paris a little. A good meal, some entertainment."

"You didn't find Mr. Gurdjieff's establishment entertaining?"

"I'm tossed out, so now it's good food, good wine and the sort of decadence you are so practiced at conjuring up. And only French women, please! No more of my fellow countrymen for a while."

"There are no French with him?"

"The French find Mr. G. absurd and do not attend his course."

"That explains how the students look, then."

"Exactly. Grinning storks and stodgy little boxes, all English. They do the cooking, too."

"Good God."

"He supervises them, so it's not terrible. But it's also not French."

We dressed, then dined in the hotel, which had an excellent restaurant. Paul agreed to go back to Germany and call on Hitler. "I wonder if I'll be shot," he said.

"With him, who knows?"

"You're not joking. You're really unsure?"

"He wants me to lure Putzi back, too. And he will certainly have him shot."

"Will you?"

"Lure him back? No. But I think you should go. If Hitler takes a shine to you again, it could be useful."

"And if he shoots me?"

"Not so useful."

"Is he going to actually fight, do you think?"

"When I left the Berghof it was full of generals and he's had me up in the Ardennes taking pictures. There are specialists in there making maps. So yes, I would think he is."

"In the Ardennes? Why there?"

"They must be planning to move a mountain division through."

At that moment, without having the least idea of it, I experienced one of my life's great failures, if not the greatest. I did not think to mention the men with the strange green wooden frame. Instead, I said, "Perhaps they intend to harass the Maginot from the rear while the main body tries to execute the Schlieffen Plan in Belgium again."

"And with the same result."

"With a different result."

"The French have a powerful army, Willy."

"They do not. I've seen them. The *poilus* look a mess."

"You haven't seen the tanks. Real monsters."

"Well, good. Hitler will get the bloody nose he so richly deserves."

I said the words, but I had seen the fury and efficiency of the Wehrmacht in Poland, men marching with robotic intensity, moving with robotic persistence across the wide Polish fields, and then seeing them lined up, shoemakers, bicycle salesmen, students—the whole of young Germany now disappeared into the dreaded field gray uniform.

We lingered over the spent dinner, smoking and drinking the left-over wine, an unfortunately jammy Burgundy very like those bizarre wines that come out of California these days. "We will sell no wine before its time," claims Orson in that Gallo commercial. Dear heavens.

He got God only knows how much money out of Carlotta to make a film version of "Dear Liar" with her starring as Mrs. Patrick Campbell, but the cameras never rolled. Carlotta's accent would have turned the thing into a farce and her heart would have been broken.

At one point he said to me, "Do you love Alf?"

I was revolted by the question and told him so.

"Then you do. I thought so. Have you ever..." He trailed off.

"What?"

"Ah! I see that you have." He gave me a steely, appraising look. "My dear boy, you must be in agony."

Speaking of masters, he was a truly superb judge of men.

And an expert in other ways, too. For example, do you see that what I am reporting here is not a conversation at all, but an interrogation?

Another of his weapons was the wide-open innocence that he could cause to appear in his face. He wore a more American than English expression, to the point that it could be rather disorienting to hear his posh accent. He seemed almost to be pretending to be himself—which he probably was. The disguises ran that deep.

"You don't speak," he said.

"I'm afraid to."

"Oh, gosh, you're a funny fellow. Poor Willy! Did he bugger you, you poor devil?"

"Certainly not."

"Never mind being embarrassed about it. I'm English. I was buggered senseless in school and did plenty of it myself. Why not? It got whipped to me when I was a first former. I gave as well as I goddamn got. How did it feel, though? We both know he's a pencil prick."

"You've gotten drunk."

"Very drunk. And, in fact—" He rose from the table with a motion so liquid that he appeared to be growing more than standing, then loped off into the lobby, disappearing into its baroque vastness. I heard him on the service phone, "Will you send up two bottles of the best La La you have in the house? Or no, let me be specific. La Turque, you see. To Monsieur Weber."

I called out, "The '19!"

"Yes, the '19, please." He came back. By that time, I had understood that he was propositioning me. I wasn't going to tell Paul a thing about what had transpired between the Leader and this little *Hitlerficker* for fear he'd try to gain some advantage somewhere along the line by spilling on me. Paul was a lovely fellow as long as one didn't mind being used to the absolute hilt.

As we returned to the suite, I told him quietly, "I only care for women."

"Me too!"

The Coti Roti came and was far better than what the sommelier had provided at dinner. I was glad that I could afford to be indifferent about money, because it probably cost the price of a small automobile.

"The night concierge here has an excellent *liste des putes. Un garcon pour tu?*"

"*Va te faire enculer*, my dear."

The drink had pushed aside my concerns about more opium, and Paul's comments had made me understand that I could be entirely frank with the night concierge.

I telephoned down for two whores disguised as nurses and two pipes. My experience of closet queens, which I now suspected Paul of being, was that they particularly enjoyed the nurse fantasy. This proved to be true, as Paul hogged both of them—and, in fact, had himself hog-tied by them.

I drank the '19 La Turque. I drank another one last week and it's still fine, can you believe it—in 1978, or rather is it 1979 now? Yes. It was just slipping along the edge of the hill. That's what one calls a great vintage.

After I finished the bottle, I smoked some opium and threw up but wasn't attended by either nurse. Then I smoked until I flew gently into a memory of being at the symphony with *muti* and *vati* and Maddy and listening to Toscanini conduct the "Scottish Fantasy" In civilization, in the long-ago. I slept, then, a black, dead sleep.

When I awoke the next morning, I hurried off before Paul could ask me where I was going.

I took the train to Calais , then went straight across and up to London to fulfill the next part of my mission. The planes were grounded by the hostilities, but the boats had resumed since Hitler had announced on September 4 that there would be no further U-Boat action in the Channel.. Even so, knowing him as I did, I was most uneasy as I watched those dark, foam-flecked waters slipping past. Worse, it was rough, and there are few things in this world more unpleasant than a channel crossing in heavy weather. Being burned at the stake would be more dreadful, I suppose, but not by much.

I found Churchill in the cavernous office of the First Sea Lord in Whitehall. It is so large that one would expect that they would keep roller skates for those wishing to cross it. I had gained *entrée* by sending in a note that I had an important paper for him and must return forthwith to Germany.

There were brief niceties, then he said "Well?" from within a fog of smoke. As he always did when not in a bath or a bed, he looked unhappy.

I took the paper I'd gotten from the Berghof and unfolded it on his desk. He peered at it, then picked it up and began paging through it. I had taken it out on the train up from Dover and was now aware of what it was.

He raised his eyes to mine. "This is useful."

Given that it was the order of battle and armament of the entire *Wehrmacht,* I could not but agree. "Good," I said.

He smiled. "Are you selling it? What do you want for it?"

"It's yours. What I want in return is a promise of your immediate attention if I should come back or even telephone."

"Most assuredly. But if you telephone, you're Mr. Fox."

That made sense. There was no such thing as encrypted telephone calling in those days.

He turned over more pages. "How did you come by it?"

"I picked it up off a map table in the Berghof."

"And do they know it has gone?"

"I have no idea."

"If I tell the SIS that this was picked up in the Berghof, they'll fear that it's a plant. If I tell them that I got it from the infamous Hitler Fucker, they'll be certain of it."

That he knew that term was quite a surprise and I felt my face burning. But then I understood where he must have gotten it. Putzi had been interrogated.

"How is Mr. Hanfstaengel faring in detention?"

"I've only read the transcripts." He went through the document again. "Siegfried has reforged Nothung, so he has." He poured himself some champagne, but offered me none. His drink was Pol Roger. For a man who was everlastingly broke, he drank the best. "I shall read some of this out in the house—unless you can tell me that my doing so will certainly get you shot."

"I can't know."

"Then I commend your courage."

"May I know if you're getting sufficient rare earths?"

"Indeed."

"I have come to you with some other documents." On the train up from Dover, I'd written out the names and registrations of all my ships. I pushed the paper across his desk. "These are ships that carry rare earths to Germany."

"I recall this discussion. I cannot sink neutral shipping."

"You can sabotage it. As First Sea Lord, you could send some sort of team."

He got up and went to a vast window and stared down into the sparse Whitehall traffic. He turned around. "Leave it with me, then. But there is something else I need. More important by far. I need you to completely stop those uranium shipments."

"That's a surprise."

"It seems that there are boffins out there convinced that it can be made into something very dangerous. You need not know more, except for one thing. There is a quantity of a substance in France that is called heavy water. Should Herr Hitler get hold of it, it will be urgent that you let us know where it is being kept. Most urgent."

"I'll stop the uranium shipments, but if they're important to him, I'll be asked about it."

He considered that. "No, I think not, then. Is it carried on any of these ships?" He waved a hand at the paper.

"The four larger vessels."

"How much have you sent him?"

"Tons. I didn't think it was of any importance. Glow in the dark watch faces."

"He's ahead of us on something I'd prefer not to go into."

"Please don't. The less I know the better." Under interrogation I would be as bad as Putzi. Worse.

Shipments continued until Hitler declared war on the U.S. In fact, the sabotage program in general wasn't effective. Ship after ship would get through. Whoever they sent to Tampico was no damned good, or perhaps a double agent. There were plenty of those in the war.

"Have you anything else for me?"

"He sent me into the Ardennes to scout terrain."

"Is it passable, then?"

I repeated the mistake of not mentioning the tank-sized frame. I said, "It's terrible terrain. But I think his interest means that he's going to attack."

"Our evaluation says that won't be for two years or more. Witness his peace proposal."

"All he does is lie."

"As Mr. Chamberlain has discovered to his cost."

"There were other Germans in there, map makers disguised as French foresters. He wouldn't be having maps made now if he planned to wait. The French will see the Germans in the spring."

He paged through the order of battle. "Yes, here, as I thought. He has a mountain division. So, very well, we'll make sure that the French are warned that a mountain division will be coming through the Ardennes. They can easily set up a screening action. He's trying to draw forces out of the Maginot, obviously."

Do you see my mistake? Remember my mention of the men I had seen carrying the green painted wooden frame? That frame was the width and length of a tank, and if I had described it either to Paul or to Churchill they might very well have drawn the correct conclusion and thus saved France and ruined Hitler. But I did no such thing. Was it ignorance or stupidity or did I unconsciously suppress it because I loved Hitler more than I hated him?

I cannot be sure, and the shame is a torment, the regret like a thousand knifes flaying me.

Eventually I got the George from Winny. The George, pinned to my breast by a dying king. I abetted the spilling of an ocean of blood and got loaded with medals. What a world.

I am in the Chrysler Building, sitting in this old office long since gone strange with ghosts. On the floor over there, I once played with a great red fire engine my father had bought for me at FAO Schwarz. *Muti* was away to see her ailing mother in St. Louis, and *Vati* preferred to take us with him rather than leave us in servants' care.

I see myself as I was then, drawing out the hose made of twine and spraying imaginary water on an imaginary fire.

To the west, the sky glows deep orange. Along the horizon there is a fiery shimmer. It is red enough to be blood.

History has a dangerous way of amplifying small details into enormous events. Gavrilo Princip shoots a pompous archduke in the breast and eighteen million victims are sacrificed.

If only I had thought to mention that frame. Or is it hubris for me to imagine my role to be so consequential? I suppose that I should say I'll never know.

Sleep does not often come easily to me, and tonight I will be haunted by tanks clanking like ghostly chains, and the Horns of Jericho howling down the sky.

In London, I returned to my hotel and spent the evening in my rooms. I thought Paul might find me, but he didn't turn up.

My journey back to Germany and the Bergh of was uneventful and life continued on the plan set out by the mistress of the house. I went back into her and Carlotta's arms, and the three of us resumed our waiting.

On November 8, a fellow named Georg Ehlers blew off a bomb at the *Burgerbraukeller* just after Hitler had finished delivering his annual speech commemorating the Munich *putsch* of 1923. Of course Eva rushed to him. Carlotta and I stayed on the mountain. Eva was with him for only a couple of days, and then almost in hiding at her Munich house. There were so many people swirling around Prinzregentplatz that she was effectively banished.

Carlotta and I stole a bit of time in Switzerland. We tried to find a way to allow her to have her much longed-for visit to New York and Hollywood, but submarine action might resume at any time. As well, if Roosevelt came into the war, Carlotta would be interned as an enemy alien.

We went to Gstaad, which was just a little town then, and skied. I taught her and kissed her and then drank hot seasoned wine with her in the evenings and enjoyed her so much. We couldn't have a pipe or anything like that, though. None of that in Switzerland. It wasn't like Germany in the Nazi era, a time when illegal rarely meant impossible, or France where illegal was not only possible, but encouraged.

The new year was brought in very festively at the Berghof, and all three of us were allowed in the party, which I recall as being a very elegant one and a great deal of fun.

Then came the spring and the new leaves nodding in the sun, and across Germany the rumble night and day of heavy traffic on the roads.

# 6

Hitler was screaming into a telephone. "Must I also direct traffic? Where's your planning, you fool! Every one of you ought to be lined up and shot. Shot, do you hear me? I mean it, General! You get them moving. Go out there yourself, flash your damnable medals, blow out the brains of anyone who's malingering, do whatever you have to do! This is an order! An order!"

When he slammed the phone down he was white with rage and shaking. I was with him in the *Felsennest* in the Eifel. It was a low bunker, spartan and cramped, ill-ventilated and tangled with a mass of telephone wires.

In taking me with him he had abandoned caution. He would tremble in the night, his skin would grow cold and a sheen of foul-smelling sweat would ooze from his pores. He would want to be held then. In his terror and excitement, his homosexual tendencies were becoming more frank. For the most part, I kept to my rooms in the town, but when he was agitated, as he was now, his *aide-de-camp* Hans Junge would come and fetch me. His silent contempt shamed me, but that was my life now. The officers around the boss acted as if I simply didn't exist. They would look right through me, even shoulder me aside in the narrow corridor of the wretched hole with its bare, swinging lightbulbs and dizzy, erratic shadows.

When I realized that the monstrous traffic jam of armored divisions he was shouting about was in Luxembourg, I was struck by a horrifying realization. Those map-makers with that frame hadn't been marking the way for the 1st Mountain Division, but rather for all these panzers.

If they were bringing their main attack through the Ardennes it would entirely surprise the French and British.

Hitler paced, literally wringing his hands. He turned to me and glared silently out of eyes made strange by too much Pervitin. This amphetamine, put on the market in '38, was being used literally by everybody, men, women, school kids, you name it. There was even candy laced with the stuff which Hitler, of course, had sitting in bowls everywhere. Hildebrand Chocolates. Carlotta once ate a box of them and shot around the Berghof for days like a crazed cat.

I noticed that his pupils were almost invisible, just little pricks of darkness in the blue. "Willy," he said, "Willy!" He threw his head back, then pitched forward over the map, breathing like a cornered animal, literally snarling.

"Alf, you need to come down. You've taken too much Pervitin."

"It's essential!"

In fact, the *Wehrmacht* ran on it. The result was that the entire headquarters staff was also hopped up and racing around. Cut orders! Send dispatches! Gather reports! People bellowed at one another in the corridor while outside motorcycles roared, staff cars snarled and men cursed. Chickens, come from god only knows where, pecked about underfoot, to the point that outraged officers would grab them, wring their necks and throw them onto the roof of the bunker.

Roaring machines, clucking chickens, shouting generals, shrieking Fuhrer—I so hoped that the whole affair would descend into unrecoverable chaos. By this point, I had been sent on numerous missions into France and had seen the allied forces, which were sparsely equipped and, it seemed to me, poorly trained as well as thoroughly demoralized. More than once, I'd seen a monstrous French tank abandoned by the roadside, disabled by some fault or accident. The French were rag-tag, but the British were not only threadbare, but armed with ancient rifles. When you saw any of their armor, like the French, it was usually on the roadside under repair.

"Willy, rub my shoulders. I'm dying. I'm dying, I tell you!"

"You're not dying, Alf, you're doing well. Putting the panzers through the Ardennes is hard but it's also brilliant."

"They're *stuck*!"

'Ah,' I thought, 'so they are sending the tanks through.' I'd thought a lot about how Paul did interrogation.

"Trust the German soldier, not the German general. You say that all the time, Alf. They'll get it sorted."

"Hoff! Colonel Hoff! Where is that man?"

Nobody responded.

Hitler moaned. "He's still up in his Storch, can you believe it? At night!"

I had heard his name and seen him about. I didn't know what his duties were but I didn't ask. One did not press Hitler for information.

He leaned back into my kneading hands and looked at me upside down. "Hello."

"Hello."

We laughed a bit. As I kneaded and rubbed—I had done it by then many times and knew just what he wanted—I wracked my brain for an answer to the question of how to inform the allies about the danger in the forest.

Getting across to France still involved going through Switzerland, which was far to the south of here, hours away by slow, jam packed and unreliable wartime trains. All the good rolling stock was now allocated to the military, and civilian trains were let through only when absolutely nothing military, not so much as a handcar, was on the line ahead. Then there was the matter of crossing into France, which now entailed a telegram being sent to the American Embassy in Paris by customs to confirm one's identity, and hours of waiting while the embassy searched its records and returned its response.

Should they fail to find a record, you could be interned or even shot as a spy, so it was one hell of a nervous business, let me tell you. The extreme politeness of the French officials always made them seem particularly menacing.

I reassured myself that the allied generals were competent men, and would be able to turn their armies to face this threat from their rear. Of course they would. Because we mustn't lose France, it was unthinkable. Civilization depended on it.

Except armor is fast. You could cut off whole armies with columns of armor as they slowly wheeled to face you.

I realized that it was urgent, and desperately so, that Gort and Gamelin be warned.

I had never felt so helpless.

Hitler felt the same way, but for the opposite reason. "Oh, god, I wish Hoff would get back! War is waiting, Willy. Hours of maddening, soul-crushing waiting. And I am not a patient man, it's not in my nature."

I thought to myself, 'the more he sleeps,; the better.' If he's not screaming into the phone, nothing happens.

I laid a hand on his forehead. He shook me off. "Leave it!"

"I want to get Morrell in here with some heroin. You've got to settle yourself. You can't command when you're this tense."

"Don't you dare tell me what I can and can't do!"

By now I'd heard that sort of thing many times. I knew not to back down. "In fact, Alf, you can't. Nobody can."

"Heroin's too strong, it'll put me to sleep for hours. Tell him to bring something else."

As I telephoned him at his lodgings in the town, a thought crossed my mind about Paul Dukes. He had returned to Germany, spent a week at the Berghof and then disappeared. During that week, he'd had a number of private conferences with Hitler that seemed to have gone well. So where was he now? If anyone could get intelligence on the Ardennes movements to the allies, it was him.

I said to Morrell that the boss needed a sedative and hung up the phone. "He'll be right here."

"You take good care of your old man, Willy."

"Don't say you're old."

"Soon enough you'll be at the center of a greater Germany, you and the sharks. But you'll best them all."

"You seem very sure of that."

"You're one of the most formidable people I've ever known. You don't whine like Goebbels or posture like Goering or endlessly plot like that damned grocer. You just get things done. I don't think any of them to this day know what you've really accomplished."

"Todt knows. Schacht knew."

"Them and a few others. Trusted men, not like the sharks."

I saw an opportunity and seized it. "You know who else knows? Paul knows."

"Ah, yes. He'll be in soon I hope. Frankly, it's waiting for him that's driving me mad."

"He'll be here?"

"Certainly here. Unless I'm somewhere else and have failed to notice." He stood up, drawing away from me and snapping his braces back across his shoulders. "Thank you, Willy, that was good." We were in his cramped, stuffy office. "I wish the girls were here."

"Telephone them. Assign them a plane and they'll arrive before noon."

"Women can't be in war. They're not like us. On the battlefield their beauty fades. They wither."

"We're far from the front."

"Tell the French that. At last report, they had a few bombers. If they ever found this place, we'd be plastered."

"We don't have air cover?"

"We do, but there's always the possibility. When I was in the trenches, I came to understand that you just never know. I saw more than one man get his head blown off without the slightest warning. Bang, gone, just like that. Or gassed. Gassed! It's the most awful agony you can imagine, choking in gas. Take it from one who knows."

He'd been gassed in the Great War, of course. Damned near killed, to hear him tell it. 'I was smothering. God, what agony!'

Morrell came hurrying in carrying his big bag. His cabbage nose was good and red. How Hitler could favor a dipsomaniac doctor like him I never understood. But look at the rest of Hitler's career. Canny though he was, he was entirely lacking in judgment.

Morrell never gave tablets. He was a believer in the injection and he was a real artist at it, I'll give him that. Despite the fact that the needles of those days were huge, he could slip one in without the patient so much as noticing.

Hitler never bothered to ask what he was being given. I needed to know, though. With no valet here, I would have to be the one to wake him in the night if he was needed. But when I asked, Morrell turned to me with the alacrity of a wary rodent.

"Linge isn't here, so I'll be the one to wake him if there's need."

"There will be," Hitler said.

"It's a preparation of morphea, something like laudanum but more refined. It induces a comfortable sleep."

"Deep?"

"In this dose, for two hours, yes. Then he'll be normally rousable. Give him strong tea."

"If before two hours?"

"Telephone. I'll remain at home."

Loading up on the *schnaaps,* no doubt. Well, good, why should I care? Maybe he'd kill Hitler and save me the trouble. I thought often, though, of the gun hidden away in the Berghof, waiting for its moment in history.

Ehlers had failed, but I wouldn't. I would deliver a point blank head shot. I had it all planned. I had dismissed Paul's warning. I could not imagine that the Nazi would survive Hitler's death.

The aide appeared. "Colonel Hoff has landed."

Hitler clapped his hands and rolled his eyes. A few minutes later, there was a flurry of activity outside the office, and the colonel came in. He wore a leather flight jacket and helmet over his uniform. His eyepatch was supposedly a wound. From the look of him, I thought he'd taken a bad strike in a duel.

He spoke the same rough sort of southern German as Hitler, and the two of them obviously got along well.

"Flying at night over enemy lines is madness."

"On the contrary, you can't shoot what you can't see."

"But you couldn't see either!"

"We dropped flares."

"Oh, and you still weren't seen?"

"The flares were seen, not the plane. In any case I can report with confidence that Seventh Army is still in position on the Belgian border. As are the Brits. There's nothing to be concerned about. They're completely unaware of the Ardennes."

Hitler dropped into a chair. A smile trickled into his face, then widened. "It's too early to be certain, of course, but I think we have them." He closed his eyes and immediately slumped forward.

I turned to Morrell.

"It is natural sleep," he said. "The Leader is simply exhausted."

"I'm not asleep. I only appear to be. It's an old trick."

"Do you want the sedative now, Leader?"

"Where's my valet? I want to go to bed. And these two have a lot to catch up on."

What could he mean? I hardly knew Hoff.

"Linge is ill with dysentery, Leader," Morrell said. "He cannot be near you."

"I forgot. Willy, come help me."

My face blazing, I followed him down the corridor and into his bedroom. I really hated walking among the many officers who were moving about, all snapping to attention and saluting as we passed. I wanted to shout to them, 'I'm not what you think, I have dignity and I deserve your respect.' That was my speech that I often imagined but never made.

The bedroom was a concrete cell. It contained an iron bedstead identical to all his others. I helped him off with his clothes. He stood naked before me. Hitler was as pale as a grub, with the rounded belly and thin arms of a man who got too little exercise. The only body hair he had was a pubic tuft.

He climbed into the bed. "Willy, I'm going to need the soldier's relief again. I'm so sorry."

"Of course, Alf." As I had at this point many times, I reached under the sheets and stroked his member.

"Maybe the girls could come after all," he said. "Keep them in Eifel. I'll come to see them."

He ejaculated and I took my hand away. I went into the bathroom and dampened a washcloth with warm water and gave it to him, then stepped out and turned off the light.

"Willy?"

"Yes?"

"Goodnight. And thank you."

"You're a funny man, Alf."

"The joke's on you, Willy. Wait and see."

I returned to his office to find Colonel Hoff behind his desk with his feet up and his tunic tossed on the small couch that stood against the wall.

"Apparently we're supposed to meet."

"What do you mean?"

"I don't know. He said to introduce myself."

"Are you serious," he said in English. "You've not recognized me?"

"Paul, my God!" It was breathtaking.

"I'm proud to say that I'm now his private intelligence officer. He doesn't like to rely exclusively on his generals."

"Do you know what's happening?"

"He's moving through the Ardennes."

"What can we do—"

He shook his head sharply. Pointing upward, he mouthed the word 'microphone.'

"—to help?" I almost choked. I'd been about to say 'warn the allies.'

He stared at me. I stared back.

"I've been running air recce," he said smoothly, "but between the two of us, I just hope my report is right. Air reconnaissance is notoriously problematic."

I realized that he knew perfectly well that one of us had to get to allied HQ on an emergency basis.

I nodded in agreement. "We could use an observer on the ground."

"That's the acid test, and the moment I saw you, I knew who that observer had to be."

"I can't get across."

"I can fly you. Land in a field at night."

"Then I walk out of the darkness announcing myself as an American? Where do I say I came from? I think that's a prescription for getting shot."

"Not if you have a car, it isn't."

"I don't have a car over there."

"I do."

"I thought your Hispano was in Dresden."

"This one is a Delahaye."

"I tried to get Hitler to buy one once. He wouldn't hear of it. Damned French buggy, was his opinion."

"He's a 770 man to his core, and quite right. It's the better machine."

"Where is this Delahaye?"

"In Spa. I used it to examine Belgian deployments but they found an Englishman in their midst too irritating so I left. One can fly in to a field along the Balmoral Road. It's protected by hedgerows, so it's quite safe. A couple of miles into Spa and there are your wheels. You wouldn't even need to go to the front, just note the numbers on the trucks in the rear areas. That would be enough."

"I could range up and down the lines, then go to Paris and send a report back via the Swedes."

"Let's see what he says."

He couldn't be left alone for long, but we took a brief walk in the darkness, in air dense with the scent of night-blooming flowers.

I said nothing about the real purpose of the mission. I didn't need to.

"Why can't you do it, Paul?"

"I can, but a British passport could cause me difficulties. If I run into the wrong sort of officer, I could be placed under guard for being a subject noncombatant in a military area. I'd get out soon enough, but it would eat time."

So it was decided. We'd propose me to Hitler as a clandestine observer behind enemy lines, but my real purpose would be to reach Lord Gort and General Gamelin and reveal Hitler's Ardennes plan to them

Hitler's usual habit was to sleep until noon, but he was too excited and was up and shouting into the telephone practically at first light.

Whenever the answers he was getting failed to satisfy him, he would send Paul up in the Storch again. Then the pacing and the shouting would start, followed by more screaming phone calls.

A Fiesler Storch was basically a powered kite, so it was completely vulnerable to fighter attack. There was a machine gun jutting out behind the observer, but it was essentially useless. This unique plane could only go as fast as a hundred miles an hour, but it could also go as slow as thirty, and needed only a hundred and fifty feet for takeoff.

It was late afternoon before the Storch's final reconnaissance of the day ended. Paul's face was grim, but his report delighted Hitler: he had spotted German panzers emerging from the forest and forming up into their attack pattern.

Hearing this, Hitler slammed his right fist into his left hand with a crack. "I won't need the doctor tonight," he said. "I am no longer in the least nervous. If we have surprise, we have them. What of the French, where are they?"

"I saw a thin line of reservists along the Meuse, that was all. I'd say that the main body is just where we want them to be."

"Excellent—and the British?"

"A bit more problematic, but I'd say that they're also in Belgium."

"But you're not certain?"

"They're more disciplined about keeping their formations out of sight from above."

Hitler grabbed the telephone. "Brauchitsch!" He waited. "Ah, there you are! I have to tell you that there are no French movements south. What do you mean, how do I know? I am telling you! But the British—have you any reports" He listened, then lowered his head and closed his eyes. Then he stood straight. His face hardened. "All right, here are your orders. The panzers are to proceed to Sedan and move directly west from there. But be careful. Any sign of British formations to their north, I want an immediate report." He put the telephone down.

"You need a man on the ground," Paul said. "A personal observer reporting directly to you."

"And that will be you."

"My British papers will be a problem in the battle area. I'll get collected and packed off home." He dropped his hand onto my shoulder. As we both knew, it had to be Hitler's idea or he would either reject it or become suspicious.

His eyes met mine. "It's very dangerous, Willy."

"I'm sure."

"How much do you know about military activities? Can you make accurate reports?"

"I'd stay in rear areas," I said officiously. "Take down numbers on trucks, that sort of thing."

"Condition of troops, weapons types and numbers, any sort of information you may overhear from officers—do you know anybody in the British or French commands? Anybody on Gort's staff, perhaps?"

"I have been at parties with Philip Neame."

"Deputy Chief of the General Staff yes, excellent. Can you walk right up to him? Will he recognize you?"

I recalled some of the parties he had chaperoned. "I would expect he would." He had once come after me with a cricket bat, for entirely justifiable reasons.

Hitler grasped my shoulders. "A man in British GHQ. Superb! You'll go? It's entirely your decision."

Inside, I exulted. How very smoothly Paul had led him in just the direction we needed him to go.

I came to attention and silently gave the salute. He nodded and turned away. "Very well. Have a good dinner in the town. Leave an hour after last light. You'll have the same pilot who takes Paul. A night specialist."

I glanced at Paul. I needed to be let down near Spa where I could pick up the car. If I couldn't get the attention of the generals, I had to telephone Churchill. I might need to go all the way to Paris to accomplish that, given the chaos in the battle zone."

Paul also realized the problem. "I wouldn't trust Henneman at this point. He's exhausted."

"Nonsense, he can take fucking pill just like the rest of us do."

"Not a fly a plane at night. But I can do it."

"You can fly?"

"Indeed I can. And we've been up so many nights, I know the situation perfectly."

"If you're sure of this.

"I'd be the more reliable of the two of us right now, Leader."

"Very well."

We went with him into the map room. He pointed to Arras. "British General Headquarters is presently here. We've put agents in a number of times. If you can believe it, you can be landed close enough to find your way quite easily. We have a communications unit in Arras as well." He wrote on a slip of paper. As testament both to his extraordinary memory and his excessively detailed management, he didn't even need to look it up. "They moved their post to this location today, so this will be good for twenty-four hours."

"How often shall I report?" I asked.

"Only as necessary. If you can get into British HQ, that is a terrific coup. I will want the reactions of the staffs as we move out of the forest. Do they understand what we are doing? And if, God forbid, they start cutting orders to reverse off their present line, an immediate radio message. Immediate! Can you accomplish this?"

He was asking for the skills of a master spy. I had no idea whether or not I could accomplish anything of the kind. But I could lie. "I would think so."

"No! Can you carry out these orders, Willy? That's what I need to know. Yes I can, no I can't." He glanced at Paul. "In many ways, he's such a boy."

"We'll soon raise him up."

"I can carry out the orders."

His adjutant came in and handed him a note.

"Ah, wonderful. My generals are assembled. Preparing surrender papers for me to sign in advance, no doubt." He paused. "Don't call the girls, Willy. I was off my head last night. The worry those devils were putting me through did it. But all is well now. I love Eva dearly, but being near a war won't do her any good." He laid a hand on my shoulder, a gesture I was finding increasingly annoying. "Willy, you have a natural bravery you yourself are hardly aware of. That's very Aryan, and to think Himmler thought you were like me."

"I am like you. I consider you an ideal."

"The filth that's in my blood."

He left the room.

"What did that mean?" Paul asked me.

"Under the Nuremberg laws, he's a Jew."

"You can't be serious."

I shrugged. I didn't want to get into it. "Let's have dinner," I said. "I might not eat again for a while."

"Ah, yes, but when you do, it will be in France."

Paul gave me a couple of thousand francs, something that had not occurred to me. I would have gone in without a *sou* to my name, I was that oblivious of the actual conditions I was going to encounter. I could draw a check on my Swiss account, of course, but it would take time to clear, and I'd have to find somebody trusting enough to cash it. Under wartime conditions, that might be impossible.

After the meal, we rode out to the plane in a taxicab. Better not to have a *Wehrmacht* driver. Paul was in uniform and so would be made a prisoner of war under the Geneva Convention if we went down. I would have to trust the American embassy to sort out my situation.

The Army Group had a number of Storches, of course. This close to the front they were dispersed in fields rather than on aerodromes.

Since they could take off from incredibly short runways, any reasonably smooth ground was enough.

"When the time comes, I'm going to be sure to let the War Office know what you're doing tonight, Willy. Hitler's right about your bravery."

"I wish you hadn't told me that. I was just deciding that I wasn't going to be in any danger."

"That's a good one."

"I'm a neutral American!"

"And you're going to be walking out of the night with no way to explain where you came from. You can't say you flew in from America."

"Lindberg did it."

"That swine, don't foul the air with his name."

Lindberg and the British were not getting along just then.

The Storch, shaped like a Piper Cub, was standing under a camouflage net. There were no lights, so it was nothing but a shadow in the field.

Paul spoke briefly with the guard, who appeared to know him.

We went over to the plane and the three of us pulled off the netting.

"Careful, don't rip the canvas."

"What canvas?"

"The entire airplane is canvas."

"Which I now know. I'm so glad."

We got in and Paul started the engine. As we rolled toward a shadowy hedgerow, I shouted, "Have you really flown one of these things before?"

"I've seen it done."

We rose into the night.

Such was the confidence of the Germans that Eifel wasn't blacked out, and it was a lovely, crystalline sight below us, with the castle looming over all, its few windows glowing softly.

Paul said, "They keep the town lit to draw attention away from the *felsennest.* If bombers show up, they'll concentrate on the castle and keep well away from Hitler's precious carcass."

From time to time as we flew, tracer came up from the forest below. "Poorly disciplined troops. They're firing at the noise of an engine. They haven't noticed that we're coming from the east. Happens every time I go over."

Some of the tracer seemed awfully close as it drifted gracefully up. The stately progress of tracer in the night is deceptively elegant.

I watched the black land passing below. There was enough of a moon to cause the *Our* to glow as we crossed into Belgium.

"Will the Belgians fire on us?"

"The Belgians are not on the border, at least not in strength."

"That's difficult to believe."

"It's a neutral country. The border with the Reich is still open."

"I can't believe that."

We flew on for another few minutes. "Can you see the ground?" Paul asked.

"No."

"Neither can I."

To give you an idea of the compact geography we were dealing with, Spa is now about an hour and a half from Eifel by car. In those days, it was three hours without border formalities, which on the German side took about thirty minutes, and were largely involved in determining that you weren't taking out too much cash and weren't an escaping Jew. In the Storch, it took us fifteen minutes to pass between the worlds.

"How are you navigating, if I may be so bold?"

"Using the compass. It's a very good compass." He pointed toward the blackness. "Ahead, that might be Malmedy. Let's have a look."

With that, he plunged the plane almost straight down.

"This isn't a damn Stuka!"

"It's fine. And yes, look, there's the cathedral."

"But what are those shapes?" There were looming areas of deeper darkness going past at our level.

"Mountains."

"Dear God, Paul, are you mad?"

"If it makes you feel better call them hills."

We went up and flew along for another ten minutes—or was it ten hours?

"All right, we have reached Spa. Are you surprised?"

"Astonished!"

"So am I, but here we are."

He began circling the airplane. We appeared to be just east of the town.

"There's the Balmoral Road, that gleam down there that looks like a river in the moonlight. I'm going to drop you on it."

"I don't see a road."

Then we were down, bouncing along a narrow tarmac. Given that the plane could land in sixty feet, we came to a stop virtually at once.

Paul leaned over the dash.

"Are you all right?"

"I'm giving thanks. I'm a prayerful man."

"That I did not know."

He lifted his head. "I've only just started."

When I got out, I practically kissed the ground.

"Once you're past the curve ahead, you should see the lights of the hotel. So far, it's not blacked out."

"How do I get the car? You've not told me."

"Oh." He dug into his billfold and produced a small bit of paper with the number 17 written on it. "Give this to the concierge." He handed me a rather large key. "This is the car key. Take a room and leave in the morning. It doesn't do to be driving about after dark, I wouldn't think."

Before he took off, we had to turn the plane around in order to face the thing into the wind. He rolled off into the darkness, there was a sudden roar and the gleam of moonlight on the rising fuselage and then I was alone with the crickets and the frogs.

Hitler, true to his obsession with secrecy, hadn't bothered to tell us that Belgium was going to be invaded in a few hours.

The hotel appeared after about three quarters of an hour of walking. It was now after eleven, quite late for a guest to appear, especially on foot and without luggage, and at hotel of the superior class like the Balmoral. And so near a war zone.

The lobby presented a sophisticated-rustic appearance, with groupings of wooden chairs with dark leather cushions. It was entirely quiet, not a soul in evidence. I crossed to the desk and rang the bell. After a few minutes, a clerk appeared. As he moved through the door from the office where he had obviously been sleeping, he drew on a weathered tailcoat.

"I'm sorry," I said in the broadest American English I could manage, "I've been at a rather late party. The taxi driver assured me I could find a room here." I handed over my American passport.

"Certainly," he said in thickly accented English. "We have nice one just in one floor. One hundred francs."

I asked for the telephone. My first order of business must be a call to Churchill. If I got him, I wouldn't need to worry about finding Gort.

"I am so sorry, Monsieur, the lines are not active now."

"There's a fault?"

"This is unclear."

"If they come back up, wake me at once."

"Yes, most certainly."

I was shown to the room, which was plain but reasonably clean. There was only a shower-bath, so I took a shower, which was in those days in Europe rather a rarity. I have never really enjoyed showers and to this day prefer a drawn bath.

I slept very poorly. Twice, I stole downstairs to ask about the phone, but the lines were still in fault. Then, as sometimes happens during a bout of insomnia, I proceeded to drop into a deep sleep at the worst possible moment.

When I awoke, it was already after eight. What a fool I was, not to have damn well ordered a call. I leaped out of bed and threw on my clothes.

Absent the phone, I had to seek out Imperial General Staff HQ and find General Neame. Hopefully he wouldn't remember me as the teenager he'd threatened to bean for being party to a country house prank that had caused him to need stitches in his left buttock. He had sat on a glass eye. It had not occurred to us that it would burst.

I felt that I should eat and was taking a quick breakfast when the manager appeared in the doorway of the restaurant. He said in French, "Ladies and gentlemen, you may wish to know that German parachutists have been dropped on Nives, and our air fields are under general attack at this time."

Absolute silence followed this statement. Everybody in the room became motionless. Then they all leaped to their feet, shouting and cursing the Germans. A woman panicked and ran for the door. Her husband, trying desperately to calm her, hurried along behind.

I went at once to the desk and presented Paul's ticket for his car. "Very well," the young man said. "It will be brought up."

The Delahaye was marvelous, dressed in light gray, low and sleek. I've always thought that the line was the most beautiful of all the cars of the 1930s, which was an era of wonderful looking automobiles that didn't work very well at all.

I got in behind the wheel. Looking out across the elongated hood, I reflected how stodgy my BMW seemed in comparison. The garage man had turned it off when he reached the steps, and despite all the luxury and beauty, it was a maddening and, under the circumstances, frightening trial to get it re-started. Most cars with electric starters in those days were also equipped with cranks, but not the Delahaye.

Once it was running, the assured surge of power when I pulled out was a relief. I drove into the town, where people were clustering on street corners and crowding into a radio shop. At that time in Europe, radios were still uncommon in private homes.

I was appalled to hear that Eben Emael, the great Belgian fort fifty kilometers north of Spa and the centerpiece of the country's defense, was under attack, also by parachutists. Waves of planes were said to be crossing the border.

Had I been wrong about the Ardennes? If the Germans were coming through here, then they were repeating the Schleiffen Plan from World War One after all. But no, Hitler had been too pleased with the tanks coming out of the Ardennes. Unless—had they been only a small force and the traffic problem in fact worsened during the night?

If that had happened, his forces would have been thrown into chaos. He could not possibly have shifted his front so soon.

As incredible as it seemed, it must be that the attack on Belgium was a ruse. The man thought on a very large scale. This attack would certainly bring the allied forces forward. But then, coming out of the Ardennes, would be an entire and entirely unexpected army which, as far as I had been able to tell, was all fast-moving armor.

Hitler had shouted into the telephone that they were to go directly west. That would take them right up to the channel. The allies would be trapped in Belgium and France would fall. It was that simple.

As I drove, I wondered if Gort was even still in Arras.

Then I had the idea of trying another phone, and began looking for a *tabac*. The one I first spotted had a peculiar automatic instrument, but the owner showed me how to press a coin in it to raise the dial tone, then dial up the number of the international operator. It didn't matter because no dial tone came.

"It must be the Germans, Monsieur, I am sorry."

I later found that it was actually the Belgian army, which had cut off all telephone service lest the Germans use the system to their own advantage.

The next thing I knew, dismayed shouts were coming in from outside. Germans had crossed the border from the Rhineland and were coming along the Leige Road, heading toward Verviers twenty kilometers to the north. There was a Belgian unit rushing toward the town from the barracks in Liege.

Unless you have been ensnared by a war of quick movement, you cannot realize how it is that life goes on around the soldiers even as they march past. A column of tanks roars into a town. Everybody disappears. They roar out again, and the grocer, the baker, the doctor, the butcher all open their doors again. Business goes on as the infantry march in. Some soldier posts a proclamation and just like that, the old country has gone and the new one is in place. If the town is large enough, a junior officer and a small staff set up an administrative headquarters, that is to say, an office of systematic looting. Hundreds of times across history, the people of this region had been looted. Always in the end the looters went and they remained, their stubborn roots dug into their stubborn earth. As Vonnegut says with such simple elegance in *Slaughterhouse Five,* "so it goes."

I jumped right in my car. Without the telephone channel to Churchill, I was in serious trouble. Reaching Arras was now an emergency of the first order, and I could not get there from here without driving through Liege. I couldn't risk the Verviers road, so I would have to take the mountain road and hope I made it to the city ahead of the *Wehrmacht*. As I knew that they would be steaming along on Pervitin, I took one myself, chasing it with a Dubonnet from the chap's little bar.

I bought a map from him that was hardly more than a tangle of lines on the page. A *Wehrmacht* map would have been far preferable, but I had thought better of bringing one in with me. Even an American would have difficulty explaining that, particularly to any Belgian soldiers who were fighting for their homes.

I had seen the chaos of war in Poland, the way that basic things that one assumed would always be available would vanish. So my next stop was a garage, where I bought four jerrycans (all they had left for sale) and filled them up with petrol. I had to stand at the end of a line already twenty long, but by the time I had finished, there were fifty more people and a dozen machines behind me, cars, lorries, a great, ungainly rural bus, motorcycles and even a tractor, a rarity in this country at that time.

I passed a butcher's and no matter my desperate rush, forced myself to stop and buy a smoked ham that would provide me with food if there was one. I got a quarter round of cheese and a magnum of local at the cheesemonger's next door, then leaped into the car and took off. I was soon out of town and traveling as fast as I dared around one hairpin after another. My urgency and the pill drove me on, but I had to be extremely careful with the car, which was not intended for this sort of motion and kept threatening to go into a skid. The BMW would have been excellent here, but it was far away—or so I thought. Life is always surprising, obviously, but in wartime in a battle zone, it really can be extremely surprising, as I was soon to discover.

When the road descended to the river bank the going was easier, but now I encountered a flood of refugees coming in the opposite direction, in their haste entirely ignoring the division of the road. So I had to drive out on the shoulder and into the berm beside it, worrying that the car would get stuck. A Delahaye is no Jeep, believe you me.

The next thing I knew, a Messerschmitt shot past overhead at a very low altitude. At that time, I'd never seen a strafing, so its passage did no more than startle me. It never crossed my mind that pilots might open fire on civilians. Nobody else reacted, either. It was completely unthinkable.

A moment later, he returned, this time flying just above the tops of the trees that lined the road. There was a sound like a fist pounding tin and then he was gone. An instant later, a horn erupted behind me. When I glanced out the rear view, all I could see was haze. Thinking that the mirror was fogged, I reached up and brushed my thumb against the glass. The horn began sounding continually.

When I looked back, I could see only steam. Then I understood that it was coming out from under the hood of the honking car. Ahead of me, the traffic had begun veering off to the roadsides. Still not understanding, I got out and stepped back to the disabled car.

Now here was one hell of a shock. The horn was honking because the driver was slumped against it. He was covered, literally covered, with blood. In the back seat were the exploded remains of children. Beside him a woman was also slumped forward dead. Blood was literally running out from under the doors. Then I heard mewling and saw that there was a kitten in a box. I reached in and pulled it out, then put the poor terrified creature on the roadside.

Completely in shock, I stood away from the car. People were emerging out of smoke, staggering, some of them on fire, others bleeding, one a man with only part of an arm. A dog raced back and forth panting, crazed with fear and painted with blood. On the berm a woman carefully stood up a stand and hung a cage on it in which there was a pair of lovebirds, both stained like the dog with blood that was not their own.

A Horn of Jericho began screaming down out of the sun. Everybody else, not knowing what it was, looked up. I leaped back into the Delahaye and drove right off the roadside.

There was white fire, then silence. An instant later, bits began falling around the car and on it, bits of metal, of flesh, of clothing, luggage.

The Stuka sped away.

My next realization was that everybody who had been in the road behind me was now gone. Where they had been was a smoking hole. Farther back, I could see cars and wagons beginning to attempt to make their way around it. Also people running forward, then stopping at the far side of the hole. Like me, staring.

It felt as if a piece had been cut out of me that I had not known I needed. But I found that I needed it now, I needed it very much. I shouted out, "Where are the lovebirds?" I shouted it again, "Where are the god damn lovebirds!"

The cage, the birds, the woman—evaporated. Great violence is generally an accumulation of tragic details.

But what to do? All that was left was the sick reek of high explosive, the stench of gasoline and the smell of blood, thick and deep. It's a smell that seeps into your soul. You never get rid of it.

Distantly, I heard the shriek of more engines in the sky, but high and far away. Somewhere the awful sirens sounded again, and then there came thuds that made the ground bounce.

I got the car moving and spent the next two hours honking and cursing and weaving. Progress was slow, to say the least, and Liege itself was a terrific jam-up of traffic. Every street looked like $5^{th}$ Avenue at five in the evening, a mass of busses, clanging trolleys, honking cars and roaring lorries and all the drivers leaning out and shouting. According to my map, I could deflect onto the road to the

University of Leige, which I did. This got me around most of the traffic and also away from the refugee flood.

I had no idea how close the Germans were. My main worry was the French border, which I thought might be closed.

I was disturbed to notice that I had thus far not seen a single Belgian or Allied military vehicle. Nothing. They were all up against the frontier, I was sure. There was nobody manning the Belgian customs station and the French let me through with hardly a glance at my passport.

The captain of the guard leaned in my window.

"What have you heard, Monsieur?"

"The Belgians were confronting them at Verviers when I left Spa."

"They're in Liege now, and our boys are coming up the road, so have a care, you'll see the French Army soon enough."

I didn't care to end up in the middle of a battle, that was certain. The car required a refill, so I went along the road a kilometer or so, just until I was out of sight of the border station, then used one of the jerrycans. I didn't want them to see my gas and go after it.

I drove on with all haste toward Arras, but soon found myself confronting a substantial column of French troops. They had with them a number of very formidable looking tanks, which were going through the fields parallel to the road. On it were columns of soldiers, wagons, occasionally trucks, command cars and units of cavalry.

Seeing the proud cavalrymen on their fine mounts, I hoped that they would not fight as the Poles had, but leave their horses and crawl into battle, which is the only sane way to fight on the modern battlefield.

The Delahaye cut a splendid figure as far as the French were concerned, and they generally made way for me. In a vehicle like that, the assumption would be that I had some sort of importance. Most of them were communists, I am sure, but this was war. Who knew what an expensive car was doing here? Could be a minister or something.

Thus I drove on into the settling light, as the fall of France—the impossible, appalling fall of France—began unfolding around me.

# 7

It was dark when I arrived in Arras, which was in at least as much of an uproar as Liege had been. The streets weren't jammed, though, but rather populated by orderly columns of military vehicles, all of them stopped. The place was in blackout and so I kept my headlamps off and picked my way along. I had no map of the city and under the circumstances didn't care to go around trying to get one, so I had to keep stopping, finding local people, and asking directions to Rue Adam de la Halle where Hitler's agents were located. Hopefully they would still be there and know Gort's position.

It proved to be a street of working-class row houses, absolutely silent, not a light showing.

There were a couple of automobiles in evidence, but certainly nothing like what I was driving. As I went along, doors opened and men and boys came out to watch. Soon I was being followed by a crowd of excited children. Some spy, dear heaven. I want to say in my defense that I was even at the time all too aware of the amateurishness of my activities. I thought that I really should have read more spy fiction. But what was it? I could only recall *the Riddle of the Sands,* a novel based around the peculiar notion of somebody thinking that yachting in the Baltic would have appeal. The story was a tiresome puzzle.

I decided not to try making a call, but instead to find a hotel, leave the car there, and walk back.

The only one I had ever heard of in Arras was the Particulier, so I asked for directions from a gent in my audience. He gave me instructions, but I suppose he was a communist because they took me straight to the river. An invitation to drown myself and my damned car, I assume.

In any case, I soon found it and managed to get a room quite easily. Everybody war running from Arras and the place had emptied out. The hotel had no car park, so I left the machine in its roundabout and walked straight back to Rue Adam.

My return attracted no interest, and this time I was able to knock on the door without incident.

It was opened by a girl of perhaps ten. She wore a neatly pressed school pinafore and curtsied politely when she saw a stranger. Her mother appeared behind her, a narrow woman with thin, evil lips and the sweetest eyes. She was loved, that woman. One can always see that in the way they move, and in the warmth of their eyes, no matter if they are pretty or plain.

When she looked at me, I felt myself in the presence of a stern angel.

I gave the signal that Hitler had provided: “I am here to see August Tessmer.”

The woman nodded, turned, and ascended the stairs that were halfway down the dim corridor. I thought I heard the child say “mama” in the English manner, but could not be sure. But then when “August Tessmer” came down to meet me, I knew instantly that he was not German. I’d been among Germans for most of the past eight years. There is about them, especially the Prussians, a certain atmosphere, a bearing if you will, that emerges from a life in profound discipline. Tessmer is a Prussian name, but this man had not been raised as a Prussian.

I said in German, “I am William Weber.” I accented it rather flatly, to sound more like a foreigner who has learned his German in school.

"Herr Tessmer" replied in exactly the same sort of accent.

I was nonplussed. Could this actually be an Englishman? In my inexperience, it crossed my mind that I might have come to the wrong house. But what would British and German intelligence be doing on the same street in a French town? No, that could not be correct. I had come to the right house and found an Englishman pretending to be a German.

I could see that he had a gun under his jacket, a small pistol in a shoulder holster.

"Please come up," he said politely, still in that accent.

If I went up those stairs, I was almost certainly going to my death. My American identity wouldn't help me now and I had no way of explaining myself as a double agent. In fact, at the time, I didn't even know that was what I was. There was nothing for it but to turn and leave.

As I did, he at first froze with surprise. Then he grunted "no" and came after me. With no idea of where I might be going, I ran away down the street. Behind me, I could hear his feet pounding. He knew that I had guessed what he was and so assumed that I would give him away. He could have no idea that I would not only not expose him to the Germans, but would protect him in any way that I could.

The fog of war is much more than battlefield confusion. In time of war, that fog covers everything everywhere and is as dangerous as acid.

Blind and desperate, I ran on. I had no idea where I might go. Arras isn't a big place and also lacks the sort of tangled medieval quarter present in many European cities.

I found myself at the river. Stopped. Nowhere to go from here. There was a car parked at the kerb. I crouched down beside it. An instant later, the British agent came rushing around the corner. He didn't hesitate. He came straight toward me, his shadow leaping ahead of him.

Might I slide under the car? No, he'd have me then. I took the only course left to me and slipped into the Scarpe. It was frightfully cold and my feet didn't touch the bottom. I knew that I couldn't survive in it for long.

Keeping close to the bank, I dog paddled as quietly as I could toward the center of the city. My clothes and shoes were weighting me down so dreadfully that I feared that I might be dragged under.

I heard him come up to the car and then stop. Taking a deep breath, I let myself sink. Knowing that my life depended on this, I forced myself to stay submerged until the hunger for air was a desperate agony and there were flashes of light in my eyes. Finally, I became dizzy. My body began to seek instinctively for breath, but I knew that I if I took one, it was going to be water.

No longer able to hold, I pushed off the oozy bottom and returned to the surface, gobbling air as soon as my face came clear. I grasped the bricks that lined the bank and pulled myself up. He was under the streetlights not twenty feet away, but no longer looking this way. The gun was in his hand.

I watched as he walked slowly away, disappearing into what had become a misty night.

I ended up staggering along the Boulevard Schuman in my dripping suit and squishing shoes, cold as all hell. At this point, I had no idea where to find the hotel.

I was now shivering uncontrollably. All at once, there was an explosion of noise, and the next thing I knew truck after truck was passing me, all of them heading east. Despite my exhaustion the sight of them drove me relentlessly onward, for I knew that this was almost certainly the main body of the French Army, and that it was rolling straight into Hitler's trap.

I tell you, I was almost insane at that point. To see those trucks passing—I cannot begin to express what it did to me. I wanted to wave them down and personally send them on the right path.

They raced toward certain defeat, full of singing men. I could think only of how to find a general officer, any general officer, either French or English, it didn't matter.

But there were no generals here. The German divisional commanders stayed right with their men. Apparently not the French.

What more can I say about what it's like to have information like that and be wandering around like a hobo? It's horrific is what it's like. It made my guts crawl and my mind twist and turn, seeking solutions that were not there. I had a piece of luck—not much, but I did come across a taxi stand with an ancient Citroen sitting in it. In it a driver snored away with his head thrown back over the seat.

"Taxi," I called as I went up. "Taxi." I got right in the back. If a French taxi driver didn't care for the look of you, he'd drive right off. I'd had it happen in Paris when drunk and riotous.

"Monsieur, what happened to you?"

"What do you think? I was tossed into the Scheld by communists."

"Ah, an ideological dispute. Are you touring? Because perhaps you've not noticed the war."

It was all I could do not to punch him in the face. "I have noticed the war, Sir. Please take me to the Particulier. I'm freezing and I feel dreadful."

"You look it, too." He started off and we were at the hotel in three minutes. All along, it had been just two streets away.

I paid him off and staggered in. "I've been tossed into the river by drunken soldiers," I told the concierge. "Please give me a room and send along a valet immediately."

"Monsieur, there is no valet here. The valet was called up last week."

"Wonderful. Then a maid. Anybody who can draw a bath for me and dry my clothes."

I was on the *premier étage* so I didn't bother with the lift, always a dubious business in rural places like this. I didn't want to end up waiting for an engineer who had doubtless been called up. I might not get rescued until 1950. There'd be nothing left to pull out but a mummy.

Once in the room, the first thing I did was to get out of the clothes.

My valise was in the boot of the car, so no bathrobe. The maid came in without knocking. She was one of those servants with a permanently astonished look. You often encounter them in hotels. She blinked at me, then went into the bath and began preparing it. I was so very glad that the room had a tub and not one of those damned showers again. To preserve her modesty, I dragged a sheet off the bed and wrapped myself up like a Roman. As I sank down into the wonderful suds, I could hear trucks rumbling, clanking noises, the rise and fall of a distant siren and a curious, vast murmuring that could have been ghosts for all I know. I never identified it, but I heard it more than once in the war years.

Thankfully the maid didn't have the modesty of the middle class, but rather the plain frankness of the *paysan*. She scrubbed my back for me but I shook her off. I only needed to get the cold out of my bones and almost immediately rose from the water. She did the valet work, wrapping Neptune in a towel as he ascended from the fragrant surf. I wouldn't have minded bouncing around on that creamy pile, but she was no Salacia, that was quite clear from her demeanor.

I at once picked up the telephone and was rewarded with a response. "I need an international operator for London, please."

"Yes, sir, I will try now."

"You'll try? But you're not sure you'll succeed, is that what you're saying?"

"Service has been unreliable for some hours."

"All right. Let me know your progress."

The maid took away my wet clothes. I told her to have the valise brought up from the car. I shouldn't have done it, because when I went down later, the ham was gone. Fortunately, the gasoline had been left behind.

The next thing I knew, the telephone set was buzzing. The room was dark and I almost knocked myself cold tripping over my valise as I leaped for it. The operator said, "there is no international service now. The Boche are on the border."

"No service to England? That's the opposite direction from the Boche."

"No service." He disconnected, and quite rudely. The maid had laid my togs out on the sofa, pressed and reasonably dry. I put on a fresh union suit and dry socks from the valise, then restored my other clothes to my back.

I don't recall the time. It was the middle of the night, but that was unimportant now. The only thing that mattered was to reach Gort or Gamelin or somebody who could communicate what I knew to either or both.

I went down. Normally, I would have had to wake up the clerk, but now half the hotel staff was uneasily congregated around his table. "Do any of you know where any headquarters are located?"

"They are all decamped."

Of course they were, and they were all rushing forward to the wrong front.

"What about the British? I thought they were in Arras."

"No, not here I don't think. No British officers have come in and we have the best dinner."

Where to go? The only person I knew of who might be able to help was that British intelligence officer waiting in his spider's web for German agents to turn up, and he would shoot me the instant he saw me.

It was now the wee hours on the morning of the 11$^{th}$, and it was then that what appeared to be luck struck me with the force of an explosion. A young man came into the lobby, and he was in the uniform of a Coldstreamer. As he reached the clerk's desk, I approached him.

"Excuse me, I'm looking for General Neame."

He turned to me. "Ah, staff officer, right?"

"Yes. On Gort's staff."

"They're coming up, but slowly, you know. The traffic."

"Will they be billeted here? Might I run into him?"

"I'm here to secure lodgings. In fact, you might get turned out, I'm afraid. We'll need the entire hotel."

Might? I was. By him. Minutes later.

I wound up slumped in a chair trying waiting as the hotel slowly came alive with English, lovely English. I was absolutely determined that Neame would get me to Gort and Gort to Churchill. And I dreamt of sugar plum fairies, too.

So there I was, waiting helplessly in a hotel lobby for a man who might or might not show up, and who I barely knew. Officers came and went and batmen began appearing with kit. In hope that a squaddie might be more forthcoming to a stranger, I went up to one of them.

"I am a friend of General Neame. Do you have any idea when he'll be in?"

"In here? Not at all. He's with Gort."

"And where is Gort, if I may ask?"

"They've gone up to Lille."

At last! It was near dawn when I left the Particulier, very damned grateful to get out of Arras. The drive to Lille was fifty kilometers through Lens, but as soon as I arrived on the road, I found a huge convoy passing. I was stopped by a white gloved military policeman.

"Sorry, not today," he said in mouthy French.

"I'm an American observer with Lord Gort. I've got to get up to Lille."

"All right." As he signaled the line to make room for me, he said, "If you break down roll out or get a push and do it quick. Otherwise, the truck behind you will shove your car right off."

"Thank you for getting me in."

He bade me drive ahead. The road was not only occupied by trucks, but by careening motorcycles, an officer jutting up out of each sidecar. As I got in among the vehicles, two of the trucks separated enough to make room for me.

Four hours and many halts later, we finally reached Lille. As the trucks went off to their dispersal points, I drove into the center of the city, a grimy industrial town. The most imposing hotel there was the Breughel. I went in and asked where I could find British HQ. I was told rather acidly that I'd have to ask the British.

"They speak poor French," I was told. "They cannot communicate with staff."

"But they are here in the hotel?"

"The generals."

"Then I would like General Neame. Can you put me through?"

"Of course. Who may I announce?"

"Mr. Weber from America with urgent business."

"It is war. All business is urgent. So you needn't have told me."

It was rather nice, actually, to be talking to a real Frenchman, sour and logical.

He shouted into the telephone, "*L'Americain! Il est la! LA!*" Then, "*Ici! Maitenant! ICI!*" With exaggerated and very ironic care, he put it down. "They're completely stupid. They'll lose the war for us. Just go. 206. No suite, he's of no importance."

I went up and knocked, and there, standing behind his batman, was Neame.

"What's this all about?"

"I am William Weber. Perhaps you remember me from some of those weekends with the Baron de Walden."

"And perhaps I do not."

"I was the American."

"Ah, yes, of course." His face darkened. "How astonishing that you've lived this long. I'd have thought you would have been killed long ago."

"We aren't in the war."

"I meant by an irate husband or father. Or have you reformed? You were a damned fantastic blackguard."

"May I come in?"

"Charlie, hide the guns and the money." He laughed a bit. As he stepped aside for me to enter he said, "Raiding the girls like that, really! Those innocent little peaches."

"Peaches, at any rate."

"Now what in the world can you be here for? You're in a war zone, you know."

"General Neame, I am no longer a boy. I am in this battle in a deep way. I have absolutely urgent information for Lord Gort. Or better if you could get me through to Winston."

"Winston! You mean Prime Minister Churchill."

"He is a friend."

The room was small, with two narrow beds and a single chair. I don't know where he kept the gleaming, wide-eyed batman who hovered nearby, looming over us. Perhaps he went into a box.

"I'll swan at that one. You must be trying to make money somehow."

"I don't need money."

"That's right, pipes, wasn't it? Wealthy American."

"Vacuum tubes."

"Plumbing of whatever sort. What can you want with Gort?"

I had to tell him. No choice. "Just that Army Group A is coming through the Ardennes. If Gamelin stays in Belgium, the entire Allied army will be trapped."

"There are thirty German divisions up against our forty and they are on the other side of the Dyle, not in the Ardennes. But where have you come from? Why do you bring this lunatic story here? I don't understand."

"If Lord Gort will only communicate with Churchill, he will confirm my *bona fides*."

"You're not getting near Gort, not through me. I don't know what the devil you're about, but this army isn't going to alter positions that have been thought out for years by some of the world's greatest strategists on the say-so of a boy in a strangely shrunken lounge suit who bears an appalling reputation."

"I fell into a river."

"Drunk, yes? I recall that you drank a great deal even when you were fifteen. You boys, raiding the gin. I never! Where have you come from, anyway?"

"I will tell you, but please understand very clearly that if this passes back to the Germans, it will mean my life."

His face grew more serious. He looked at me askance.

"Give me your word, General."

"Very well, you have it."

"I have come from the *Felsennest*."

"Which is what?"

Amazing that they would be so completely ill-informed. "It's Hitler's HQ in Eifel. Guderian is going through the forest. Believe me."

"Guderian is armor. His forces will be supporting the infantry, not going off on some mad chase through the forest. What would they be after in there, anyway, rabbits?"

"They have concentrated most of their armor into a single army group. It's going to burst out behind you and race all the way to the channel."

He considered. "Then we'll simply collapse its flanks. So even if it happens, what does it matter? They'll still lose. In any case, only a lunatic would try that, and Brauchitsch is a good general."

"Hitler is a lunatic."

"He's the dictator. He's not commanding the army."

"Right down to the battalion level, I assure you, and he is a genius. A horrible genius. He will encircle you out of the Ardennes and France will fall."

He stood. "I will take this to Lord Gort. That I can promise you. Nothing more."

I stood as well. Perhaps I hadn't failed, but I wished that I could see Gort personally. "I ask you again for an introduction to Lord Gort."

"Really, young man, how dare you! I've given you my word."

'And,' I thought, 'as the Frenchman so accurately stated, you are unimportant.'

"Where is Gort?"

"You say you came from the Germans? From Hitler?"

"Yes."

"I'm beginning to think you should be arrested."

That must not happen, so I left at once.

But where to go?

Then I thought, communications would certainly still be open in Paris. I could attempt to reach Churchill through the British embassy.

I also needed to report to Hitler, who would be getting uneasy. I wouldn't tell him that the station in Arras had been turned, only say that I couldn't manage to make contact.

I set off in the quickly deteriorating Delahaye. It was a vehicle for quiet roads and easy streets, not for the rough and tumble it was getting.

It took me four hard, complicated days to reach Paris. Every mile I drove, I heard the Horns of Jericho in my head and hated those heartless German boys in their planes. I did not want to hate them or hate any person. But in such times innocent hates innocent and they all fall before the elegant tracer that fills the sky.

As far as I could tell from the chaotic accounts in the papers, the Dyle Line was still holding, but the Germans were also at the Meuse, perhaps across it. There was simply no way to tell.

I went directly to my beloved Crillon, where I was well known enough to cash a check, and thank God, because I didn't have a *sou* left in my silk lined pockets. When I walked up to the desk, Monsieur Georges looked me up and down with rising eyebrows.

"I've been in the north."

"So shall I send along a tailor to your suite?"

"Please."

"You can go up. Your wife is already in."

I opened my mouth. I closed it. Had he mistaken me for somebody else? Rather than discuss the matter, I drew out my checkbook and said that I wanted twenty thousands. This was not an unusual sum at the Crillon and thankfully he cashed it without the slightest concern. When times are unsure, there is nothing like a Swiss bank account. I know all about all those other offshore affairs, but one can count on the Swiss. I have been in Swiss banks now since 1932, and my father before me for another twenty years at least. Between us, that's 60 years.

As I went up in the lift to find out who in the world had decided to become my wife, I felt a lot better with my pockets loaded with cash. I assumed that it was one of the whores I'd had here. Probably a poor Jewess, terrified that the Germans might win and looking to shelter with her American friend. Well, if so, I'd get her out if I could.

Maybe there were still flights. If so, she could go to Spain. The trains were hopeless, of course. During war, never bother with the damn things.

I'd been given one of the large, unforgettable keys, so I simply went in.

A sprite flew at me, embracing me with her arms and her legs. Incredibly, impossibly, it was Carlotta.

"Oh my boy, I thought you were dead, I was so afraid!"

I stood her before me. "How in the world did you get to Paris?"

"I drove in our car."

So now it was "our" car. "But the border—how? It's impossible."

"Not for me. I've got a damn good cunt and I can fuck my way anywhere. If I'm condemned to hell, which I assume will be the case, I'll fuck my way to heaven, I can assure you."

"Good God! But you can't drive! You're an absolute menace."

"Don't be mean. Anyway, the car works. Still."

"Still? What does that mean?"

She strolled into the living room and took a cigarette from the box on the table before the couch. She lit it. "Aren't there places that repair those things?"

"What's the matter with it?"

"Not much. It still goes. How do you make them go backwards? I know it's possible, so don't lie."

"You don't know how to reverse and you got all the way from Munich to Paris? But you must have needed to park. How could you do it?"

"I was careful. I parked on slopes. What else could I do? Anyway, one of those silver things is in the boot."

"Silver things?"

"The one that runs along the front. It became involved with a fence."

"You must mean the bumper."

"Possibly."

"Dear God."

"I'm so glad to see you, Willy."

"Oh my dear sweet—" I held her again and it was so lovely. "How wonderful! Just wonderful!"

"You really want me? I was afraid you'd be mad."

"Not at all! And forget the bumper. All is forgiven."

"Also the other one?"

"Ah. Yes, certainly."

"All right, then everything is forgiven. The door and all of it."

My poor little sportster! "Yes, yes, all is forgiven, my love." I kissed her hard and long, my heart swelling with gratitude and joy—just joy! She had moved heaven and earth to do this. My dear, dear woman. I have never since known such a moment as holding her then, just holding her.

"But how could you have bought petrol? Come to a hotel? Anything? Do you even speak French?"

"I'm not sure."

"You're not sure? How can you not be sure?"

"If they don't understand me I cry. Then they understand me."

The French male, of course—a weeping woman, young and beautiful, of course he understands. She could have robbed her way from bank to bank across the whole country and received only a kiss on the hand.

So here she was, my brilliant, inventive, determined and profane Carlotta, bringing to me the most profound testament of love I had ever known.

"I had to point to dishes on the menu and kept getting peculiar shit, so the first thing we do before the nice long fuck that's coming my way is you take me to dinner and you order me a fine schnitzel."

"This is France. They have no schnitzel."

"That seems very strange. But look at that smirk. You're lying, of course, you bastard."

She did very well, as it turned out, with a nice peppered beefsteak.

I have a soft place in me for people who are actually helpless but get by on bluster. It's one of the reasons I am so in love with my Carlotta, and have been for so long. She was an orphan, helpless, a

Jew, doomed, and yet somehow she ended up in the Berghof with Hitler at her feet. And now here she was having traversed a war zone in an expensive, temperamental automobile with only the vaguest knowledge of the enemy's language—which, in any case, she spoke with such a thick German accent that it might as well have been another tongue entirely.

In times of trouble, the first thing that crosses the mind of France is, 'what about the food?' At this point Hitler's gimcrack empire had not yet descended on the French, so the food was still superb. I took her to *le Restaurant Vefour*, a wonderful old room in a corner of the Palais Royal. It is quite marvelous now that the veneers have been restored, but in 1940 its faded elegance gave it an air of mystery, almost sadness, as if the shadow of *le temps perdu* lingered there.

Contrary to legend, the food was not appalling and the list was quite good, really. An advantage was that the decline the place had endured meant that its clientele could no longer afford to raid the cellar, so I got up a bottle of Latour '89 and it was very fine. It was one of those wines that age to perfection and then acquire immortality. I believe that the vintage is all gone now, but if it isn't, I would guess that even at 90 years, it's still redolent with the scent of spring rain and old books, and that flavor so subtle that it seems almost like a memory of wine rather than wine itself, but a memory rich with imagination and full of dreams.

I thought that a beefsteak, simply grilled, would not tax the chef too much, and they brought it with some nice runner beans as I recall, and we left the place quite happy and satisfied.

As we were walking along beside the formidable flank of the Palais, the air raid sirens began the mournful call to death that would soon become the song of Europe. Carlotta had not heard them before.

"What's that racket?"

"An air raid coming in."

"Oh. Will it come here?"

"Paris is a big place, but in war the law of chance prevails."

"Can't you ever say anything simple? Eva says you're too damn smart and I think she's right."

It never occurred to either of us to take shelter, and in any case there was no place to go. Paris was not prepared for bombs. The *drôle de guerre* had been too *drôle* for anybody to think of preparing bomb shelters. Anyway, this was Paris, the heart of civilization. Surely not even Hitler would blow it up.

They never imagined what I knew, which was that Hitler did not believe in civilization. He was an apostate, or worse an esthetic heretic. For example, he knew a great deal about art. He knew the works of Klee, Picasso, the Dadaists, the Surrealists, the Impressionists. He knew them all and detested them all. No visionary exploration for him. Art should reflect form, that was all, and then only ideal form. Anything else was horrible to him. The interior search that is the living soul of art was something that he consciously rejected. He knew civilization so well that he knew just exactly how to rip open its chest and tear out its heart.

The bombers were in the distance, their droning barely audible. There were some explosions, we heard them—thuds like the distant footfalls of a wandering giant. Carlotta clutched my hand and I held her around her shoulders.

"I want to be home with Eva in our house in front of the fire. We've been drinking your whiskey-*schnapps*, you know, and when her sisters aren't there we make love. Do you mind?"

"Of course not."

"I worry that you would be jealous."

"I'm jealous of missing the fun, but I don't think she's your lover."

"You don't know us women. You know nothing about us. We've grown very close, she and I. She's my dear friend now. She cried when I left."

"You had such terrific fights."

"You know Alf made Goring aryanize me. He didn't want to do it himself, it would have been too obvious that I was his courtesan. When I wouldn't screw that old bag, he issued orders for me to go to Mauthausen."

"What the devil? When?"

"As soon as you and Alf left. The next thing we know, here comes a car up with a pokey little man in it with papers for me to go to a transport in Munich. Eva said, 'how dare you, this is the home of Adolf Hitler. You can't come in here with papers like that.' So he left. She telephoned Alf in the *Felsennest* and he put a stop to the whole affair."

I was appalled, and I also wondered what was really behind all this. Was it simply Goring being vindictive, as he certainly was, or was some deeper game being played that would end with my lover being shut up in one of those dreadful places?

"Carlotta, did you escape Germany? Is that really why you're here?"

"I'm not sure. Maybe."

We had walked all the way to the Seine and were now strolling toward the Pont Royal. The blackout had come down and the stars shone overhead. They sparkled in the river, in its darkly flowing waves, and I thought that it must look to the pilots up there like a starry road into the Louvre where *la Giaconda* gazed into her darkened gallery, the Tuilleries and the fine private houses full of hidden wonders, the homes of rich and cultured Jews set in the high points of the Marais, the Sorbonne, a center of education since 1257, and so much more. A starry road into the very core of human culture, and I felt a sickness crawling within me.

I must say that we created a Doisneau image while sitting on a bench along the *quai*, kissing like teenagers. I found Carlotta so thrilling then that it was almost impossible even to glance at her without becoming absolutely frantic for her. I still do, of course, but when we were young—when I was a boy—I could fulfill my desires until she would breathe happily in my ear, 'Oh, Willy, you're breaking me in half.' And I would say, 'shall I stop?' and she would reply, 'don't you dare stop. Do it more.'

We went into in some dive club and listened to a negro playing on a clarinet and drank cognac, then found a taxi in the midnight hour and went back to the hotel. Our rooms were warm and so very comfortable. We called for a maid to draw a bath in the great tub, and bathed one another, lingering in the intimate places with our hands.

She had come and oh my what a joy.

I decided not to call for any opium or hashish. I'd been going on Pervitin for days and I needed to be cleansed internally, I felt. So I got a bottle of icy cold Pol Roger in honor of Churchill and we had a supper of caviar and oysters, and they also brought tiny cakes filled with berries and with them a split of a luscious Yquem, as I recall the '26.

We made love in a leisurely, frank way. She said, "Kiss me like Eva does." Between her legs, in the scent and taste of her, I dreamed on the mystery of the body while she smoked and ran her fingers in my hair and moaned my name, and to the north of us in that starry night, men died.

# 8

In the predawn hours of May 12, the iron cobra of Army Group A slid out of the Ardennes and headed for the Meuse, with the French none the wiser. The Germans had successfully come down out of the torturous dark hills and into the easy plain. It was perfect ground for tanks, farmland that presented little obstruction.

I had no idea that it had happened, no more than Gamelin did or Gort, Daladier or Churchill.

Also on that morning, I went to the Swedish Embassy. As always, it was obviously under surveillance by men in black Citroens, the *Sûreté*.

So be it. Once inside, I went to the communications station to prepare my cable to the Chancellery. It was not to be addressed directly to Hitler, of course, but rather to Frau Junge, one of the secretaries. The communications officer said to me, "Herr Weber, there is a call to make."

"A call? What sort of call?"

He handed me a slip. It was to a number in Stockholm. He gestured toward the telephone that stood on his desk in the small, crowded space.

"Is this not listened to by the French?"

"They say not. We're a neutral power, as you know."

I asked the switchboard to connect me, and listened as the call was handed off to a series of French operators. Then, distantly, I heard a Swedish voice calling *"Halla! Halla!"*

I said in German, "this is Herr Weber."

The answer was silence, then more clicks. To my astonishment, I then heard somebody very familiar. "Willy!"

"Alf! How can this be?"

"Are you well?"

"All well. Arras—"

"No, cable about the vacuum tubes. The phone is too expensive. Is Carlotta safely with you?"

"She is. The Crillon took her in when she said my name. It's a wonderful place, my favorite hotel in the world, I believe."

"When you didn't report, she was afraid. We all were. Don't tell me anything about her journey although I'm sure it's a fantastic story. We'll all enjoy it later. Just keep those tube orders coming. This is the time to make money on both sides of the line."

He rang off.

I was stupefied. Was there nothing the Germans couldn't accomplish? But I was also touched. He must have moved mountains to make this call possible, and must have been waiting for it, probably for days. If only he had been a good man, or even a somewhat decent man, I would have loved him as I wanted to love him, like the father he wanted to be, and in the secret moments of which we did not speak, the strange one who needed me.

"Tube orders" obviously meant cables, so I wrote one out about my travels, saying of the unit in Arras simply that it could not be contacted. I told him about the confusion of the Allies, the growing flood of refugees, the fact that I had seen General Neame and determined that he knew nothing at all about the Ardennes. I dared not leave that meeting out. There was no way to tell what Hitler might or might not know of my movements.

I then went to the British Embassy and managed to get an audience with an embassy secretary.

"I must be put through to Number 10. It's an emergency."

"I have no authority to do that."

"Telephone and ask them to say to the PM that it's Mr. Fox."

"He is very busy just now," the fellow said archly. "There's a war going."

"If he hears my name, he will come on the line."

"The ambassador disapproves of this sort of thing. I have no idea who you are. You could be anybody. Any fool, to be frank."

"If I'm a fool I'll be unknown to him, so when he hears my name he won't do anything. Then you can cut off the connection. There's no loss to you, no possibility of embarrassment. But if you don't do it, I can guarantee that you will regret your decision for the rest of your life."

"I must get the permission of the ambassador. He's not in just yet, so you'll need to wait."

I ended up sitting in one of the huge chairs in the baroque lobby, smoking cigarette after cigarette and trying to keep myself from descending into madness. The more time passed, the more I feared that I had been abandoned to sit here until I gave up and left. At great length, though, perhaps two hours, the secretary returned.

"You are authorized, Mr. Weber. You may have your call."

After all this, finally! I thought I would faint as I got up from the chair and wobbled away to his office.

The secretary, prim in his tight collar and now nervously efficient, made the call. I listened on the auxiliary earpiece that is on French phones, to a disquieting succession of operators, ending with the mellifluous tones of a gentleman at the Number Ten switchboard.

"This is Mr. Fox for the PM," the secretary said, his voice burbling with mirth. Then Churchill's unmistakable voice said, "Willy, yes?"

The secretary thrust the receiver at me with such force that he almost struck my jaw.

"They're coming through the Ardennes."

"We have that."

"Not just the mountain division."

"No?"

"It's Army Group A. The panzers. All of them."

"You're certain of this? Because what we have on the map is a reconnaissance in force moving toward Sedan."

"That's no reconnaissance. That's the most powerful assembly of armor the world has ever known."

Silence. Finally, "Is that all?"

"It is."

"I'll get on to Daladier."

"He must tell Gamelin to reposition enough divisions to break their flank."

He hung up abruptly.

The secretary was staring at me, his eyes as blankly helpless as those of a mouse. I left immediately.

Within hours, the news was everywhere. The *Boche* were on the Meuse, ready to cross it and break through to Sedan.

As I walked along the Fauborg St. Honore, heading back to the Crillon, there was such a silence that one could hear the sad murmur of the pigeons. Hardly a car passed in the street. But as I approached the hotel along Boissy d'Anglais, I could see traffic along the Champs Elysees, and it was strange traffic indeed.

There were horsecarts filled with children, wagons piled up with dressers and mattresses and coops of chickens, a little girl in school greens carrying a tired puppy, a boy leading a donkey, trucks and cars and an unruly herd of goats being managed by a frantic dog and a tall, exhausted man in a once-fine suit of clothes.

I passed the hotel and went to the corner. As far as I could see along the great boulevard wound the vast column of silent, hollow people and plodding animals. A Roller turned carefully into the Rue Boissy. Inside, I could see an entire family, the father long-boned in the way of the French aristocracy, the mother with head high, in the back seat three children with their hands folded, sitting silently.

The vehicle stopped at the Crillon. I walked along, curious to see what might transpire there. As I came into the *porte cochere*, I saw a large hole torn in the top of the boot. It was a crater big enough to fit my fist. It was so fantastic, so improbable, that I could only stare at it, the great wound in the deep gray paint of the wonderful machine.

Then I smelled something—a sour, organic odor. The car's runners were caked with soil that was sticking to a deep red, dense substance, which was slowly oozing to the ground.

A bellhop came smartly out. He opened the boot. Inside was a shredded wreck of clothing and bits of luggage.

Then I knew. The oozing substance was old blood caked with dust. That was what was causing the meaty sourness that filled the air. The luggage had been ruined by the bullet that had passed through the trunk.

These people had been in a strafing, but the blood was not theirs. They were not injured, I could see that. They must have driven through it, or even over the dead. In war, the dead are dead and one goes on. Reverence is for peace.

I went into the hotel. The children sat in the chairs that were directly across from reception. In fact, the lobby, while large and ornate, was not grandiose. At reception, the father was speaking with the clerk in a low tone while his wife looked on, a petite, uneasy statuette.

"Sir, I am so sorry, but you must understand the circumstances of the hotel also. We are directed to take the checks only of familiar customers, and you have not been here since 1928. I am truly sorry."

"I am a member of the ancient nobility. My checks are good, let me assure you."

I thought that I might offend him, but if he was turned away here he would be turned away everywhere. "Monsieur," I said, "I am well known here. Give me your check and I will give my own to Georges."

As I spoke, he stiffened. I could almost smell the sour acid of his umbrage. His head had risen—but then he slumped and turned. A gray eyebrow rose in his collapsed face.

"Then I can only thank you."

There was a desk for the writing of checks, and we went there. I said to him, "Your wife is quite dark. May I know if she is Jewish?"

The eyes, glittering with suspicion, made me think that I was making a mistake. But then the tears came.

"You must not stay in France. You must go on to Switzerland. Start first thing."

"I have nothing in Switzerland. In any case, the trains aren't running."

"Take your car. They'll let a Roller in."

"It has little fuel."

I thought of the petrol in the Delahaye. "I have jerrycans. I'll give them to you."

"But Monsieur, this will all cost a great deal of money."

"I'll extend you a loan of a hundred thousand."

"A hundred! But Monsieur, I may be unable to repay. We are near Sedan. The Germans might confiscate my property, burn the chateau. Anything."

There was certainly a shroud settling over Europe. He was right about that. But he could not know that it was there, in part, because of my own actions. He would not leave here without that money. "It will be very hard for your wife and children if you stay in France."

"But France cannot fall, not all of it. Paris will not fall."

"I know something of these matters. Trust me when I tell you that, short of a miracle, France is finished."

I had already in Poland seen the shadow that comes into the faces of men who expect to die. It now settled into his. His eyes fixed on me, but as if he was seeing into himself from a great distance and wondering if anyone was there.

I wrote a check for a hundred thousand. The clerk silently took it into the back. A moment later, the manager appeared, Monsieur Charles, who had known me since I was a little boy running about with a toy bomber in my paw. He looked at me with a twinkle. "We don't have any casinos open, Monsieur Weber."

"My wife is shopping."

"Ah, then of course! Do you want two hundred? Three?"

"Even she is not that fast."

We laughed, if uncomfortably, and they brought ten packets of ten thousand each out of the safe. I had no briefcase, so we wound up putting them in a sack, which I gave this man, whose name I did not yet know.

When I received his check, I saw that he was the Comte de Malouet. He died in 1954 in Geneva. His children and wife are back in France. Their estate now includes a wonderful *relais* where I have stayed. They did not recognize me and I did not introduce myself. His check I cashed in the fireplace in my suite.

Over the next days and weeks, I continued sending cables to "Doctor Heer" via the Swedish embassy. Every day that passed brought more frightening news, and Paris began emptying out. At first it seemed somewhat as if Sunday had come early, but then cars began to jam the streets, all going south.

I cannot imagine how it would have felt to be a Jew in one of those cars. For the French, change was coming and with it some danger. But for the Jews, it was death and they knew it.

On the last day of May, two things happened. Churchill visited Paris and I was arrested by the *Sûreté*.

Boulogne and Calais had fallen earlier in the week and the allied armies were trapped north of the German lines. Huge columns of refugees were now pouring through the streets. What had been a torrent had become a deluge. History records that of the 39,000,000 people in France, 8,000,000 were on the move at that time. There were 340,000 Jews in France, more than double the population of 1935. This was due to emigration from other parts of Europe, and the fact that Britain and the United States would not allow them entry.

It is not within the scope of this memoir to elaborate on the reasons that British and American doors were slammed in the faces of the Jews during their time of need. Suffice to say that, as far as the United States is concerned, the refusal is a stain on the Roosevelt Administration and in particular the State Department of Cordell Hull.

My arrest was not dramatic. Actually, Carlotta and I were dining with some English people we had run into in the Crillon, the Mays-Heanes. There was now difficulty crossing the channel unless you had a rowboat, so they were uneasily stuck in Paris. They had no car, the BMW was ruined and the Delahaye had no gas, so I couldn't do much to help them. In any case, the refugee-choked roads were dangerous and not only because of strafing. There were thieves out too, ready to rob corpses or, barring that, you.

We were in la Coupole. I was rather surprised to see a man approaching in business attire. My first thought was, 'how can he be in here, he's not properly turned out.' My next was surprise. He stopped at our table.

"Good evening," he said pleasantly. He turned to me. "Are you Mr. William Weber, the American?" he said in fair English.

I stood. "I am Weber, yes."

"Will you be so kind as to visit this gentleman at nine tomorrow, if you will. Sharp, please."

He handed me a card. When I looked down at it, I saw that it belonged to a Captain Louis George of the *Sûreté.*

“ Yes, of course. But is something wrong?"

"Very much is wrong, as you must see in the news, Monsieur. And there is also a discussion that Captain George wishes to have with you."

We were just at the beginning of an evening with some promise, but now this had really sobered me. Carlotta, who had been discreetly quiet, asked, "What is this?"

Carole Mays-Heanes said, "Sh! Somebody's going to shoot us."

"That was a polenta. A fucking polenta, am I right?"

"A security officer. They want to question me."

"A lot of good it'll do 'em now. We'll be in Paris any frickin' day." She folder her arms. "Damn Alf."

I said no more, but obviously the situation might be very dangerous. The dinner and the rest of the evening seemed as if they were happening to another man, a trivial drama unfolding on a distant stage. We ate, we danced, we went to some sort of circus, of all things. I recall a dancing bear being overseen by an elderly Jew who obviously loved the old creature very much. He had a gray head, his bear a gray muzzle. The bear was called Dauphin. Yes, I remember that.

Our story for the Mays-Heanes was that Carlotta was a Jew and we were on the run from the Nazis. Ha, if they had only known who we really were! They were pokey little people, really, but an enormous comfort to be within those uneasy hours. There is something extraordinarily reassuring about the English, I think, especially in difficult situations. They always retain their self-confidence, even when to do so is entirely absurd.

Back in the suite, I think we smoked the last hashish in Paris. Carlotta and I got into some Chinese robes that we had, while the Mays-Heanes remained resolutely dressed.

"Oh, dear, what can the matter be," Carlotta said.

"What's that," Jimmy Mays-Heans asked, "what's she saying?"

"That she's a lesbian and would like to kiss your wife's ass."

"Hell, she could kiss my ass in a moment."

Carlotta snarled, “Why’s he looking at me like that? What’s he saying?”

"They want us to be the first to strip," I replied.

She dropped her robe to the floor and danced like some sort of Indian snake charmer.

"We had best be off," Mays-Heans said in a very clipped tone. He'd taken off his dinner jacket. Now he put it back on.

"Nonsense," his wife said. "I might like to have my ass kissed. Nobody's ever done it or ever will, knowing you."

"Well I won't, you're right about that."

"She's dying for you to eat her," I said to Carlotta, still in German.

"Ah, good, I'm in the mood!"

The English girl, all pink and blushy, disrobed, little knowing that she was in the clutches of advanced decadents like us. But it was 1940 and in such times, decadence assumes an extraordinary importance and becomes an easy part of life. Outside, the whistle of bombs, inside perhaps only a moment to live. If you’ve ever wanted to do something, you’d better do it right now.

In the end, the four of us were hardly decadent at all. We lay on the big bed and smoked our hash and stroked one another's slim young bodies and traded stories of better days.

There was a distant thudding. Insistent. Then voices, raised, angry. The click of a lock. Somebody had opened the door in the living room.

As I rolled out of bed to see what was going on, a man in a threadbare coat barged in. I wish I could report that Captain George was some sort of Inspector Clouseau, but there was nothing comical about him. His long face was grim. More than that, it was red and his eyes were bloodshot. And the man was furious.

"May I help you?"

"You were called for nine sharp. It is now the noon hour. You must come."

"I want to telephone my embassy."

"No. There is no requirement for that. We have you as a spy and if you don't come of your own accord, I will have you brought."

"What's he saying? Is this the polenta?"

"A *Boche*!" he shouted.

"She's a Jew and my wife. We're running from the Nazis."

"You visit the Swedish embassy and send cables there. You have made a telephone call into Germany."

"I am trying to extract our funds."

"You are in the Crillon and you're worried about funds?"

"I am an American. I have five hundred thousand on deposit in Germany. Because my wife is Jewish, they will not release my money to me."

"What is your work? Why are you here?"

"I am in shipping. Also electronics. And we must leave. We must somehow get out of France, and so must they." I nodded toward the terrified Mays-Heans. "They are English."

He gave me a long, careful look. I thought, 'he has believed nothing.'

"Mr. Weber, have you ever been in Arras?"

The question completely gobsmacked me. Completely. I must have gaped. I'm sure I did. Should I tell the truth? No? I was absolutely at a loss.

"I see that you have. What were you doing there?"

"Seeing a friend and bringing back a friend's car."

"Be specific."

"The friend I saw was General Neame, on Lord Gort's staff. The car is a Delahaye that belongs to another Englishman, Paul Dukes. He is a British diplomat presently in Berlin awaiting exchange. The car is in the garage."

"All of this is clever, and all of this is lies."

"It's entirely true."

I was then arrested. But rather than being taken to the Security Police Headquarters, I was driven to a small office in a side street. Carlotta followed in what might well have been the last taxi running in Paris. The Mays-Heans disappeared from our lives. Years later, I ran into her at a party in London given by Bertie Willys, who had just been knighted for managing rock stars. She said that her husband had been killed in '41 in the siege of Tobruk. She was rather cold, I thought. I assume that she now knew what is believed to be the truth about me. She was remarried to a man who looked as if he'd been stuffed into his clothes by a sausage maker.

I was immediately suspicious of this so-called police office. This was Paris, their city. They wouldn't interrogate a dangerous spy in an office that looked as if it had been put together day before yesterday,

Carlotta stared from the cab as I went in. If she'd had a pistol, I am sure I would have been a free man. I also knew that she would wait for a time, then burst in making demands in her rough Berlin slang, and at the top of her lungs. How that might go over, I had no idea, but I suspected that it would not be well.

As we passed under the arch where the concierge had his flat, I felt myself prodded with what I assumed was the barrel of a pistol. For the second time in my life—and in a few days—I was being menaced with a gun.

Although the hell I had been going through since I returned to Europe was maturing me fast, it was not making me fatalistic. I had no intention of giving in to these people and every expectation of getting myself set free.

We went into a pokey ground-floor flat, then through the sitting room into a bedroom that had been made into an office by the removal of the bed and the addition of a desk that might have been new during the time of the Second Empire. When the occupant of the office looked up at me, I got another terrific shock. It was the British spy who had chased me in Arras.

And now there was yet another. In Arras, when he spoke German he had sounded to me like an Englishman. Here, speaking English, he sounded like a German. So who were these people, Abwehr or SIS? Was I being somehow tested by Hitler? It was certainly conceivable.

"You're not French," I said. "This isn't a *Sûreté* office."

"Where have you come from?"

"This isn't a legal arrest. You're simply holding me at gunpoint."

"Why did you go to that particular address in Arras?"

"I'm an American citizen, protected by the laws of the United States. I demand to telephone my embassy."

"You visited the British Embassy. Why?"

"Why do you think?"

He leaped to his feet and slapped me so hard I flew against the wall.

Silence followed until a third man entered the room. It was the embassy secretary who had facilitated my call to Churchill.

"We know you came out of Germany. We know you did it in a Feisler-Storch flown by a double agent called Paul Dukes."

I went to my feet.

"Sit down!"

I remained standing. The secretary stood face to face with me. There was sweat along his upper lip. His eyes were liquid.

At that moment, the event I had been dreading happened. Carlotta appeared in the doorway. In her long black leather coat, spiked heels and black veiled *chapeau*, she looked like some sort of updated Mata Hari character out of the movies. Until this moment, I had not realized that she had dressed for the part.

Both the secretary and the man with the gun were facing me and did not notice her appearance. As the one behind the desk started to rise in reaction, the one with the gun put a hand on my shoulders and tried to jam me down into the chair. To my own complete astonishment, I slung a roundhouse punch right into his jaw. He dropped like a sack of potatoes.

The secretary cried out and tried to reach past me to get his gun, which had gone sliding across the floor.

As he reached down, Carlotta grabbed his ears and forced his head down as she raised her knee. As he came into contact with it, his nose cracked like a small firework exploding. Wailing, he clutched it with both hands, and then there she was standing in the door with the gun pointed into the room.

"Willy, I'm fuckin' scared, what do I do?"

The man behind the desk had half stood. He raised his hands. In German, he said, "Don't squeeze the trigger, *Fraulein*. That's what makes it discharge."

"You think I don't know how to use a pistol? Asshole."

He breathed out between his lips. His hands were raised to the ceiling. "Please go," he said. "There are no further questions."

"That's right," she said, "no further questions."

"May we have our gun returned, please?"

She laughed. "Come on, Willy, let's go tie one on."

The fellow with the broken nose had somewhat recovered himself and was coming to his feet.

"*Nein*! *Bleibe*!"

He froze in a half crouch. "I'll be fined for losing my weapon," he whined. Everyone was speaking German, and this one sounded like a native. Odds were increasing that we were in the hands of the Abwehr, in which case my troubles were far from over. The embassy secretary had heard at least some of what I'd said to Churchill. If he was a German agent, Hitler might well be informed of my treachery.

I was beginning to understand that espionage is truly a darkness of mirrors.

"You think I'll give this back?"

"We won't do a thing. We'll take it and you can leave."

"Well, all right." She twirled the cylinder, expertly extracting the bullets into her palm. She tossed them into the room.

I thought that this was extremely foolish, and indeed the interrogator at once drew his own weapon from his pocket, a Beretta automatic.

"All right, this is finished," he said. He gestured toward me. "You sit down. And you put the pistol on the floor."

"Five," she said.

"Excuse me?"

"There are five bullets on the floor." I heard a click. She had pulled back the hammer on the revolver.

Smiling slightly, he replaced his pistol. He stood. "Very well."

When we returned to the street, the taxi was gone. No Paris cabby will tarry long.

As casually as she might have been leaving a shop, she began strolling along the sidewalk. "Let's go back to that river. It's so pretty at night. Is it nice during the day?"

"Carlotta, thank you! I had no idea—"

"Bulls are all the same everywhere, either they want to screw you or knock you over the head with a billy. Or both. Anyway, that guy didn't know what he was doing with that Beretta. If you weren't in the way, I'd have taken it right out of his hand and kept it. It was a nice gun."

I realized that growing up in Berlin during the Weimar years made situations like this seem perfectly natural to her. Who knew, maybe she'd even been in a gun fight or two. Hitler might have Old Shatterhand but Carlotta had reality.

"He might follow us," I said.

"He will."

I hurried toward a taxi stand I saw in the distance. She continued to stroll.

"Come on!"

"Why? No matter what we do, he'll catch up."

"If we got a taxi—"

"He'll show up at the Crillon."

"We'll move."

"Two days and he'll find us. He's a German, he's not going to give up."

"You're sure?"

"Germans look at life one way, French another."

"He could be English."

"Have you ever seen an English who looked at a woman straight? I don't think so. No, he's a German. They look at women like they look at food. The whole time we were there, he was making a meal of me with his eyes."

"What about the French?"

"The Frenchman creeps about in the garden of women, sniffing, touching. Not the German, he never touches, he consumes."

"And Americans?"

"Panting dogs with big grins on their dog faces. You get an Ami, you say two hundred marks and he pants and grins." She nodded, wagging her tongue.

"Do I get a big grin on my dog face?"

She gave me a light tap on the arm. "Usually."

I would once have been insulted, but the last bit of my naïveté had died beneath the screaming Horns of Jericho. When I closed my eyes at night, that great crater in the road, pocked with bits of people, floated into my mind's eye, bringing with it the animal wariness of wartime.

Perhaps I should have hated Hitler for it. It was his fault, he did it. In fact, he'd done it all. But still the scale of it all made the direct connection hard to see. From the *Felsennest* to that crater was a direct line. But it didn't seem that way. When one was in the riot of it, there was a sense of inevitability about the war, as if it was a fatal doom that emerged out of all men rather than out of the lunatic imaginings of a single one of us.

So you plodded along. The war was the war.

The hell it was, though. The war was him. Hitler was the war and the war was Hitler, a game of lives being played out on his maps and in his mind.

We found no taxis at the first stand we came to, none at the second, either. By this time the Germans were already in Calais and Paris was a ghost. Only a few relatively wealthy people remained, walking their dogs, sitting in the Tuileries Garden with their newspapers, waiting quietly for the anti-Communist and anti-Semitic Germans to arrive and impose what they hoped would be a reasonably comfortable occupation.

We needed to hurry back to the hotel and flee to new accommodations, but she knew nothing of the Metro and I knew less. The maps in the stations had been covered or removed lest the *Wehrmacht* ride in on the trains, I suppose. War is also absurd. The ridiculous is in constant competition with the grotesque for one's attention.

So we had no choice but to walk. As our pursuers had a car, we dodged down along the river. There was no road down there then, so they would have to follow on foot, or—which worried me more—go on ahead and intercept us. I didn't fancy trying to jump in this river. The Seine, if you have not seen it, is a fast water, and the rains of autumn had caused it to rise.

Carlotta, enjoying the stroll, was in no hurry.

"Please come on!"

"What's the use? We're caught. He let us go because he can find us again."

"We can go south with the rest of Paris. We can get out of here."

She rolled her eyes. "What we're going to do is go back to the hotel, get a nice meal and wait for him to turn up. We have to let this play out, Willy. He's German. On our side. He'll figure that out eventually."

I stopped her. I took her by the arm and made her face me. "Carlotta, there's something else. Something you don't know. One of those men is a British embassy secretary who knows a secret about me that will get us both shot if it gets back to Alf. Shot or worse." And there was worse in that war, believe me. A bullet through the heart was an act of grace.

At first, I didn't think she'd heard me. But then she hunched her shoulders and sped up.

"Carlotta?"

"Shit! Shit! Shit!"

"We're in a war. We have to take sides. I have to do this."

She turned on me. "We're whores! Whores don't fight in wars. That's where we make our dough!"

"I am no whore."

"Aw, go fuck yourself. Why do you think you're so rich?"

"I—"

"You're rich because Alf made you rich and he did that because he's in love with you, and he is that because you are a whore and you seduced him."

I sat. There was no bench. I sat on the ground.

"Oh, no, none of that. If we have to escape, we have to fuckin' escape." She held out a hand and dragged me upright. "That Abwehr guy's gonna be along any second."

"You know he's Abwehr? How do you know that?"

"I seen him."

"But do you *know*?"

"Sure, he used to come into Madam Kitty's. He liked me to wear a man's jock strap. God fucking knows why."

"But he said that? He said he was Abwehr?"

"The spooks all brag. They can't tell their amazing stories, so they insinuate. Snark snark. But yeah, he's an Abwehr. He's in the Paris KO. Oh, shit, I wanted to fly home to Alf with a bunch of new dresses and presents for Evie and everything, and damn you, *damn you*!"

"He can't be allowed to defeat France. France is civilization. And what about your fellow Jews? Look at what's going on with them."

"Nothing new there. Jews get fucked over. It is what happens."

I drew *Judea Capta* from my pocket. "Do you know what this is?"

"Gold. Great. Give it to me. Maybe I can pawn it and get home that way. If I still have a home."

"This coin was minted two thousand years ago by the Roman emperor who sacked Jerusalem and sent the Jews wandering through the world, which they are still doing to this day."

"They're not wandering, they're getting stuffed onto trains and sent east to die."

Those were chilling words. "Where did you hear that?"

"Jew talk."

We had reached the Pont Neuf. I thought if we went up to the Rue de Rivoli, we might find a cab or a bus to the Crillon.

In the event, we got to the hotel with no trouble from our pursuer. He had backed off. So he was watching.

We lunched. She said, "This may be my last meal I'll ever get to eat, so I want a huge heap of caviar and the best champagne in the world."

He goggled at her. It was her German, of course.

I said, "Monsieur, I am American and my wife is Jewish. We are escaping."

"Ah! Oh, she gave me a start."

"Understandable. Bring us each a service of Beluga, some cold poached salmon and champagne. And the best, really. Ask the sommelier. Cost doesn't matter."

He went away.

"Am I gonna get guillotined because I'm a *Boche*?"

"I told him you're my wife and an escaping Jew."

"This Jew ain't a Jew anymore, as you know perfectly well. And she intends to escape right back to the Berghof and continue the delightful life of a minor deity."

"I said it to keep you out of an internment camp. You're an enemy alien here, remember."

"Just until Alf and his boys arrive."

"*IF!*"

"Cigarette me." I gave her a cigarette and lit it.

"Here's how it is," she said after her first long drag. "You fix this. You fix it up with Alf."

"I'm caught. It won't work."

"Oh, you! You are such a child. Understand me, little boy. Alf wants to be fucked by you, and he thinks about it all the time. Let me assure you of that. Any lie that enables him to bend over and take your dick up his bunghole will work. He'll forget all his spy shit so quick you won't even believe it."

The idea of screwing that monstrosity in the ass was without question the most dreadful thought that had ever entered my mind.

At that moment, the hotel manager came to our table. "Monsieur Weber," he said gravely, "Madame. You should know that the *Boche* have surrounded the British army at Dunkirk, just above Calais. They're finished. We are collapsing and the Germans are on the road to Paris." He looked at Carlotta—and I realized that his expression was exactly as she had described a Frenchman's would be. He bent forward and smiled slightly, just as if he was regarding flowers. "Madame must flee."

The news had appalled me. If the British lost their army, what would prevent Hitler from conquering England, too?

The food came, and with it a Pol Roger '99, and perhaps the name on that bottle was what gave me the inspiration that now flashed into my mind.

"I have it," I said. "I can fix this."

"You can fix what?"

"All of it."

"Then do it. Because it sounds like Alf's gonna be here any day."

I had made a very complex decision, which you'll see unfold over the next pages. It was the hardest decision of my life, and it led in the end to the ruin of my life.

But I have a life and above all, Carlotta has a life. In that sense, my destruction has been my victory.

# 9

We couldn't go back to the room. In fact, we had to get out of there at once. I'd given up hope and had simply been waiting for the Abwehr agent, but no more. Now, with this news, at all costs, I had to get to the Swedish Embassy before the agent found me.

"I have to go."

"Not without me you don't."

I couldn't imagine it, but I'd sooner try to herd a famished tiger than resist Carlotta. I stood from the table. "Impossible. It's going to be dangerous."

"You don't know shit! You've never lived on the *keitz* I grew up in. Well, now all of Europe is my *keitz*, so you'd best learn. When there's trouble, us Lauras stick together. Strength in numbers." Incredibly, her eyes were wet. Absolutely wet. She continued, "Baby, I love you and if I'm gonna lose you I want to see it. Because then I'll turn around and I'll walk away. But if I don't see it, I can never walk away. I'll wonder, and wondering is loving and that's rat-face hard if you can never find out where the wondering ends."

I held out my hand to her and we walked out like that, hand in hand. Elegant young lovers in one of the most elegant settings in the world, we crossed the lobby like two angels, to an observer beyond any idea of danger, fear or pain.

I said to the doorman, "Are there any taxicabs?"

"There are none, Monsieur."

"And the damn Delahaye is out of gas."

"We can take your car, it has some."

"I thought it was ruined."

"Screw you. It still goes."

"Even backwards?"

"If you think you have a sense of humor, think again."

When the garage man brought it around, for a moment it looked all right, but then I saw that the bumpers had been tied on with wire and under the new wax, the sides were all scratched and the top was patched with sticky tape. They had done their best, but my poor baby was now a jalopy.

"You see, it's fine! Anyway, where did you say we're going?"

"The Swedish Embassy."

"I can't go to an embassy dressed like this. I've got to change."

"You look perfectly fine. Beautiful."

"This is a skirt, you idiot. You can't appear in an embassy in a skirt."

I was trying to save the BEF and she was worried about her appearance. "They won't care at all, not at a time like this!"

A slinky little Citroens pulled up. I'm sure you've seen them in movies, and thought that they were rather ominous. In the flesh—or the tin, rather—they were most ominous.

We both looked at it. The doorman said, "Perhaps you should go, Monsieur."

She got into my car. "I'm going to be embarrassed and I don't care to be embarrassed."

"It can't be helped."

As we pulled out I saw a couple alighting from the Citroen, and perhaps that's all they were. Perhaps.

I say that I was no longer naive, and that is true. Still, I was far from being a trained agent. Instead, I was an innocent explorer in the labyrinth of espionage, and thus unprepared to navigate it. For it has some quite unique qualities. It is not just a labyrinth, for example, but a labyrinth of mirrors. The problem is that if you fix only on the first image you see reflected, you don't see enough to help you. But if you try to sort out the multitude of images sweeping around you, then you see too much to understand anything. In my experience, the truth in intelligence work is an elusive, often invisible suggestion hidden in a flood of lies.

Having come to Paris throughout my life, I knew the city well, and drove easily through the empty streets to the Swedish Embassy. To get there, we had to pass the *Invalides*. I said to Carlotta, "There is where Napoleon is buried."

"Good. I wish him good riddance. That bastard Titus, too."

For a moment, I didn't understand. Then I did. "I thought you didn't know anything about the Romans." Titus was the son of the Roman Emperor Vespasian and had been the general in charge of the sack of Jerusalem.

"You don't know what I know. Anyway, I'm a German. We're not like Americans, we're educated."

I drove on. What she had said was very true and made me obscurely sad. I'd seen public gallows in some towns in Germany. Stocks, in one case with some poor Polish worker hanging in them, his face swarming with flies. The Germans are good at towns. They create lovely towns.

As I got out of the car, I said to Carlotta to wait for me.

"No, not at all." she said. "We cannot be separated for a second. Not a second."

I didn't want her raging at me in German on a Paris street corner just now, so I took her with me. We were soon in the communications room, with the same technician I had seen before.

Either this would work or the moment I rang off, Hitler would order his henchman to shoot me dead on the street as I left the embassy.

"Please place a call through to Dr. Heer."

"I will try. The lines are up and down."

They would be. They passed right through the area of conflict in northern France.

Then he was there. "Doctor Heer!"

"Yes, hello?"

I took a breath. This was an extraordinary moment in my life. Maybe at last, I would accomplish something that mattered.

"I have news. Our rival in England wishes to parley."

"You have spoken to him?"

"I telephoned him."

Carlotta frowned at me.

"Ah," Hitler said. "Do you judge him to be sincere?"

"I can't be certain, but he has reason to be."

He laughed. "The association hasn't been very profitable for his company."

"Yes, their wasted product covers ten acres, I hear."

"That's quite a few trucks—I mean, truckloads."

Here it came. Either this would help the BEF or I would find out that Hitler no longer trusted me. "My thought is if we let him keep his personnel, he might be inclined in the end to make a deal with us on territories and so forth."

"But you have no assurances?"

"He's a slippery character."

"And how is your assistant? Mine is missing her a great deal. They work together closely, you know."

"I do know that. If you're coming soon to the hotel, bring her."

"Yes, she'll enjoy it. Things will be very peaceful by then."

There was a silence in which I could hear faint chuckling. I realized that the absurd coding conversation was delighting him.

"Very well," he said more seriously. "Is there any more?"

"I want to approach the Germans."

"And sell those devils vacuum tubes that would aid their war effort? I should say not!"

"Very well, Doctor Heer, you're the boss in this."

We rang off. Carlotta said, "Who was that?"

"A business associate in Stockholm."

"Why do you want to approach the Germans? We are the Germans."

"Figure of speech, my dear."

As we returned to the car, my heart was flying. I sensed that he had believed every word. If so, this might be a triumph. There were nearly half a million British soldiers encircled in Dunkirk. If Hitler let them go as a signal that he was open to peace talks, the BEF would be saved.

In the event, that is to a degree what happened. 384,000 British and allied soldiers got back to England. The Dunkirk beaches were hammered by the German air force, but Guderian remained behind the dunes with his tanks and all of those men were successfully brought home. I've often wondered if Johnny Scott-Ellis was among them. I really should try harder to keep up, but to be frank, it's almost unbearable to me to be around people who believe that I was Hitler's boy-toy, but to my face pretend that they don't, then at the first opportunity cut me dead.

Perhaps I had some sort of a hand in Dunkirk and perhaps I didn't. It could be nothing more than Guderian's tanks needing to be refueled.

We remained in empty Paris, in the increasingly silent hotel. Rationing and curfew would come later, and foodstuffs were plentiful. If one did not worry about the closed cinemas, theaters and concert halls, life proceeded in a reasonably settled manner.

Many of the clubs and cabarets, while still open, could not offer their headliners, who had fled the city, even Josephine Baker, who had been working, as history has recorded, for the *Deuxième Bureau,* picking up tit-bits of useful gossip at the many parties to which she was invited. As he Nazis closed in, she had retreated to her castle in the south, and that was the last I knew of her during the war. The story of her distinguished and courageous career in resistance fighting can be found in the history books.

One looked in the papers and especially listened to the BBC for war news. Where were the Germans today? The allies?

On the 12th, Reynard declared Paris an open city and the government evacuated to the south. June 13th was a Thursday, and one of the quietest, saddest days I can recall.

All the shops were closed, so Carlotta could not continue what I laughingly described as her "buying surge." She was obsessed with getting matching clothes for her and Eva, which I doubted would be much appreciated. And indeed, in future years we had to arrange a system of signals so that they wouldn't come down dressed identically. If they'd had pistols, they would both have died in a duel sometime in mid '43.

When we went down to breakfast on the 14th, there was hardly any staff.

The waiter said, "Monsieur, the *Boche* are in the Champs Elysees."

"But the war isn't over. France hasn't capitulated."

He hung his head in silence. We took a quick croissant and a *cafe noir* and went out to see. And there they were, an immense column of fine looking young men, clean shaven with polished helmets and excellent rifles, marching three abreast as General von Breisen, sitting on a really fine chestnut, motioned at them to hurry along.

"It's Sixth Army. That's von Breisen."

"He'll be bald soon."

"What happens when I go bald?"

"Don't."

Nearby, I heard the voices of young Americans excitedly calling out the numbers of the various units as they passed.

"Listen, Americans. Let's go see," I said. As we threaded our way through the crowd, a young man yelped and leaped away from me. Carlotta gave him a well-placed kick that projected him off the curb. A military policeman immediately came over.

"Keep moving," Carlotta said. "Fuckin' dipper had his paw in your pocket."

I reached in. My wallet was gone. "Shit!"

"Here it is." She handed it to me. "I went to dipping school but it's no good, you get caught too much. That guy was a gypo. All they know is dip. That's their calling."

The thief had disappeared. The *feldgendarme* once again stood with his legs spread and his hands behind his back, watching the sparse crowd of dejected Parisians watch him.

This was Sixth Army, the conquerors of Poland, who would become the conquered in Stalingrad. That great column, strong, young, spotlessly turned out, marched endlessly past.

"They look like hunters," I said to Carlotta.

"They're soldiers. Obviously."

"I mean the horses. I suppose that they've been taken off some of the big estates to the north. Fine animals to be pulling artillery."

I heard an American voice call out, "76th Infantry!"

"Hello," I shouted.

"Oh! Oh look, chaps, another one of ours. And his lady, oh my yes!"

"What are they saying?"

A Frenchman shouted, "A *Boche*!"

"No, a refugee," I shouted back. "Leave her be!"

"A *Boche*!"

"And a refugee and a woman!"

The Americans had converged on us. "Who are you?" one of them asked. "What's going on?"

"I worked for IBM in Berlin. This is my wife. She's a Jew. We had to leave."

"Well, I work for GM right here in Paris, and I don't think I quite approve of a white man with a Jew wife. Right, fellas? This guy's got a Jew for a wife."

"Here comes motorized!" another shouted. "60th, see there—60th Motorized!"

Low armored cars came roaring along three abreast, spewing out copious clouds of fumes. They were followed by artillery being pulled by trucks—Fords.

"Boy, nobody's gonna beat this crowd," one of the fellows said.

"What's he saying?" Carlotta asked.

I replied in German, "That he's an asshole, as are they all." Then I said to him in English, "No GM trucks?"

"*Opel* is our brand. Best truck in Europe."

"Maybe if you're lucky they'll buy more. Win the war with them. Then you won't have to worry about anybody being married to Jews."

"What's that supposed to mean?"

"No Jews."

"That shit. You sound like the New York *Times*, always whining. I have to tell you mister, we don't need Jews. Nobody does." He spat.

I popped him on the nose. Not as hard as I could have, just enough to send him sprawling among his friends.

"Willy!"

I grabbed her arm and pulled her away with me into the crowd. People had seen the fisticuffs, of course, but they were French and as the argument had involved *le Anglais* it didn't matter.

He was right about his trucks, though. Had it not been for the stout Opel truck, the *Wehrmacht* would never have made it to the gates of Moscow. Too bad for Hitler that they weren't given anti-freeze before they left for Russia. Had the *Wehrmacht's* vehicles been provided with it, his forces would have taken Moscow, I would think. This is an example of why I always say that the reality of history is to be found in the details.

Another example is that a Japanese scout plane during the Battle of Midway had a broken antenna. A single screw was missing. Because of that, the plane's report of the location of Nimitz's carriers was never received by Yamamoto. Therefore, the Japanese lost the battle and the war. For want of a few thousand gallons of anti-freeze and Germany is defeated. A single screw lost and down goes Japan.

We never see these things, which is what about history that fascinates me the most. I suppose that it's because I am a ghost in history myself.

We walked back to the hotel where the concierge handed me a calling-card. It was for a Helmut Greise, a personal card and so no indication of his business. It offered us a dinner this evening at eight in 6, Rue des Colonels Renard. This was the Paris flat of G. I. Gurdjieff.

We discussed it. Who was this man and what could he possibly mean offering to give us dinner in an obscure side street in an undistinguished corner of the city. I thought it better not to mention the name Gurdjieff.

"Greise. Could he be that agent?" she asked finally.

"I think that's exactly who he is."

"Let's see if we can buy a gun and shoot him."

"Buy a gun in Paris today? That seems a fool's errand."

"Ask the concierge. He can do all sorts of things. He got me *etsch* while I was waiting for you. Plus girls. I didn't want boys, I didn't want to be disloyal."

"Don't use heroin."

"It's relaxing. It's very nice."

"Just don't! Don't!"

"All right. You can't blame me for doing something to help me sleep a little bit while you fucked around God knows where!" She grabbed me. "The only thing I ever had is you. You're stayin' with me. If you go on expeditions for Alf, then we go. Eva feels the same. She's ready to fight, too."

"She can't come with us."

"With Alf! She wants to be with him. Fight side by side! Women are good in war. We don't care. We're excellent killers."

"Have you ever killed anybody, Carlotta?"

She met my eyes. I think that I have never seen such innocence in a pair of human eyes. If I'd been a police investigator, I would have completely melted. "Why do you ask that?"

"I'm just curious. I know so little about your past."

"What if I did?"

"I'm glad you survived. Because I know you. You wouldn't kill anybody who wasn't trying to kill you."

"I threaten to kill you all the time."

"That's different."

She turned the innocence off, but slowly, like somebody turning down a lamp. Now she regarded me with a poisoner's stealthy gleam. "Is it?"

That was Carlotta, desperate for love and full of guile. Even before we were married, I put her in my will. I never let her know it, though, God no.

She had some marijuana which she had been smoking by meticulously emptying cigarettes of their tobacco with a tweezers, then refilling them. The tobacco, of course, she saved for future need, keeping it in a little silk bag she'd gotten in some shop.

By evening we had discovered that even the food supplies of the hotel were running low, and the idea of being given a dinner interested us both a good deal more than it had.

"I hope there's a *bombe*," she said.

"Too many of those about already. Let's hope for a *gateau*.

"Alf doesn't care for *gateaux*. He prefers a *bombe*."

"He's not here and I am, and I prefer *gateau*."

We drove along the Champs Elysees and around the Arc de Triomphe into the Avenue de Grande Armee. The Germans were gone. The Sixth Army was not an occupying force but rather had been in pursuit of the retreating French, and was by now far to the south. They had come first along the Avenue de Grande Armee and right through the Arc. I wondered if one day they might go back out that way.

The Rue des Colonels Renard is an undistinguished little street near the border of the 8th. The building itself was trying to be imposing, though, with Rococo balustrades that, instead of adding the intended impression of elegance, made it seem rather desperate.

"It's quiet," Carlotta said as we parked on the curb.

"All Paris is quiet."

We looked up. In my dinner clothes, I felt quite exposed. One cannot run in evening shoes. For her part, she was once again wearing the black silk that she favored for evening, and very high heels. We were, in fact, entirely helpless.

"Maybe we shouldn't do this."

I said to the concierge that we were here at the invitation of Monsieur Griese.

"No such person here."

"Ah. And yet we have his invitation." I displayed his card.

"No, Monsieur, no!"

I was careful not to speak to Carlotta. Out here away from the center, German was not going to be a good choice of language, not at all.

We noticed the lift coming down, clanking rhythmically as it descended.

I took her arm. I was ready to pull her out and run right back to the car when the door opened and the Abwehr fellow came out.

"Ah, you came," he said in French.

"What's he saying?"

Sure enough, the moment she spoke, the concierge bristled.

"Never mind," I said, "she's a refugee from Hitler."

Growling to herself, the woman backed toward her door.

Griese said, "You've met Georges Gurdjieff. He's making the dinner. You mustn't miss it. It'll be the best dinner you have in Paris."

Carlotta frowned. She couldn't make out the French, but she'd heard that name.

"Before we go in," I said to him, "what is this about?"

He shook his head. "Monsieur Weber, you and I will never know the truth about one another. In our world this is not possible, as I am sure you understand. I may work for the Abwehr, you for the SIS. It may be the opposite, or we both may work for both. You could be anyone and I could be anyone. Maybe you work for Stalin or Roosevelt or maybe they all cross your palm and, for that matter, mine. But here it's different, in this house. Come up and you'll see."

Carlotta had slipped behind me. "What's going on? Where are we?"

"It's the flat of that Lebanese rug merchant."

"I thought I heard the name of that old prick. No proper German food then. Only odd stuff."

Griese smiled gently down on her, as if she—who had overpowered him just the day before—was some soft little kitten. Or perhaps it was fear.

We ascended to the flat on the 2nd Floor. The door was opened by an Englishwoman I had seen in the Prieuré, a Miss Gordon. She smiled quite broadly and said, "Helmut, your friends did come! Welcome!"

"What in hell..." Carlotta muttered as we entered a room fitted with cushions and thrown with Oriental carpets. It was exactly like Gurdjieff's apartments in the Prieuré.

A boxy, once attractive woman appeared. "The American," she said, "the man of mystery, who came out of the dark."

She was introduced as Jeanne de Salzmann, whom I know to this day as Madame de Salzmann, and regard as a great spiritual master. If my soul may be saved, it is my inner work with her that is saving it. She has taught me how to truly feel remorse.

A male voice said, "With three of us here and you, too, Carlotta, we can't play chess with our lives. Too complicated."

"Good evening, Paul."

"You're dressed for *La Coupole*. Didn't you know where you were bound?"

"To take a dinner. I saw no indication that I shouldn't dress."

"Willy is very proper, Helmut. He hasn't been at war long enough. But Helmut and I have been sparring for ten years at least, intellectual pugilists trading rounds."

I now understood the reason for this lunatic dinner. These men were enemies of one another, but I had secrets from both of them, and they had banded together to attempt to find me out.

"You know, gentlemen, my game isn't chess. Chess is a game of search. One searches with one's mind, for the one perfect move. I'm an American, which makes my game poker, where one lies with one's face, and looks for the card so high that it will take him home."

Paul said, "Funny boy! In your case, that card is in your pocket."

"What do you mean?"

"Shall I spell it out?"

"You have no idea, Paul. None." I turned to Helmut. "Do you know how it is that I came out of the dark?"

He smiled. Paul made the smallest of signs to me, hardly more than the tick of an eye. But it spoke eloquently: 'Lives are at stake here. Have a care.'

I wondered if Paul had been arrested by this man. Could he be a prisoner?

Others came in. Except for Miss Gordon, no English anymore. They brought low tables and big, elaborate cushions. Some sort of perfume, a scent from far away, filled the air. Then Gurdjieff swept in. As he was settling himself in some of the cushions, he saw Carlotta. He came back to his feet, I thought rather painfully.

"Oh," he murmured. He took her hand in both of his, then dropped it. "This one." His eyes twinkled. "She is too thin! Like English, always too thin. We shall give her a good dinner!"

"He's talking about me, I can tell and I don't like it. Tell him to either shut up about me or talk German."

"Mr. Gurdjieff does not speak German," Helmut said. "He only imagines that he does. Please understand this when you converse with him."

"Ah, your shoes," Gurdjieff continued in French. "What? Two hundred francs? Mm?"

As Carlotta couldn't understand a word, she only smiled warily.

"He is interested in your shoes."

"Oh, one of those."

"No, in their value."

He said, "She is *Allemand* like you, Helmut." Then, to Carlotta in his "German": "I am a little Germanian."

I said, "He means that he speaks some German."

"No he doesn't."

"I am shoes in pawn, mark. Mark. Franc."

"What?"

"I think he needs money." I turned to him. "Monsieur, do you want two hundred marks."

"We make dinner for *l'argent*."

"We're meant to pay for the dinner, two hundred francs."

"What a chiseling old shit he is!"

Helmut laughed. "He will tell you about his oil wells soon."

As indeed he did. We ate a fine meal of *beshbarmak, shelpek*, and various cold meats and a quite complex chopped salad which contained cucumbers, tomatoes, onion and many herbs in a redolent dressing. It was Gurdjieff's own special salad, which I still have on occasion. The wine was, unfortunately, one of those Greek horrors that they inexplicably infuse with pine oil. I've always thought that they must have been trying to make gasoline when they came up with that stuff.

Helmut and Paul and I parried no further during the meal. On that particular evening—I believe it was June 17—the Reynaud government had already quit Paris but the Germans had not yet established their occupation. So it was still an open city, really without any laws at all. Two million human beings were waiting, breathless with fear.

The dinner was followed by honey cakes and thick, lovely coffee. It was already a great rarity in Germany. Soon in would be unobtainable in France, also.

Gurdjieff asked me if I had enjoyed myself. I told him that I had. I made no reference to Carlotta, who had obviously been ready to leave the moment we arrived. He then said, "I am making loans against the production of oil well I have in Texas. Will you do this?"

"Ah, Texas. I have friends there. Where is your well?"

"In the center."

"Central Texas?"

"Yes, exactly there."

"It must be the only one, as there are none in central Texas that I know of."

"You seek to work on yourself. That's why you come here. Rich is hard. Eye of needle. Ego robs you. You and young woman."

"He's looking at me and talking again and I really hate this, Willy! Let's go."

"His eyes just happen to be glued to you because you're so beautiful."

"He's peculiar and the food was unspeakable and it stinks in here and I'm ready to go."

As we were making our goodbyes, Gurdjieff said one of the strangest and most remarkable things I had ever heard.

"In our solar system, certain substances emanate from the sun and the planets in the same way as those emanated by the earth, making contact at certain points in the solar system."

Not understanding French, Carlotta continued to leave. For a moment, I followed along, but the words stayed with me. We were in the corridor when I stopped. Paul and Helmut were right with us.

"Carlotta, wait."

"Certainly not."

"Please."

"What's going on?"

"He said something in French that was rather remarkable. I want to ask him a question about it."

"He says many remarkable things," Helmut said.

She came close and whispered to me, "I need to be fucked senseless right now." Her arms came around my neck. "Let's go."

"Just one moment, please."

"Shit! OK. Always your way, you're the one with the cash."

I stepped back in.

"Oh, well, have you changed your mind? I will sell you the oil wells."

"What did you mean?"

"Come and sit."

"Carlotta, come in."

"*NEIN!*"

"We'd best stand."

"She has strength, yes?"

"Much!"

"Ah. Now listen quick before she beans you. There is a materialized image of the all-highest in our atmosphere. But to communicate with it requires great concentration. If you have enough, you can enter into contact with it. Like a telephone."

To this day, I do not know what it is, but I know that it is. In my years in Mr. Gurdjieff's practice, I have had glimpses of other realities.

I gave him some money, a few thousand francs that I had in my wallet that night. During the war when I went to Paris, I always gave him some. He needed it. They hid the Jewish members of their little group. As an Englishwoman, Miss Gordon, was interned in '43. Fortunately for her, she wasn't Jewish, but she died anyway, right after the war, exhausted by her ordeal.

At the time what he'd said seemed quite incomprehensible, even mad. It has taken me years to begin to sense that the living world around us is more than what we can see.

On the street, Paul gave the BMW a long look. "Is that running?"

"It is."

"Let's walk a bit," Helmut said in French. "There's a bar along the way."

"Carlotta," I said in German, "they want the bar."

"All right, good. Let's get drunk, gentlemen, what say you?"

As we walked along, Paul briefly took her hand. "I'm glad you're alive."

"Am I?"

"You're walking, talking."

"Being alive is different. It's more." She reached into my breast pocket, took out my flask and drank from it. "Ach, what's this now?"

"Absinthe, I'm sorry."

"Horrible!" She spat into the gutter.

"You have absinthe in a flask? I never heard of such a thing."

I replied, "So now you have, Helmut."

"She understands no French?"

"Perhaps a little."

He shifted to English. "This?"

"Not a word."

"You live right there in the Berghof, yes?"

"You're the intelligence officer."

We reached the little bar and took a table. There was a gramophone playing somewhere, not in the bar itself. Except for us, there were no patrons. We took cognac and Helmut cut a cigar, not a very good one. Havanas were already unobtainable in Paris.

"Do you ever wonder that somebody in the Berghof might just shoot him?"

"Not at all. It's well guarded." But not from my own pistol. Helmut had suddenly become interesting in a new way. Was he an anti-Hitler conspirator? Was that really why he and Paul were together?

"He sends everyone away, though."

"What do you mean?"

"When you're there. The four of you."

"I've never noticed."

"Do you think this war is good?"

The waiter brought the cognac. I lit cigarettes for me and Carlotta.

"It's really very rude," she said, "leaving me out."

"I'm so sorry," Helmut responded in German. "I'm always annoying people by trying to perfect my English. But with these two here, it's irresistible. May I plead for a few more moments?"

"Yes," she snapped. She turned away from us and stared out the dark window. "Oh, Willy, maybe there's a radio. See if the waiter will turn it on. I'd love to hear some news."

"It's all French here."

"Oh, yes, stupid French."

Helmut said in English, "Is she a loyalist?"

"To a good meal, a bed and money in her stocking. She's a whore."

Paul said, "A very exalted one, to be sure."

"The Queen of the Night," I said. Then to her in German, "We're saying you're the Queen of the Night."

"If you don't stop talking about me in languages I can't understand, Willy, I'm going to slap your face."

"Mine, too," Helmet said.

"And mine, please," Paul added.

We got a laugh out of her at least. "Men! You only grow up physically."

"Now listen, Willy. I'm going to be frank."

"Careful," Paul said.

"No, no, he's with us. I can see it. Willy, if you had the chance, would you be willing to murder him?"

I pretended shock and confusion. "Excuse me?"

"He's going to destroy Europe unless he's stopped. Europe, Willy!"

"You don't know that."

"I do and so do you!"

"A man's life is ended, and at my hand. So what happens then?"

"You become a hero of the world. You'll receive every decoration for valor there is."

"I, or my corpse?"

"But do you want to do it, Willy? Do you long to?"

He was playing out his chess game. I stuck to poker, lying carefully. "I haven't thought of anything like this. I don't know what to make of it—or you, frankly."

Through the whole exchange, Paul had remained silent, looking from one of us to the other as we spoke. He was like a man watching a duel. I'd tried to find some sort of signal from him, some means of telling me what this man was really about, but hadn't detected the slightest frown or nod, nothing that might have communicated his feelings.

The conversation—or rather, verbal chess game—continued for a few more minutes in the same vein. Finally, Paul said, "I have another place we can go. More entertaining."

At this, we returned to the car.

"I'm sorry it's a squeeze. The back is a bit of an afterthought."

I drove along to the Champs Elysees. I'd be glad to get back to the hotel and give Carlotta a dose of what she was longing for.

"An idea," Paul said in German. "Given that this might be the last sweet night in Paris forever, why don't we walk a bit along the Quay?"

"I'm sick of walking," Carlotta said.

"Ah, but the moon in the flying clouds, my dear, the dark quick waters, then some excellent *etsch*, what do you say?"

"No heroin," I said. "Too much of that."

"Then opium. I know you kids love that."

"We can get opium at the hotel."

"That commercial stuff from Morocco. This is the original smoke of dreams, right from China. And a marvelous spot, a luxurious den, hidden away. The most exotic people in Paris. I promise a night of complete abandonment. This is just along the Pont d'Alba."

"I don't want opium," Helmut said.

"I think you do. It makes people so talkative."

What an odd thing to say. That was the last thing that it did.

Carlotta protested no further, so I turned into the Pont d'Alba.

"Here," Paul said. "Park here."

"Where is it?"

"Right across. Best not to leave the car over there. It'll sprout wings and fly away."

I parked along the roadside. As we strolled across the bridge, there wasn't another car or another soul in sight.

Carlotta and I were walking in front, Paul and Helmut behind. They were speaking together, laughing a bit. I was trying to make out what they were saying when I heard Helmut make a sort of grunt. Then they were silent.

The moon stared down, bright and amazed, the waters rushed, a night wind made the lamps hiss. A dark object sped away in the current.

"I'm cold," Carlotta said. As I had for Eva so long ago in the forest, I took off my dinner jacket and wrapped it around her shoulders.

"You know, I'm afraid I've made a mistake," Paul said. "I've just remembered that the club I was thinking of has closed. Perhaps we should call it a night."

She turned around. "You walk me and walk me and then it's closed. I wouldn't have minded some top quality smoke." She looked past Paul. "Where's the Nazi?"

"He stepped off."

I knew at once that the dark object I'd seen in the river was him, his head above the swirling water. Without so much as a sound, Paul had thrown him off the bridge.

I thought at once of the wife somewhere, the children at this moment waiting deep in Germany, the lovers, the friends, the life he had left behind.

Ian Fleming knew Paul, of course, and some of his personality went into 007, especially the sardonic little quips that followed his exploits.

Helmut had indeed 'stepped off' right into the Seine, tossed there by some Ju-Jitsu move of Paul's.

My skin had gone dry and the night frigid and unwelcoming. As we returned across the river, I sought another glimpse of that bobbing head but saw only the waves.

There was little chance that he would survive. The quays would prevent him from getting out. He'd struggle and tire and eventually drown. As has been the case with so many others, he'd eventually be found tangled among the rapids downstream, a bloated ruin, likely with his eyes eaten out by crows.

Paul and I continued to speak in English. I trusted Carlotta then and I trust her now, but every secret is a burden, and why burden her?

"What of the other two?"

"Shipped off to Blighty on the morning blimp. They'll hang."

"And Helmut was really a danger to us?"

"To you possibly."

"But you're not sure?"

"You're in a business now in which nobody is ever sure. He knew too much. That was his guilt."

"But if he survives?"

"With a broken neck? No."

"But how? There wasn't a sound."

"Shaida Way."

And you are, I am sure, wondering what that was. So am I. I have been seeking the Shaida Way for 35 years. Not a clue. He said later that it was a practice perfected in the Tibetan monastery where Gurdjieff had been a student.

"I'm so tired! Willy, can you carry a person?"

Carlotta was petite like Eva, the exact opposite of the sort of women Alf publicly favored, so she was fairly easy to lift. I carried her like a bride and she put an arm around my shoulder and laid her head against my chest.

"What are you talking in English?"

"Nothing much. What happens to the British embassy, that sort of thing."

"They get shot?"

"Diplomats are exchanged."

"Will Paul be shot?"

"I don't think so," he said lightly. "Remember, I also work for Herr Hitler and the work I do for him is very useful." Then, in English, "There's another matter. Heavy Water. I believe Winston told you about this."

"Yes."

"Talk German, don't leave me out!"

"We are discussing things that don't translate easily, my dear. Whether or not I can somehow manage to get my mother to Germany for her heart. The best treatment in the world is there." Then, in English, "We need to find it and get it out. It's an absolutely urgent priority."

"What is it?"

"That I'm not told. It's about 1500 gallons of water in shielded containers and it's somewhere on the coast. Normandy, we think."

We reached the car. I gave Carlotta a kiss on her cheek and put her down.

"You're a strong one," she said happily. "I had an alphonse like that when I was a kid. I loved him to carry me and I love you to carry me."

As we got into the car, I said, "Who is this alphonse? Should I be jealous?"

"Of a Jew somewhere off in whore camp? I don't think so."

Lost to history is the fact that the roundups from the underworld *keitz* were all sent to a special section of Dachau that was called *Benilskamp*. The SS held tea-dances there.

"Put me off here," Paul said as we reached the hotel.

I pulled up.

"Why not come in with us? Have a nightcap."

"A nightcap with you two will lead even the strongest man astray.

Anyway, we're on Berlin rules here too, now. I've got to go to my own little hide-hole."

Carlotta laughed. "What's to your taste, old man? Have your bubble blown?"

"Oh, my dear!" He got out, but then leaned in my window. "Where's my Delahaye?"

"In the hotel garage without fuel."

The doorman let Carlotta out, and I followed Paul.

"Is it otherwise running?"

"Absolutely. But there's no petrol to be had in Paris just now."

He switched to English. "I'll cable Hitler. They'll fuel it up when they get here."

"Do you know the date?"

"They'll establish occupation in Paris tomorrow. They've already secured Le Bourget and there's an SD unit setting up in Avenue Foch. I don't know when the official surrender will take place. Whenever the Frenchies have had it in the south."

I really felt like crying, I have to tell you. I said in German, "So there you have it. He's beaten the French."

"We won? Is that really true?"

"We won, Darling."

"Aw *fuck*!"

Paul said, "You're not proud of the soldiers? It's quite an achievement."

"Germans in Paris? Have you been to Berlin lately? It used to be so fun, but not now, not since Alfie-boy took over. It was amazing, the art and everything. A new world was being born. A *real* new order, not this bullshit we have now."

Carlotta's capacity to surprise has always been considerable. I thought to myself, 'if I say you're a whore with a heart of gold,' she will hit me, hard.

Paul said, "Well well, you're the proverbial whore with a heart of gold."

Her purse came up and hit him in the side of the head so hard, if he'd had false teeth they would have flown out of his mouth and across the street.

"'Strooth! That *hurt*!" He staggered, holding his head with both hands. "Gad!"

The doorman, being French, did nothing to help and remained completely silent.

"You killed that man. What about his kids? Ever think of them?"

So she'd seen. She'd given no indication. Carlotta seems to be many things, but what she really is she never seems to be. After all these years of knowing her, I have come to think that she can only see what is true. She cannot have illusions. In her, the truth is like a light that she can never turn off. Harsh light. And it has been like that ever since she was a child.

He put his hand out to her. She looked down at it. He said, "I will take his children with me till the end of my days, them and all the others."

She pushed him in the chest. "You oughta be like us. Willy and me, we're on the easy plan. Fuck toys. But you're too old. Also too English, like a big pink bag full of roast beef."

Paul slipped off into the dark. His head was down and I couldn't tell if he was laughing or crying. Of course, it's possible to do both at once, I suppose.

When we went in and I was getting our key, the desk clerk said, "Your father and sister have come. We let them into your suite."

Slowly, side to side, the room swayed. Then for an instant I was terrified for them. 'But they're Americans just like me,' I told myself. My surprise brought anger with it. Why hadn't they told me? Then the most extraordinary joy washed over me. *Vati*! My *vati* has forgiven me!

Would he accept Carlotta? Oh, yes, *Vati* was a Freethinker, of course he would! Maddy would love the joke of it, and when she discovered how I loved Carlotta, she would love her, too.

In the lift, I said to her, "My father and sister are in the suite."

"Really? That's peculiar."

She was right. It wasn't so easy to travel to France just now. In fact, the German radio was trumpeting the fact that a U-Boat had just sunk the Lancastria off Saint-Nazaire. But *Vati* was a resourceful man. When he wanted to do something, he did it.

By the time we were at the door, I was shaking so much that Carlotta took my hand. "Willy," she said. "Be proud before your people. You're a man doing a very hard thing." She whispered, "But let's be careful with our secrets."

"Absolutely."

I tried to calm myself and couldn't, then put the key into the lock, twisted it and opened the door.

Inside, it was quite dim, only a single lamp burning. Under that lamp sat a woman reading a book. She raised her head.

"Oh good!" She stood up and came toward us. "But be quiet, he's so very tired and he's finally sleeping."

She was not my sister and the man here was not my father.

"Evie!" Carlotta said. They flew into one another's arms.

# 10

Now, none of what follows here is in history. Hitler is in history. Alf is not. It is often said that he never once went to a bombed city. That is not true. He was often in bombed cities, but in disguise. What did he feel about them? Anger and desperation. He told himself that it was happening because the German people were not strong enough to take their true place in the world. The Aryans were proving to be inferior after all.

So he was usually rather accepting of the catastrophe. It was their fault, not his. Even so, I have seen him leaning against a wall, weeping in the small hours, with the hoses hissing and the stink of burnt flesh in the air, and the night wind moaning in the ruins.

There were extensions for his mustache, glasses and a hairpiece that concealed his characteristic mop. The only giveaway remained that prominent nose of his. But a lot of people have big noses.

There were a few close calls, such as that evening in Horcher's, but to my knowledge he was never unveiled.

When Eva and Carlotta had finally stopped weeping in one another's arms, Eva said, "He's absolutely dying for it. So you be ready when he wakes up. Really give it to him, Carlie, give it to him hard and long."

"I'll add some stuff. I've got some new ideas. Has he been fucking you at all?"

"He says he can't. He says the war has taken it out of him."

She smiled softly. "When he's nice and hard, I'll send him out to you."

They were sitting side by side on the couch. Eva turned and kissed her cheek.

Silence fell. "Any cards in here?"

I went looking for some in the drawers of various tables. No good. It was now past midnight, so I doubted that the staff could find us any.

"We've got some hashish, some opium."

"We'll be asleep when he wakes up."

"Not with hash," I said.

"We can strip and play with each other," Carlotta said. "We can play with you, big boy."

In preparation, I ordered up champagne, caviar, salmon, cheeses, a box of Calissons and a cold chocolate Charlotte.

So here we were in the middle of a war in the middle of the night playing with each other like children at the game of doctor, in a setting of the utmost luxury.

Hash is one of my oldest friends now. Good hash overtakes you. It lifts you into the arms of love, slowing everything down and softening and brightening the world. I, at least, recover my sense of humor when I am high on hash. My guilt seems something I should keep in my pocket, a black kerchief wrapped around *Judea Capta*. And as for life unfolding, I am filled with compassion. I see the way we need ourselves with such acute tenderness. I feel the spirit of the plant as a moral guide.

Oh, but goodness, we always had such a nice time together, the three of us. I had—and have—no interest in the sexual mores of the middle class. I'm an aristocrat and like most of us, exactly as morally unformed as those at the bottom of the social order. I am much more concerned about whether or not my cuffs are properly shot than where my dick goes. I still admire the ideas of Magnus Hirschfeld. He originated marriage counseling, gay liberation, gender reassignment and sex therapy. In other words, he was a compassionate man, and that's what I strive to be, a compassionate man.

We did our first really serious threesome on the floor of the living room in that suite, covered with a big silk quilt we'd dragged in from an empty bedroom.

Why didn't we use the bed? That was before the king sized bed appeared, therefore it was too small.

The girls took turns sitting on me and seeing how many strokes it would take them to come. For my part, hashish slows down orgasm and thank God. They would have beaten the dickens out of me if I'd come before they were finished with their play.

It was a sweet hour, surrendered as we were to the pleasures that the body has been created to give. One must not resist the body or push away its needs.

Carlotta, of course, having that strain of dominatrix in her, always had to face sit me until I was practically going unconscious. Meanwhile, Eva stroked my shaft. She was a connoisseur of the penis. Before she met me, her biggest catch had been Hermann Fegelein, but now that I was in her life, she would say, "Hermann's good enough for my sister, but not for me." In fact, Gertl and Hermann married. In the last days of the war Hitler had him shot, poor fellow. There was no real reason. He was like a raging child at that point, swatting insects to serve his anger.

"Oh, now, what's this? I can't leave you three alone for a moment."

He stood over us, staring down with merry eyes. He wore only a silk nightshirt.

Carlotta said, "What are you doing up?"

"I heard squishing sounds and came out to see who was squishing who."

She arose from our pile, lifted his nightshirt and cupped his balls in her hand. "You're seeing all this and you're still as soft as a little worm."

"I know it. It's dreadful."

"No worse than usual." She took him by the hand. "Come on." As they went toward the bedroom he'd been using, she said to Eva, "Get the other bed made up and get in it. I'll have him to you as soon as I can." As she closed the door, I heard her say, "ditch that nightshirt and go lie in the tub. We can't do it on these nice—" The door closed. A moment later, there was a loud pop and a stifled cry. Then silence.

As we made up the bed, Eva looked at me with melted eyes. She was such a pleasant, comfortable woman. She wasn't like Carlotta, so at ease with command. 'I've tried to cane him,' she told me once, 'but my arm gets weak, I can't do it.'

"Willy?"

"Evie?"

We hopped into the bed and screwed like a couple of rabbits. Gosh, I remember her so fondly. What a waste to go so young the way she did. But I almost did, too, and Carlotta. We were not intended to live, none of us, precisely so that a memoir like this one would never be written.

But you're not going to get rid of my Carlotta so easily. When she goes, it will be because nature took her, or somebody shot her from too far away for her to be able to lure them into a nice fuck instead.

We were still lying wrapped in one another's arms when Carlotta appeared, towing Alf along by his little weenie.

"Oh, now what," he said.

"Oops!"

"It's just a little fun," Eva cried.

"I'll leave you to it, Alf."

"Nonsense. Stay." He came into the bed and I thought with dismay that Carlotta's prediction might be about to come true, and he would want me to enter him.

"Oh, how warm it is!" he said from within the sheets. He kept his surroundings cold, but always preferred a very warm bed.

He came in between us, and I had the uncanny experience of feeling his naked skin against mine.

He said, "You know, Himmler is always doing archaeology to find out German past. What an ass he is. The Italians and the Greeks have pasts. We have no past. And this is why this is what we should be doing, just like this."

Carlotta was glaring down at us with folded arms.

He continued. "We're making a new world. New everything. New ways of sex. This is why the young are with me. The *Hitlerjugend* and the *Jungmadel* get up to this sort of thing all the time. We encourage it!"

Carlotta lifted the sheet. She looked down at his penis, which had gone flaccid. She sat on the edge of the bed and slapped her hands against her lap. "Come on!"

"What do you mean?"

"You know, Alf. Exactly. Come on. Now!"

He looked at me. "But, wait."

"You know the rule. Politics and sex are not to be mixed in my presence." She slapped her lap again.

He licked dry lips. His eyes were wide. "You can't compromise my dignity! I'm the leader!"

"I'm waiting."

"No. Absolutely not. Not in front of people."

"It's Willy and Eva, for God's sakes. Come on!"

"Look, it's coming up. We don't need to go through with it."

"The longer you make me wait, the longer it takes." It was fun to watch her face. She was trying not to laugh. "Eva, go get me my brush, it's with my *toilette*."

"Not that, that's too much!"

"You'd better hurry or you'll earn yourself a two cigarette smacking. You'll be redder than a baboon."

Now I burst out laughing. I couldn't help myself.

"Alf!" She pointed.

He lay across her lap like a miscreant child, except that he wasn't little. He looked like a great, fat fish of some kind.

Eva pulled up a chair and sat across from them to watch. She gave Carlotta a cigarette and took one herself.

"No smoking!"

They lit up, and as they did, I realized that this was a scenario that they had acted out before.

Carlotta began, and the blows were heavy, the smacks like explosions. Although corporal punishment was not part of my upbringing, I could well imagine how much they must hurt.

With her cheeks flushed, her cigarette in the side of her mouth and her eyes at once calm and forbidding, I have to say that she looked completely in control.

When he put his hand back, Eva grabbed it and held it. As his cheeks reddened, he became frantic, shaking his head and cursing, then shouting.

I found it appalling. It wasn't sexy to me at all.

Finally Carlotta said, "Now." She stopped. He leaped up—and presto, the treatment had worked!

Eva clapped her hands and immediately lay down with her legs spread for him. They got to it. Carlotta sat in the chair and put her hand between his legs. She glanced up at me. "You, come."

I walked around the bed to her.

"You see?" She held the base of his shaft between thumb and forefinger. "You do it."

I shook my head and grimaced at her.

"Do as you're told!"

She pulled her hand away. I could see that the shaft was softening. She said, "Willy, check him out, give it a feel, tell me what you think."

Oh, God, I can't believe it, that I have actually gotten to the point in my life where it's time to say this. But here is the truth: I did it. I put my hand there. I felt it as it ran in and out, in and out.

I said, "It's stiffening up."

"Good. Alf won't need another spanking. Just as well, your butt's really trashed, fella."

The pumping increased. His breathing—he was gasping—became furious. He reared back and cried out and Eva cried out with him, and then he sank down on her.

An instant later, he turned his head. I could now see one eye. It looked at me, blue and penetrating. Cold eye, like a reptile gazing, empty. "You whores, get the fuck out of here! Get out!"

"Alf?"

"GET OUT! GET OUT!"

Carlotta took my hand. "Come on, Willy. Game's over." She led me into the living room and closed the door. "Let's have a bath. I feel dirty."

"Is he—what's going on?"

"We have to get out of the way now. These are children, these men like this, still entangled in guilts from childhood. But he's had the fantasy that started across his mother's knee when she was heating up his butt with her paddle and causing his prick to heat up against her leg. Lying in her lap, he experienced the greatest pain he's ever known—the fire of it and the humiliation of it—at the same time that he was feeling that indecent, illicit pleasure, the greatest thrill he's ever known."

"And now?"

"He's in there pretending to be the lover. Romancing her and kissing her and trying to impress her with his sex brags. How well he did. Lothario with a *rotzbremse*, God help us. We don't have to witness that saccharine display, thankfully."

"How can she love him?"

"You've never loved or you wouldn't ask that question."

"I love you."

"One day I hope you will."

"I do. Now!"

"You love with a boy's love. It could fade like the dew. His love for her is a man's love, and hers a woman's. What's between them will never fade. He lays before her all of his weakness, inadequacy and perversion and she's still there, in the face of his truth. In return she offers what she has, the simplicity of her adoring soul."

"That's very high sounding and incredibly condescending."

"Come on, let's have a bath. We need to wash Alf off us. That smell! What the fuck's the matter with the man?"

"Satan."

"Really, Willy, I'm surprised. This is 1940. We are no longer superstitious."

As I strolled into the bathroom, she blocked my way.

"Oh, Willy, *damnit*! Go and wait."

"What the hell—"

"Now!"

As I returned to the bedroom, she slammed the door. I could hear the water running and, of all things, her singing. It was some light song. She sounded like a little bird, chirping and gay.

There were sounds of scrubbing, more water splashing. What was the matter with the damn place anyway, that it needed her to act the maid?

"All right, entry!"

When I opened the door, she lay naked in a tub full of bright, sparkling water, surrounded by bubble islands. The room was filled with rose-scented steam, but also another odor, very faint, that I had smelled more than once in Hitler's places.

"Has the plumbing gone wrong?"

She undulated. "Come in, come in and be a fish with me. I know some French, did you notice?"

"You said 'entry'. That's English. It means an entranceway. The French is *entrée,* enter."

"*Betreten Sie das Bad. Schnell!*"

I got into the great tub opposite her. She smiled. So lovely, like a flower opening. "Are you ready again?"

"Of course. Yes."

We churned like a paddle wheel, spilling out a great deal of water. But when we were entwined together in that water made holy by the splendor of our young love, we were steaming away the dreary awfulness of weird Alf.

I thought, as we splashed about, laughing and kissing, of the flashing waters of morning somewhere to the south which would have given up a body, dead Helmut Griese, by now drying among the reeds, ready for the sacramental ministrations of the flies, which would bless his eyes and his nose with their eggs, soon to hatch out the maggots of their love.

## 11

Eva and Alf had spent themselves and come out again, and the four of us lay naked on quilts on the floor of the living room, our bodies gleaming in the pale early light. Alf turned over on his back and put his hands behind his head.

"Isn't it wonderful, Willy, what I've done? Willy, such an accomplishment! The French, the Danes, the Dutch, the Norwegians, the Belgians—they must be so happy, so very glad that National Socialism has finally freed them from the burden of democracy and the cruelty of capitalism. But do you agree?"

"They are very afraid, I would think."

"Oh, certainly. That's a given. They need taming. Breaking like horses. The Germans are strong. The Germans can do it."

"Taming like horses, or like little birds?"

"Oh, my dear son, such an idealist. If we tried that, they would kill us all. No, a firm hand—" His eyes turned to Carlotta who lay with her eyes closed. He lifted her hand and held her palm to his lips.

She evoked a maiden's blush, then drew it away and turned over.

"A firm hand is what they need," he said.

"Don't alienate them."

"Of course I will alienate them—the ones who don't understand and won't. What else can you do with incorrigibles? Willy, we're making a new world. Of course there will be casualties."

"Like Herr Pappenheim?"

"After all these years, you bring him up! I ought to slap your face, Boy, but all right, yes, like him. I wish he wasn't dead. Of course I do! You think me a monster? I'm anything but. I'm the kindest man who ever lived! That's why I am willing to do what is hard."

I was naked or I would have touched my beloved *Judea Capta*, which had become for me a talisman from a future that might never be, when Hitler was gone, the demon vanished like smoke torn away on the wind.

Eva said, "Dawn is here and we all need more sleep. Willy has opium, Alf. Let's get down. Completely, totally down. For a little while, just forget."

"What? Forget what?"

She was silent.

"Evie, I love you so very much. I'm sorry about what it takes to make me able."

"Oh, Alf! We have these whores. We're fine!"

"I'm so ashamed. It should be different. If it was any real sort of a man, it would be."

Carlotta said, "Oh, now Alf. Just because you're butt's stinging, you can't put it out of your mind. Take it from me, the men who do best are the ones who have the courage to admit their true needs, then close the door. Take Josef. You don't see him bellyaching about the fact that he likes to lick cigars girls have smoked with their cunts."

Silence fell. Alf's eyes brightened. His lips fluttered into a smile. Then we all burst out laughing and we were hugging and even in this situation, not unlike being buried alive, I felt relief. She had said exactly the right thing to free him from his guilt, and therefore to free us all.

"Willy's got the usual fantastic dope," Eva said. "Not only opium. Also hash, *etsch*. We did some of the hash earlier and it was wonderful."

You should do *etch*," I said to Hitler. "Take the edge off." Lovely to see him become a heroin addict. Useful, too.

"I've got to go back to OKW, they can't do anything without me. The soldiers don't understand. They are conquering countries. I'm not. I'm bringing joy. Willy, I am the bringer of joy!"

Eva said, "Oh, Willy, I am so happy. So happy for our dear Alf!"

Alf said, "Come, let's kiss us, the four of us, the family that we have made, me and you and you and you."

We went together in the middle of the sitting room, amid the Rococo *putti* and the ivory walls and the gorgeous green draperies woven with eighteenth century huntsmen in their wigs and astride their bounding horses. Our faces touched, him and we who were within him and of him kissed, and he lingered his lips on mine, hungry for me—and then proceeded to expel a terrific burst of gas.

He reared back and shouted, "I'm no poet!" Then he said, "That quack Morrell!. Sometimes I think I ought to have him shot."

"Good, shoot him," Eva said. "He's dirty and he has thick hands. He smells like somebody who doesn't bathe. And those stenches from his horrible medicines! God preserve us."

"You can go to him feeling awful and he sticks you with an injection and in five minutes, you're damn right. Geniuses often stink. They forget to bathe. It's part of being a genius."

"You bathe and brush your teeth constantly and you're a genius."

"I'm peculiar in the opposite way from the usual."

Carlotta went and got the red Moroccan case in which I kept my hash and some little pipes and opened it on the table.

I telephoned down and ordered the '98 Y'Quem, another Charlotte as the last one now stood melted on the sideboard in the dining room, and a selection of *petit-fours*. Then I added caviar omelets and *cafe noir*.

Everyone hid for the waiter except me. I wrapped myself in the quilt to take the order. Once he had left, we piled up on the floor under the quilt and smoked hash and Alf ate all the sweets. The rest of us had omelet.

"He's asleep again," Eva said. "Thank God. Two days ago, they telephoned me from the *felsennest* to say that he was completely beside himself. When I went there, I knew that we needed you, too, Carlotta."

"Mm."

"You girls have completely exhausted him."

"Your busy fingers helped."

"Is he a homosexual do you think? He was certainly adamant about outlawing it."

Carlotta laughed. "Oh, you're all sort of homosexual, you men. If you got tied to a tree and another man stroked your dick, even a very ugly man, I bet you'd shoot off in ten strokes. Five."

The hash was hitting us nicely. I closed my eyes onto a long spring afternoon somewhere in memory.

"You're making that up," Eva said.

"If I'm making it up, ask your friend Fegelein."

"No!"

"It was his idea. I didn't think it up."

"But who—"

"The gardener at Madame Kitty's. He did it for a couple of marks. Then he jacked him off and wouldn't stop, and your lover body tried to get the Gestapo on his ass."

"Did he?"

She snorted derisively.

We all drifted off, one after another, heaped up together in the quilt. The floor was hard but the hash made us indifferent to things like that.

When I woke up the sunlight had changed from bright silver to waning gold. I ate some of the Charlotte in my fist and drank wine out of the bottle. The Y'Quem was so subtle and complex, that it was almost like ingesting a living spirit. Then I drank two cups of cold *cafe noir* and lit a cigarette.

A few moments later, there came a cry from inside the quilts, "No smoking, please, I am begging you!" His head emerged. I didn't stop. I'd only just lit up.

"You should learn. It's good for you."

"I know how to smoke. Hell, I smoked like a chimney during the war. But the more I stay away from it, the more horrible it comes to seem. The smell, the ugly look of it—it's ghastly."

"You don't stop Carlotta."

"Who could stop Carlotta? Anyway, she looks exciting when she smokes."

"Willy, you two jabbering about cigarettes makes me want a cigarette." Carlotta lifted two fingers from within the depths of the quilt.

Alf leaped up. "Now everybody's smoking!"

"Be careful, I'll make you smoke. I could do that, you know."

"Oh, why have I done this to myself?"

Carlotta said, "Never fear, we are only the stuff dreams are made on. You'll wake up one day and find us gone, and miss us so."

"Alf, does anybody know how to reach you?"

"Bauer."

"And where is Bauer?"

"A room downstairs."

"And OKW can reach him?"

"Yeah yeah! Shut up about it. And don't worry, I'm going back. But you stay here, Willy. I want you to observe and report. The *Sicherheitsdienst* will have communications established later today. You can telephone me from their offices."

"Very well."

"There's another matter. Girls, you aren't supposed to hear this."

"I'm completely asleep," Carlotta said. She was reading the novel Eva had brought with her. Eva herself was having a bath.

"There is this Heavy Water. Have I mentioned it?"

I was immediately alert. Entirely. "Possibly. But what about it?"

"There is some in France. We don't know exactly where. Are you in touch with Paul? Is he here in France?"

Carlotta said, "We dined with him last night in the flat of that rug salesman who's supposed to be such a *fakir*. It was ghastly."

"I thought you were supposed to be asleep."

"I lied."

"What is she talking about? Rug salesman?"

"The Levantine *neger* who fascinates the Haushofers."

"Oh, God, them and their rug salesman. They babble on about him constantly. Wake up! We must wake up! And do you know when they say it? While wide awake! I gather you were given that *neger* food."

"I found it all right."

Carlotta stretched, her body gold in the late light, arching herself. "I found it pure shit."

"We're not finished, Willy." He turned to go into the bedroom where his clothes were piled.

Carlotta said, "Look at you, Cherry Cheeks!"

"Sh!"

"Who cares? It's only us. He saw it. He knows."

"It's terribly embarrassing."

"Remember not to strip in from of Lenge, then. He'll know instantly that the leader has been spanked. He'll think your mother has returned from the grave."

"Were you spanked, Alf? I never was. Well, a bit."

"I was spanked. My mother would lie me there. She'd spank me then knit or shell beans with the bowl on my back or whatever and I'd have to wait for more. It took an hour sometimes, all the swatting and waiting like that. It soothed me, though, somehow. You're not in control then, which is rather wonderful. But the pain part—not so wonderful."

Carlotta got up off the floor and sat in a dining chair. "Come on." She pointed to her lap.

"Not in front of the whole place!"

"Which is Willy and Eva unless she's withered away in that bath. And what do they care, they've seen it."

"Still, not in the middle of the daylight right out in the room."

She shrugged. "All right, you're not being punished so I'm not insisting. I just thought lying across would relax you. Remind you of being over mommy's knee."

"Kubizek's writing a book about me. I warned him if he put any of that crap in it, he goes into the system. He would watch her do it to me. I hated it but what could I do?"

"Suffering fascinates children," I said. I was in plenty of fights to know that.

"We tortured little field mice and stoats we caught. Baked them alive. Suffocated them in smoke boxes. Did you do any of that? Finding us at that sort of deviltry, that's what caused my mother to get so angry. I remember her punishments, but when my father was involved, my mind simply goes blank. It's a blackness, what he did."

There it was, the beginning of his psychopathology. That blackness was the barrier that had trapped him in childhood. I think that this is part of why he chose gas for the Jews, because of the suffering involved. Slowly choking in those chambers—its unthinkably horrible. They claim the gas was for efficiency. I don't think so. I think he got a grotesque thrill out it. Hitler liked death, especially slow death. He enjoyed the deaths of others and was indifferent to his own.

He went in and dressed himself quickly. Dressing was easy for him, he hadn't been raised in a sea of servants. To this day, I worry if I've done everything right.

"Willy, come in."

This time he closed the door. "They won't understand but better that they not hear. The Heavy Water is important. Very important. As Paul plays both sides of the line, he probably knows where it is. I want you to get that information out of him."

I knew not to equivocate. "I will," I said.

"Soon as possible. It's on the French side of the line, we know that. But where is another question. Probably somewhere along the coast by now. They won't want us to get hold of it, not with all that uranium you've so brilliantly acquired for us."

"It's just a matter of curiosity, so don't spill any state secrets, but what's all this about?"

"I can only tell you this. It will end the war in ten seconds flat. And not just this war. All wars. Russia, America. Who has it, holds the future in his hand." He stared at his open palm, then closed it into a fist.

"I'll get you the information immediately."

"All right. I'll take the girls back with me. We'll leave at once. Eva! Come help me with the hair, we're leaving."

"Glad you came."

He put his hands on my shoulders. "Willy, forgive me what I am."

"There's nothing to forgive, Alf. In America we have a saying, 'you play the cards you're dealt.'"

"But it's so absurd. I feel like such an ass. But in those moments, as much as I am suffering, I am completely at peace. Only then. All the marvelous potions Morrell has to offer are nothing compared to Carlotta."

"She's quite something, Alf. There's only one of those."

"Don't I know it? Aryanizing a Jew whore! Fortunately, Goering will do anything for money. He got half a million marks out of me for it, you know. More for his silence." He reflected. "Do you think he's competent at anything?"

"No."

"Nor I. But he understands airplanes, at least. His ministry is appalling, though, I will say that."

Carlotta put up a terrific fuss about separating from me and, as was generally the case, got her way. After they had gone, she slumped onto the couch. "At last." She lit a cigarette and smoked ostentatiously. "Back to normal life. That man is so *meshuga*. It must be a sign of contempt from God that he has been chosen to run the world."

"I certainly can't disagree there."

"And yet you seem so loyal."

"As you said, I'm a whore. And all of those things you do—I know I've asked you this before, but you must have some sort of feeling about it."

"I've just done it for so many years for so many men. Jews and Catholics, they're the ones for the beating of the ass. At least that one is light. Try sitting under some big fat Jew across your lap. Not at all pleasant."

"Catholics can be fat."

"I don't care. Let's talk about something else. I'm off. Not working now."

I went to the telephone and called the flat of G.I. Gurdjieff. To my astonishment, Miss Gordon answered. Her French was all right, but her fruity accent gave her away instantly as English. "You shouldn't be talking down the telephone! Don't you know you could be interned?"

"Who is this?"

"I'm sorry. William Weber. I'm trying to find Paul Dukes."

"He's unable to come, I'm sorry."

"But he's there?"

"Yes."

"Tell him to telephone me at the Crillon as soon as convenient."

"Yes."

"And tell Mr. Gurdjieff to assign somebody else to answer the telephone. What can he have been thinking?" I hung up.

I went across the room and sat beside Carlotta, who looked as if she was about to ascend into the shaft of sunlight that was making a golden halo in her hair. I kissed her cheek, causing her to wriggle a bit, then gaze into some inner distance. I could almost hear the Madonna's venial mind clicking over: 'Tenderness. What can I get out of him now?'

I soon knew. She said, "What was Alf on about?"

"State secret."

"So what? Tell me."

It crossed my mind, just fleetingly—but no, Carlotta couldn't also be a spy. But of course she could be. In Hitler's house, anyone could be.

But who for? Stalin? The SDP? The allies? Or for Hitler himself?

I could not know, and that reality, in that moment, soured me deep. An inner innocence, only visible now because it was dying, "ran and faded through the brightening air," as old Yeats so eloquently mourned.

"Come on, tell me, I'm curious."

"He told me to keep it to myself."

"So now you're a fuckin' Nazi."

"I just don't see that curiosity is enough. You have secrets I'm curious about but you don't tell me."

"I oughta slap your face."

"Look, fuck this. I don't want a fight. And come up with a new threat. That one's getting old."

"Then tell me. Go on!"

"It's some stupid thing I don't know anything about or understand at all. Heavy Water. It's something Paul's supposed to know about. I've got to get in touch with Paul."

"Does Paul work for Alf?"

"You're scaring me now! You sound like some kind of goddamn fucking spy yourself."

"Little boy, if I was a spy, you would never know it."

Now what was I to do with this?

"Are you?"

She touched the tip of my nose. "I think we're on the same side."

"Which one is it?"

The telephone rang. It was Paul, and I made an arrangement to see him in a cafe near Gurdjieff's flat.

She refused to stay behind, of course.

While we spoke English, she folded her arms and fumed—literally. She kept blowing smoke in my face and announcing loudly that she was bored.

"If you keep speaking German, they're going to poison us."

She had been about to sip her Pastis. "Thank you." She put it down.

I called out to the bartender, "I'm an American. My wife is a Jew. We're refugees."

He shrugged and turned away.

"Damned Frogs," Paul muttered. "They're going to love the *Boche*. They're all a bunch of Hitler fuckers anyway. Sorry!"

"I don't care."

"Anyway, Gort saw a chance to break right through Guderian's flank at Arras. Would've won the war with four divisions. So Weygand agreed. But what does Bilotte do? Not a thing. We march off into the breach and he sits. So this chap Rommel's in there and he doesn't sit, not a bit of it. He beats us up and kicks our asses out and off they go, all the way to Calais."

"I thought Bilotte got killed."

"Auto accident. Arranged, no doubt, by the Abwehr. Dead men and their tales. The old fucking story."

"Hitler wants to know where the Heavy Water's located."

"I'll bet he does."

"Are you getting it out?"

He said nothing.

"I have to tell him something."

"Well, why not? It's in Bordeaux. Crazy Charlie Howard's in charge. Half is already aboard a steamer. They sail at midnight."

I glanced at my watch. "If I tell him at seven, will that work?"

"You tell me."

"I don't know, goddamnit!"

"Relax!"

"How?"

"You have a point there. Don't relax. Tell him at nine. Has to go through channels, they have to dispatch some kind of recce in force because we're still behind French lines. So yes, nine."

At nine, I telephoned Hitler at OKW and told him that PauI had located the Heavy Water. I gave him the correct information in every detail.

As a matter of history, the Earl of Suffolk, Charles Howard, got what was then the world's entire stock of heavy water and most of France's nuclear scientists across to Falmouth. The Nazis arrived about two hours late, and Paul and I were both thanked by Hitler for the effort we had made.

Would Hitler have used it to build an a-bomb? I think so. I think that they knew more about nuclear weapons than history has disclosed. With it, he would have absolutely annihilated Moscow, Leningrad, London and, if he could reach it, Washington. In any case, he would have won the war. No question in my mind. He had in the Condor a plane that could reach America nonstop. One had flown from Berlin to Brooklyn in '38.

The Nazis at once began manufacturing heavy water in Norway again. They knew what the bomb was capable of. Hitler knew. Fortunately, the process is slow.

Carlotta and I remained in Paris through the first week of the occupation. I dutifully reported to Hitler about the attitudes of the populace as they came straggling back from the desperate run to the south. They weren't very happy, but they also weren't very sad, I have to say. It wasn't until later when the dreadful occupation government had alienated so many and the allies were on their way that the tide began to turn. Not that the French were cowards. Far from it. But France is nothing like the vast Russian wilderness, dotted with marshes and forests for a partisan to use as cover. France is a metropolitan country. The only real cover is in places like the Norman *bocage*, but they are far from any cities where partisan activity might make a difference. In many parts of western Russia one could walk out of a city and hide in a marsh or forest a few kilometers away and be practically undetectable. In France a few policemen with dogs could find you in short order if you were near a city.

The French did it anyway in the end, getting their fingernails torn out and being hung up on meat hooks, poor brave fellows.

We were glad to return to Germany where the fall of France had transformed the atmosphere from sullen apprehension to amazed delight. When Hitler went west, the Germans did not go with him, not in spirit. They remembered the bloodbath of 1914-1918, both the horror of the trenches and the suffering at home.

But then he won. Incredibly. Impossibly. Next thing we knew, the Berlin shops filled up with French wine and cheese and all manner of clothing, wonderful things that were inconceivable to the Germans.

I divided my time between Wannsee and the Berghof. I'm ashamed to say it, but I screwed Alf many times. I did exactly what they whispered that I did. The more powerful he became publicly, the more private abnegation he required. Carlotta taught me to just get used to it and treat it like a job.

I fell more and more in love, frankly, with both women and they with me and with each other. We were a tightly bonded secret tribe of what the world would call decadents. When Alf came home, we absorbed him and completely dominated him. To us—three young, vitally alive people to whom he had revealed himself entirely—he was like a peculiar old toy of a man. We played with him exactly as if he was a toy. What were we to think? We were callow and shallow and here was the supposed king of the world kneeling at our feet. He was a big laugh. What was happening in the distance had nothing to do with us. We did respect Eva's love for him, because it was real. But even she enjoyed our games. She enjoyed watching Carlotta work him over. It made her hot. Me, too. I was often wild for Carlotta after watching some outré scenario or other.

There was only one thing kept secret, which was what went on in the upper room above Eva's flat. That, Carlotta would never say and that Eva and I were never allowed to witness.

I know how completely this image of him flies in the face of the public impression of the austere, explosive man of unlimited power, at once grand and terrible and so impressive. But it's true, quite simply.

He was indifferent to the lives of others, but that doesn't mean that some part of him didn't feel guilty about taking them. It wasn't anger at the core of his being, or ambition, even. It was that guilt, for the cruelties of his childhood, for his homosexuality, for all the lives that he was destroying.

Nature, as Emerson so eloquently demonstrates in his essay "Compensation," requires balance. So the more cruel Adolf Hitler became, the more humiliation he required.

It was not long before the victories faded, and in the brutal winter of 1941 when he came to understand the true peril that he and his strange, twisted Reich were in, he would scream and scream, twisting like some sort of a man suffering a seizure, scream until blood sprayed out of his mouth.

The staff would congregate in the driveway, biting their fists, clustered together like frightened kittens. We never let him know they heard. He would have had them shot, every one.

# 12

It is October. It is 1976. October 14, 1978. I am sitting outside the Malibu house. I've been here for hours. I'm in some Plymouth or something. Nothing she'd expect to see me in. About half an hour ago I saw her and it hurt. How can she be so beautiful when I am so old? She was wearing a bathing suit with a little skirt on it and her legs were long and gleaming, her body looking absolutely delicious, and yet she's only two years younger than I.

She picked up the habit of exercise from Eva. Obviously, she still works out and swims and all of it. I suppose she goes to Gstaad still. Lots of closet Nazis there to admire society's dark and secret woman of legend.

It's lovely that this old body can still ache for a woman. I go through long periods of being almost a Trappist, but then I go to the whores on 17th Street, the kids working their way through college. They screw with mechanical indifference, one old man after another.

That's my sex. That's my love. It's all of me that is left out of my grand and exotic life.

I look at the house. Mostly from the Pacific Coast Highway, all you can see are the garage doors and the back entrance. When I built it, there was a splendid garden here, full of exotic plants that grow in sand and thrive in the sea wind. Bulldozed by Franklin Delano Roosevelt.

I'm crying, damnit. Old fool! I came all the way out here to try again but I can't do it, not and be told to get the hell out again. Her voice is just like it was when we were kids, it's so beautiful. Her arms, her bosom, her eyes all so lovely. Those eyes—what they've seen—what I know and others don't—I love her for our shared memories. I love every bit of her, gorgeous body and flawless soul. For she is flawless—not in the conventional way of lies and pretenses, but in the way of the true path. She's sacred. I know it. Others despise her but I know it.

I'm finally dying, I know that, too. The doctors can't find what's wrong, but I'm turning into a dry old leaf. I feel sometimes as if the wind is blowing through me. I awaken weak, as if I have sunk in the night to the bottom of a well.

How can I bear to fall into that dreadful dark without some hope that this angel—the only one who can save me—will reach out her hand?

And yet my ego glues me to the car seat. I don't want to be laughed at, scorned again. "Swing out your schlong, old man, I'm in the mood to throw up."

She is a coarse, stupid genius. All the dirty, dreadful things she did were only professional. They didn't stain her at all.

I want to die right here, right now in this car. But I can't enact p'howa, not like Paul did. Of course he was a fully conscious man, a true master, and I'm just...me.

From the day in the Chancellery that Hitler signed that contract until this day, I have done nothing but make money. I am worth, at this moment, just shy of a billion dollars. My worth is contained in lists, endless lists—a telephone book of possessions, investments, on and on. And it all starts with Alf.

The most evil man in the world was also one of the few people who ever truly needed me. I have needed many and seen them die—my father, his finger pressing the trigger, the bullet flashing into his temple, Maddy in the storm-ridden *Pole Star* on that lunatic voyage to nowhere, Dieter, the bastard, and Eva, of course, by her man's side.

I must get out of the car, step up to the back door and knock. I must say to her, "Carlotta, I am dying and I must speak to you a last time. We must not let it end like this."

Her eyes will go empty, I know. I will see all of her from the little, scared medicine of 1932 to the grand demimonde of 1940, to the street hustler of 1946 and now, the sweet-scented Malibu princess of 1976. I will see all of her and she will know that, and she will try not to love me for it, and that will make her hate me all the more.

But why, my darling? You are lovely in your truth, beautiful in body and soul. Your life is a moral glory.

Oh, hell, what a sentimental old sap I've become. "Moral glory." How is it that I've spent my entire life idealizing a venial, mean-spirited whore like her?

It's hot in here. I've made it stuffy with my cigarettes. After 20 years on the wagon, I've decided to smoke again. When as you pass fifty and glimpse the shadow line ahead, you abandon your pleasures —no more cigarettes, no more drink, no more dope (or just a bit, say, on some endless flight in your lonely, hissing airplane). You get healthy. You will defy death! Run, bike, swim, ski. And then one day you look at yourself and you think, now *that* is old and then you think, 'I want a damn cigarette, why not?'

Now, while attempting to will myself to get out of this car and walk over to that door, I instead busy myself with another cigarette. The truth is that few things are nicer than nicotine when one is dealing with unpleasant realities.

Everybody smoked like maniacs during the war—all except Alf, of course. All he had was that pipe. The day he decided to add the axe to the guillotine he was wandering about the house in his BVDs smoking it. And when Himmler came along after the Wannsee Conference, he smoked it while they discussed insecticides.

I sit here. Toss the cigarette out. I wish opium was easier to get. It stank and gave you terrific headaches—at least it did me—but the high was so lovely. If I had some I could go back to the hotel and get a pipe going and...oh, my. My mind is instead drawn down into the murk, and as the darkness gathers me, I remember.

At last I drive away. If I stay too long, she will notice. She'll assume that it's another detective and I'll get a curt letter from her secretary asking me to stop watching her.

I'll go back to Manhattan, I suppose, and resume my seat on the Literary Walk.

I don't take in shows, go to movies, any of it. I do read a bit. Saul Bellow diverts me. I enjoyed as well *Catch-22*. It turned out that Joseph Heller and I had a mutual friend in Speed Vogel, and I gave them a lunch. Taciturn, of course. Perhaps Heller had it in his mind to write about the *Hitlerficker* and was disappointed that I wasn't more obviously louche.

Inevitably, my mind is drawn back as if by magnetic attraction to my manuscript. All through the flight back, I make notes on a yellow pad.

Ugly though they were, but truly also, those were the days when I was alive.

Through 1940, the war rather pottered along, at least in our little bubble. There was rationing but we weren't affected. Bormann built a big hothouse at the Berghof, so we were supplied with every kind of vegetable and legume. Even American corn, can you believe it? (Of course, after the declaration of war against the US, that was no longer cultivated.)

Eva and Carlotta and I would get up a hunting party with some of the SS and go out into the mountains for boar and deer. But one had to be careful. If there was one thing that would infuriate Alf enough to impose punishment even on those close to him, it was violation of the *Reichstierschutzgeset*, the animal rights laws. One thing that was safe was to hunt with Goering, which we did some of. He was even more obsessive about animal rights than Hitler, except when it came to his emulation of the aristocracy, who continued to hunt on their estates without regard to the NSDAP and its laws.

You couldn't boil lobsters, even. I never knew what happened to the French with their force feeding of their geese. I don't recall much *pâté*, that's for sure, and after *Barbarossa*, there went the caviar, which had been plentiful before. I managed to get some out of Iran at great expense to my Swiss address, along an unreliable route through British protectorates and then Italy. Italian aristocrats have a real jones for it, though, and the postal authorities, recognizing the packaging, would steal it and sell it to them.

When we got it, we really did enjoy ourselves. Opium and hashish continued to come up from Morocco quite easily in 1940, and Eva experimented with growing marijuana in the hothouse, but it was limpid stuff.

The winter of 1940 was appalling. The cold was so brutal that even the railways became frozen and coal and foodstuffs could not be transported to the cities. Most people had a week of coal or less put by in their cellars, or even just a scuttle full in their flat. Rationing was strict for them, but not for us. The great houses put by a winter's supply in September, so I was not affected. Down the street, though, the Goldsmans were still resident, as he could not escape from his complex merchant-banking operation without becoming completely impoverished. Neither could the Reich displace him so easily as his international correspondent banks doubted the legality of such transfers. Had the bank been aryanized, it would have collapsed. Being Jews, though, their coal allotment was in no way able to heat their magnificent establishment. Their pipes burst and their mansion spent the winter behind a curtain of ice-sickles, their windows glowing pitifully at night with the few lights they could manage to keep on.

No-one realized that he was secretly putting gold aside in Switzerland, bit by bit. In the spring of '41 they defected, leaving the bank, as far as its Swiss, Turkish, and South American correspondents were concerned, without legal ownership. As nobody would deal with it any further, its assets were sold off in bits by the ministry, but really it was a disguised failure.

They're back now, the fourth generation in that house. They were one of the few families who were trapped for that long who survived intact.

It was in August of '41 that I had my first real argument with Hitler. The Luftwaffe was in the process of losing the Battle of Britain by then, and the bombing of civilian targets on both sides had just begun.

All German cities were then blacked out. Travel after sundown was hazardous in the extreme, so I was in my house in Wannsee. I'd been making friends in Berlin, and had given a dinner to Freddie and Lally Horstman, whom I was cultivating. Their *salon* was one of the few places left where people still observed the niceties of civilized behavior. Among most people, an awful sort of familiarity had developed. One found oneself being called by one's Christian name by people who had been introduced five minutes ago. *Sie* had been entirely abandoned. Everybody was now *du*. It was unnerving.

At any rate, later that night there was an air raid. Nothing like what was to come, but it seemed pretty terrific at the time. Carlotta, who was still indifferent to her own danger, went up to the roof to watch. It was a lovely late-summer evening, very pleasant but for the bombers passing over at practically treetop level. This far from the center of the city there was no danger from flak splinters, which seemed to kill somebody or other practically every raid. Still, I wanted her to come in.

In the middle of the raid, the bell rang, followed by frantic banging on the door. My butler ran to answer, thinking probably that it was the Horstmans, driven back by the raid.

It was Hitler.

My servants had never seen him here before. They were unaware even of our acquaintance. So poor Fritz leaned back on his heels and gave the salute with such force that his hand slammed into the door jamb.

"Get out of my way," Hitler snarled as he barged in. I was at the top of the stairs and went running down when I saw him.

"Alf? My God, welcome! Welcome to my house!"

He stopped right in the middle of the foyer. "Planes," he shouted, "where are the planes?"

"I'm sure they're up there."

As I arrived at the foot of the stairs, he waved a sheaf of documents. "You bastard! You shit!"

"What? What are those?"

He thrust them into my face. It was an Abwehr report on British aircraft production. "They have whatever they need and I get nothing from you! Nothing!"

"You do! You get all we have."

"Except what goes to your fuck-buddy Churchill. I know you, you little whore. Do you think I'm stupid?"

"You're the least stupid man I've ever known." I tried to lay it on.

"Oh, shut up with your flattery. So why can't we build planes? You tell me."

"I presume that you wouldn't be here if it wasn't because we lack enough high strength steel."

"And why not? Where are your shipments?"

"They're coming regularly. I haven't seen a single ship sunk in months."

"The English offload more than we do. Why?"

"I'm not sure."

"Then find out. Also, I want to know what each ship in each British convoy is carrying so that we can destroy not the ones full of cooking oil and left shoes, but the ones that matter, the tankers and above all the ones carrying ores and rare earths. Do you hear me?" He grabbed my lapels and shook me. "Find out, do you hear?"

"But how? I'm not equipped."

"I knew it! I knew what I would hear! You damn fat little pig! I've made you rich, and what do I get in return? Deceit and betrayal, nothing but that."

Carlotta appeared at the top of the staircase. "What's going on?"

Hitler pointed at her. "All right, here it is. Mauthausen! There's an arrest warrant on that kike whore of yours. Mauthausen!"

"She's not a Jew."

"A Jew is who I say is a Jew and she's a Jew."

She came down the stairs. "Wait a minute! Fuck you, both of you!

If you're fucking pissed off at me, Alf, I'm right here. What's your goddamn beef?"

"Listen to her! Speaks to the leader like I was some kind of a fucking dog. Let me be clear, Willy. You get me what I need and in the quantities I need, or she's fucked."

At that moment, a bomber roared over at an altitude so low that the house jumped on its foundations. Moments later a flash filled the windows and thunder rolled.

He practically leaped at me. "Berlin! Berlin! You've done this to me, you fucking *shit*! And of course the whore, the whore is a Jew conniving behind my back, whispering her treasons in your ear at night, you stupid boy. It's you, yes, of course."

She stepped up to him and slapped him so hard he reeled away.

Silence.

"Oh. I see. Disrespect of the leader. That's an act of treason, punishable by death. The axe!"

"Alf, Willy is doing a brilliant job of getting his ships through. Do you know that they often come with the British convoys, protected by the enemy's own destroyers?"

What was she saying? It was a good idea, certainly. I'd never thought of it. We relied on floodlit neutral crosses like the rest of the contraband ships steaming through British controlled waters.

He looked to me, then back to her. She stepped closer to him and took him by the arm. "Alf, come upstairs, we'll sit together. You need to relax. This raid is just a bunch of noise, that's all. How many bombers do the English have? A hundred? Two? We'll shoot them in the end, all of them."

His silence continued to frighten me. He'd made a terrible threat against the woman I loved more than my own soul. Somewhere in the bureaucracy there was probably an order deporting her to Mathausen, just waiting for a signature. A sword hanging over her, or really an axe poised above her long, pale neck.

"Come on, Alf."

"What are you going to do to me?"

She smiled at him and ran her fingers through his hair. "Whatever I think you need. And what will that be? We'll talk. I'll decide."

He bowed his head and sighed a long sigh. Then he nodded.

Off they went into the upstairs. Somehow she had captured him again and saved herself from the jaws of the lion. But for how long?

For my part, I went into the servants' area. I found Maria and Fritz sitting at the kitchen table with a bottle of *schnapps* between them. The housemaid I'd taken on to help them was long gone, drafted into some service or other.

"Now you know a secret of mine. The leader and I are close friends. Carlotta is his friend also, who brings him solace. That's why he's here. You could hear how upset he was over the bombing. As we all are. But you must understand very clearly that this is a private business. Completely private. You are not ever to mention his presence here to family, to friends—and I know you're Catholic, so not to your confessors, even. He has great strains in his life, as you must realize. Usually we are together at his home in the mountains. But now that he has come here, he's likely to come again. Fritz, when you open the door to him, let him in silently. Do not speak to him or salute him. Take his wrap and then come back here. If you're wanted, there'll be a bell. Is all of this clearly understood?"

Fritz leaped to his feet and threw a salute.

"No, no! Not here! Not ever here, especially not in his presence. This is a place of refuge, understand that, for the man doing the most difficult job in the history of the world."

He sat down so abruptly that I thought the chair would burst. Then such a flush overcame him that it seemed possible that he was having a heart attack.

"Now Fritz, just wait. Calm yourself."

It was not until sometime later that I discovered the actual reason that he was so unsettled. The two of them were members of the anti-Nazi resistance, my two good German servants. One afternoon in a corner room in my cellar when I was inventorying my liquor stores, I came across a small hectograph press taped to the top of one of the shelves. The gelatin was clean, but there was an *Edelweisspiraten* meeting notice that was ready to be reproduced, hidden in the lid of the hectograph tin.

Of course I was completely shocked. Then afraid, both for them and for me. Then I was so very proud of them.

Inevitably, a few months later, the Gestapo showed up at my door, a chap called, with supreme irony, Hermann Hesse. Some "unusual activity" had been reported at the house and he wished to have a look around.

"What sort of activity?"

"That's why I'm here. If I may step in."

I let him in. "If you tell me more, I can help you. It's a large house."

"Automobiles late at night."

I went into my study and telephoned Himmler. "There's a chap of yours here. The neighbors have noticed Wolf's car coming and going late at night and they've reported it."

"Willy! How nice to hear from you. May I offer you a luncheon?"

Drat. "I'd be delighted, Heinrich."

At the lunch, he seemed fairly affable. Once he had understood that I was supplying something of vital importance to the war effort, he had backed off my case. Or so I imagined.

Anyway, the Gestapo never returned and Fritz and his wife survived.

They had been servants to the former owners. They despised Hitler and considered me a thief in this house. I will never forget their faces when the Kreislers returned, the streaming tears of joy with which they greeted them and the looks of stone cold hate they turned on me.

So be it. I didn't try to ingratiate myself. The reasons not to hate me were—and remain, in my opinion—very small indeed when weighed against those that justify such hatred.

The raid by now had ended, and the all-clear was sounding faintly across the lake, the glow of the searchlights dropping away and the calls of night birds returning to Wannsee. I went upstairs to look in on Carlotta and our client. They were in the bathroom.

Although among the four of us almost all barriers had fallen, I still left them to the bathroom business by themselves.

By that time, he would often sit in a chair beside the bed and watch Carlotta and me make love, or Carlotta and Eva and me. When he did, he would weep, and I would feel his cool fingers between my legs, holding the base of my shaft. The barriers had indeed fallen, but for one, which was the one that concealed my betrayal, and it was obviously in jeopardy.

As I think I've already made clear, his accusations about the rare earths were entirely accurate. I was shorting him in favor of the British, who were indeed getting their supply from me.

I knew full well that this was enabling them to build more planes than the Germans, and faster and more powerful ones. The Spit beat the 109 in almost every parameter, save for fuel management. The Spit Mark I had a gravity-fed carburetor which would cause the engine to cut out in a dive, while the 109 had a fuel pump located in the center fuel tank, a much more advanced arrangement.

On that night in October of 1941, he went from screaming threats at us to lying naked before her, kissing her feet and telling her how much he adored her. She sat quietly, a princess for whom the groveling of her slave was simply a matter of course. But why not? He'd been doing it since she was eleven. That is to say, nearly half her life. Even as a medicine she'd been a dominant. The role she played made her assume that others would defer to her in life, as we usually did. As I do to this day. To be sure, her professional life has drawn out the princess in her. But in bed she opens, she is warm. In bed, she is a woman surrendered.

For my part, as I waited for them to come out, I calmed down, finally losing interest even in whatever lurid scene was unfolding behind the closed door.

I fell to recalling with pleasure the dinner I'd had. There was a rule in the Horstmann's circle that politics were never to be discussed, but that did not mean that I couldn't tell them my memories of Hoover and share my thoughts about Eleanor Roosevelt's reading matter. For example, like Eva, she enjoyed *Gone with the Wind*. Of course, Eva never read the book, only looked at the movie, which she watched often in the Berghof. Toward the end, it became a nightly obsession for her.

I had installed a projector in my music room and put in some American-style easy chairs I'd found in a shop in Charlottenburg, so we would watch it here as well when she came.

Nowadays, that theme music drives me almost mad. But when I do hear it, I can't stop listening. I'm compelled. My ghosts float in on the melody.

When I reported the confrontation with Hitler to Paul, he got back at once to his own superiors and it was decided that I would increase shipments of just *praseodymium*, the rare earth most crucial to aircraft engine manufacture.

When he saw the numbers go up, Hitler practically wept. He called me a hero. When I told him that the ruse of slipping our ships into British convoys had been Carlotta's idea, he was ready to give her an Eagle, but it was not an award allowed to women.

So, no Mathausen for now, but what about the future? And what of me? I often wondered if we who knew so much about him had a limited lifespan. Geli had, and so many other women. And he and Ernst Rohm had almost certainly been lovers at one point. I thought then that there would be an end to this one day, when he decided to protect his memory from our testament.

Before that happened and no matter Paul's request, I would kill him. I swore it to myself. I would kill him before he killed her.

Of course we didn't slip our ships into British convoys. The War Office decided which of our ships got through and which didn't. Churchill allowed the increase in *praseodymium* only to preserve the integrity of my espionage operation.

Very late, when they had come out and the three of us had been together naked for hours, lounging in my big bedroom, chatting quietly, Carlotta said in the most vulnerable tone, her voice trembling, "Alf, don't threaten me anymore."

He sat up quite straight and covered his genitals with his hands. She walked to him, a long-legged angel in the soft lamp light. She drew him from the bed. He knelt before her. She pressed his head against her chest.

"Hear that," she said, "that's a human heart. They beat like that. Yours, too. Everything that we are depends on it. Do you understand me?"

He nodded. So there they were, the lithe yet petite girl looking down on the man with his head on her chest, and in that moment, I saw what I believe to have been the only real spark of love within him.

He could be screaming threats one moment, and the next his anger would pass like a rushing storm. But not always. Sometimes he wouldn't let it go, and then the men of death would come and another life would be sacrificed to his child's flaring temper, a leaf running to forgetfulness.

But life is a weave, and as I attempt to unravel the knots of the past, the one that presently entangles me keeps getting more and more complex. And so now I must withdraw from our wartime life to the present, where I have just lost something too precious ever to lose.

And yet, it is gone.

It is a wonderful, hot afternoon here in Manhattan. The summertime soothes my soul. There's nothing going on socially, so I don't feel left out. I still lunch at Jack and Charlie's every three days and dine at Zoe Chase's when she's got a cake in the window, and I still express my pleasure when her husband pours me a glass from his jug of Gallo. I wish I had the guts to wear spats like he does.

Carlotta has exiled me. After my last session sitting in my incognito car failing to get up the nerve to knock on her door, she knocked on mine. I had flown back to New York, then at once returned for another go.

I was staying in my usual bungalow at the Beverly Hills Hotel, one of the most discreet ones, well at the back of the property. I'd been lying on the bed for hours, considering whether or not I might be able to find some restaurant open if I went out. It was around one in the morning. I would call room service, they were there, but I wanted a beanery, something like Norms. I was wondering if the one in the Farmer's Market on Fairfax was open when there came "a tapping at my chamber door."

Had I called for room service after all? No, I was sure not.

"Who's this?"

"Carlotta. Open up."

"Oh my God."

"Open the goddamn door!"

# 13

There she stood, the beloved of my soul, her face as ever shaped like a heart, her lips held in the expression of kindness that is so deceptive, at least to me, her eyes at once hard gray and gentle blue. They seem to toss aside the curtain behind which we hide, and penetrate into the places we would rather not expose. When you see them like I did in that moment, suddenly and unexpectedly, they almost knock you over.

For the first time in twenty years at least I was looking upon her in the flesh. She was sixty three years old and appeared not a day over thirty. (Of course I may be lying to myself here. The eyes of love do that.)

"Oh, come in."

She strolled into the center of the living room and glanced around. "What a dump." Aping Bette Davis, of course, from "Beyond the Forest." I was a little embarrassed. Such obviousness was not up to her usual standard.

"It's the closest nice hotel to you. The ones in Malibu are pretty minimal."

"Willy, I want you to meet my husband."

That was a lightning bolt flashing through me. "Carlotta, I'm your husband. Our marriage is still quite legal."

"She's not that kind of husband." She turned toward the dark doorway and made a sweeping gesture. "Angela, you can come in now."

A tall woman with blond hair, very closely cropped, moved into the light. She wore black slacks and a tie-dyed t-shirt. She had the exquisitely proportioned face and faintly wild eyes of a classical sculpture. If you want to see her, go to the Louvre and look at the Diana of Gabii.

She waved her arms and said, "Smoke, yuck!"

I rushed to throw open windows.

"Never mind, the damage is done. You shouldn't do that, though, it's vile."

Drawing Carlotta down beside her, she sat on the love seat with which those suites are furnished.

"May I offer you drinks?"

"'Course not," Carlotta said. "We're not here to indulge in outmoded social mumbo-jumbo. Willy, you're to quit lurking around my house. You've been there seen there."

"I was trying to—I wanted—" I looked at the woman/man. I could say no more.

"I'm living a different life now. You're part of the past."

"We have a past, though. I still—" I stopped. I couldn't say it, not with this extraordinary piece of human statuary guarding her.

"You're dead to me, Willy. It's like talking to a ghost."

"I'm alive. It's Eva and Alf, they're the ghosts."

"Who?" Angela barked, turning to her with an air of accusation, even threat.

"I have no idea. Some friends from the past, I suppose. He led me around by a social nose ring for years. I lose track."

I was desperate. Frantic. My mind was seething with defenses, with attacks, anything to relieve the agony of loss I was feeling. And then I acted in a very stupid way. I said, "Angela, if you will get up and walk out of here and never come near either of us again, I will write you a check for one million dollars. Right now, this instant."

Her face flared into an expression of the amused derision. "You're right, Carlie, he's a complete asshole." I thought, she's cruel by nature, and Carlie will pay for that.

"Willy, you've been warned. The bottom line is this. I've had a lawyer look into this business. There's laws against stalking."

"I can't stalk you, I'm your husband!"

"You don't recognize Angie, do you?"

I looked again at her. "No."

"This is Angela Truro."

"No bell ringing, I'm sorry."

Angela made no sound but she didn't need to. The Diana of Galbii was sneering at me with her eyes.

"Well then you don't need to know any details. Suffice to say she's a major star and we happen to live next door to each other. When you sit outside my house, you sit outside hers. Stalker."

I so regret it now, but I leaped up and shouted at them to get out. Stupid fool, I should have done almost anything else, continued to bargain, begged, anything. But I shouted and they left, and I heard them laughing together as they walked down the little path, hand in hand.

I dream now that, if only I had been more diplomatic, we three could be the same as Carlotta and Eva were with me. Why not? It was fun then, it would be fun now. Let her be married to Angela, this beautiful, extraordinary woman, for now I know all about her. She's a great actress and not only that, at just the age of 30, already a novelist of note, obviously a brilliant woman. I'm proud of my Carlotta that she can gain the affection of such a one.

Angela Truro, Carlotta Weber, wife and wife, man and wife? What does it mean? All of this structure that used to seem so defining has faded for me. It happened a long time ago, really. I was married for years to three other people, after all. Since one of them happened to be Alf, after he and Eva died, Carlotta and I preferred to forget. We thrust the whole matter from our minds. And yet it deposited within us both a silent conviction that the meaning of relationships is not in these arbitrary structures—engagement, marriage, all of that—but rather in the chemistry of people and the mystery of the heart.

I know that in the eyes of most, nothing I can say can be valid and nothing I have done or can ever do can be good, simply because I have been intimate with Adolf Hitler. I accept that. I believe that it's right and just. But looking deeper is also right, and in such depth the moral shadings change. Not to excuse Hitler. Nothing can excuse Hitler. But to make moral sense of what happened, yes.

So here I am, having circled this long distance from 1931 to 1978 and seeking to slip an apology past myself in yet another clever way. I'm human so I want forgiveness. I am also a moral man, so I don't.

Over the next two weeks, I detached myself from Carlotta and Malibu, but not immediately. I rented a different car and drove past the house, back and forth, gazing at it and longing for her. I was mawkish, of course, but at least doing it this way I wasn't noticed.

Because my love loved her, Angela Truro came to seem a sort of goddess to me. I went to all of her movies when they appeared, and rented tapes of the ones that were not currently playing. Her beauty and the hardness of her heart made me feel desperately alone and isolated. I wrote her effusive fan letters and sent them care of Carlotta.

I lived in the hotel for another month, but soon gave up my excursions to Malibu. If they noticed me again, I thought that they would have me arrested and throw the book at me.

Finally, I telephoned for my plane and took off from the Santa Monica airport, resolving this time not to return. On the way to Teterboro, I inventoried all of the different conditions of sorrow that I knew. Carlotta and Eva had been lovers, and that hadn't bothered me. It was different from this, though. The four of us possessed one another. I possessed nothing of Angela and Carlotta.

I wondered what happened if one leaped out of an airplane. But there would be the inevitable second thoughts on the way down, so no.

I'm trying to get out more. I cannot spend my life sitting under the portrait of Carlotta in my study or working in my office. It's not hard for me to go days without leaving the apartment. Day? Months. I'm more reclusive than Howard Hughes, although not so unkempt.

There are art galleries opening down in the rag district south of Greenwich Village, and I recently enjoyed myself down there for an afternoon, compulsively buying paintings I don't want in order to get smiles from the pretty gallery managers.

Now I'm back from a walk in blazing hot Central Park. I stopped into the Met and looked at the Dutch landscapes for a while, then went over to the carousel and watched the children riding round and round. The cheery music made me go away.

But there had been a moment of pleasure standing there, and such moments always take me back, but not to pleasures past. They take me back to the whistle of bombs and crying in the streets. That's forgotten, of course, in the distancing photos we see now, or the documentaries or the descriptions of people's reactions.

By the fall of 1940, the raids were often lasting all night. It had become obvious that the fantastic outpouring of flak did little to stop them. The English bombed either from very high or very low. As always in Wannsee, it was something that happened in the view, not in the silence of our night.

After one particularly spectacular raid, with flak rising in fountains and the bombs sounding like a Midwest thunderstorm, I went into the city. Carlotta was like Alf. She preferred to be shielded from such things. But I was curious.

My car had been reasonably repaired, and I had no interest in exposing it to what I thought might be a difficult driving situation, so I took the train in to Potsdamer Platz. From my roof, it had looked as if most of the bombs were falling in that area. The Zoo Flack Tower had been blazing away.

History records only so much of life. Even a historian who includes diaries and witness testimony is limited to what his sources might say. But I was there. I walked in those streets.

One thing that has never been recorded is the way it smells after a bombing. There is smoke of course, the sharp, thick odor of burning tar, the cold smell of brick dust, but above it all, pervading everything, is the sweet-sour stench of high explosive. Once you have had that in your nose, you cannot forget it. Like cyanide, it's a dangerous smell. But the weeping, the tears—that's what they absolutely never write about.

When I came out of the station, I saw along the Potsdamer High Street mountains of rubble and heard a general chorus of tears. They were working, throwing bricks aside, trying to open the street, and as they worked they were crying, men, women and children. It was already cold that October and these people had lost the little bit of shelter they had. They knew that they would not get it back, and that winter was upon them.

I know that it could be said that I shouldn't write about the suffering of the Germans when the Jews were suffering far more terribly a few hundred kilometers away. But I did not yet know that the Jews were there, so I reacted to the suffering that I saw.

A *Hitlerjugend* shouted, "You, pitch in, get to work!" And just like that, I ceased to be the exalted friend of Adolf Hitler, a prince in a distant realm, and became just another miserable soul on a gray, miserable morning with bedsheets drifting along the street like ghostly memories.

I didn't hesitate. One could get hung from a lamppost or shot in those days. That boy had a gun at his hip and I was sure that he wouldn't hesitate for a moment. I at once started throwing bricks into the rising heaps.

I remember the feel of them against my hands, rough and dry, some still warm, and how surprisingly heavy they were.

A man came along. He was carrying a woman. Her face was gray with dust, her left leg and arm were both akimbo and at first she seemed dead. But her eyes were flitting about with the nervous intensity of a bird's. Both of their faces were covered in tears, pale lines streaked through the dirt.

They drew a few glances but nobody helped them. These people saw such things every day. Maybe he would make it to the hospital in time and maybe not. So be it.

After about fifteen minutes, I said to the Hitler Youth, "I've got to move on. I have to get to my ministry."

"Yeah, sure, go on. Thank you."

As I left the bombed area and approached the Tiergarten, there was Berlin again. It wasn't as bright as before the war, but the shops were still there and still appeared to be stuffed with goods. It was an illusion, of course. The regime compelled them to decorate their windows so that everything would look attractive and prosperous, but not to actually sell any of the goods on display.

There were ice cream shops with no ice cream, clothing shops with full windows and empty racks, butchers with posters of cuts of meat in their windows, toy shops with lovely displays but nothing to sell.

The park was undamaged still, but as I walked along a path, I noticed underfoot twisted shrapnel splinters, thousands of them, a dusting of deadly hailstones. All of that iron, I thought, bought with gold drawn out of the hills of the Sierra Madre by men I had never seen but who were my men, shipped in my bottoms all the way to Europe, then transferred to the Swedish mining companies who in turn pulled out the iron ore and sent it along the Norwegian coast from Narvik to Herr Krupp's mills in the Ruhr.

So he made money and I made money, and two little girls dressed identically in pink played tag in the walkway. Farther along, other children hunted for cigarette ends and others still tossed a ball back and forth in silence. There were no longer any dogs. Already. And, in fact, I was surprised to see so many children. Hitler had made the *Kinderlandverschickung,* the children's evacuation, mandatory after the terrific September 24 raid. But in fact chaos was much more the norm than order in the Third Reich, and all but the most serious rules were there to be broken. Not many people were willing to trust their children to a state that had been discovered to be gassing the mentally unfit. What if their little ones were declared delinquent and incorrigible while in the care of National Socialism?

Some were sent, of course, but many more were not.

Living in the Reich, I saw with my own eyes how much anarchy there actually was. The endless examples of petty thieves receiving draconian punishments and blackout violators getting terrific fines that were regularly published in the newspapers have been taken to be fact by historians. Judging from the way life was actually being lived around me, I would say that a lot of them were fictions.

During the next week, the horrendous war winter set in. By November, as I recall, the entire continent was an absolute deep freeze.

As time went on, Hitler became more and more paranoid. He began to understand that the British were exactly as perfidious as he had always claimed, and therefore started to fear that they might have agents hidden in his immediate proximity.

Fortunately, this suspicion did not extend to me and Paul, at least not always. He had seduced me and captured Paul. It simply never occurred to him that these brilliant strokes might in any way be compromised. He trusted his genius implicitly, fool that he was.

His primary focus became a fear of poisoning, first in the Chancellery and later at the Wolf's Lair. He had a squad of young women who tasted his food in Rastenberg. If you can believe it, his meals would be kept hot for him while everyone waited around to see whether or not they would die. That was our world. Death everywhere, so much so that it became ordinary. They never died, though. As I was to discover and very soon, there was a reason that Hitler was not assassinated by allied confidential agents. Once he had won France, Churchill no longer wanted him dead. In fact, there were times when Paul Dukes discreetly protected him from German-originated plots, and when the Stauffenberg bomb went off, a shiver of fear passed through Whitehall until it was discovered that he had survived.

As much as possible, he wanted us close by. He came to love the Wannsee house and was extremely careful to keep it as much of a secret as he could. When we were in the Berghof, the building had to be cleared for privacy, which meant only that the life guard remained at a discreet distance, often just outside the doors. But in Wannsee there was no life guard. As far as they were concerned, he was asleep in his apartment in the Chancellery, or with his sister in her little flat.

I didn't want him to spend too much time away from Carlotta. I wanted her to continue to be an essential ingredient in his life. The idea that he might send her into the camps because of my plotting caused me to lie awake in the night, my arm thrown over her sleeping body, so small and vulnerable curled up there in our bed.

Rather than deal with the roads, when we would go back to Berchtesgaden, we would fly. As long as we were discreet, the Hitler Flight was generally available to us. He no longer had just the one plane, but a number of them, six I think. There was also the special train, but it had to stop running in November because the rail lines were frozen. In any case, he used it throughout the early fall to travel in France where he was establishing the machinery of terror, and then to Florence where he had a furious meeting with Mussolini.

It was at that meeting that the German war was lost, another fact that is little remarked in history. When Mussolini invaded Greece and the Balkans, he both surprised Hitler and infuriated him. But there was nothing Hitler could do about it. And indeed, within weeks the little, ill-equipped Greek Army had rolled the Italians all the way back to Albania. For a time it looked as if Italy might fall to Greece.

So Hitler, who was deep into planning for Barbarossa, was forced to protect his southern flank by sending the *Wehrmacht* into Yugoslavia and on to Greece, and to protect Crete with parachute soldiers.

The result was that Barbarossa, commencing the next summer, was delayed by about six weeks. Had the Germans arrived at the gates of Moscow in September rather than October of '41, they would have taken the city and won the war. Had Mussolini stayed at home in 1940, that's exactly what would have happened.

Great events slipped past like great ghosts haunting the borderlands of my life. When Hitler went to Florence, Eva and Carlotta raged because they had not been allowed to go. They wanted to shop. There was no rationing in Italy and the shops were still full of nice clothes, perfumes, smoked meats, wines, and all the lovely fruits of that country. Unlike Germany, Italy had not been methodically stripped of manpower by the army. Plenty of men had gone, but plenty more had not.

For its part, Germany was now filled up with what we now think of as slave laborers. They certainly didn't view themselves that way, except, of course for the Jews and the west Europeans. The eastern Europeans were better off than they had been at home, and being paid more as well. Workers in heavy industry also got better ration allotments than ordinary people, so many Polish and Ukrainian workers were actually better fed in the Reich than they had been at home.

As ordinary Germans got thinner and thinner and forced laborers did not, they would be spat upon in the U-Bann and sometimes even needed police protection to keep people from stoning them with bricks from bombed out buildings.

Hitler travelled almost constantly across the autumn and into winter, but on December 28, he arrived at the Berghof for a month's stay.

It was very snowy as his motorcade climbed slowly up the steep road to the house, chains clanking.

We had decorated the house for his arrival with pine garlands and our tree with Eva's lovely Christmas balls which she had been amassing for years. It stood on the raised area just above the great room, decorated balls of every description, St. Nicholases, sleighs, children at prayer, gamboling deer, even tiny ice caves made of blue glass. The pine branches and wreaths and, above all, the tree filled the entire house with pine scent. It wasn't particularly warm, though, as the advanced heating system Hitler had ordered from America when the house was being built had proved to be a fiasco. We had to rely instead on a big boiler, fireplaces and wood stoves. So there were plenty of cold spots, to be sure, and when the wind blew Hitler's study became an icebox.

It didn't much matter to him. He liked the cold and in fact, when he was later in the Wolf's Lair, he kept his private rooms as cold as possible at all times. At the Berghof, he was constantly telling the staff not to over fire the stoves.

The icy weather had inspired Carlotta and Eva to buy coats and wraps, and they sailed around in clouds of mink, ermine and all manner of exotic fur. I think there were even chinchilla vests, as I recall.

After the fall of France, Goering got all the good cognac and champagne for himself and sent the inferior stuff to us, so I had gone to his house and bought cases of Moet and Pol Roger and Hine Cognac from him at fabulous prices. I didn't care to go through a Christmas without decent drink, and I also planned to have a goose as well, no matter how much Alf yelled about the "stench" as he called it of meat cooking.

He burst into the foyer in a long black leather trench coat and a lovely cashmere scarf about his neck that I had given him, and his mustache completely frosted. True to form, his car had come all the way from the airfield with the top down. Kempka behind him exhibited an air of studied indifference, which would have been convincing enough had he not been shivering like a schoolgirl.

Blondi bounded in behind them, accompanied by the latest brace of pups—which he had solemnly promised Eva he would leave in the kennels.

He shouted out, "I'm home and I'm ready for some Christmas cheer."

Instead, the dogs started rioting immediately. Blondi and Eva's rugs Negus and Stasi, who had been roaming the house, were never friendly and a great cataclysm of barking and snarling erupted.

"Stop it, stop it!" Eva shouted from within fog of white Ermine which Carlotta had teased her about by calling it the "Stoat Coat."

"The devil, here I am home and what sort of a greeting is this? Barking dogs and a shrieking snow-leopard!"

I rushed up and collared Blondi while Eva took the rugs up to her suite to shut them away.

From the back staircase, I heard Carlotta call out, "Are we alone?"

"Yes," Hitler shouted, "unless somebody's bought an actual leopard instead of just the fur."

"This is Ermine," Eva said sweetly. "Anyway, leopards are not white." She gave him a very pretty, very 'come hither' look, and I could see him lean toward her.

"There's a great crowd of generals arriving," he said. Outside, more chains were clanking and engines growling.

Unfortunately Carlotta had no way of hearing that, and came sweeping down across the great room in a shining black mink coat, ankle length, with a diamond necklace from Van Cleef and Arpels that I had given her. It was a splendid piece of gold *passé-partout* worked with little diamonds, and absolutely *au courant* in that time. It had better have been. To this day, I remember the price of a hundred thousand francs.

I'd given Eva one as well, except that hers was worked with rubies as well as diamonds. So I'd walked out of Van Cleef that day with my wallet lightened to the tune of $5,000 for the necklaces and another $5,000 for the lovely bracelets and rings worked with ruby and emerald and sapphire "flowers."

"Oh, we have to have these for the winter! It's like wearing spring right on your finger."

"*Oui*, Madame."

But notice those numbers. Ten thousand dollars. In 1940 it was an awful lot, but to me essentially nothing.

Under the open coat, Carlotta was naked. Eva would never have come down naked. That would have been impossible for her. She was a traditionally domestic woman of *mittleurope*, publicly discreet and at the same time a complete savage, but only behind closed doors. Carlotta was a complete savage wherever she happened to be.

Eva looked Carlotta up and down. Silently, she came closer. Hitler and I watched, neither of us foolish enough to interfere.

"This is the home of the leader," she said to Carlotta. "You can do anything you please in Wannsee, strut around naked or whatever in that whorehouse. But you will never repeat this performance here again."

I realized that I had been remiss in not inviting Eva to Wannsee often enough, and now Carlotta had to pay.

Of course she did not pay. She was Carlotta. So she opened the coat wide and said to Alf, "Merry Christmas Noble Wolf!" If you say Adolf as a name, that's all it is, but if you use a different inflection its meaning comes out, which is "Noble Wolf."

Eva stomped her foot. Alf started to laugh. I put my hands up, warning him just in time. At that moment the door flew open and generals began parading in, one after another.

For once nonplussed, Carlotta ran away. I followed Eva up into her rooms. I was soon to understand that, around the trappings of Christmas, amid the carols and the celebrations, Barbarossa was in planning, the greatest military operation ever known.

While we drank the champagne and the cognac and Hitler ate *bombes*, *frappes*, *gateaux* and chocolates and brushed his teeth four times a day, he and his generals spent hours after hour poring over maps that were rolled open on the table beneath the great window. After dinner, though, the house was emptied and we Christmas ghosts appeared, candles were lit on the tree and we sang, me in my indifferently tutored tenor, Alf in his gruff baritone and Eva and Carlotta in their bell-clear sopranos. Many carols, *Kommit in Hirten, O Tannenbaum,* all of the standards. We even sang a fantastically absurd *pastiche* of *Stillege Nacht* , with lyrics like "Silent night, holy night, all is calm, all is bright, only the Chancellor stays on guard, Germany's future to watch and ward."

As we sang it, reading from a little book of Nazified carols that somebody had sent in as a gift, Alf and I met one another's eyes. The girls were taking it completely seriously, singing with the fierce sweetness of rival angels. But then we arrived at "Adolf Hitler is Germany's star, showing us greatness and glory afar."

The two of us fought it for another moment, then burst out laughing. Eva was furious and stomped her foot at us. "Have you no respect for the leader?"

"Certainly I do," Alf said.

"Well you don't show it at all. That might even be a crime, that laughing like that."

"Ah, if it is, I'll arrest myself, my darling." He put his hand on his heart. "Promise."

"I like it," Carlotta said. "I like songs about you." Coming from her, that sort of fawning sounded very much 'off.' Clearly, she had not forgotten the Mathausen threat, either.

This resolved me to do something I had been avoiding. I had to confront Goering, who had been the first to bring up Mathausen, after all. I felt sure that Hitler would never have mentioned a specific camp if the suggestion hadn't come from somewhere, and that somewhere was the fat boy, no question, maybe even with Eva's prodding.

Things between us were less frigid, and for the same reason that I was now Himmler's bosom pal. Hitler had told them of my importance to the war effort. They detested me, I'm sure, but everybody hated everybody in the upper reaches of Hitler's government. He wanted it that way, a scrapping weasel gang, always at each other's throats. At any given moment, he knew precisely who was at whose throat and why. He played the instrument of the leadership like some sort of discordant harp. The important thing to him was that they never band together.

Of all the books Hitler read and the influences on him, I continue to believe that the most important was Darwin. Recently I've seen refutations of this, but I was in Germany then and Darwin was not only not banned, his theories were taught in the schools. Hitler's copy of *the Origin of Species* was extensively annotated. I saw that. He also had the Darwinian Ernst Haeckel's *The Riddle of the Universe* and, in the library at Prinzregentplatz a portfolio of his *Kunstformen dur Natur*, his marvelous drawings done to illustrate principles of evolution.

What one could never forget about him was that if you weakened, you were lost. He would not help you. They all knew this perfectly well, which is what made the whole government such a snake pit.

At any rate, Goering was coming over daily for the conferences and I began to look for a moment when I could buttonhole him for a private meeting. As I was *persona non grata* in the downstairs when guests were present, this took some patience. I disliked being around the generals anyway. In the *Felsennest* where such details were forgotten, I had found their open contempt an agonizing embarrassment.

When they went out in groups onto the terrace to smoke, I would watch to see of Goering might go off by himself. My plan was to hurry down into the kitchen, cross through the cellars and come up via the delivery entrance. On that side, there was a narrow outside stairway to the terrace.

They smoked hard and didn't stay long. The cold was fierce. Insulated though he was, Goering would stand about fiercely sucking a cigar and slapping his shoulders. He wore a huge Crown Sable coat, one of many furs he owned. For such an outspoken anti-vivisectionist, the idea of banning fur or being against its use had apparently not crossed his mind.

One afternoon I saw him well out on the terrace gazing at the pristine snow that covered the mountains. Nobody was near him and I acted at once, passing down via the servant stair and then through the roaring kitchen and out.

The steps were not often used and were icy, and I very nearly fell. Under those conditions if I'd gotten myself knocked out, I would have been dead in fifteen minutes.

I walked up behind him. "Good afternoon, Hermann."

"What! You! What the devil, Willy, where did you come from?"

"I want to talk for a moment, Hermann."

"How dare you keep addressing me like that. I'm *Reichsminister* to the likes of you, *Hitlerficker*."

"You were Hermann in the Roth Forest."

"I'm in uniform now. These meetings are official. Get on with it."

"Stop threatening Carlotta."

"Who? Oh, yes, the kike whore. We don't want kikes around here, not in wartime. Things are getting serious now."

"She's not a Jew. You signed the papers yourself."

"The boss couldn't. I had to cover. Anyway, she's going. Eva detests her and can't stand having her in the house anymore. I'm transporting her as soon as the weather clears."

"To Mathausen?"

"For a kike whore? I should say not. Poland. We have places in Poland now."

"I thought the Jews were headed to Madagascar."

"Oh, sure, call it that. Madagascar, yes!"

"She's not going anywhere."

"You little prick. Don't you dare speak to me like that."

"Has Alf ever told you what I do?"

"He doesn't need to. I know you poke him in the bunghole. Matter of fact, you ought to go, too." He smiled. "Maybe you will."

"I won't, and neither will she."

He shrugged.

"Let me put it this way, Hermann. There is a reason you can't build enough airplanes. A reason you had to give up on England."

"And it has nothing to do with a kike whore and a worm like you."

"You will find that statement to be wrong."

I turned and went struggling down the stairs. He stared after me, silently puffing on his cigar. My throat had filled with acid. This had gone much farther than I had imagined. But at least I'd found it out.

I enjoyed Eva. We were friends. But she was a bitch and a half.

It was after three when Hitler was finally alone in his study and the house was empty of guests. I went across.

"Willy, what a nice surprise. I was just wishing you'd come in. We're planning magnificent things, Willy! We're going to completely revise Europe." He got up from his desk and came over to me. "Come, sit, I'll tell you about it."

I knew that if he started I wouldn't be able to get a word in for hours. I said, "Eva has convinced Goering to send Carlotta into the system. As soon as the weather clears, she's going to be deported to the east."

He was silent. Did he already know and had he agreed? With him it was extremely difficult to tell anything for sure. As an actor, he could conceal himself with exquisite skill.

"Alf?"

"EVA!"

She had probably been lingering at the door, hoping for just such a call. She appeared at once.

He pointed to the telephone. "Call Carlotta in." His tone was curt.

"Alf?"

"Do it!"

She picked up the instrument and dialed our room, which was 7 on the intercom. "The leader wants you."

"Give me that!" He snatched the phone from her. She was now ice pale. "It's Alf. Alf wants you." He hung up and said to Eva, "You are never to go behind my back to a creature like Goering. That pompous pile of shit!"

"Alf, I—"

"Silence! Don't you understand that Emmy loathes you? She considers you a cheap joke, and yet you go over there plotting to put my one person I can count on for relaxation into a fucking gas chamber!"

What had he just said? But no, I'd heard it perfectly clearly.

They went on arguing, as if Eva already knew it, too. No horrified cry of '*gas chamber? What is that?*' But that is exactly what was in my mind.

"I just wanted her out of the way. I thought with a war on it was dangerous to have a Jew here."

"SHE IS NOT A JEW!"

"All right!"

"Go in the records all you want. You won't find a damn thing except she's pure Aryan. It would be entirely illegal to kill her. And let me tell you something, if you were to have arranged that, I'd have had you laid out under the guillotine. How do you like that?"

A wet spot appeared in the chair into which she had collapsed. Tears were flowing from her eyes. "Is it her, is that it? Is she to replace your Eva? All right, then I kill myself. You won't need any fucking guillotine." And she bawled.

I noticed that Carlotta was standing in the doorway. How long she had been there, I didn't know.

"A row?" She came into the room. "Now listen to me. Nobody speak for a moment. I have no idea what's going on here, but I do know that this family is precious. It's unusual, sure, but so is our situation. We're here to keep Alf strong and happy. No rows!" She spread her arms. "Come. Family hug." Eva came to us hunched like an old woman. Carlotta pressed the small of her back until she was straight and we were, the four of us, face to face. "Now I don't want to hear another word about it. Not now or ever. Whatever it was, we're more important to us than any argument. Yes?"

Hitler said, "Yes."

"Eva?"

She gave a little, interior nod.

"I'm not hearing you," Hitler said.

"Yes! YES! All right?"

"Willy?"

"My family, always."

So there we were in the deep of the winter night in Hitler's frosty study with Barbarossa staring down at us from the wall.

Carlotta said, "Tomorrow is the eve of the new year. We must have a carnival. Get the Speers over, they like to have fun and we can all see them. Yes, Eva?"

"Yes, a good idea." She managed a smile. We broke our hug.

Hitler went to the window. "Turn off that lamp. Come."

I switched off his desk lamp, which was the only light in the room. He threw open the French doors and we stepped out into the bitter air. Before us stood the Untersberg arrayed in winter glory, glowing with the light of the setting moon.

"Never forget this, why we are here. Oh, Willy, hug your girl, she's trembling like a rabbit." He took Eva to him. "Barbarossa, he is with us, awakening in the mountain. I can feel it. And I can feel another thing. No, I prophesy it, and I am always right. I am *always* right! 1941 is coming. It will be the greatest year in all of history, the greatest year for the world and for the Germans." He chuckled a bit. "My God, it's cold even for me."

Thankfully, we returned to the interior.

"I'm frozen," Carlotta cried. She opened her blouse. "Look at me, my boobies are perfectly blue!"

"Let's have a bath," Eva said. "We'll fill the big tub and all have a steamy bath."

And that is what we did.

# 14

It was not long after I returned to New York from that dreadful trip to California and the confrontation with Angela Truro that there came a stern knocking at our door. My new butler, David, hurried past my office where I was gathering information about the next events I would address in this memoir, which were Operation Barbarossa and the horrifying reappearance in my life of Dieter Junger.

David is of the new breed. He has a "Walkman" and he jogs mornings before I arise. He has brought new names into the house such as "the Who," "Stevie Wonder" and "Steely Dan." The roaring they get up to can be heard at times drifting in from the pantry, but he always silences it when I draw near.

I have become an old fossil, I suppose. I'm sure that he cannot begin to imagine what this dry old skeleton was like in its youth. Can you imagine me saying to David, "I made love to Adolf Hitler?" The world is a funny place, but too often in quite horrible ways. If there is a god overspreading us, he is a sardonic and baleful fellow. Or girl. I am now aware of feminism.

Which was as well, as David came into my room and said,

"There's a huge, unbelievable movie star here. I didn't know you knew Angela Truro."

I gathered my surprise into myself. "You should say, 'A Miss Truro is here, Mister Weber. May I announce her?'"

"Shit! That's easy to forget."

The next thing I knew, Angela appeared in the doorway. But how can I say it? She had about her an atmosphere that I had not noticed in anybody since the days of the Third Reich. She was ominous.

She came striding in.

"Wow, Cezanne, Seurat, and is that a Klee? Carlie said you stole a bunch of paintings during the war." She raised her eyebrows at me, then sat down across my desk.

"The Cezanne was purchased at a Christie's auction, the Miro—it's not a Klee—from Gagosian in Los Angeles and the Seurat also at a Christie's auction."

"So you sit around in room with five million dollars worth of pictures, about? Ever heard of Biafra? Places like that?"

"I don't know."

"OK, please forgive me. You're too up there—" She fluttered a hand over her head "—to be aware of trivia like starving children." She bowed her head.

Her overstated affect would have worked well enough on stage, but it was far too broad for a small study like mine. What I was seeing was not real. That was very clear.

"Would you like a coffee, Miss Truro?"

"From the cutie in the suit, sure."

"Cook will prepare it. David will serve."

"Who's Alf?"

"Is Carlotta with you?"

"Carlotta is in St. Bart's. She has a house there."

"I didn't know."

"Who is Alf and who is Eva and mainly, who are you?"

"You have my name and address. You're here in my house."

"You know how little there is out about you? I had my PA looking through microfilm at the library for the past two days. She didn't find a thing. There was a Weber who died in 1946. Was that you? Are you living some kind of weird anonymous life?"

I am not mentioned in my father's obituary. I am not in the papers, not since I was in society in the thirties, where my name appears here and there in lists of ball attendees, or as having been on one crossing or another.

"Why do you care about people you never knew, Miss Truro, who are dead?"

"I want to know her. Where she's been, what she's done, where her passions lie." She paused. "She's obviously German."

"Yes, she was born in Germany."

She considered. "So then was she there during the war?"

Back in the fifties, some in Hollywood had known. In my opinion, that had been the main reason she couldn't get work back then, that and the accent, of course.

Could this woman be a Nazi hunter? I'd had one meet me in Paris in 1955, a man called Evan Berg. I'd been terrified, but it had turned out to be Dieter he was after, and, sadly, for good reason.

What should I say? I had no idea what Carlotta might have told her. "You've flown all the way across the country looking for nothing. I don't know what she did during the war."

"She has a hole in her life, then, because she won't tell me, either."

"The past, what does it mean? What if she was some kind of a Nazi? It's over and done with now."

"She doesn't even have a maiden name. You can't find her anywhere, either."

"Why do you even care? People come and go in each other's lives without having to be investigated."

"You understand, there's a statement that's gonna be made. It's a statement about women and it's a statement about marriage, and the press is going to want to know who the hell she is. And I don't want that to turn out to be something bizarre."

I sat there looking at this flashing Diana my wife had somehow attracted, and wondering if there could be anything more bizarre than us and our old, destroyed family.

"She has a penchant for experiment," I said. "The four of us were like a four-way couple. We considered ourselves a family, we lived together, we slept together, we all fucked. Does that illuminate anything?"

"It doesn't tell me who she is. It doesn't tell me who they were."

"Then say something ridiculous! Say it was Hitler and Eva Braun. Alf and Eva. The press is going to laugh and forget about it."

"No, they are going to continue to try to find out who this person —this *woman*—who I have married on a beach in Malibu, California actually IS! And I don't know and I can't find out and I love her."

"As do I."

"Well you're sure not gonna be in our family. We're adopting, as it happens. Girls. No place for some male in that."

It had never crossed her mind that she had just heard the truth. It was simply too impossible. Paul Dukes, god rest him, was an expert at disguise, but the concealments of history are greater than any disguise.

Sometimes I wonder if anything we imagine that we know of the past is really true. But when you see its bones, you know that something was there. Treblinka was blown up, but you can still feel their presence if you walk among the right stones, packed together in the dark, in the heat, in the stink of the fumes.

David came sashaying in with a coffee service.

"I don't drink coffee, it fucks up your skin."

"You should wear more hats. You put tinfoil in them, you age much more slowly."

"I've heard that. But I don't like hats."

"Just the tinfoil, then. It would work."

"Yeah, listen, I get that you're not going to tell me anything. Ok. But this is my last stop. If I can't be sure that something isn't going to come boiling up out of her past when her name shows up in the papers that makes me look like a complete moron for marrying her and trying to have a family with her, then I'm gonna go on down the road, and I'm gonna tell her you're the reason."

I felt many pangs. A pang of relief, a pang of fear, a pang of regret. But then I thought, 'my love wants this. It's no crazier than what we had with Alf and Eva. In fact, it's less crazy. Much less. And it's innocent.' And I wanted to cry.

"I want her to be happy."

"Good, then who is she, for the love of fuck?"

"Do you perhaps come from a military family?"

"No, I was raised in a convent, ok? I picked it up from the nuns."

"Angela, I want more than anything in the world for my wife to be happy. And I think she will be happy with you. In fact, I know it. You have many things in common. But the truth of her past—who Alf and Eva really were, for example—that's unfindable. I will tell you one thing about her. She may have already told you this, I don't know."

"She's really good in bed. That's what I know about her."

She was that, my Carlotta. Is. An expert with both sexes and all comers.

"In Germany before the war, things were very hard. When she was eleven—"

"Year?"

"Um, '31, I believe. About that. She was what they called a "medicine." That's a child prostitute."

"Has she always been a prostitute? That's what my husband says."

"Hardly! I was an intelligence officer. She was a beautiful woman in her twenties. I was in the Allied Control Council. I did her *Fragebogen* interview and released her under the classification of Exonerated Person. Then I took her straight to dinner and the rest is history."

"And what was her name then, before she was Carlotta Weber?"

If this paranoid maniac got her name, it wouldn't be long before she located the real records of the trial, and they weren't pretty, obviously. Intimate of Adolf Hitler's. Lived with him. Granted Aryan status early in the war. In other words, a Jew who lived in Hitler's House.

No, that record paints an ugly picture.

"Officially speaking, her record is sealed, as she was a minor at the time."

"If she was eleven in '31 she wasn't a minor in the war."

"All I can say is the record is sealed."

"Why? Is it classified?"

"That I don't know. I've always assumed that it's because part of it involves abuse that took place when she was a minor person. Who is your husband, if I may ask?"

"An asshole who lives in Denver and thinks he can play the guitar. He's got two kids of his own that I do not like, and I don't like him."

"But you've confided in him. Told him about Carlotta."

"I've thrown her in his face, yes."

"As she threw you in mine."

"Pretty much. It's a technique. I like it."

"Do you know anything at all—anything—about human love? Have any feelings whatsoever?"

"When I'm in character and that character is in love, you see love."

"That's a truthful answer, thank you." From it, I saw that she was like Alf. That was why Carlotta was attracted to her. It was a familiar emptiness and Carlotta was comfortable with it.

I understood that the woman sitting across my desk from me was a psychopath.

"Do you despise all men, or just me and your own husband?"

"I want to scare men. I want them to feel woman power."

I have come to understand, a little bit, feminism, and to feel real pride that women are beginning to demand that they be accepted on terms that suit them. I'm not entirely sure if Angela's brand of it is really feminism or just anger, but I felt the hopefulness in it, and liked what I felt.

"Angela, would you like to fuck? Would you like to fuck me right now?"

"Fuck a smoker? No way. And you've got a hell of a nerve. I mean, fuck you."

"'Show me a rose or leave me alone.' I'm a hopeless romantic."

"Shit on you and your misogynistic garbage romance. You're an exploiter just like the rest of them, only you know it damn well or you wouldn't have hit me with a proposition like that out of nowhere. Shock effect, right, maybe it'd get you a little sack time with one of the most beautiful women on the planet. No wonder Carlotta detests you, and boy, I'm telling you, she sure does."

Those were hard words to hear, but I knew that they were true. Carlotta detests me. And what's worse, she's right to. And even worse than that, she has rejected me, a loving and gentle man, in favor of a steel-hearted psycho so much like Hitler that it's uncanny.

I know why. She could control Alf, and she can control Angela the same way. She's getting old and coming to the end of her beauty. She feels vulnerable. She doesn't want a lover, not a real one like me. She wants a supplicant like him. The only thing that would ever have separated those two was what did, which was death.

Just as she had enslaved him, the king of the world, she has enslaved this woman, the queen of Hollywood.

What is worse than being in love with someone you cannot have is also being impressed by them. As a little Jewish whore, she wrapped Adolf Hitler around her finger. Now, as an eldering nobody banging around in a big old house by the sea, with nothing distinguished or important or even particularly interesting about her, she has done the same to the hottest star in Hollywood—and not only that, another woman.

I found myself wondering if Angela had been a lesbian before she met Carlotta. I thought not, and then I wondered if she guessed for a moment that Carlotta was herself straight? Again, I thought not.

"You can be sure that Carlotta's record will never surface."

"And yet it's not classified."

"No."

"So you were spies? Is that it?"

"Yes."

"But it was a long time ago. They Nazis are toast. So what's the big deal?"

I had led this simple creature to precisely the point that I wanted her to go. Now I could save Carlotta's relationship with her, or ruin it.

"There is an extensive Nazi underground in this world, and one of their bullets has Carlotta's name engraved on it. She is a very brave woman and you should consider it an honor to know her.

She looked at me a long time. "Shit," she said at last, "I need a cigarette."

I lit her up. "I thought you were anti-smoking."

"That's Angela Truro. She doesn't smoke. My real name is Glenda Morris and I do, OK?"

"Fine by me. I don't care."

"How did you get so rich?"

"Inherited. I'm exactly the sort of drone I'm sure you despise the most."

She stood. "I have to say, I'm glad I did this. You're a complete piece of shit and it's been really, really unpleasant, but she told me it would be. I'm satisfied, though. It's gonna be OK."

I followed her along the hall.

"Expect headlines," she said with a sigh. She dropped the cigarette on the floor, crushed it out on my lovely parquet, stepped out into her waiting entourage and was gone.

She'd believed my lie, but if she delved deep enough into my own wartime record, she'd find that I had testified at the trial of a Carlotta Krause. And then she'd find the truth.

But where were the records? Library of Congress? No. National Personnel Records Center? Could be. But most probably in Germany, in the Federal Republic's archival files, where they were not going to be easy to find, assuming that they could be at all.

Only if social whispers surfaced would anything go wrong. And even if they did, I was much better known that Carlotta. The studio types who had known about her right after the war were long gone, having drunk and smoked themselves to death by 1965 at the latest. Maybe Bette Davis knew, but she'd never say a word. She'd understood Carlotta's dilemma, and anyway, she was too private to get mixed up in a scandal at her age.

David came and took the coffee things away and went back to whatever they spend their time doing in the servants' area, reading, fornicating, stealing silver, I don't much care. Blowing grass, as I sometimes smell.

I raised my window. There was the roar of the street, but sometimes you can hear the carousel even here and that makes me close it again. But as I didn't hear it, so I looked down. Do you think on the way down, remember things, or is your mind simply blank? How long, I wondered. Not more than a few seconds, not like a plane. No time for second thoughts here. But I'd have to do it out the kitchen window, into the air shaft. I wouldn't want to dent a car.

The air smelled of fumes, but also a little green. They'd been mowing the Sheep Meadow earlier. Now, coming up from below, I heard excited squeals. Angela was departing.

It occurred to me that if I was going to do it out the front, this would be the perfect moment. But off she went, three limousines for one goddess. You'd think if she was a real goddess, there'd be even more. At least five.

August heat, New York, 1979. Not feeling too well, but then again I'm never feeling too well, am I?

You know, tonight I think I'm going to go down to Therese's Little Secret. Have I ever mentioned the Little Secret in these papers? It's a hidden after-hours place in a basement on Lex between 47th and 48th. You're expected to come in high and yearning for something gooey and sweet, so I'll smoke some marijuana before I go down.

The last time I was there, I saw Thomas Berger, the author of *Little Big Man,* a book I enjoyed a good bit. The film, too. Secret though it is, it's not exclusively a celebrity place. More cognoscenti. People who know this city rather well.

You go down under a brownstone and thread your way through a cellar packed to the rafters with books, newspapers and magazines. In the back is a tiny room, four tables, and a little garden that will be open on a night like this.

Therese tells stories and her shockingly ancient waitress Queenie, cooks, or rather concocts, and serves. You can order anything, a hamburger, caviar, a *bombe*. You'll always get a vanilla soda with two cherries and Miracle Whip. I once ordered *pâté* and was told that I could have it, but only if I brought my own goose and force fed it myself.

Therese is involved in a lawsuit with one of her neighbors over who owns the cat that lives in both houses. I worry about her. I want to know if she's won.

If I don't go out, I'll fall asleep early and then I'll dream and that I don't like to do. Nothing can stop the legions who approach me in my dreams. I've tried suffocating myself to see how it feels and it's awful, a frantic agony. I think of the children who felt that. The mothers trying to help their babies in the naked, stifling dark.

Do you know what he said when I asked him about it? 'Gas?' he said, 'what gas?' I said, 'Jew gas.' He manufactured a fatherly smile and replied, 'Oh, that. It's delousing gas. They use it in the prison system.' Then he shifted the subject. 'Why do I get so angry? I can't seem to control it. I worry about myself, Willy.'

Ah yes, indeed, but that winter of 1940 was the last time he didn't really have reason to fly off into a rage.

Wartime, as I have mentioned, is a different sort of time. Peacetime is regular. It flows with a predicable cadence, days and nights, weeks and months, seasons and years and cycles of years. In wartime, a day might last forever or be over in an instant. The weeks and months fly, fueled by rumors and changes and warnings and tragedies. People disappear into new people, changed by battle or bombs or just the endless, ceaseless suffering of it all. People disappear altogether. And then there is the waiting, when the sun stops in the sky and hell reigns eternal.

By the summer of 1941, the bubble in which we lived was growing less stable. Sometimes there were no chickens, no eggs, no geese at the Berghof. There was always asparagus, though. Always. I avoid Europe entirely during spargle season when there seem to be a few spears on every plate. Horrible stuff, it tastes to me like his mouth.

After that brute of a winter, the spring of 1941 in Germany—the dawn chorus greeting the sun, the warm, green days and the slowly fading evenings—made one feel as if one was being kissed by the world.

I had tabled my plan to assassinate Hitler. If I did, I felt certain that I would be killed at once and Carlotta shipped off to what I now knew would be gas.

In any case, Paul was right. If sanity prevailed among the Nazis, at this point, a negotiated peace would likely mean that they kept at least half of Poland and the north of France. Any survival of the Nazi state was anathema.

Watching him and being with him in the weeks when he was there, I longed more not love him than to hate him. I did hate him, that was foundational. But the damned horror of it was that I also loved him still, despite everything.

When he played at being the father, it was so very hard for me. I missed *Vati* every moment, and when he was assuming that role, for those few minutes it was so very nice for me. But then I would remember what he was and I would feel a rage so intense that I wondered if I would always be able to control it.

Shortly after the fall of France and before the Mathausen threat, I had made a final decision to go ahead with the murder.

Millions were dying. The *realpolitik* of protecting Hitler in order to defeat him was grotesque. It was morally ignorant. I would not go along with Paul and Churchill.

I began to think of ways. But there was an immediate problem. Hitler was not at home. The Berghof was under construction again. Something was always being built or changed. At present, a subsurface bunker was being dug out and an elaborate machine installed on the roof that would produce a fog bank to conceal the house from bombers. Radar stations and listening posts were being constructed in the mountains.

The reason for this was that new ultra-long range version of the Halifax bomber had been introduced by the British, and it was feared that it might be able to reach the mountain retreat.

After he left in January, he was back only for a day or so at a time and when he did come, he arrived in a cloud of bureaucrats and generals, his government traveling with him. The sort of quiet, private time that I needed did not come.

During his long absences, Eva was disconsolate. Carlotta was bored. The three of us now routinely slept together. It was the way we lived. Hitler preferred me to stay there. He wanted me to be intimate with Eva. Any jealousy had been trumped by his fear that her loneliness might move her to suicide.

There was a notable event in May when Rudolf Hess, now elaborately crazy and in obvious need of psychiatric care, took off in a Messerschmitt with the plan of working out a peace plan with Churchill. He already knew about Barbarossa and like most of the others was convinced that it would fail unless Germany was allowed a completely free hand. Large formations in Western Europe, the Balkans and Greece had to be freed up, and the only way to do that was to make peace with Britain.

I could have told him that Churchill wouldn't make peace, but his astrologer convinced him that the moment was right and off he went.

As it happened, this event occurred during one of Hitler's flying visits, and led to the most extraordinary and, frankly, interesting temper tantrum I ever saw enacted by anybody. Unless somebody's life was at stake, or their career, his tantrums could be quite entertaining, especially if one was as familiar with him as we were. It was sickening, though, to see the ease with which he could end men's lives. He would yell, "That one, that fool Schmidt, take him out and shoot him!" Or "That idiot, that so-called professor, he's another incorrigible, put him under the axe!" Such things might happen anywhere, during a conversation or while he was reading reports, at any time.

I came to understand the real reason for legal process. Formality slows matters down. Procedure respects details, which in turn encourages discovery of truth, which is usually hidden in them.

For a time there was hope that Hess hadn't managed it, that he'd crashed into the sea. When we got word that the BBC was announcing that he had turned up in Scotland, Hitler literally leaped into the air. He threw himself back and forth bellowing, "Hess! Hess!

Hess!" A frantic telephone call to Canaris confirmed that there was no agent in place in Scotland who might be tasked to assassinate him.

He wasn't just aware of Barbarossa, he knew a great deal about it, most particularly the dispositions of the troops and the numbers involved. I might say that at this point that there can have been few people in Germany, including Stalin's many spies, who didn't know that something was up. Troop trains were rattling up and down every line in the country. Hurried goodbyes on jammed station platforms were a daily routine everywhere. Long convoys of trucks crowded the *autobahnen*. The men of Germany were being separated from the women, and sadness lingered as an inescapable, teary mist in every eye. Lale Andersen had recorded a song in 1939 called "The Girl Under the Lantern," and it was at this time that it became popular as "Song of the Sentry." It is now called "Lily Marlene."

I think of all those young fellows when I hear it. Deluded, crazy boys marching off into the lunatic dreams of Adolf Hitler. How can the world be as it is, when one man, armed with obviously insane notions and maniacal ambitions can inspire a whole country to make the mistake that the Germans made?

At the end of *Barry Lyndon*—what a movie, I saw it a few years ago—there occurs this epilogue: "It was in the reign of George III that the aforesaid personages lived and quarreled; good or bad, handsome or ugly, rich or poor, they are all equal now."

So also the German boys and the Russian boys, the American and British and French boys, the Australians, Indians, New Zealanders—all of those who fell, equal now.

Anyway, the tantrum developed into quite a show. He leaped, he shouted, his eyes bulged, he wept, threw himself about, cursed Hess blue, searched in his mind for scapegoats, on and on. Over the course of the next few days, his rage would periodically erupt again. When it was just us, we would hold him and he would shudder like a cowed dog. As always when he was out of sorts, he shouted at Blondi over the least mistake the dog made, and swatted her with his whip.

Gradually, though, matters went back to what one might call normal in the Berghof—a sense of looming danger.

About a week after Hess's defection, the former American ambassador to Belgium, John Cudahy, send a letter requesting a visit to the Berghof to interview Hitler for a book he was writing.

Late one night when we were alone in his office, Hitler read me the letter. We sat across from one another in the social area of the study. There was a single light on, the green-shaded reading lamp on his desk. We were both in deep shadow. The night was extremely quiet, too late even for the howl of the wolf or the snort of the rooting pig.

"Willy," Hitler said, "I want you to listen from your room. Tell me if you think he knows anything of the plan. How far has Hess gone, that's what I must know."

"Would Cudahy have been likely to have heard anything from the British?"

"He's quite well connected and he has very suddenly requested this appointment."

"Ah, then I see."

The new intercom on Hitler's desk could be set so that he could listen in on any box anywhere in the house, or could direct sound from the study into one.

"I'll listen," I said.

"And Paul, where is he?"

"I'm never sure. I can telephone his flats." He had one in Berlin and another in Munich."

He wrote on a paper and handed it to me. "This is his telephone number in Berchtesgaden. If he's there, have him come up and listen with you. But don't tell him why. I want your impressions of him, also. What does he know?"

"He must know something. The entire country is clearly mobilizing."

"Something is not exact! I need him to be convincingly misinformed about Barbarossa so that he'll take false information to Churchill. That's what I need. After all, we could be going into the Balkans only. That's what Paul needs to believe."

Barbarossa must not happen. Millions of lives were in the

balance, millions of young men and boys on both sides were about to be murdered. No, it could not go forward.

It was time for Hitler to die.

Just yesterday, I had examined the gun, which was hidden in a drawer behind Carlotta's vast collection of undergarments.

"Are you concerned that Churchill will inform Stalin?"

"What an idiotic question, Willy. He most certainly will. Of course."

"Very honestly and with all respect, I disagree."

He leaned forward in his chair. "And your reasoning?"

"Capitalism wants the destruction of communism. Churchill would like nothing better than to see Germany do to Russia what she has done to the rest of Europe."

"Which is why that lunatic should be with me instead of blowing up bombs all over the place!"

"My point exactly. If we let Churchill find out about Barbarossa and he doesn't tell Stalin, which he won't, then we have something to hold over him—the fact that he betrayed Stalin and therefore should side with us. Must, because now Stalin will never trust him again."

He considered. "How would Stalin know that Churchill has withheld the information?"

"He will know," I said. Instantly, he looked at me sharply. I saw my mistake, but now it was too late.

"You seem very certain of that," he said. The undertone of menace in his voice was unmistakable.

"I am very certain that Stalin has spies among the British. Half of them are communists anyway."

He descended into himself. At some length, he said, "But not among us?"

"I wouldn't think so."

"Carlotta is a communist."

"That isn't my impression at all."

'Oh, yes. When she was young, we both were. Very much convinced."

"When she was twelve, perhaps, or fifteen. She's absolutely loyal you, Alf. I see it in her every moment."

"In love?"

"As much a whore ever can be, but yes, certainly.

In a calm, businesslike tone that I did not feel at all, I continued, "I think that the moment of Barbarossa is an ideal time to get a peace with Britain."

He made a tent of his hands. Then he raised his eyebrows. "Let it never be said that the Americans are only good for poker. That's a very nice chess move."

"We give Churchill the date as a sign of good faith. Take him into our confidence. A joint effort to destroy Bolshevism once and for all. I don't know the date, of course, but if it's far enough in the future, perhaps we could even convince them to send an expeditionary force to fight alongside us."

"Ha! The innocence of youth!"

"It could happen."

He fell silent. Finally, he spoke again, so softly that I could read nothing from his intonation. "The true date. And he doesn't tell Stalin. You are sure?"

"Excuse me?"

Without warning, he leaped out of his chair and stood over me. "YOU ARE SURE OR YOU ARE NOT, YOU STUPID FUCK!" He twirled around, then glared down at me, his eyes bulging, his face purple. "ARE YOU SURE ARE YOU SURE, GOD DAMN YOU!?"

I fought my pounding heart. "Yes, Leader, I am sure," I said as calmly as I could.

He rushed across the room and threw himself down behind his desk. "Willy, if we do this and Stalin is lying in wait, I will have no choice but to shoot you."

"I'm right. I'm quite sure."

He stared at me, his face a shadow in the low light.

"Alf, my loyalty to you began in 1932, when Paul told me how you would rearm Germany and prevent Stalin moving west. And I have seen this happen, and so has he, and that is why we are both loyal to you and to the higher power of human happiness and freedom that you represent."

"Ha, you must have a speech writer you keep in your ear!"

"No, it's true."

"Yeah? It sounds fucking rehearsed." He jumped to his feet. "Salute, Soldier Willy!"

I jumped up also, and threw the Roman salute.

He came back to me. While I was still saluting, he ran his fingers down my cheek.

I dropped the salute.

"Such beautiful skin," he murmured. "Beautiful boy..."

He took my hand and held it against his own cheek. "I like to be held. We do in our family, you know. Ernst used to hold me. He would lift me in his arms and put me in the bed and I could just close my eyes and give it all up."

Then he bent forward. I could no longer see his face but I could hear his wracking, bitter sobs. "This is terrible," he choked, "a terrible, terrible thing!"

He went to his knees and embraced me around the waist.

I laid my hands on his head in silence.

Though there was a volcano of joy within me, I concealed the elation I felt. I had convinced Hitler to give up the Barbarossa dates to Churchill and therefore Stalin. I felt sure that Churchill would tell the Russians at once. The Red Army would be waiting for the *Wehrmacht*. Without surprise, the Germans were going to have a devil of a time. And if Hitler was dead there would be no question: Goering or Himmler, whoever won the war between the rats that would follow the assassination, would withdraw the troops.

So thought the boy, anyway, as unaware as he still was of the way history has of subverting the expectations of us little pawns, arrayed on its board before kings and castles whose motives not even they can guess.

But this moment of surpassing elation was also one of surpassing fear. I knew very well that killing him would end my own life. Escape would be impossible. Carlotta, too, would almost certainly die. I could only hope that it would be quick for both of us.

'Two lives for millions,' I thought. A fair bargain.

The next evening, we had Paul up to the house for a dinner and then in the morning to listen in on the Cudahy visit. When he arrived, he was decked out in full *Tracht*, right down to a *gamsbart* in his hat.

Hitler took one look at him and laughed aloud. "You look more German than any German!"

"I admire the look. It's handsome."

"You and your disguises. Perfidy! It's just natural to you English."

After the meal, we went to the map table where Hitler showed Paul the whole plan. He pretended that it was a sort of brag—'look, fifty divisions here, ninety there! Stalin will run squealing off behind the Urals'—that sort of thing.

Hitler was a master deceiver, and to make it work, he never directly told Paul any date. He wouldn't have considered that strong enough intelligence to take directly to Churchill. No, to believe in a date enough for him to actually give the information to Churchill, Paul had to believe that he was stealing it.

Thus the paper showing it was left lying in a dispatch box, upside down to Paul's position at the map table. Hitler watched as Paul made an effort to read it. Once he had succeeded, he casually closed the dispatch box.

Paul said, "This must be soon."

"Oh, soon, yes." Hitler gave me a twinkling glance. "Let me ask you this. What if we give the date to Churchill? The real date, you know." He laughed a little. "Not the one you just read upside down." He took out the memorandum and gave it to Paul.

It was a proposal for joint German-British combat operations against Russia.

"This is a surprise."

"The date is next July. Plenty of time for us to conclude the stupid war we're fighting and sign a peace pact. Then there could be a new BEF, this one against our mutual enemy."

"You leave me breathless."

"All right, all right! What do you think of the goddamn proposal?"

"It's remarkable."

"It's also impossible to send through diplomatic channels. I want you to take it to Churchill personally."

"Yes, of course, I see that."

"What's our likelihood of success?"

"I have no idea. He would certainly welcome a way out of the war, though."

I realized that Hitler was lying, both in this and with the date that had been on the paper. Both were false. His olive branch to Churchill was nonsense, just designed to confuse the issue, and the hidden date also was false. His real purpose was to get Paul to believe the hidden date.

He was, in other words, desperately afraid that Hess had given the real date to the British and didn't believe for an instant that they wouldn't tell Stalin.

He hadn't believed me last night, not a word of it. And he didn't believe a word Paul was saying, either.

He had reached the same situation that had driven so many Roman emperors mad—he could no longer trust anybody at all. He was thus alone within himself, not just wandering like the rest of us in the labyrinth of mirrors, but doing that entirely and completely alone.

"So all the troop movements we're seeing now are for the Balkans?" Paul asked.

"For the most part."

I have to admit that it was fascinating to observe this master manipulator and this master deceiver at work trying to outwit one another.

We spent a fine afternoon chatting with the women. Hitler and Paul dared one another to swim in the cold alpine pool below the house, but neither would get up to it.

I don't recall the dinner. The food at the Bergh of was always unexceptional, and the wines, unless it was one of mine, were indifferent.

After dinner Hitler listened to the BBC while Paul and I and the girls played *Skat*. I was interested to see that Hitler seemed to listen carefully to an evening drama, and wondered how much English he knew. I had thought none, but the truth of that became just another mystery about him.

Later, after Eva and Carlotta had retired, Hitler lapsed into one of his rants. Until about three, the two of us listened to him rhapsodizing about how amazed the German people were by all the victories he had delivered to them, and what a joke the Italians were when compared to the Germans, and how chastened his generals felt now that they understood that he'd been right all along. "That's what you can count on about me, I am always right. Always!"

Finally he wound down and leaned back in his chair, gazing up at the ceiling. "Can't you feel it? It's out there beyond the stillness, the power. My guns, my tanks, my men." He closed his eyes. His breathing deepened.

I called the valet, who came in and began undressing him. Paul and I went across to the back of the house, passing the SS guard in the foyer, who gave us a smile and a wink. "Finally, eh?"

"He's excited," I said. "It's an extraordinary time."

"Willy, get me reassigned. I'll do anything to get to the front."

"You want me to ask him, Karl?"

He nodded.

We went on up. I said to Paul, "You're sleeping in the Chamberlain Room."

"That fucking asshole! Put me somewhere else."

"Not for me to choose."

We parted and I went into the dark of our room, warm with Carlotta's animal presence. I was just settling down, wishing that I had opium—and then I thought of the gun.

I froze, my finger on my collar. I should take it out now. I should use it. This was the ideal time, especially with Paul here. If anybody could succeed in helping us escape, it was him.

I went to the drawer when I kept it and quietly opened it. Pushing aside the undergarments, I exposed its gleaming darkness to the thin light coming in from outside.

I looked down at Carlotta, pale and perfect, the line of her jaw suggesting a higher geometry, too beautiful to bear.

I did not get into bed beside her, but rather sat in one of our two hard chairs, silent in the dark. Closing my eyes, I listened to the faint sounds of Paul at his *toilette*, then the fainter hooting of owls. Somewhere far down the mountain an engine churned. There was a light tank kept hidden from the road, always ready. I could imagine its interior, dimly lit, a couple of SS boys in the hard seats, their conversation desultory. I remembered the sizzle of burning men in Poland. That had happened just last year, but it now seemed an eon ago.

Somewhere deep, a wolf howled, followed by the yapping of its pack. I watched the moonlight crawling across the top of our desk. A shaft of it illuminated Carlotta's sleeping face, making her look like an exquisite ghost.

I got my dark blue silk robe from the closet and drew it around me. I dropped the pistol into a pocket.

I opened our door, silent on its hinges, and looked up and down the corridor. At night, there was only a single bulb lit, and another over the bathroom and w.c. that the lesser rooms like ours were meant to share.

How vividly I remember walking along the corridor and down the stairs. I was barefoot, I had forgotten my slippers. I did not move furtively, but rather stepped boldly along. Making no attempt at stealth, I hurried along.

The floor was cold downstairs, the rooms quiet. Crossing the great room, I saw Karl lying on the couch. There was a faint odor of cigarette smoke in the air.

He said, "Hey, Willy?" A question.

"He called," I replied. "He wants to discuss an idea."

"An idea?" he said, laughter in his voice. "Enjoy yourself."

I climbed the front stairs. Wotan would die now. The god would die.

I passed Eva's room, then paused. Her heart would be broken. Her love for me would turn to hate.

So be it, she was a fool.

I went into the study. No light was on. This room, where I had had, had received my Eagle and had so many intense, sometimes terrifying encounters with Hitler, was silent. Filled with ghosts, though. They were ranked before me in their millions, silent boys in steel helmets, Jews behind barbed wire, all the great horde of victims prepared for the coming sacrifice.

Our gods are not outside of us as we imagine, but lie waiting within, ever ready to awaken, and National Socialism was Wotan returned to life in Hitler. He was lying now on the narrow bed in the next room, Wotan himself.

I went to the doorway. Hitler's bedroom was so silent that for an uneasy moment I thought him gone. But no, there was a lumpen mass there, and soft snoring from beneath the quilt.

I approached the bed. He lay with his mouth open, his head turned toward me. His face, like everything on this side of the house, was presently lit by a shaft of moonlight. In that sere light, it looked dry and old. Vulnerable.

Now. I could do it now. I closed the fingers of my right hand around the pistol. I slipped my forefinger around the trigger.

He was dreaming. I could see his lips moving.

I stood like a statue. Screw me, I hate saying it, but I loved the man. Oh, god, but I did, but I was going to do this. I would kill him now.

I started to lift the gun from my pocket. Another moment, a quick shot, then, I decided, a shot into my own mouth. Leaving the world together, me and Alf. Appropriate.

I took the gun completely out.

He sighed and turned his head.

I raised it. This was death to me, too, right now. The seconds passed. I stared down. He stirred a bit and I thrust the pistol back into my pocket.

At the same moment, his hand came out from under the quilt and searched the air. I took it, and he closed his fingers tightly around mine.

"Willy?"

"Alf?"

His eyes were dark sockets. Open.

"Why, Willy?"

Why what? Had he seen the gun? "You called."

"No."

"I must have dreamed it, then." I felt sweat break out all over me. I caught my breath, then leaned down toward him. I had to do something intimate, something more than friendly, and I had to do it right now.

I touched his forehead. "You sleep, Alf. You need it."

His hand gripped mine more tightly. He murmured "my boy...my boy..." And he was asleep again, or appeared to be.

I said, "*Vati.*"

The soft snoring returned. I turned and left him then, and went back down and across the great room where Karl now slept on the couch, and back up to our room, to its warmth and to my love. I returned the gun to the back of the desk drawer and laid my head down on the desk and wept.

I am still ashamed. Even more, now that the entire history is clear to me. My failure is like acid inside me.

When I slipped into bed, Carlotta turned to me. Pleasantly aroused, I was at once ready. She pressed her mouth up against my ear and said, "You asshole!"

"What?"

"Doing that! The goddamn gun!"

"I didn't—"

"Don't you dare disobey your orders. I'll fucking well execute you myself."

I leaned away from her and looked at her face in the dark. She gave me a little smile, all innocent. I thought to say something—to ask—but then I thought perhaps not.

She pulled me close again and resumed talking right in my ear.

"Where's the gun?"

"In the drawer."

"Keep your voice down. Whisper!"

She got out of bed and went to the dresser. "Stupid fuck," she muttered. When she came back, she once again pressed her mouth to my ear. "You think they wouldn't notice that it's been moved? They would notice. I've replaced it in exactly the same position it started out in, and you can thank me for your life."

But surely nobody came in here. Nothing was ever disturbed. "Who, Carlotta?"

"Your fucking jolly SS friends, that's who!"

I was at a loss.

She grabbed my wrist with ferocious strength and again whispered against my ear. "They search every inch of every room every fucking day. Understand this. Don't be deceived by this place ever again. You are in Hitler's house, Willy. *Hitler's house*!"

I lay a long time awake, wondering about her words. "Follow orders...execute you myself..."

What was she? And, for that matter, what was I? I'd had no orders, just a diffident comment from Paul that the British didn't want him killed.

I realized that we were a cell, we two, and Paul was our handler. That causal comment had been an order, and one so strict that my counterpart here was willing to kill me if she came to believe that I would disobey it.

But that was only the beginning of the story of the gun.

As was our habit, Carlotta and I joined Hitler for his breakfast and our lunch. Eva prowled the forest or crawled about in her gym, which was in the cellar near the bowling alley. Hitler so detested any slight sign of fat on a woman that she never stopped exercising. Carlotta, of course, neither exercised nor gained an ounce. Generally, she'd start with my food, then go for Eva's and even Alf's. We got hers, if we were fast.

We sat in the alcove together, the four of us. Hitler, I noticed, had been discreetly watching me the whole time. I was terrified, of course.

There is something to be understood," he said. "Henceforth, nobody approaches my suite unless called, and if you are called, inform the guard. They will ask my valet to find out if you can come ahead."

"I thought you called me. I heard you."

He leaned toward me. "Never come in unless I call! NEVER!"

Carlotta said, "Willy, what the fuck?"

"I heard him on the intercom. I'm sure of it!"

"Not possible," he said, "it's on my desk and I was in my bed sound asleep. As you saw."

"Maybe I dreamed it." I tried to catch his eyes with mine. He looked away. "I suppose I just wanted it to be true."

A snort from him, nothing more. Was I losing his trust? No way to be sure.

We continued to eat, or they did. I couldn't manage, I was too frightened. It didn't matter anyway. Carlotta ate mine, too.

I no longer knew who Carlotta really was, or what was actually happening in this house. It appeared that she also worked for the British.

Later that day, she "accidentally" spilled the drawer, thus making certain that any movement of the gun would be concealed. Nobody took it away. Nobody moved it again. It lay there, waiting to spring its surprise.

Speaking of which, when Barbarossa commenced, Stalin was indeed surprised. The last train loaded with grain passed from Soviet territory into the Reich while the Germans were storming the border.

I often think of it steaming along the rails, the sleepy engineer leaning out, the huffing old engine looming away into the dark, and the soldiers in the steel helmets watching it disappear down the line.

Stalin was so surprised, in fact, that at one point he ran off to his dacha near Moscow and simply hid.

After the war, sitting together in Quaglino's in London, I asked Paul if he had given Churchill the date.

"Absolutely, the dispositions, the date, everything Hitler told me."

"He told the date? I don't recall that."

"One of the first things one learns in spy school is how to read upside down. Apparently he wasn't aware of that. The whole schedule was lying open for fifteen minutes. Upside down, but I read it all."

"I thought that was fake."

"Perhaps he did, too. The dates on it were correct. Every detail was correct."

"So the date and all went straight to Stalin?"

"Stalin was told nothing."

"Paul, why not?"

"We intended to let the dictators hack each other to death, then intervene after they had bled one another white. We could have stopped Russia's bleeding by going into Normandy or even Calais in '43. It was quite possible."

"But Tunisia was chosen instead."

"Exactly. The long way round. The hope was that the Soviet Union and the Reich would kill each other while we took our time in North Africa and Italy. After the war, with neither dictatorship menacing Europe, that sunlit upland Churchill spoke so eloquently about in 1940 would come to be. Alas."

"That's not in any of the histories."

"Certainly not. The history of war is what the victors want to remember. I am telling you the truth, which is a very different matter."

I am no friend of Bolshevism and have a horror of the USSR, but if the allies had invaded Europe in '43, millions of lives might have been spared. If the British divisions that were available in England in 1943 and the American forces that were sent to Tunisia had instead gone across the channel before the Nazi defenses were prepared, an attack on Calais would have almost certainly succeeded.

So the Barbarossa got date to Churchill and all the German dispositions, and it did absolutely no good.

That meal at Quaglino's was, I believe, in the autumn of '47. Paul had been shooting in Anglesey and had, to great his surprise, come in with a good brace. He had hanging for his birds in Quag's, so we dined on them, lovely and high, and drank a satisfying Ausone. In my old wine notes, I give it two checks and say, "'34, thinning already." But I recall it now as being very fine, soft and richly complex, not even close to being over the hill. Memory makes the heart grow fonder, that old saw. It's annoyingly true.

When Paul and I went into my room at the Berghof in order to monitor Hitler's interview with Cudahy, I opened the door into a cloud of cigarette smoke and a riot of women.

Eva, Gretl and Carlotta were all half dressed, trying on clothes and smoking away as usual.

Paul, ever the proper Englishman, shielded his eyes with a hand and turned away.

Eva and Gretl left happily enough when we explained what we had to do, but Carlotta sat down in one of our rather hard little chairs, folded her arms and said, "Tell me what you're listening for. I'll help you."

I had wondered before if she was spying for somebody. Now I went further, asking myself who she might be reporting to. I thought Paul, apparently. But was that really true? Hitler had called her a communist. She could even be spying for the Social Democrats, for that matter.

I didn't want her hurt. I said, "Carlotta, the Leader doesn't expect you to be here."

She crossed her legs.

"This is very serious business, Darling."

"Don't you 'darling' me. I'm staying. I can be of use where those empty-heads can't."

So the interview started. Cudahy was polite, even courtly in his manner. He inquired about whether or not Germany would ever invade the United States, an idea that Hitler called "silly." Cudahy then asked if he would invade Russia.

"Never! It's impossible. I can say that history has a lesson here for us, in the fate of the Teutonic Knights and, of course, Napoleon. The USSR is a friendly power. We respect the integrity of our friends."

Cudahy had moved on to other subjects, but a little too smoothly, I thought. So did Hitler, so did Paul. It made the next few weeks an uneasy time. I kept hoping to see reports that Stalin had redeployed his armies. But they never came.

On June 22 at 3:15 German Time, the *Wehrmacht* jumped off with 104 infantry divisions, 19 armored divisions, 15 motorized infantry divisions in three army groups. It was a total of 3,800,000 men including allied forces.

Carlotta and I, Eva and Gretl and the third sister Ilse and their parents were all in the Wannsee House. Hitler had told us that he would be there in the evening with a great surprise, and to have a family celebration ready.

We assumed we knew the surprise, as Goebbels had read Hitler's proclamation announcing the invasion in the morning newscast. But we did not know. The actual surprise was a terrific shock to me, and led to the second great argument I had with Hitler.

Over the course of the day, the house was quiet, with papa Fritzl reading a Karl May novel and the women listening to records and dancing together. In one's home, it was legal to dance as one pleased. If you can believe it, there were detailed instructions regarding what was and wasn't legal in public. Of course, no *negermusik*, but it went farther than that, as I recall. No more than 20% of a band's performance could be devoted to fox-trotting, for example. That I do remember, and plucking of the double-bass was prohibited as being "inimical to Aryan musicality."

A Czech novelist called Josef Skvorecky published an essay recently that contains a number of absurd rules, such as, "Strictly forbidden is the use of instruments alien to the German spirit /(e.g. so-called cowbells, flex-a-tone, brushes, etc.) as well as all mutes which turn the noble sound of brass-wind instruments into a Jewish-Freemasonic yell /(so-called wa-wa, in hat, etc.)"

I wrote him in regard to this, and he insists that these rules were distributed in all Prague music venues in 1943. Real or not, they do reflect the National Socialist attitude to jazz quite accurately.

Scat singing was definitely out. No singer in any publicly visible Berlin cabaret would dare to scat. But not at home, and Eva's mother could scat like Ella Fitzgerald, so when I say "the girls were dancing," you must form a picture in your mind of completely forbidden records blasting out of the Victrola with Franziska standing beside it scatting fabulously and smoking a black cigarette in a long holder while the four girls jitterbugged like fiends.

There were plenty of underground clubs where anything went. And how do I know? Because old Alf would install his hair and off we'd go to really unwind in one illegal place or another.

I know that I've written much here that will seem fantastic. The Hitler of my memory hardly squares with the Hitler, say, of William Shirer or Joachim Feist. That Hitler—the ranting, crazed bureaucrat—was only a suit that he wore.

History is not the real world, history is a story about it, and most of what Adolf Hitler was and did in his private life is not part of the story. That this vulnerable, elaborately perverse and frightened little man has become a distant, unreachable symbol of power appalls me. Hitler was a genius, but so flawed that he was at the same time an idiot and a monster. I saw him racing along in his Mercedes with his arm smartly erect. I saw him naked on the floor and slobbering on Carlotta's feet.

Then came the first night of Barbarossa. We were in Wannsee. I recall celebration and shouted glee from the street.

I danced some, drank champagne and longed to know what was happening.

I was constantly watching the door, hoping that Hitler would arrive in a state of shock and dismay. I hoped to hear, 'Stalin knew! We'll make it, but we're tied up on the border.'

The worry was so impossible that I went upstairs and for the first time in months took a heroin tablet.

I went out and looked at the lake with Carlotta, who, after dancing had become uncharacteristically quiet. Normally, if you are anywhere in her general vicinity, you are hearing her, I can assure you.

The sun had risen an hour before, and there were a few sails on the shining water, not many, but they conferred a lovely, if false, sense of peace. I sang, "By the sea, by the sea, by the beautiful sea..."

"What song?"

"English ditty."

"It's no good."

"All right, as you say."

"You don't sing. You just sort of talk long." She imitated me. It wasn't pleasant and indeed, I cannot sing at all well.

Like two school kids, we held hands. I said to her, "What do you think will happen?"

"A lot of really cute boys are going to get killed, that's what I think will happen."

I thought of the gun and now of the order not to assassinate. I thought of Carlotta's 'I'll execute you myself."

We stood hand in hand, in the rising dawn. No blood sky to report, no bombers, nothing but a normal morning, as I am sure will be the case as well, on the final day, when the world comes to an end.

# 15

I used to have quite a large number of photos from the war years. None from the Berghof, of course, as they were all destroyed in the bombing and fire. But pictures I wanted to look at, felt compelled to look at. They were nothing special, no secret collection, just things I had seen here and there and clipped out of newspapers or wherever.

These were not the terrible battlefield stuff that Hitler would show me on my first visit to the *Wolfschanze*. Those images were all collected by Abwehr conspirators as part of a plan to use them as war crimes evidence against the Nazis after the war was finally won by the allies. Unfortunately, they were found by the Gestapo in '44 and burned along with thousands of documents that would have provided evidence of war crimes committed not just by SS, but by tens of thousands of *Wehrmacht* personnel and civilians on direct orders from Hitler.

One of them came up in *Signal* magazine about a month after the start of Barbarossa. It shows a group of Russian soldiers standing in one of the wire cages that were set up across behind the German lines to confine the two million of them who were captured.

They are not yet thin and bearded. In fact, they might have been put in just that day. They stare out, some of them looking fierce, others as if they are waiting for some instruction, some order. One has his fingers in the wire. I can see the idea that is in his mind: this wire is thin, the *steppe* out there is vast, maybe I can run...

What happened to them was really very simple. They were not fed, they were not given drink. They were left to wallow in their own piss and shit, not even provided with latrines.

Those men in their millions, perfectly good human beings with lives and hopes and love in them, were left to die in conditions worse than those that befall abandoned dogs, who at least can forage for garbage.

I wish I could say that Hitler was simply indifferent to suffering. But that wasn't the case. He not only cared, he cared a great deal. He enjoyed it. Normal people evolve an inner witness. This is a part of them that watches and evaluates as they live out their lives. When I met Carlotta, for example, she had a very undeveloped inner witness. But she is a brilliant, striving human being and now has an exquisitely evolved observer within herself, who directs her toward experiences of deepest richness, such as the love she has found with Angela Truro. I regret it so very much, but I nevertheless see the beauty of it, and wish them well.

Hitler, by contrast, even in his middle years, was still like a five year old when it came to empathy. He would have been the sort who found it fascinating to push needles through captive insects. I think I've said already that he referred to Jews as insects. Certainly, he thought Slavs were of little more consequence than beetles, and he enjoyed the idea of them trapped in those cages out on the *steppe*, where the bees sang in the meadows and the flowers nodded prettily. Deiter Junger told me that they would try to catch insects that flew past, to eat.

All of my life, I have loved Russian literature. When *Vati* and I read together Turgenev's *Torrents of Spring*, I lived within Sanin and loved Gemma so much that I can to this day taste her mouth and smell her hair in the house of my imagination.

I have the highest regard for that tragic, brilliant people. When I look at the faces in that photo—the defiance there, the grandeur of the souls—my heart is agonized.

In the evening of the first day, we went into the study to listen to the BBC, but they did not have a very informative bulletin, just a comment that Germany, after claiming provocation, had invaded Russia, "on a broad front."

Then, in the wee hours, he came, the car purring along the street, the brakes squealing slightly as it stopped, then a shadow leaping out and cavorting up the walk amid the night blooming flowers.

I opened the door to him (the servants were long asleep) and he came hurrying into the foyer. He threw his arms around me and uttered a great, wracking sob.

"Willy," he said, "Willy my boy—oh, my son—we have taken three hundred thousand of them in a day."

My heart just crashed. Crashed into the depths. I said, "Alf! My God, how fantastic!"

"Oh, it is! It is, absolutely. Even Brauchitsch smiled a bit. Not a lot, mind you, but I saw it, the corners of the mouth twisting up, oh yes! The Bolsheviks, they're done for. Oh my heavens, we're rebuilding the world, Willy. It's wonderful. Wonderful!"

We went through the formal rooms and into the salon at the back of the house. From here in the day one could look across bobbing gardens to the sheer, crisp lake, but at night the great, soaring windows were dead black.

"Where are they?"

"Some units are twenty and more kilometers in, that's where."

"Not our soldiers."

"Who?"

"The prisoners. I'm curious. How do you accommodate three hundred thousand people like that—I mean, just the water they need for drinking, it must be tons. And the wounded, and food—all of that."

He rushed to the window and glared out, his hands tightly clasped behind his back. Then he whirled around. "You are the great-grandson of General Albert Weber?"

"Indeed. He was my father's grandfather."

"Then you know what a wonderful Indian killer he was."

The general had a scalp collection which was kept in our attic in the St. Louis days. I remembered them all too well, in boxes neatly labeled according to the tribe and band that had harvested them. (There were apparently characteristic techniques dictated by custom.) We boys used to go up and hang them out on the rafters, some blond, some dark.

"I do."

"Are you not proud? He was a genius of the white race, was he not? Opened Wyoming and the Dakotas, drove those squat, ignorant savages to ground and shot them dead, yes? Didn't he?"

"He was one of the bloodiest, yes."

"And what of the buffalo? What did he do there?"

"He and Sherman killed them all."

"And why, Willy?"

"To starve the Indians."

"So you could have the land, and you took it, the white Americans, Germans and Swedes and English and Irish, you went out in that land and worked and built your magnificent country. And I'm proud! I'm proud to know a man in whose veins flows the blood of that noble champion of the white race. A pure Aryan, too. Unlike you."

"What does that mean?"

"Just that your lying, fucking goddamn hypocrisy comes from only one place, which is that nasty little bit of Jew blood running in your veins. Oh, yes! I have protected you, Willy. Himmler wanted you dead, dead, dead! 'Take the gold and kill the Jew,' he told me." His eyes all but burst out of his face. He screamed, "Shit! Shit on you!"

"Now, wait a minute. I haven't even said anything yet. I just asked a question."

He rushed up to me. "You stand right there. Don't you move an inch." He drew his hand back and slapped me across my face. I stood it and I swallowed the anger that it brought up in me because I still thought that I could help by being so close to him—that some way, some time, I could either trip the bastard up or convince my newly discovered superiors to let me kill him.

He slapped me again. He tossed his forelock out of his eyes and strutted.

"There now, son, that's chastisement. Do you accept the wisdom of your father, who is showing you your moral weakness?"

I took a breath. Another.

"Say it!"

"I do."

"Apologize to me."

"I apologize to you."

"I apologize to you *my father*. Say it!"

"All right! Yes! My father! I apologize to you, my father."

"Of course we're not going to give them food and water, no more than you gave it to the Sioux and the Comanche and the Kiowa, and for the same reason. What is that reason, son?"

The agony was amazing. The Indians—it was an extraordinary crime—my own grandfather was one of the worst of those criminals—and yet our whole country rests on it. It does!

"The reason!"

"The reason—"

"Go on?"

"We couldn't have settled the land if they were there." I could barely mutter those true, terrible words.

"Precisely. We are going to do for our savages exactly what General Sherman and General Weber did for yours, which is to deprive them of all means of survival. Then we will colonize that beautiful land with which in the thousands of years they have had it, they have done no more than your red Indians did with the golden prairies you took from them. I can see now in my mind's eye fine German farms stretching forever, and we Germans never hungry again. Never, never, never!"

I was silenced. It's true enough that one evil does not justify another, but it certainly undercuts the force of an argument. I had no way to debate his logic.

I remembered singing "Home on the Range" on autumn nights when I was young, out on the prairie at the end of a deer-hunting day with fine racks strapped to the hoods of our great Cadillacs and Pontiacs and DeSotos, and the venison dressed by the servants and stored in the trunks, and the girls close because the night had grown cold. Here is what we would sing:

"The red man was pressed from this part of the West
He's likely no more to return,
To the banks of Red River where seldom if ever
Their flickering camp-fires burn."

Now Hitler smiled at me, and warmly. He knew that the smile that followed an outburst was a powerful tool. Sure enough, I felt a flood of relief.

"Willy, there are thirty million Germans ready to go. That's flat. And do you know why? All of your wealth rests on the bones of savages. As will ours. In a sense it's regrettable, of course. Lives are lost and it's unpleasant."

He touched my face.

"My boy, your cheek looks like the skin of an apple!"

"You have a strong right arm, Alf."

"It's the saluting, no doubt." He ran his fingers along my jaw. "I haven't broken anything?"

I opened and closed my mouth. "It still works."

He threw himself against me. "Hold me," he murmured. "Just a moment."

I put my arms stiffly around him. The usual odors wafted up, greasy, strange.

"Willy, Willy, Willy, I want even champagne. Yes! I want champagne." He was still for a moment. "Your arms—you're so strong, my son." He leaned his head against my chest.

He stepped back, all but shaking me off. He turned back toward the dark of the sleeping house.

"Hello! I'm home!" he shouted into the silence. "Wake the house, Willy, push the servant buttons, we need to have a triumph!" He hurried into the hall and shouted up the stairs. "I'm home!"

Lights came on. A ghost floated past the balustrade above.

It was Eva and as she appeared at the top of the stairs, I saw a glory of womanhood, her red-blond hair flowing about her face, her body caressed by a dress like a concealing memory. She came running down and threw her arms around him and kissed him hard.

Silently, Carlotta followed. Eva was in white, she in black, but the designs of the dresses were identical. I had never seen them before but I knew who had made them, of course. Again, it was the genius Schiaparelli. One woman light and full of day, tripping along in dancing slippers, the other darkly striding on tall spikes.

What a thrilling theatrical the two of them presented, and the knowledge that they had conceived it and arranged it and gotten the designer to help them made it all the more exciting to both of us. I had to contend with my trousers. Alf flushed redder than my cheek.

"Sh!" Hitler said, "the others—where are they?"

"Nobody's talking but you," Carlotta said.

"That's right. Oh! You two. My goddess and her—" He paused. He looked upon Carlotta with sheep's eyes, his *rotzbremse* puffing out with his smile. "—her genius."

"I'm smart," Eva said.

Carlotta laughed.

"You have the manners of a pig."

"And you're as arrogant as a peacock, Eva. But the female peacock is very plain. Don't forget that."

"No squabbling on my night of triumph! I've already fought with Willy."

Both women looked to me.

"It's finished," I said. "We're all over excited."

Fredericka and the girls had now appeared. They were in their dressing gowns. They were not so often around Hitler and weren't used to his preference for the night.

I said, "Come into the salon. There must be a toast." I rang for Fritz.

A few moments later, Fritz rushed in wearing a sagging boiled shirt, a cockeyed tie and a wrinkled tailcoat. He looked like Emmett

Kelly. To his credit, though, he had a service of champagne and caviar, all correctly presented.

"A *bombe*," Hitler shouted, "at once, a huge *bombe*!"

Fritz rushed away. Did we have a *bombe*? I'm not much for sweets, so I wasn't sure.

We had a solemn toast. Hitler screwed up his face after sipping and peered into his glass. "Is this all right?"

"A *Cliquot* '18? I can assure you, it's very much all right. In any case, I bought it from Hermann and he knows his wine."

He grimaced at it. "If you put sugar in this stuff, it explodes. But anyway—" He raised his glass. "To the German soldier!"

We all repeated, "The German soldier!"

We sat before the fire, which Maria was building up very nicely.

I let my heart sink. If Stalin had been forewarned, it hadn't helped, had it?

There was a silence, more than a little awkward. Finally Papa Fritzl said, "I gather that it's been a good day."

"I got three hundred thousand captives before the sun set. And we are running after them still, right through the night." He slapped his fist into his palm. "That's how it went!"

As he described the day's battle with his usual—and astonishing—grasp of detail, I for the first time came to really understand the stunning scale of the thing.

His gruff voice rattled of the names of units—the 292nd at Seklatchoa, the 263 reaching Bran'sk in a matter of hours. "And all on the other side of the Bug. 'We must cross the Bug on the first day, they told me, or we will be in trouble. Well, how about the first hour? Yes, it's true. And do you know why? Because of me! Oh, yes! Of course, but who else?"

"It went like this. I saw a few months ago—oh, perhaps last December, I don't know—that the Finns had possession of all sorts of captured Soviet materiel. I just glanced at the inventory and saw it immediately. Thirty thousand Red uniforms!"

"So, do you know what that means? Can anybody guess?"

He waited. I knew that they must have been used to costume

commandos, but said nothing. Steal the narcissist's moment from him and he will not forgive you.

"Of course you can't! It takes a certain cast of genius—military genius—to see a thing like that. I bought them at once."

I noticed, as he spoke, that his eyes kept flickering toward Carlotta. She noticed, too, and another development of Sexschaparelli's design became evident as she crossed her legs and the dress slid off her knee, leaving that beautiful object gleaming in the soft lamp light.

"The way it is, at three-fifteen in the morning, thousands of commandos crossed the river. The Russians thought nothing of it. They didn't see the intelligence in our eyes, of course, not those meatheads. Savages, yes, Willy?"

I nodded.

He waved a hand in my direction. "Let me tell you, Willy understands what we're about. He did it to his red Indians. Shot, starved, burned, imprisoned in camps where they remain to this day. And the result? 'Amber waves of grain,' yes, Willy?"

I nodded.

"And we shall have them, too!"

He said to Fritzl, "How about you, will you farm?"

Fritzl was a teacher. "Um, I suppose, yes."

"Then I grant you a hundred thousand hectares in the new Germany!"

"I don't know the first thing about farming."

"Then find out, you damned sloth!"

Fritzl straightened. "Yes, Leader!"

"Anyway, what a perfect day for campaigning it was and we took full advantage from the Black Sea to the Baltic. Can you imagine? Tremendous! Oh, so many extraordinary stories. I can tell you now of the 18th Panzer Division, a clever business I thought of. How, I asked myself, am I to get tanks across a river where there is no bridge?

"Well, simple enough! I had the 18th Panzers fitted with breathing hoses for the engines and one-way exhaust valves, that's all. And there they went, right across the Bug in a mass of bubbles."

"Wonderful, just wonderful! And another thing, can you believe this, the Russkis went up in fruit trees to snipe at us. Right out in the middle of orchards. There could be no escape, and they were cut down wherever they did it, up and down the line. Oh, yes, all of them! What stupid creatures they are. Even more so than the Red Indians, more subhuman than those lumps!"

I guess he had forgotten about his favorite Karl May hero, the compassionate and daring Indian Winnetou. He used always to say that when he and his friends played at Karl May stories in the forests around Linz, that he would prefer to play the Indian.

I replied to him, "I would imagine so."

"Indeed, it is so! No imagination needed. And in any case, how can creatures like that even have imaginations? That's a human characteristic."

I assume that Tolstoy, Dostoyevsky, Tchaikovsky, Bulgakov and all the others had been shot out of the fruit trees along with the other savages. Pushkin.

He paused, then stood and paced to the dark windows. "No stars?"

"It's the blackout paper you're looking at."

"Oh, of course, what am I thinking?" He looked from one of us to the next. "My family! How proud of me you must be!"

"So proud," Eva said. "What an accomplishment! And did Stalin get taken prisoner?"

"Stalin?"

"In Moscow. We've taken it, have we not?"

Hitler smiled, went over to her and laid his hand on her head. "My dear woman, that must wait a few weeks. But let me tell you this. We will take Moscow. We will take it all. Those simple creatures cannot stand against us any more than the Indians stood against Willy's ancestor. Am I not right, Willy?"

"I am sure of it, Wolf." (The Brauns did not know him as Alf, only Eva and Carlotta and myself.)

"As am I. We will have our land and make it heavy with the fruits of the tree and the field, just like the plains of Iowa and Illinois,

Nebraska and Kansas. Even though I am staring into blackout paper tonight, I can still see the vision before me of those broad plains swept by rain, full of golden wheat, and the German tables laden with bread and surrounded by children, blond and strong and pink!"

"And even a few with brown hair and big noses, I hope," Carlotta said.

His eyes went wide. His mouth dropped open. Then his hand went to his nose and he roared out a great guffaw. "Let's hope very few of those!" He surveyed us, his expression curiously innocent, like that of a child who believes he has done right, but bears a deep, nagging doubt. "Well," he said, firmly shaking it off. "We will have Russia. We will have that glorious, golden plain. I am never wrong and I am not wrong now. I am never wrong!"

# 16

The idea that Hitler might be defeated had become impossible to believe. I felt absolutely emasculated. I was a failure, a rich, useless drone.

But nobody can imagine the future, nobody can know before it happens that it would be possible one day to look up and see a thousand bombers plunging across the Berlin sky, or smell the hideous sour-sweetness of the long rows of bodies in the streets, or, at the end, hear the women screaming in the rape rooms that were set up by the Red Army in any ruined apothecary or hairdresser's salon.

Carlotta was in one of those rooms for a week, instructing the other girls how to take it in the ass, how to take it in the cunt again and again and not be torn apart, how to lean out of a slap so it doesn't bruise, how to lie as soft as a jelly beneath pumping bones.

But who the hell cares, am I right? Because they were Germans and they knew, they all goddamn good and well knew. Of course they did. Toward the end, Goebbels made sure they did. This way, they would fight and fight and fight because they believed that for the Germans surrender was death. The Morgenthau Plan was trumpeted by every organ at his command. "Germany to be left an agricultural region! Depopulated! This means you and the ones you love!"

It is a testament to the humanity and deep goodness of the American people and their leaders that the Marshal Plan was enacted instead. It is testament to the wisdom of that plan that Germany is coming back so fluently, recovering at last the genius of the civilization that the Nazis trampled down.

But it was not that way then. If there are folk tales in hell, they are stories from the Germany of those days.

Sometimes I dream that I am slipping into the night air, flying like the Lost Boys over the chimneys of the Darling house, but it is not the Darling house and the smoke does not smell of toasty coal.

The collectors of hair, of teeth, of spectacles, of shoes and belts. The collectors of bones and the grinders of bones, round and round their mills whirring and the dust on their skin, the dust in the air, men breathing the dust of their sons and wives and daughters. The spreaders of bone dust bending along the rows of cabbages, and the heads growing rich and green in the short, exquisite summer of the Polish plain.

"I've been a whore all my life and here's how you take it in your ass and don't let him rip your bunghole when he pistons you. And here, this one, she's bleeding from her cunt. Hold her upside down for half an hour. If it stops, she lives, if it doesn't put her out in the snow, death by cold is quicker."

She saw old women screwed until their hearts gave out. She saw girls screwed until they were in pieces on the slick floor. She herself was broken, her precious womb destroyed. She had dreamed of four of us, we two and our boy and our girl. No.

In London later, when she was saved but still little more that a pair of owl eyes in a cloud of mink, she said to me, "There are dead inside me, my love, many dead." As those eyes gazed across the ocean of a restaurant table, I thought, 'they stare into a dark I cannot see.'

Ah, but that was later. All later. Wars also have their summers.

By August of 1941 it appeared to me that the Germans were going to win their war in Russia in a matter of weeks.

Despite the danger, I was cutting back *praseodymium* shipments again. I communicated to Fred Miles in my office in New Mexico from Bern, but I dared not be explicit. He had to read between the lines that I wanted him to start shorting Hitler again.

Not long after we resumed this sabotage, Paul Dukes made me aware that the Abwehr was looking more deeply into the matter. British agents in New York reported that an Abwehr team had appeared there, and then travelled on to New Mexico.

The only thing I knew of there that might concern them would be my mining operation. Meanwhile, month by month, British aircraft production was rising while German production continued to decline.

Hitler had come to blame the fact that he'd had to withdraw from the Battle of Britain on the production shortfalls. Initially, he'd blamed me, but I had managed to confuse him about why they were occurring by pointing out that Goering's ridiculous Air Ministry so chaotic that it was a mystery that they produced any planes at all.

Fritz Todt, the very efficient Minister of Armaments, had sent me a letter complaining that I was failing to provide the amount of rare earths agreed, which was entirely true. I had played the supply problems card as convincingly as I could. But they could read newspapers. Todt knew that I was lying.

A second letter demanded that I make good the contract or face sanctions in the form of reduced and, eventually, withheld payments. If I didn't comply, those sanctions would cause me to end up myself paying for the shipments I was sending to Germany, the last thing I cared to do. The threat amounted to a gun at my head.

Worse, if Hitler discovered that I wasn't just shorting him, but sending the praseodymium to the British, that gun would be fired right into my brains.

There was only one thing to do. I had to show Todt books that confirmed that Germany was getting all we could produce, and also provide an affidavit from Fred that would affirm that we were doing all that could be done to maintain and increase production. But no doctored books existed and Fred had no idea that they might be needed in Berlin. I dared not call him or cable him something so explicit and damning, and therefore decided to travel back to America, this time on the Pan American flying boat that was then offering a service between Lisbon and New York.

I remember it as a decent air service, the first one I'd been on that had food anything close to that on the Graf Zeppelin, but with the added advantage that the thing was both heated and air conditioned, not just the latter—if you could call the constant draft in the Zeppelin interior air conditioning.

Over the period from the late summer of '41 and into the autumn, I was in America, and what a relief. Living under constant oppression is like living in constant pain. Until it is gone, one does not realize how debilitating it actually is.

Under such circumstances, sighting the Statue of Liberty from the window of that droning airplane was among the most moving moments of my life. We soared past her at close range, past the torch raised in the sunlight, and I thought of 'yearning to breathe free,' and of all the people who have brought themselves here in abnegation and fear and made lives that were worth living, and contributed in each small way to the immense triumph that is our nation of immigrants. I thought also, dismally, of the Indians and General Weber and the dark side of our country.

The world is not made of black and white anything. It is a place of compromise, and often a cruel place. America is ours, yes. We took it. And here I was striving to prevent the Germans from doing that precise thing in Russia. All moral truth is moral compromise, I told myself. That our evil exists on the tumbledown reservations and in the sorrows of those hearts did not mean that Hitler was justified in doing the same.

Gosh, though, his argument had been silencing to me.

I thought of the president in the White House, and how it is that I have never known of a president who failed to reflect the dignity that is associated with that august office. There is something about winning a fair vote cast by a free people that causes a man to rise to his best state, I think.

My first mission was to go to Washington and again attempt to meet with Roosevelt. By now, I was certain that the Jews were to be wrecked in every place the Germans controlled. You could see it in the streets, in the sadness in their faces, and their children, wide-eyed, looking about, confused. Once I saw a little one laugh when a storekeeper struck his father's backside with a broom. The father had ambled away like Charlie Chaplin so that his child would not be frightened.

The reintroduction of the yellow patch was occurring all over the Reich, the form of a Star of David against a yellow background being mandated. Many Jews, to enable themselves freedom of action as best they could, were wearing it on their backs. Later, of course, it became mandatory to wear it as an armband. The yellow patch had been off and on part of German life since the time of the Holy Roman Empire, and to see it reappearing in modern civil society was most disheartening.

Setting foot on American ground was truly wonderful. I could see the other transatlantic travelers around me literally blossoming, some of them—the four lucky refugees—shedding tears. To fly on that plane took not just wealth, but great wealth, and getting as far as Lisbon with enough money to fly had been, in each case where it happened, a miracle.

Others, like me, were businessmen hurrying along to waiting cars. In my case, a humble Skyview Cab.

I didn't stop in New York longer than to have a bath and a meal. The next morning was rather rainy, so I decided not to risk the planes and took the train to Washington.

Once again, I found myself ignored by the White House. I could manage a meeting with the Prime Minister of the British Empire, but not my own president. He had very many more supplicants than me, I suppose.

I managed to get a few minutes with Cordell Hull. I was still a bit worried about the Nazi sympathizers in the State Department, but some of Hull's anti-Nazi statements reported in the press had reduced my concerns. At the time, also, Hull's own anti-Semitism was not publicly known. By 1941, he knew very well what was happening to the Jews of Europe. He didn't need me to tell him a thing. In '39, he had refused to allow the Jewish refugees aboard the liner St. Louis to disembark in the United States, thus sending them back to Germany to their eventual deaths under the Nazis. In 1940, he was told frankly by Henry Morgenthau, the Treasury Secretary, that a group of Romanian Jews would be killed if they were not given visas and allowed to come to the U.S. Morgenthau attempted to facilitate their applications, but Hull prevaricated—in my opinion, with the clear knowledge that his delays would lead to their deaths. And indeed, that is exactly what happened to them.

So I was deceived by the public Hull, never imagining that the private one was actually facilitating the murder of Jews.

I recall that he was a dour man with an ugly air of arrogance about him. He'd been raised in a log cabin in Tennessee, and had brought with him from that hard childhood, it seemed, not the equanimity of an Abraham Lincoln, but the bitterness of a Simon Legree. This man, who was instrumental in the founding of the United Nations, had a side to him that was, quite frankly, vile.

Fortunately, I did not importune with him on behalf of the Jews. Anti-Semite though he was, I was at least right about his not being a Nazi sympathizer. Indeed, he had been disgusted, according to the newspapers, by the shrill anti-American propaganda that had come spewing from Goebbels' organs after Fiorello LaGuardia had spoken out against the regime's anti-Semitism. Goebbels had gone so far as to denounce American women as prostitutes, this man who spent so many of his evenings surrounded by German ones.

When I entered Hull's office, he did not stand, but rather sat with his arms folded, glaring up at me from beneath a wilderness of eyebrows.

"Good morning, Sir, thank you for seeing me."

Silence.

As he did not ask me to sit down, I remained standing. I said, "I have a business that trades with both Great Britain and Germany, and I know both the prime minister and the chancellor. I am here to offer my services."

The eyebrows went up. "What in the world can you mean?"

"I am often in Hitler's presence in social situations. I spend a good deal of time in his private company at his residence in Bavaria, the Berghof. I can offer insight."

"We're not at war with Germany."

"No, but we may be."

"I don't see that happening."

I thought better of mentioning Lend-Lease or the frenetic rearmament that was taking place. I did not think it wise to get into an argument over foreign policy with the Secretary of State.

"If it does happen, though, I want you to know that I am a resource that might become useful."

"The European states employ spies. That's one of the most unattractive things about them. Not to say un-American. We content ourselves with diplomats."

"If war comes with Germany, there will be no American diplomats there."

"And you won't be there, either, young man, because you won't be trading with the enemy. That is illegal now and it will be illegal in the future." Now he did stand up. "Good morning."

"Remember my name. I can easily be contacted through the Weber Shipping Organization in Los Angeles."

As he remained silent, I also wished him a good morning and left. He really was one of the most unpleasant men I have met, displaying all of the pugnaciousness of Churchill but none of the guile, and certainly none of the wit. To this day, I find it difficult to respect him even given his distinguished career. He is among the men who had a chance to help the suffering Jews and instead blocked their way. Quite frankly, I think it's unforgivable. For my own failure in this regard I fault myself. But I did try, and would have given my life to my effort, had that fate confronted me.

I was certain that war was coming to America. I thought it might start any day. Given his public statements, Roosevelt was just waiting for a provocation. Should an American ship be torpedoed with great loss of life, for example, I felt that he would declare war.

After that dreadful meeting, I thought to fly back to New York and connect with Maddy. But if I did, I feared that I would see *Vati*, too and I couldn't bear it, not now that I had this grotesque new father and was giving him a perverted version of a son's love. Perverted, yes, but still love, and not only that, love that in its pure form belonged to my real and honored father. I felt a traitor to my own blood and the man I revered most in the world.

God, to tell you the truth, I didn't think I could bear to look at him. My shame was agonizing. That's the only description I can give it. Agonizing!

How I wish now that I had seen them, for I would not lay eyes on Maddy again until *Vati's* funeral in 1946, after which our relationship was forever changed. She blamed me for his suicide. As this is not entirely wrong, I was never been able to find my way to reconciliation. To this day, I wonder if she took *Pole Star* on that misbegotten circumnavigation to escape from the humiliation of being my sister. I can only say that I am grateful that she left young Albert in school at Andover when she did, as he would have been lost, too, and with him every scrap of family I have in the world. As it is, though, there are now Albert's boys and one day they will have children, too. I'll be a great-uncle, albeit of Martins rather than Webers, and at a distance. But they will be in the world. That is my blessing and my comfort.

Given that I lost my whole family to the curse of Adolf Hitler's friendship, I would argue that cliché of the Faustian Bargain is entirely true. From the day I signed Hitler's contract in his Chancellery office to this, there is an unbroken line of accumulating wealth. Right now, I think that I am worth more than two hundred million dollars, if you can believe it, and that's just the liquid assets. If everything was sold up tomorrow—every house, every ship, every office building and warehouse—I am sure I would clear something like half a billion dollars.

Despite all of my wealth and all the power I had as a confidante of Hitler's, I could not turn the great rudder of the world. The dark ship plunged heedlessly on through the blood ocean that is named History.

So, instead of trying for another reconciliation, I went west, telling myself that speed was of the essence—which turned out to more true even than I suspected.

When one is living a complex life, things like the danger of arrest and death can seem quite abstract. But my actions under German law —and for that matter, American law—were criminal. I was defrauding the Reich, pure and simple. Even if I was in the United States, if they entered a criminal bill against me I felt sure that they could get an extradition order. And it was pretty clear to me that they would have no difficulty getting Cordell Hull to execute it. He'd ask Edgar Hoover to arrest me and back I'd go, this time in manacles.

On my way to California, I stopped briefly in San Antonio to reaffirm my contacts there. I flew to Dallas, then took the Katy Railroad south, as San Antonio then had no municipal airfield. This proved to be a delightful service in bright red cars called the Katy Flyer. I enjoyed a good luncheon while passing through the flat Texas landscape in the blaze of summer. I particularly recall the Katy Coronets, little cornbread fritters served in a silver basket. To this day, they can be had at the San Antonio Country Club, as can the Gold Brick Sundae, also from that service, which consists of ice-cream with a type of Louisiana chocolate poured over it that becomes a shell when hardened. They are all that remains of the M.K.T.'s Texas Special trains, gone since '59.

I found my San Antonio friends markedly less enthusiastic about Hitler than they had been on my previous visit.

"Why that yellow star? That is mean," was Sam Spiers' comment. I had to agree. I suggested to him that he cash in his Mefos. He was surprised by this. "Hitler's winnin' the war, and I'm makin' a nice piece of interest. They're about the best thing I have after the oil."

"They might not last."

"What does that mean?"

"It means that Russia is a big place."

I spent a few days in that affable city, which has since become my second home. I played a good bit of Bridge, thank God, and sipped bourbon sours on the breezy veranda at the San Antonio Country Club. Nobody spoke of Hitler, which, in that world, was really the same as an insult to the man. Goebbels' shrieking about the "nigrifcation" of America and his atrocious characterization of American women had not gone unnoticed.

In their very polite and southern way, the San Antonians attempted to gently steer me away from what they thought of as my approval of Hitler.

One evening at the Spiers' home, I found myself dining with Ephraim Frich, the rabbi of the local synagogue, Temple Beth-El. I don't know how I had been described to him, but he was stiff and unforthcoming, confining his conversation during the dinner to generalities and bland pleasantries. He made only the briefest reference to relatives in Germany. Spiers at once suggested that I might be able to help them get out. Of course, I agreed at once to do whatever I could. The one thing that could still move Jews about in the world of 1941 was money.

I was given a list of addresses. When I returned to Germany, it turned out that none of them had ever heard of Frich. It was simply a random group of desperate Jews who had written to friends and relatives in America asking for help. I got most of them down to Italy, seven families in all, equipped with enough money to grease the rails further along. I do not know what happened to them after.

In any case, after hearing of my willingness to help, he asked me for a lunch. We met the next day at a local German delicatessen called Schilo's, which is there to this day and still much the same. Sauerkraut, pea soup and bratwursts.

I committed him to absolute secrecy and told him as much of my truth as I dared. He hardly needed to be warned about the situation of the Jews of Europe, but I said to him that it was liable to be worse than anybody could imagine. By way of that, I also told him of the fate of Ludwig Pappenheim and showed him *Judaea Capta*.

"Rabbi Frich, Herr Pappenheim is only one of thousands, I believe."

"How many thousands?"

"I have seen Jews hanged in Poland simply for being what they were. I think it could be very many."

"Ten thousand? As many as that?"

That seemed a large number. But the camps were large places. "I don't know," was the only answer I could give. And what if I'd said a million? Five million? Or all?

He wouldn't have believed me. In point of fact, I wouldn't have believed myself. Such a thing couldn't be comprehended. It never even occurred to me, not until years later, on an awful October night in the Berghof.

So I left the man with the number ten thousand. At the time, it seemed a disgraceful lot of innocent people, and I feared that I was exaggerating.

I returned to Germany in October of 1941, armed with Ditto copies of all my ledgers from 1937 on—except, of course, that they were all fakes. Fred and I had created them over the summer. Like any good salesman—and Fred is a fine one and a fine businessman—he can work a good fiddle.

The real books were now being kept in the safe. I thought that the Abwehr team might well visit the office at night, and I didn't want them to find them. The originals of the faked set were kept in a glass fronted bookcase in the bookkeeper's office.

We also concocted memoranda to file from Fred documenting continuing shortfalls in production dating from 1938 and blaming strikes, equipment failure, seams playing out and so forth.

On November 1, I arrived back in Berlin. On October 3, Hitler had made a broadcast saying that the Soviet armies were essentially destroyed and that the war would soon be over.

But by the 15th, it was raining across the whole of the Moscow *Oblast*, and, in fact, throughout western Russia. What would become the second terrible winter of the 1940s was already developing.

When I landed at Templehof on a plane of the Hitler Flight that had been sent to Paris for me (I had flown up from Lisbon on the German Diplomatic Service aircraft), I found the city enveloped in a clammy fog, with wind whipping in from the east. I thought immediately that this was a bad sign for the Germans. Since Hitler's optimistic pronouncement in October, there had been no further word about what was happening at the gates of Moscow. So, clearly, the *Wehrmacht* had not taken the city.

I went at once to the Armaments Ministry, lugging my books with me in two large brief bags. As one could not in those days rely on air schedules, I hadn't made an appointment with Todt, but he didn't keep me waiting.

He was, however, in a dark mood. As I went through Fred's counterfeit reports, I offered the good news that we were hoping to increase production in a few more months. A lie, of course.

"Hoping?" he said in a dull, disinterested voice.

"Well, expecting. But you never know in America. Strikes are common."

He muttered something to himself, then rose up from behind his desk and motioned to me with his hand to follow him. As we walked down one of the ministry's endless corridors, he said, "Herr Weber, it is not possible for us to win this war, so while I thank you for the effort you're making, you must understand that it's quite useless."

As one learns very quickly to do in a dictatorship, I made no suggestion of assent. "Does the boss share this opinion?"

"More or less. He's trying a last throw at Moscow, but the weather —" He waved a hand. "So cold petrol freezes, can you believe it?

"I've never heard of such a thing."

"Gehlen—do you know him, the intelligence chief out there?"

"I know the name."

"He gave us bad estimates of Russian strength. Very bad."

Gehlen is another of those secret heroes whose full contribution is undocumented and therefore has never entered history. I believe that Reinhard Gehlen was somehow aware of Churchill's policy of bleeding the dictators and faked his intelligence estimates in order to make sure that the Germans would not win, but also that their defeat would cost Russia dear oceans of blood.

"Is this Gehlen a traitor?"

"He's an intelligence officer with bad sources. Air reconnaissance that isn't read correctly. Production estimates that assume that Stalin has no factories beyond the range of our aircraft, or armies or any damned thing. To dear Reinhard, Siberia is a wasteland. That, as it turns out, is untrue."

We had reached the end of the corridor. As we turned and walked back, he said softly, "You are to see Admiral Canaris."

I did not like the sound of that. "And why? I have nothing to do with military intelligence."

"You may find that you have more than you think to do with it."

That caused my stomach to do a very swift roll, I can tell you. There are moments in any life when one feels very far from home and very alone, and this was one of them.

"All right, then I shall. But I'm curious. What can he want of me?"

He shook his head. We were back at his office. "Thank you for the books. I'm sure they're quite in order."

"Please read them."

"Why? If they weren't in order you wouldn't have returned."

"I'll get the supplies up, you'll see."

As he went through his door, he nodded vaguely. Then the door was shut.

I was tired, very tired, suffering from my usual airplane fatigue. I had managed little more than an occasional doze since I'd left New York four days ago. I'd wanted to stop in Paris, but Hitler had enjoyed the Crillon so much that he had made it *Wehrmacht* HQ. Some damned general or other now occupied the suite I and my family had been staying in for most of my life. In fact, some general or other now occupied every suite.

I'd been assigned a car from the Leader Motor Pool and, since I had no message from Canaris, went at once to Wannsee. Right now I was ready for Maria to draw me a bath and Fritz to pretend that he could valet me. Since I'd discovered their traitorous activities, as far as I was concerned, those two brave souls could do no wrong.

As soon as Fritz opened the door, I smelled cigarette smoke—good tobacco. In fact, my tobacco.

"Carlotta? Eva?"

"Fraulein Carlotta is in the solarium," Fritz said. Then, accusingly, "She's made me tear down the blackout paper."

I hardly heard him, I was running. And there she was in palest green, her legs crossed, her knees gleaming, her face turning to me, eyes full of the powdery intensity central to her astonishing beauty.

She leaped up and jumped into my arms. A long, wracking sob shook her. “Willy, you’re home, my darling. *Home*, oh, I never thought you’d come back.”

“Of course I’d come back.”

“Who would come back from America? Only a complete idiot.”

“Or someone in love with a marvelous woman.”

She leaned back and peered at me. “And?”

I took her chin in my hand and kissed her. We stood in an embrace. Then, with her usual flare for the romantic moment, she leaned around me and shouted, “Eva! He’s here! You can come down, I’m calling truce. Truce, Eva!”

“What truce, what are you talking about?”

“From one to six she’s upstairs, I’m downstairs. We share the house, but not the same parts at the same time. We’re trying not to kill each other.”

“Oh, good, I’m glad to hear that.”

The next thing I knew, there was a clatter on the grand staircase and Eva appeared. She also flew into my arms.

“Willy! Willy! Oh my God. Oh, dear God!”

Carlotta said, “Don’t exaggerate, it makes you look a fool.”

“Shut up, you.”

I laughed. “So I see you two are still in love. That’s one nice thing.”

Carlotta wiggled a finger. “She’s in love with this.”

“How dare you!”

“First, I desperately need a bath. Then we go to Horcher’s.”

“Oh, not Horcher’s,” Eva said. “Hermann might be there.” She raised her chin toward Carlotta. “He hates her.”

“I hope he is there. I’ll spit in his fucking food.”

Ah, I was home, home for sure!

Actually, I thought it might be rather pleasant at Horcher’s if the Goerings were there. Eva hated Emmy, as I have mentioned, and

Hermann obviously detested Carlotta. So any time Eva and Carlotta were confronting the fat and his spouse, their battle with one another was put on hold.

We went upstairs and it turned out that I didn't need any maid service or valet. The girls got me unclothed and dipped into a hot tub *tout suite*.

"Want a pipe?" Eva asked when I was deep in lavender suds.

"I'll go right out."

"So what? When you want to burn it off, sniff some coke. You'll go from out to in immediately."

And so it began again, our druggy, careless life, so luxurious and such fun.

I don't recall a dinner. Was there one? I only remember that deep in the night I awoke because of a tickling on my face. When I went into the bathroom to have a look, I discovered that my eyes were pouring with tears. I felt nothing, neither sad nor happy. I thought to myself that my soul was crying.

The next morning, I was summoned to Abwehr HQ in Tirpitzufer Strasse to meet with Canaris. His office telephoned the house at ten o'clock in the morning. Fritz woke me with the call.

It was a deeply clear morning, a radiant sky spreading the illusion of peace in sedate Wannsee. When I arrived in the breakfast room, Eva and Carlotta were sitting across from one another drinking coffee. Waiting for me was the Hitler breakfast.

"Fritz," I called, "can you bring me sausages, a boiled egg and a coffee as well?"

"Of course, Sir."

Coffee was now rare in Germany, but here at home, there was always plenty of everything. I had been issued a permit that allowed my servants to shop in the *Spezielle Lebensmittelgeschaft*, the food commissary reserved for high government officials. For us, it really was as if there was no war, and now that the British bombing had all but stopped, it was easy to live as if the Eastern Front simply didn't exist.

"We thought you took only zwieback and chamomile," Carlotta said sweetly.

I noticed that they were sitting with hands across the table and pinkie fingers entwined. "So, I see that you've once again seduced each other. Did you have a hot night?"

"Actually, fell asleep in the tub," Eva said. "So there was nothing for us to do but play girlie bed-games, which we do every night anyway."

"To be fair, I have been flying for days. Halfway across the world."

"We're not at war with America," Eva said. "Why can't we go and see it? We both want to so much. Take us in the flying boat."

"Alf would not be amused."

"He's never amused, not anymore. Since summer, he's changed completely. He's got that Morrell quack poking him with needles all the time and I think he's killing him. He's stooped! My Alf, can you believe it? Anyway, he's spending too much time in that hole they've dug in Prussia."

"The Wolfschanze?"

"Exactly. When we go, it's to an awful old castle in Rastenberg. He won't let us near his wretched bunkers. 'War is no place for women, blah blah.'"

Carlotta said, "That castle is full of ghostly Teutonic Knights lurching around. You hear unearthly screams."

"It's true, the place is eerie and horrible and Willy, in the summertime, the mosquitoes are a phantasm."

"He wanted her to be naked and walk the halls," Carlotta said.

"I had to cover myself in Dr. Zinsser's Lotion. I smelled like it." She fell silent. Her eyes dropped. "He was disappointed in me."

"She's lucky. Lately I have to wear a leather butcher's apron and clomp around in boots. All my pretty clothes, and off I go lurching around in that junk."

And off I went after a final slug of coffee off to see Canaris.

Abwehr HQ was next to the *Bendlerblock*, the headquarters of the *OKW*. While the *Bendlerblock* was an enormous complex, Abwehr HQ beside it was a narrow, gray shadow of a building, so nondescript that it could be nothing but an intelligence annex.

Canaris did not have the usual enormous baroque office with a huge desk on a dais that one so often saw. He sat at a plain army desk with the standard photograph of Hitler on the wall behind him.

As I entered, he stood up and gave the Hitler salute, which I did not return. "I'm a neutral, remember," I said.

"Please." He indicated one of his office chairs and I sat.

"How may I help you, Admiral?"

He reached into his desk and brought out a folder. Silently, he pushed it across to me. When I opened it, I saw photographs of a familiar office: my own, in Los Angeles. They'd been taken with flash so, just as I suspected, the Abwehr agents had entered in the night.

"Please look through them."

The third one was my safe. It was wide open. Some of the ledgers were still inside. Others were not.

I looked up at Canaris. "What's this supposed to mean? Why would you break into my safe?"

"Herr Weber, we know."

And now here it was. I was caught. I hoped that I was keeping a blank face. I hoped that my crashing heart could not be heard. I hoped that the drought that had entered my mouth would not rasp my voice. "And what is it that you know?"

"Just that you are keeping two sets of books. One for the Armaments Ministry and another for yourself. We have compared the figures. You're cooking your books, Herr Weber."

"The two sets contain identical figures."

He smiled. "You have charged us for more material than we have received, and we have paid."

He said nothing about the British sales. So, did he not know? But no, he had to. He must have seen the truth, it was as plain as day in those books.

"We took photographs of the pages," he said carefully.

"I don't see them here."

"No. They've become lost."

"Lost? So then how can you accuse me of cooking my books?"

"I have the sums." He pushed across a ledger sheet. The numbers from the two sets of books were identical. I no longer understood what was going on here, and so remained silent.

"Herr Weber, get a better safe."

I realized, in that moment, that Canaris was also a traitor to the Reich. He wasn't threatening me at all. He had indeed seen that I was selling to the British, and he was warning me to be more careful.

"Yes," I said, "that sounds a good idea."

"There are other agents in America. Himmler's, for example."

At that moment, had he concluded the meeting, I don't think that I could have gotten to my feet. My knees were jelly.

"It must be extraordinary," he said.

"What, exactly?"

"Would you like water? You sound very dry."

I took the glass gratefully. I wouldn't have minded a stiff whiskey, too, but I didn't say that.

"I was saying, Herr Weber, that your line of work must be extraordinary. May I know how it is that you get the ore you send us through the blockade?"

"Neutral flagged shipping. Mercy crosses. The usual."

"Except that usually doesn't work. But in the case of Weber Shipping, yes. Your ships lead charmed lives, it would seem."

Churchill knew that if supplies were cut off altogether, I would lose my value to Hitler and thus also my usefulness to the British. Also, I suppose, he wanted Hitler to be able to build just enough of an air force to keep himself from too early a defeat.

So my ships did indeed lead charmed lives.

"I'm lucky."

He laughed aloud. "Of course you aren't. There is luck in war, oh yes. But not that kind. That kind of luck doesn't exist at all, in fact. The British let you through."

"What?"

"Oh, don't be silly. Up to this moment, I've thought you one of the cleverest men I've ever met. Don't disappoint me."

"Very well. I do have an arrangement with Churchill. I lie to him and he believes my lies. In return, my ships get through."

"Have you told Hitler of this?"

"Certainly. We worked it out together. It was arranged through a British double agent. As far as I know, at least."

"Who?"

I recognized that I had to be careful here. The wrong answer could cost Paul his life. "Only Hitler knows."

"Not Himmler?"

"Possibly. But I think only Hitler."

"You could help me by finding out."

There, a trade offered. He kept my secret, I gave him Paul. But I had no way of telling where that would lead.

"I will," I said.

"Then we'll revisit this soon." He got to his feet and held out his hand. "No salute," he said, smiling. "You're a neutral."

I stood up and shook his hand. "Thank you, Admiral."

He clicked his heels and gave a slight nod.

A few minutes later, I found myself back on the street and in a state of near collapse. I thought that I must have come face to face with what was probably the most powerful traitor in the Reich, and that he knew that I was also a traitor and had signaled that he would protect me, but at a price. He needed to know the name of that highly placed double agent. I thought, 'He can't be planning to expose Paul, there's nothing to expose. Hitler knows he's a double agent and uses him as such.'

So it was to protect himself from Paul that he wanted to know the name. I wondered if he would kill Paul. If he seemed a threat, he might well do. The Abwehr was liberally supplied with assassins.

Canaris managed to keep up his charade until 1944. At that time, a member of the "intellectual opposition," one Johanna Solf, was having tea parties at which seditious discussions took place. A Gestapo infiltrator, Paul Reckzeh, who attended one of these parties in '43 turned over evidence to Himmler that eventually led to the execution of everyone involved except Herr and Frau Solf themselves, who miraculously survived the war. This became known in the Reich inner circle as "the Frau Solf Tea Party Incident."

It affected Canaris indirectly, due to the fact that a number of high-ranking Abwehr officers were in attendance at the meetings. This, combined with the catastrophic under reporting of Russian strength, caused Hitler to become more and more suspicious. The final straw was when numerous Abwehr officers were implicated in the July 20, 1944 von Stauffenberg bomb plot. The Abwehr was dissolved and Canaris finally executed along with the plotters, even though the evidence against him was indirect.

In my opinion, he did some very brave and important work on behalf of freedom.

But that was all coming later. I was left to wonder, if lost, who had found the damning photographs, or if they were really lost at all, or in some Abwehr vault waiting to be used against me if that became necessary.

When I got home, I found the house filled with roses, its air swirling with their scent.

I have described this house perhaps too little. This is because I have also disguised the name of the family who have regained possession of their property, the same as I have changed the names of other non-historical persons who crossed my path in those times, primarily those who worked against Hitler or who were persecuted by him. The names of the ones who worked with him I have left intact.

I have done this because there is still a substantial Nazi underground, and they are quite capable of carrying out assassinations and so forth.

The front door opened onto a broad oval foyer with a double staircase sweeping down in two great curves from the second floor. The foyer was floored in woods of various types, inlaid in an intricate and elegant geometric design that was copied from a house in Pompeii. In the center of the space there was a magnificent oval table on which was set a broad-mouthed Ming Dynasty bowl worked with images of fish leaping from the ocean. Under the staircase was an archway that led into the sun-drenched sitting room that Carlotta liked to inhabit.

It looked out through many-paned floor-to-ceiling windows onto a view of the back garden and beyond it the lake. Hung in the foyer were two of my Van Dycks that I'd had shipped over from the States, but the house was filled with Watteaus, Ruisdales and Fragonards. Apparently the former owners had been collectors. In the attic, there was a Klimt, one of those brilliant florals of his.

The sun room was done in yellow, with casual cushioned furniture in gay floral patterns. One could lie in there on a chaise and believe, on a sunlit afternoon, that it really was Antibe or Cannes.

The Ming Vase was bursting with deep red, yellow and white roses, and as I walked around to the sun room I saw that more vases had been brought out from the cellar and filled with more of them.

"Is it the Festival of Roses from the South?" I asked Carlotta.

She looked up and said, "I need spectacles, I think."

"Of course, go into town and be fitted. Why the roses?"

She threw her head back and stretched like a sleek feline. "We're happy, and so we decided the house must be filled with roses."

Arms came around me from behind, and Eva whispered in my ear, "You're our best fun. When we're with you, we're so happy."

"Why, thank you, that's very sweet and the house has been transported. It's joyous with the sun and the flowers."

Carlotta said, "We bought five hundred of them."

"Ah, but do you need more? Are there any rooms that lack roses? The toilets, the cellar?"

"I'll have you know that he talked down from twenty marks to ten, so it wasn't even very expensive."

"Twenty marks, no it isn't." Except that it was *per stem*. Ten thousand marks to brighten up the house for a day.

"In the shops a stem is thirty, assuming you can find one."

"She terrified him with her foul mouth, that's the only reason she got a good deal."

"Fuck off, Eva."

They got Fritz putting on fox-trots and we danced in the afternoon light amid the roses.

Eva whispered, "Why not naked? Let's dance naked."

"Poor Fritz, his old heart!"

"Oh, he sees us naked all the time. We run around the house without clothes when you're not here to enjoy us in our dresses."

I sent Fritz away and I could see in his eyes that he was grateful to go. Then we took off our clothes and we danced naked, two graces and a guy.

The sun dropped westward and in the settling light of afternoon, the telephone rang. I grabbed it so that Fritz wouldn't have to come in to our little sorority house.

"Hello, Willy, and why haven't you called me?"

"It's Alf," I said *sotto voce*.

"It's dreary here, the sky is never clear. But tell me, when are you coming?"

"In the morning."

"Oh, excellent. Really excellent! We've got a lot to discuss. I've really needed you. These people here, they all fear me or they're like Speer and Himmler, full of calculation." He snorted. "We'll put our feet up, you and me, and chat."

"I've missed it so very much, Alf."

"You say that—the word 'very'—that's good to hear. These people listen because they must, that's all. I find myself compulsively keeping them up all night simply because I know they don't want to be there."

"Speer adores you."

"Yes, and if I actually was Wotan, he would act exactly the same way toward me. He's a wonderful architect, a genius. He's going to build our Germania! But you can't chat with him. We do not chat."

Hitler was always uncomfortable with the telephone. The fact that he'd remained on the line this long was testament to his loneliness.

I said, "The girls are here with me and we're all completely naked."

"Oh, don't tell me that! Now I'm dying to be there!"

"They filled the house with roses, Alf, hundreds of them. It's like being in the garden of the gods."

"Tomorrow, then. Bring some roses."

"And the girls?"

"Of course, in the castle. I'll come there for a dinner if I can break away."

With that we rang off. I said, "Unfortunately, you're going to be in the castle again."

"Oh, wonderful," Eva said, "I'm so happy."

"At least the mosquitoes are gone," Carlotta said. "Look on good side of it."

When morning came, there was a fog. The weather Hitler had complained of had extended during the night over all of Germany.

Aircraft being grounded, we took a special train which was reserved for officials. It left from the Gesundbrunnen Banhof in the late afternoon so that it could pass through the Polish Corridor during the night. The thing ran like the wind, as Polish partisans were a real danger. Even Carlotta was careful to keep the shades down in our suite.

We dined together on an English beef roast done to a perfect, blushing turn, with a shamefully young *Petrus*, quite unfinished and suffering from being cellared on a vibrating train.

Eva said, "Eat well, Willy. This will be the last meat you see until we're out of Alf's range. He's becoming more and more fanatical about it."

"And everything else. That shitkicking quack's running the show now. He sticks him full of black stuff that smells like Horlicks."

"You get in all the horlicks, you bitch."

"Yeah, and you get the fucking, so don't complain."

"Anyway, it's not available anymore. You can't get Horlick's here."

"Oh, the genius has put two and two together and made four instead of three. I can only congratulate you, Eva, dear."

"I'll make that creep doctor shoot some of his cow shit right into your blood."

"Such a wonderful mood! If you're in your period, Alf's gonna be pissed."

"Oh, shut up."

So off our little circus went, spatting through the hour of the wolf, and onward into his lair.

# 17

When we finally pulled into Gerdauen, it was late evening. We had been slowed by some unknown problem, probably a partisan action along the line. To my dismay, I discovered that, while the girls would be going to the castle, I was to meet Hitler in the Wolf's Lair.

I hated the humiliation of being among the OKW officers. They would show their contempt for the *Hitlerficker* in blank stares and silences. To make matters worse, it developed that I would need to wear a uniform in the compound. I knew that this would only intensify their disgust.

So, while Eva and Carlotta went off to the castle where they could bicker with each other and love each other to their heart's content, I was driven alone through the sodden, gloomy Masurian forest to the *Wolfschanze.*

The *feldgrau* uniform tunic that I wore carried no insignia. In this regard, it was exactly like Hitler's—above any need for insignia.

Kempka had picked me up in Hitler's 770. He'd brought the tunic, which I put on in the car.

"You've come at a good time. No midges now."

"Lucky for me."

"You're the lucky one, always."

Given the unsureness and complexity of my situation, I immediately wondered if he meant more than he said. I remained silent, helplessly letting the acid build in my gut.

We passed through what appeared to be—and was—a trackless, sodden wilderness. Rain mixed with snow and sleet was falling. Hitler had said in the summer that the war would be over by October, so I wondered if the soldiers had winter supplies. Knowing the National Socialists, my best guess was that nobody had thought of that. 'The Leader says the war will be over before winter, so there's no need to spend money on winter clothing.' That's how they thought.

On our way through the forest, we passed signs saying *Askania Werke*. I didn't inquire. Maybe *Askania* had some sort of lens-making facility out here and maybe it didn't.

Kempka said, "And now prepare your eyes for the lens factory!"

"Really?"

"No."

In the end, we arrived at a road barrier manned by SS in tailored uniforms and spectacularly polished helmets. On the other side, looming, camouflaged shadows began to appear, dark structures, their windows shuttered. Here and there, a figure hurried through the snowy mist.

The *Fuhrerhauptquartier* was behind two further barriers.

The complex consisted of squat concrete buildings, dark, square blocks that were mostly windowless. It looked like a village in the land of the dead.

Kempka stopped before a dark, lowering structure, silent. "He's in there," he said. "I'm going to the dining hall. If he wants me, tell him to ring." With that, he stepped away and was immediately enveloped in darkness.

I walked up to the door of Hitler's bunker. A single SS guard stood watch. As I approached, he snapped to attention. Nothing was said. There was no salute. He reached over and pressed a bell-button. From inside, I heard a shrill jangling.

A moment later, the door opened. It was one of his secretaries, Frau Junger.

"Herr Willy, he's been pacing! He'd decided that the train had broken down."

I stepped in to a chamber fitted with thick chairs, a mahogany table and some floor lamps. On one of the gray concrete walls there was a fine Titian, "the Pastoral Concert." I had seen it in the Louvre.

The ventilation system made a dull rumbling noise. Fraulien Junger wore a sheepskin overcoat.

"Willy! Good, I never thought you'd be back. America is far away."

"Not so far with airplanes. From New York to Berlin it was only four days."

"And in the middle of a war! You are a resourceful man. Come, come into my wolf's lair." He nodded to Traudl, who went out the front door.

As I walked behind him into the next room, I saw that Eva was quite right. He was stooped. I also thought that his left foot seemed to be dragging a good bit more than I had previously noticed.

What was taking such a toll on him, the war only, or the war and the quack?

"Sit, sit," he said.

I took a seat. He stepped out. "I've got to brush my teeth," he said. He might to do this time and again, all through the day, but even so, when you got near him and the Hitler odors appeared, one of them was always his sour breath. I don't think even Satan could stink in all the ways that man did.

This room was more intimate, the floor carpeted with a fine Kazakh and some indifferent tapestries covering two of the walls. On the other two were paintings, an Achenbach with mountains and a roaring stream and a Werner Penier of the limitless *steppe* with a tiny farm lost in the middle of that grassy sea. I imagined the German soldiers consumed in that vastness, out there in the cold. Poor fellows.

He returned, stood in the doorway for a moment, then clapped his hands and lifted a smile under the *rotzbremse*. I went to him and embraced him. He leaned his head against my chest, and it was so very pitiful, as if a monster had found solace.

He pulled back, took me by the shoulders and looked me up and down. "Tears, even," he said.

There were tears. When he had leaned on me I had been powerfully flooded with memories of *Vati* and Maddy and *Muti* and happy days of long ago. Sitting together reading Whitman in English, Schiller in German, Rimbaud in French, and Dante in that flowing, supple Italian of his that so enchants the heart. And *Vati's* pride in his children—in me. It was agony for me at that moment.

Hitler said, "You feel your father's pain?"

"Yes," I said, both telling the truth and lying at the same time.

"You have been with Todt and he told you, yes?"

I nodded.

"Let's take off these stupid costumes." He threw off his uniform tunic and I mine. "Sit, come on, we need to face this together."

I sat across from him.

"No," he said, "closer."

The four chairs were arranged in two groups on either side of the table. I sat in the one beside his.

"I understand your books are perfection."

"I have a fine manager."

"Is he with us? Do you know?"

"We're businessmen together."

He was silent for a time. Then he said, "Did Fritz tell you how much it would take for us to win?"

"He said we couldn't."

"And the reason is that it would require an expenditure of five hundred billion marks a year for the next three years at least."

I'd never heard a sum so large even mentioned before "That's beyond comprehension."

"Completely. There's no chance of reaching any such sum. We could print the money, then there we are, back to 1928. But there are things he doesn't consider. I already have nearly two million guest workers and still factories, farms, businesses of all sorts, are screaming for more! Marks aren't bodies. That's what Todt and the others don't understand."

I had to work really very carefully not to let him see any slight indication of the joy I felt in the plight he was describing. Speaking of Schiller, I could literally hear his "Ode to Joy" in Beethoven's gorgeous setting resounding in my head. The soul of my beloved homeland, my Germany, would in the end be released from this monstrosity. I could see it now, a gate opening into the light, but what I could not see was the agony that lay waiting for us on the path to that bright place.

Never forget this: when a demagogue captures a country, he captures its soul. To break his hold, that soul must also be broken, which is the hardest human thing.

"What are we to do?"

He reached his hand out to me. I took it. He leaned back in his chair and closed his eyes. "They asked me for a political solution. You are the only person on this earth to whom I can say, 'help me. Is there one?'"

"A peace with Stalin when we have half his country? I don't think so."

"Then Churchill? I'd rather make that peace anyway." He grimaced, sucking air through his teeth. "Stalin is pushing me back now," he said in a tight, clipped tone. "Maybe in August a peace with him, yes, but not now, you're right. So Churchill? Is there anything there?"

I wanted very much to tell Churchill that the Nazis had concluded that they could not win. I wanted to warn him against any temptation to negotiate. I had come to understand that every single cell of the Nazi cancer had to be eradicated.

I said, "I could go and see."

"Mm. I've thought about that. You can meet with him, yes?"

"I would think so."

"Do you think there's any hope? He seems absolutely fanatical."

"I don't know, frankly. He also hates Bolshevism. He could be tempted by the idea of leaving Stalin in the lurch."

"We would agree to leave the Middle East to him."

"The oil? Can we?"

"I'm going to go against my instincts and let the generals settle into the defensive for the winter. The soldiers have no winter clothing as it is, and the weather's so awful that we can't get any to them. Next spring, I'll run south and take the Caucasus. So, no need for the Middle East."

"Our abandonment of that region would be most interesting to him."

"Also, the Japanese are going to move south. They're going to take the Dutch and English colonies in the Pacific. It won't be difficult for them. They haven't lost a war in 3,000 years."

"And the American colonies?"

He glanced over at me. "What do you imagine?"

"America will declare war on Japan if its possessions are disturbed."

"Indeed. Then I'd be in another situation I want nothing to do with."

I waited for more, but he was silent. Did he know then about the Pearl Harbor attack plan? I have often wondered.

Finally, he spoke again. "So we try. Without the need to guard against England, our requirements will be reduced. Todt's calculations will change." He took his hand back and rubbed his chin. "You know what I'm thinking?"

I didn't know but I did care, very much. He had given me a gold mine of intelligence just now. I wanted more, as much as I could get.

"I'm thinking about the girls."

"Ah, they're at the castle."

"Thank God! How are they?"

"They are fighting as always and wonderful as always."

"Ah. Willy, I need them badly. Carlotta...that relief! And the warm arms of a woman who genuinely wants me."

"So let's go. They're right there."

At that moment, the door to the study opened. Dr. Morrell came in. He strutted along, bursting with officious self-importance.

Hitler jumped to his feet. "How dare you!"

"It's time for your injection, Leader."

"You knock! You go back and knock!"

He opened a black case on the table and withdrew a gold syringe. "This will help you."

"Don't you dare defy me. Do as I say, then we'll talk about whatever the hell it is you've brought."

Morrell paused. He glared at Hitler. Then he closed his bag, turned and left. He did not knock. He did not return.

"There he goes. He just wants to put me to sleep, anyway, and I don't want to go to sleep. I want to go to the girls. He's a genius, though. You should ask him for an examination. He can do wonders, believe me."

"What does he give you?"

He laughed. "I haven't the slightest idea. I have a symptom, he eradicates it. That's how it works. I had dysentery a few weeks ago. Running back and forth, back and forth, I nearly wore holes in my shoes. He confined the illness to a few days. Might have killed me, otherwise."

"We wouldn't want that."

"Now he'll pout, damn him. Morrell! MORRELL!"

He reappeared.

"What is it, a sleeping injection?"

"You have very full schedule tomorrow."

"I have a more important one tonight. My family is here."

"Are you fatigued, then? I can change that."

"Hop me up? I don't need hopping up."

"Very well. If you have any need, call me, I'll be in my rooms."

"Thank you, Doctor."

Morrell withdrew.

"*Shalom bayit*. Do you know it?"

"Yiddish? No."

"Of course not. I heard it when I was a boy. 'Peace in the house.' I don't want Morrell angry with me like everybody else around here. Angry, fearful, pretending. It's sickening. The German is a weakling, and he's the strongest there is!" He stood up and put on his tunic. "Let's go like the wind, Willy Weber!"

As we left, Hitler pressed a button on the wall beside the door, and when we went outside, Kempka was already pulling the car up.

Snow was falling in dense sheets, and its whispering silence filled the air. Everything was covered with its curious glow. No lights shone anywhere, of course. The Wolf's Lair was under the strictest possible blackout restrictions.

Hitler leaned in the driver's window. "The castle, Kempka. Can we do it?"

"We've chained the tires, so yes, I would think so. About two inches are predicted."

We got into the car.

"The meteorological service is as superb as the intelligence service, so hopefully it won't be twenty inches."

"Ha, let's hope for the best, Boss."

"Raise the window, Erich. I'm sorry, but we have to discuss state matters now." He said to me, "I never care to do that. National Socialism is socialism after all." Hitler usually rode in front, and even now, he made sure that his servants often dined with him.

"The night is beautiful here."

"Not before Moscow, though. Those boys are really taking it on the chin. Ten degrees and more below and I can't even get them a few winter coats, not with the railways frozen!"

I reflected with silent disgust—and, at the same time, relief—on the degree of mismanagement involved there. And hubris. Hitler had been so certain that he would win by October that it now appeared he would lose by January.

This was the night of December 6.

"How is she?"

"Eva?"

"I know how Eva is. She writes. Carlotta does not write. I sometimes wonder if she can."

I recalled the heart-rending letters I'd received from her on my recent travels. One of them was simply three pages of 'come home, come home, come home,' repeated again and again in her precise and nicely formed *Sutterlin* hand. She had only the first few years of school. But she was very dedicated to her own mind. The book she'd been reading in Wannsee, for example, was Spengler's *Decline of the West,* which she had pulled out of Hitler's bookcase in his study at the Berghof. In fact, there were piles of his books scattered around in our room, Spengler, Goethe, Schopenhauer, Cicero in parallel text, many others. She longed for the *Allegemeine bildung* that her chaotic life had denied her.

Hitler had leaned far back in his seat and closed his eyes. He said softly, "I have so longed for them. You cannot imagine the relief." He chuckled a bit, then whispered, "I feel so guilty, Willy, and yet I've done nothing wrong. I look and look into myself and there's nothing there. I've done nothing wrong."

I prefer not to give myself credit. It's an unattractive habit. But I must say that I am proud to this day that I managed to suppress the burst of astonished laughter that exploded within me when I heard that fantastic statement.

"You've made a great effort to follow your beliefs. Herculean."

"But exactly! Exactly!" He was quiet again for a time. Just when I thought that he'd dropped off to sleep, he said, "I used to go to the Excelsior for the medicines. Theirs were always the best. And one day, they sent this one to me. She knocked and I opened the door onto a baby Aphrodite. She strode in, glanced around, glanced at me, then dropped down into a chair and said, 'all right, Mister, what's up?'"

"You probably were."

"Oh, you may be sure of that!" Another long silence. "Most of them were frightened of my needs. They would shake and pour with sweat. Not her. I was so embarrassed by myself that I would whisper to them. She said, 'Oh, don't bother with all that mumbling. Just say it. I don't care.'"

"That's Carlotta."

"Through all the women I have ever known, she has been there, the shadow they must not see. Except for Eva. Eva knows everything about me, and yet she stays. And yet, when I see her, I see love."

Theirs was certainly the most tragic love I have ever heard of.

"Do you think I will lose the war, Willy?"

"From what you and Todt say, it seems possible."

"But do you think I will? Personally, do you think that?"

Coming from him, it seemed a very dangerous question, and I answered carefully. "You transformed a wrecked country in to the most powerful state in Europe in six years. You have resources that other men do not possess."

"You should be in the diplomatic service! I should send you to flummox the Turks or somebody."

"I think it's possible that we will lose. Given Todt's expertise."

"As matters stand, he's right. We cannot win."

"As matters stand."

We arrived finally at the castle, a great relief to me. Chatting with him about matters like this felt like defusing bombs. At any moment, he could erupt.

I'd expected some sort of gloomy medieval pile, but instead I found a modern lobby dressed with warm, blond woods and leather furniture, the effect very masculine.

"Alf, this is lovely."

"We refurbished it for the Olympics. Wait until you see the suite."

As we approached his desk, the nodding clerk snorted, opened his eyes, then leaped to his feet.

"Heil Hitler!"

Hitler said, "Open the bar for Herr Kempka and be certain that his room's in order. If anything comes in for me, give it to him. He'll decide if I'm to be disturbed, his decision final."

"Yes, Leader!"

"All right, Ernst, you're free for the night."

"It's not night any longer, Boss. It's morning. Three o'clock."

"Whatever time it is. Nobody comes upstairs. Telephone, don't knock."

"Yes, Leader!"

As we ascended in a lift to the top of the castle, Hitler muttered, "Yes, Leader, no, Leader" in a wheedling singsong.

I thought of how many people lived by those words. Men were giving their lives for him right now, from the gates of Moscow to the sands of Tunisia. Yes, Leader!

We knocked on the door of the master suite. Carlotta opened it.

A vision. Her eyes were so artfully shadowed that their innocence looked entirely and startlingly real. She lifted her lips into a startlingly childlike smile, her teeth appearing like pearls in their trembling blush.

"Well, fuck all, here they are at last. I thought you'd frozen to death out there. I was already planning the funeral. A big coffin and a little coffin side by side." She drew us into the room. "Let's look at you, Alf." She looked him up and down. "You're better." She hugged him. "My boy was sick!"

"Yes, he told me,." I said.

"Don't let that quack of yours kill you, Alf. I'll punish you with a stay in hell if you do."

"Where's Eva? Eva!"

There came distant thudding.

"She's in the closet in the bedroom."

"In the closet? Eva?"

"I put her in there. She was annoying me."

Hitler was taken aback. I confess, so was I.

"Eva," he called, rushing into the bedroom.

Carlotta said, "Key's on the dressing table."

He let her out.

"Oh, Alf, she's a monster, she was trying to suffocate me!"

"Why would you go in the closet? You don't have to obey her."

"She has a gun!"

I was so shocked to hear this that I almost needed to find a chair. She had the gun out of the drawer! With her! I said, "Carlotta, give it to me."

"No."

"Yes!"

"How did she come by a gun?" Hitler asked. There was laughter in his voice, but why? What in the world was the truth, here?

She pointed her chin toward me. "It's his. He hides it in the back of my underwear drawer."

"Willy?"

"Himmler gave it to me for protection when the three of us were alone at the Berghof. Years ago."

"We might need a gun. We're near the front."

"We're seven hundred kilometers from the front," Hitler said. "Now give it over, and apologize to Eva."

She flounced to the dresser and pulled it out from under a stack of panties. "All right! And I'm sorry, I overreacted, OK. Just get off your high horse for once, please, Evie my dear."

Hitler unloaded the pistol. He looked down at the bullets. "Well, well, guess what?" He held out the handful of bullets.

I was mystified. "What?"

"These wouldn't have done much good."

"What do you mean?"

"These are wax, look at them."

Now I did collapse into a chair. The gun had been a trick. If I had tried to shoot Hitler with it, he would have been injured, but only slightly. He certainly would have survived. It was only a test of my loyalty and had never been anything else. And I had come so close, I had been in his bedroom with it in my hand! I was so shaken that I very nearly vomited.

Carlotta pointed a gun finger at me. "Bang bang."

All along, she'd known. They both had. So *now* who did she work for? Was it really him in the end? She'd been with him and keeping his secrets since she was eleven. Maybe she was the most loyal Nazi of them all. But I could not believe that of her. I simply could not, I loved her too much to believe that of my brilliant, beautiful angel.

Hitler tossed the fake bullets in a wastebasket and the matter was forgotten, although not by me, I must say.

Neither woman ever explained why Eva had been shut in the

closet at gunpoint, and Alf and I respected our ignorance of women enough to know not to press the matter.

It was now four o'clock in the morning German winter time, nine in the evening in Honolulu. Two hundred miles to the west of that island, a battle fleet steamed at flank speed toward the horizon, still dark, where the sun was soon to rise.

## 18

The four of us fell to playing about, I suppose. We usually did. As with everything involving Hitler, the pattern never changed. He either went off alone with Carlotta for a time or, if humiliation was to be involved, Evie and I watched. At such times she would get so hot that she would squirm and sweat and color pink. Of course she enjoyed me, too, but he was the man she loved and having him in her, little though he was, was infinitely more pleasurable to her than being excavated by my piledriver.

Looking back, I envy my young self, still innocent enough to take the pleasure that was there. It was guilty pleasure to be sure, but God, what pleasure it was! Power is an aphrodisiac, and both Hitler and Carlotta were extraordinarily powerful human beings. This is why loving them and receiving their love was so delicious. To feel Carlotta surrendered in my arms or see Alf, beet red and begging to be entered—it was an amazing experience. Both of us felt it, both me and Eva. We had a secret that not even they could share. It was the secret of how delicious it was to be needed by them.

Late the next morning under a bright blue sky, Hitler went off to the *Wolfschanze* and its bad news, and Eva and I went skiing.

There were no mountains in that flat, dismal region of East Prussia, so we had to content ourselves with going cross-country in the birch forest that came almost up to the walls of the castle. Carlotta, who had declared Oswald Spengler "a prick-sucking weasel with the brain of a frog," preferred to stay behind and continue to read his book, presumably to confirm that she had chosen the correct descriptive epithet. Hitler was expected back after evening tea, at around midnight. Of course we knew that would actually be more like three, but we were unbothered. We were used to him. It was the secretaries and generals who staggered about the *Wolfschanze* with gaping eyes.

To be fair, he rarely pontificated to us like he did to them. The moment he began, say, his standard discussion of vegetarian cooking, Carlotta ostentatiously went to sleep in his face. If he persisted, she soon started snoring. He would say, 'Are you really asleep?' She would say, 'Yes.' He would say 'I gather that I'm boring you.' She would say, 'Five more minutes of this and I'll be dead. Then you won't have to worry about boring me.'

As Eva and I arrived back at the castle, both of us ready for mulled wine and some time listening to the delightful military request show *Wunschkonzert fur die Wehrmacht*, I saw an unexpected sight, a muddy 770 pulled up at the *porte-cochere.*

"He's back," Eva said, "how surprising."

He was not back. The car was for me. And not only that it was his personal Mercedes with Kempka slumped behind the wheel smoking a cigarette, which he flipped away as soon as he saw me coming.

"Never mind, I don't care if you smoke," I called.

"Shit, then I've wasted a good butt. Get in. He wants you right now."

Carlotta came onto the porch. She was in a sheer blouse and hugged her shoulders in the sharp wind that had come up. "What's this?"

"I'm going back to the fort."

"Aw, damnit."

"Don't kill each other while I'm gone, please."

"We won't," Eva said, "fighting's just a hobby. We do it to pass the time when there's no boy-toy to entertain us."

"That stupid gun. I could have had fun shooting you with it and I didn't know it."

"You shoot me with anything, sister, and I'll see you in prison."

"You would've thought you were dead but it would've just left a bruise. It would've been fun."

"Carlotta, I'm a lot stronger than you are and I'm warning you, the day will come when I put your lights out!"

I got in the car. As we pulled away, I could see Eva rolling Carlotta in the snow. I believe that there's a medical term for their relationship. It's called 'homosexual panic.' The fact that they were incandescent with desire for one another terrified them.

Pleasure shared is always pure. That I was taught at my father's knee, and that has always been my creed.

"You're going too fast, Kempka."

"No, Willy."

If he'd been authorized to tell me anything more, he would have.

We went not to the *Wolfschanze*, but to the Mauerwald OKH HQ about 20 kilometers away. Kempka stopped at "Fritz," the high command's staff center.

"Ok, get out and open my door, Kempka."

"Screw you, Willy. He's in there biting heads off. Watch out or yours'll be next."

We had a gruff, bantering sort of relationship like that. It was how the *Hitlerficker* managed to hold his head up with the intimate retainer. I liked Kempka. When I used to go a lot to Germany in the fifties, I never missed giving him a dinner. We used to laugh a lot. Why not? We weren't bad men. He wasn't, anyway.

I went into the HQ's big map room to find it filled with generals. Hitler was sitting at the far end of the room in his shirtsleeves and glasses. He waved to me to come closer.

As I entered, every head turned toward me. But the familiar contempt wasn't there. No, there was something else. As I crossed the room, I put my finger on it. They were wary.

That scared me.

I'd put my uniform tunic back on, so when I approached him I stood to formal attention, clicked my heels smartly and gave him the salute. Still on the phone, he returned a desultory wave.

Then he put it down. He stood. "The Japanese ambassador reports that they have hit eight battleships. All are either sunk, burning, dead in the water or beached. One, the *Arizona*, has exploded." He looked up at me. Into the silence he said loudly, "Willy, close your mouth."

For a moment, that silence was like the interior of a sepulcher. Then a smile tinkled into his face and the entire room rocked with laughter.

I don't think I ever remembered to close my mouth.

I thought, 'the Japanese attacked us.' But that was in the Pacific, a distant theatre of war. It had nothing to do with the nightmare unfolding here.

"What has Roosevelt done?"

"He speaks to congress soon. We shall listen and find out."

As the speech wasn't rebroadcast on German radio, we listened over the BBC. Most of the men present spoke enough English to understand. Hitler didn't have a word of it. As I heard his words leaping through the whistling static of the shortwave broadcast, I was stirred by the deepest patriotism. It wasn't only Roosevelt's words but the power in them that moved me. I thought of Lady Liberty out there in New York Harbor with her light high and her words for all time, "Give me your tired, your poor and your weary..." and how we Webers had come into her arms not a hundred years ago and been given the chance to lift ourselves up. I thought also of the tragedy of the St. Louis in '39, and the Jews returned to Hamburg and now deported somewhere to the east, and the lines before every American embassy in Europe, and the polite young men saying 'no, no, no' and Cordell Hull exulting in the secret darkness of his soul.

"This is a day that shall live in infamy," Roosevelt said.

"What is it, Willy?"

"He's complaining that they were surprised."

"And he's angry?"

"Very."

"What does it mean? Will he attack us, now?"

I heard him say how "the American people in their righteous might will win through to absolute victory."

I said, "He's equivocating. He sounds indecisive."

"Ah, as I thought. The nigger nation is afraid."

"Yes." I listened. "Now he declares that they are at war with Japan."

"And us?"

"No, not us."

Hitler considered this. "But what do you think? Will he?"

"The speech is over."

"Willy, please think carefully. Give yourself time. If I declare war on him, will he come here? If we only do that and nothing more?"

I thought quickly, feverishly. Roosevelt would not declare war unless provoked, and he absolutely must come into the European conflict. If he didn't Stalin might sue for peace or Hitler, the genius facing hopeless odds, might win after all.

If Hitler didn't declare war, I feared that Roosevelt would not come. So I said the opposite of what I believed to be the truth. "If he declares war, he will come. He'll have to. But if you do it, he will only meet the demands he must."

"Churchill's demands?"

"Churchill has been making demands for a year with no result. He'll react to things like passenger liners being torpedoed, exactly the same as Wilson did. The two men are much alike."

He was silent, then. He stood up. "Gentlemen, we've both got our gentle ladies waiting for us at the castle, so we'll bid you goodnight."

We went out to the car together and began riding. He said to Kempka, "*Wolfschanze.*"

"Not the castle?"

In the dark, his hand slipped close to mine. When I turned toward him, his face was six inches away and he was staring right at me, those baleful eyes a study in, to my horror, desire.

He had hidden his real intent from the soldiers by claiming we were off to see the girls.

I almost retched in his face.

The car went on, its chains clanking, occasionally sliding in the snow.

I have never known what effect our brief conversation had, if any, but his declaration, which I heard on the radio in the castle the next afternoon, was the sweetest music. When he unleashed the American colossus on himself any slight chance he might win was over.

Had the Japanese and Hitler not drawn the United States into the war, vast numbers of human beings would have lost their freedom for generations.

Only free societies matter to the growth of the human soul. Dictatorships are wastes of the human spirit.

Stalin had almost sued for peace the previous August. Only the ferocity of the winter had made him hesitate. But the *Wehrmacht* was still strong and if it once again wrecked his armies in the spring, there would have again been that temptation. No more, though. With the United States committed to the European Theatre, Stalin would never quit.

And now, after all these pages, I am going to write out a description of what remains, to this day, the single most unpleasant experience I have ever had. I can tell you that this was a very, very wretched creature, this Hitler. You may think you already know that, but you don't. Had he not been powerful, he would have been pitiful. Thus when I look back, it is with a mixture of hatred and pity. I confess that the pity is something I wish I didn't feel, but I also think that, if I didn't, I would be the less for it.

To write this, I have come to a place of peace for me, of comfort, which is my bench on the Literary Walk. And, to my delight, the old woman who often sits on the opposite bench is there. We have developed a nodding acquaintance. The warmth of New York's anonymity has always given me pleasure, and as I nod and she nods, it does so again.

The reassuring roar of the city fills my ears. It's a life-ring, this sound, the noise of life going on anyway, no matter what. Above all, free life in a free country where one can journey wherever one needs to go, in thought, in speech, in travels.

Like all demagogues, Hitler was a narcissist. He believed himself too completely. Inside, he was hollow and afraid and so would constantly blare out, "I am never wrong!" The truth is that he was like anybody, sometimes yes and sometimes no.

As we were riding, he lifted my hand onto his knee. He stared straight ahead. I could see that he was sweating from the brow. I did not move my hand, just patted his leg a bit with the tips of my fingers. In response there was a choked gasp. He started to remove my hand, then stopped and left it there.

Was the theme tonight to be homosexual panic here, too?

In those days, I was a very different person. I found homosexual intimacy disgusting. The years of life have changed that. I'm still more keen for women than for men, but as I matured, if somebody wanted to make love with me and I found them appealing, I'd generally give it a go, and no matter which sex. Men are fun, too. It's all far more joyous than we let ourselves believe. Too bad, really. The great seer Meister Eckhart said in the 14th Century, "God laughs and plays." It's hard for our prudish world to face, but that has something to do with sex. A lot, I think.

I didn't think that then, though. Not at all! We have anti-nausea pills now. I wish we'd had them then, because I can tell you, I had to fight it on that night. Hard.

As we went into his bunker, I noticed that there were no SS around. He turned on the light switch, which raised the lamps and made his living room seem somewhat warm, actually.

"Where is everybody?"

"I told Traudl and the others that they could sleep. They so detest being with me at night, I'm giving them a respite."

"Why do you say that?"

"Because it's true. Everybody hates being with me. I bore them but they fear me too much to let on. They hate the war and they blame me for it. They don't see that Stalin was about to attack, or earlier that France and Russia would eventually have struck us across both borders at once if I hadn't put a stop to it. They don't see any of that, they can't, they haven't got my perspective and they're just people, not like me. They're not geniuses."

"I find you very interesting, Alf."

"I know you do, I can see it. It's quite a relief." He moved toward the bedroom. I followed. But could I see it through?

I felt I must. My every action must be to gain more of his trust, not diminish it. As to becoming an actual *Hitlerficker*—if that was part of it, then I was damn well going to do it.

My head was chock-a-block with valuable intelligence. I needed to get it to Churchill and I needed the latitude to do that. This depended on trust. I could not let the side down now.

He sat on the bed and patted the place beside him. I joined him.

"Alf, have you ever done this before?"

He closed his eyes and leaned his head back. "Oh my God, thank God. I was afraid you might not be understanding, and I can't say it. I have such difficulty saying it."

I then said the hardest thing I had ever said in my life. My whole being was transported with loathing. "Just relax. Let me take care of it."

"Have you ever done it before?"

"I was in boarding school. We used to bugger each other raw."

He gasped. He gasped again. "Do that," he whispered, "do that."

I was tempted to demand that he speak up, but I didn't. I stood him up and lowered his trousers, then had him lie across the foot of the bed. Fortunately, I managed to get myself up by imagining the way it felt in Carlotta.

"Are you going to do it soon?"

"In a moment. Have you any grease? Petroleum jelly?"

"Look in the bath."

All he had was that thick hair tonic he used, so I worked a bit of it into his rectum with my finger. I kept at that for a while, then lay upon him and slid into him. When he felt the energy of my onslaught, he reared back and shouted my name in a hoarse, swelling voice. Then he slumped down.

When I was done, I got up, went back to the john and cleaned myself off, then got back into my trousers and shirt.

He said, "I am..."

"What?"

"So grateful."

"Ah. You're a great genius Alf. Geniuses are complex. I'm glad I can help you."

"You're so matter-of-fact. It doesn't bother you? I don't disgust you?"

"You're here alone in this terribly difficult situation. You have to have help releasing the tension."

"Oh, yes, that's it. That's exactly it."

As he sat up with his trousers still down around his ankles, the door opened and Morrell walked in.

He stopped. He stared at Hitler. Then, slowly, he turned his eyes to me.

Total silence. Everybody frozen.

Then Hitler leaped off the bed, lurched forward and, cursing deep blue under his breath, dragged his trousers up, jumped like a spider across the room, picked up a wooden chair and hurled it at Morrell with all his might.

"Stupid jackass! What did I tell you? Did you not hear?"

Morrell dodged the chair, which slammed against the wall and shattered into a dozen pieces. If it had struck that fat old man, it might have killed him. Happily, it didn't. If Hitler had stopped getting his quack treatments, he might have become healthy enough to conduct the war effectively.

"I—yes, Leader! Yes!"

Hitler grabbed him by the collars. He began shaking him, banging the back of his head against the wall. "Never! Never! Never! Do you hear?"

"I hear!"

"YOU DO NOT HEAR! YOU DON'T HEAR ONE DAMN THING!"

"You need to calm. Calm!"

Hitler literally bared his teeth. "I ought to hang you, you stupid, pompous little shit!"

"No, Leader! I am only doing—" He coughed, then sobbed.

They were face to face. Hitler was as red as his flag. Morrell poured with sweat.

I continued dressing. I felt indifferent to their battle. Wishing as always for a valet, I went into the bathroom and busied myself tying my tie.

Outside, I heard Morrell say, "Your breath is ketonic. You need an immediate injection."

Hitler spoke softly and mildly, too low for me to hear much. But I knew that it meant that the storm had passed. I got my jacket on and went out looking not very presentable in the lounge suit I'd put on after skiing. I travelled so much in those days that my trunks were always behind me.

"Please step out," Morrell snapped. "The leader is having his injection."

I lit a cigarette.

"Don't you dare!" he shouted.

"Leave him be!" Hitler bellowed.

I sat back in the still-unbroken wooden chair and closed my eyes and smoked, reflecting that this was an unlivable life, but I had nevertheless to live it. What I had just done had changed me, more deeply, perhaps, than a boy of that age could know. But I did know this: I had gained the trust of this man who trusted nobody. I could save lives with that.

And yet, looking back and contemplating the degree to which I ameliorated or did not ameliorate Hitler's vast crime, I feel that only the most rigorous possible moral standard is applicable, and by that standard, millions and millions of times over, I and everybody else who worked against him failed.

Thus I have kept only my Nazi Eagle, not my Intelligence Medal and not my George, and I think that was the right thing to do. The symbol of my guilt is more important than the symbols of any courage I may have shown. That and the warning I carry in my pocket, *Judea Capta.*

The next morning, the 9th of December, the four of us flew from Rastenberg back to Berlin. He would make his declaration against the United States in a few days. Before that, I was made a German citizen and issued a Reich passport. It would enable me to continue to travel in, as Hitler was fond of putting it, "the countries I have in my pocket." My US passport would suffice for the rest of the world.

I didn't bring the matter up with him, but I decided to get Eva and Carlotta false Swiss papers when the opportunity arose. He and I no longer spoke of it, but we both knew that the offer that he had decided to make to Churchill was his last throw. If it was refused, the war would not be won by Germany.

I sat with Eva and Carlotta in the distinguished visitors area in the *Reichstag* to listen to his declaration of war. Eva wept, the tears rolling down her face. Carlotta's eyes blazed with triumph, for I had explained to her what it meant that the United States was now going to fight Germany.

As always, we remained in the shadows at the following reception. I watched him receiving congratulations and telling all comers that victory was certain now, endlessly repeating that Japanese had not lost a war in 3,000 years.

Indeed not, but they had never fought the United States, either.

Back at the Wannsee House, Eva asked, "When will they come to get you, Willy?"

My journey to London had been arranged. It was to start in the morning with a trip to Switzerland.

"I suppose about ten, why?"

"Do you know if you'll be in a prison or a *lager*?"

"What are you talking about?"

"Oh, listen to her," Carlotta said, "she thinks you're being interned. What a silly goose!"

"I'll have you know that I'm not a silly goose. I know the law, which is more than can be said for you, it would seem."

"Eva, I've been taken in by the Reich. I'm a German citizen now."

"Oh. Oh! Why didn't you say? What a wonderful thing for you! We need to celebrate!"

So we spent the evening drinking champagne. Goebbels showed up with a tart and we did a good deal of dancing. He was an awful man, true, but he was also a charming companion, socially quite capable. His infirmity caused him to dance like a piston, plunging up and down, but he was game for it.

Word always spread when there was an impromptu gathering in that tight circle, and soon Kempka appeared with the very fetching actress Dara Daranowski in tow. I kept waiting for the Himmlers to come through the door but they didn't, thankfully. Ever since we'd made him Charleston in the Berghof, he had avoided us decadents.

Around two, Hitler burst in wearing nothing but his military tunic in the cold, and with frost coating his mustache.

"My Leader," Kempka cried, rushing up to him and dusting snow off.

"I thought that's what I was, too. But I had to take a taxi. The driver looked in his rearview and died of a heart attack."

"What?"

"It's a joke, Ernst. He drove away. He never realized who it was."

"But you were to sleep in the Chancellery tonight."

"I can smell parties, you know, from far, far away."

Once he had appeared, it became the battle of the *negermusick*, with Carlotta putting on every American negro performer we had and Goebbels rushing to put German standards on instead.

He said to me, "Willy, is there anything you have in here that isn't illegal?"

"What can I say, I'm an American. We're all mad for Cab Calloway."

Eva managed to get Alf onto the floor. This was always amusing to watch. He was worse than Himmler, worse even than hopping Josef. He danced like a man stomping out a campfire.

And so we passed another glittering night in that time of dying. I could imagine *Lily Marlene* echoing along the trenches of the wintered-up *Wehrmacht* a thousand miles away, and their Russian counterparts, strong and warm, dancing their own wild dances on the ice of their land, and the Japanese exploring the government houses of the Dutch and the British in the bright Pacific afternoon.

# 19

And now it has come time to do another of the hard things that I have set myself this task to do. I sit in my place of safety on the Literary Walk, remembering. My old friend is across from me, eating her sandwich, she and the pigeons and a feral cat who does not seem to concern them in the least.

Earlier it rained, and now the trees that overhang the walk are a dripping bridge of leaves. I slip back across another bridge, this one made of Octobers, last year, the year before that, more years, then a march of years, all the way back to 1942. I mentioned this day before, October 14, 1942. And now it's time.

The most terrible sin is one that you do not know until too late that you are committing, and which you then cannot understand how to stop and can never hope to make right.

Eva and Carlotta and I were on the Obersaltzberg, Alf was in Vinnitsa in the Ukraine. The Germans were in the process of taking the industrial city of Stalingrad, with the expectation of shortly crossing the Volga and storming northward, this time attacking Moscow from both the west and the south, and at last winning the prize.

Late in the previous year, I had indeed gone to London, threading my way down to Portugal and taking a and had spoken to Churchill. It had proved to be a complicated and dangerous journey and it wasn't one I wanted to risk again. I'd flown to Paris, then taken a train to Madrid, a long, wearying journey with many stops and even more frequent unexplained halts. I'd found a flight to Lisbon, and from there caught the BOAC service to London. I'd made sure to send a cable from the German embassy to let Hitler know which plane I was on. Even so, we'd been looked over by some Heinkels while crossing the Bay of Biscay. Nerve wracking.

When I finally met with the PM, I told him of Todt's belief that the war could not be won, and Hitler's reaction, and his offer to withdraw from the Middle East. He had responded, "Do you think he would really leave?"

There was something in his voice I didn't like—a sort of avidity. I hadn't expected this. Far from it, I'd expected absolute resolve. No deals, Hitler and his Nazis had to be destroyed.

But then I considered of all the people he was responsible for, their lives being lost every minute, of the tottering empire that was also his responsibility, and I thought, 'of course he'll take the deal.'

That must not happen, so I lied to him, as I already had many times in this war, to both sides.

I replied to the question, "He laughed and told me to use my American poker face when I proposed the idea to you."

"But if he didn't leave, then the agreement would be moot. We'd have to see the Italians and the Germans get out before we'd do anything."

"Oh, he'd get out. But then after he defeated Stalin, he'd go right down to Iran. He'd take your oil from that direction instead. Then he'd have you."

"If he defeated Stalin."

I told another lie. "Once you're no longer a threat, he plans to take his troops out of Norway. He'll defeat Stalin easily."

"Take this back to your friend. He must return to the 1918 borders. Then we can talk."

"He can't back out of Russia. Stalin will follow him all the way home."

"Then in the west."

I knew that Hitler would agree to this immediately. It would mean peace in the west, and another version of the catastrophe that I would not allow.

I returned to Germany via Stockholm, a harrowing flight on an RAF plane followed by another harrowing flight on a Luftwaffe plane. Both sides had agreed not to attack such flights, but I had no faith in that, and indeed, a few weeks later Messerschmitts shot the RAF flight to bits.

I did not tell Hitler the truth, either. I said, "He wants a return to the 1918 borders. Then he'll talk."

"But not in the east?"

"In the east also, yes." And now stop, please. Read that sentence again. With those words, I gave up millions of lives. Had I given the two men their true positions, there would have been peace in Western Europe. There would have been no Casablanca Conference and the decision to fight the Germans to unconditional surrender would never have been taken. To this day, Hitler's grotesque Third Reich would have some sort of life.

When I uttered them, we were in the *Wolfschanze*. It was about two in the morning. Bormann was in the room, the secretaries, some others. Todt had just been killed in a plane crash, and I believe that was the night that Speer began to despise me.

"He demands that we abandon everything?"

"So it would seem."

He leaped up from his chair, then lifted it and hurled it, once again narrowly missing Morrell, who had come in from the anteroom where he had been preparing the sleep draught.

"That devil! Lying English shit! Oh, we'll get to England all right! We'll get there and he'll be strung up, you wait and see! Oh, yes. Him and his champagne and his fucking cigars, always drunk, that one! Bad habits, can't think clearly. Not a bit of it! Going back to those borders would wreck National Socialism, which he knows very well. The Russians would chase us all the way to the goddamn channel. That shithead! Stupid fuckface!" He turned on me. "You, you're no diplomat!"

"I'm not, no."

"It borders on treason, I'm telling you. Treason! If you couldn't do it, you shouldn't have gone."

"I succeeded."

"Go to hell!"

"If we make progress next year and Stalin capitulates, he'll capitulate too. We know that now."

"And you know that because you're some kind of a goddamn soothsayer, I suppose. Don't tell me it's astrology. I should hope not."

"He offered a negotiation. Don't you hear what I'm saying?"

"Not acceptable!"

"Not now, no. But he's open to the possibility, and now we know that. When we defeat Stalin, he'll be singing a different tune, you wait and see."

"God, Willy, I just—the man makes me furious. But you're quite right. It was a dangerous mission and you've done well. You're to be congratulated."

I hoped it wouldn't come to that, of course. But the war was a much closer thing than it now appears. Much closer. If America hadn't come in, Stalin would probably have thrown in the towel after Voronezh in July of '42. Had that happened and Churchill once again faced Germany alone, he would certainly have negotiated. Had Pearl never happened, Hitler would have won the war in the summer of 1942, and this despite the forces arrayed against him. Even if Stalin had held out, if Churchill had accepted an offer of the Middle East from Hitler, Stalin would have sued for peace, America or no America.

It was that close, a couple of sentences, a few lies.

I remember on that night the inner woe I felt. I so wanted all those young men out there on all sides to be able to go home and live out their lives. But the stakes were simply too high. Churchill's idea of keeping the two dictators at one another's throat was the right one, and he must not back down.

Hitler got up and went toward his bedroom, he called back to me, "Come on, Willy." And there I was in front of them all, the male prostitute obeying the call of his master. I was mortified beyond words, but also conscious that I must not allow even the slightest blush.

I stood up and walked off, forcing myself to hold my head high. As I closed the door, I heard a brief burst of laughter, instantly suppressed. It had been the voice of Albert Speer, I was sure.

After that, Speer literally writhed with loathing whenever he was in my presence. Once, I intentionally brushed my hand against his, and watched him holding it as if it had been injured for the rest of the conference we were in. As soon as he could, he rushed away to the washroom.

He never stopped being a Nazi, no more than did Von Braun or any of the scientists the United States brought over to jack up our scientific prowess, men like Hubertus Strughold and his ilk. They are Nazis still, every one, let's not kid ourselves. And another thing, if certain of them knew about this book, I would be under threat, I am sure. I don't know what I'll do when I publish it. Move to the Congo, perhaps.

I am glad that I acted as I acted in preventing an outbreak of peace. This is because of something that happened at the Bergh of a few months later.

It was on a quiet autumn afternoon in that October of '42 that the horror that Hitler's ideology was really revealed to me.

It started with an SS man appearing at the door, seeking permission to enter. The Officer of the Day sent word in to Eva that a *Sturmbannfuhrer* Junger was here on leave and wished to see the house.

I was most disappointed. I had hoped that Dieter was gone from my life.

Eva would never say no to a soldier visit like this, and she let him in at once. So here he came, a much older man now, with prematurely gray temples and a badly smashed ear, the skin still an angry red. He dragged a bit as he walked. Although he was actually two years younger than me, there was not the slightest trace of youth left in him.

National Socialism was largely a youth movement, and I could see in Dieter's appearance how it was sucking all the joy of their young days right out of the German kids. He shortly explained that he'd been in an explosion, which was the source of his disfigurement and infirmity. In later years, he told me the truth, which was that he was attacked by a Jewish wrestler who was on his way to the gas.

To Eva, he was simply another brave officer who wanted to see the legendary Mountain Court. When strangers came, Carlotta and I stayed out of the way. Without ever so much as hinting of her relationship with the leader, Eva would show such a man the public rooms of the house and let him step out onto the terrace, perhaps even open and close the great window for him. She would seem to be some sort of docent or manager.

I was just mounting the stairs to our wing when I heard his voice, soft now, no longer full of excited pride. But I recognized it instantly. He was asking after me.

Carlotta came to the top step. "What's going on?"

"Dieter is here. You remember Dieter."

"That sweet guy. Sure." She came down the steps. "Still in the SS?"

"Let's see."

We went across the great room to the foyer and there he stood just as I have described him. He didn't click his heels or make any salute or anything like that, but only rather solemnly shook hands.

We went into the sitting area. There was a nice fire going and the atmosphere was really very pleasant. Eva said, "We were just having coffee. Would you like to join us?"

"Real coffee?"

"Very real." It was completely impossible to get by then, only available to the highest levels of government or the richest families. Coffee was number one on the list in the black market, even ahead of Cubans.

We were always uneasy in the presence of strangers, and the

conversation was stilted. As Eva said nothing at all, Carlotta asked him where he was stationed.

"In the east."

"Are you *Waffen*, then?"

"No."

I knew what that meant. He was working in the camps, poor fellow.

Catching my eye, he glanced meaningfully toward the terrace. After a bit, I said, "Let me take a walk with my old friend. We go back, we two, all the way to '31."

Eva stood up immediately. "Well, then, I'm going downstairs and bowl." Between summer sports season and winter sports season, she did this every day, and climbed about in her little gym that was down there.

Carlotta did not. In fact, this was her classical period. She was having me teach her Latin and we were reading together in Horace. I have always loved the sylvan illusion of his odes, composed as they were in the ferocious, filthy and immeasurably difficult world of the Roman metropolis. Illusion in literature captivates me perhaps more than it should.

We would work with the Odes and imagine our future together. Our plan was to marry and have children. She wanted boys by the dozens. I wanted girls, just as many. "Hundreds of little Carlottas," I would say. "I would be in heaven."

"Too much fucking cursing. A house of blue language."

"They will look like you but speak as I do."

"You talk like a textbook. No accent. People ask, 'where is he from?' I say Uranus.'"

"Not mine. His."

"I wish I had a dick. I'd love to put it up him."

That's how we would talk—intimate, vulgar, delightful.

Death rather haunted her thoughts. Once she asked me, "Will we ever die, Willy?"

I said "Lovers never die. Lovers are forever." That was a few days prior to Dieter's appearance, a day when the sky was infinite and we drank hot wine, full of spice, in the afternoon. The night before, the three of us decided to play at camping, and spent the night on the floor of Alf's study under a quilt.

Looking back, it seems so terribly silly, but not at the time. It was just our normal life.

How vast time seems when one is young, but on that next day, just a few hours hence, my youth was going to end. It was a Wednesday, and as I have said, very clear and cold. A day of extreme clarity, every leaf etched, every stone gleaming.

I went out onto the terrace with Dieter. If I could convince the girls, I thought the four of us might wind up spending an evening together that he would be unlikely to forget. Us whores always find one another good company, as no acting is then necessary.

To make the prospect even nicer, the Germans hadn't yet lost Tunisia, so there was still plenty of hashish and cannabis in the house. Heroin, too. We'd fuck his brains out and shoot him full of it. He'd go back to Auschwitz or wherever he was stationed with quite a story to tell, but no ability to remember what it was.

Actually, his post was the worst one, Treblinka. They were already doing it there. The previous July, they had taken 300,000 Jews from the Warsaw ghetto and done them all. The month previous—September—trains had begun moving from all over Europe toward the camps.

At Treblinka, they had a tank engine exhausted into a barn that had been sealed up with tar and reinforced to prevent the victims from kicking their way out. In there, it took about fifteen minutes. But it also used a lot of fuel. In the end, they used the gas there, too. It was important that the exterminations be profitable. The SS collected gold, sold hair and clothing and glasses frames, anything to make certain that the despised Jewish profiteers in their dying turned a profit for the state, even if they were impoverished Poles and Russians. Those were just profiteers in disguise, you see.

We stood at the end of the terrace and smoked. "Your cigarettes are wonderful, Willy. Everything you have is always so good. Even those women! Is one of them yours?"

"Carlotta."

"The prettiest, of course! She must keep you good and warm at night. You should see the trolls the SS send us. Right out from under a bridge and into the female barracks."

As he spoke, he drew something out of his pocket and put it into mine.

Dieter?"

"It's a film. Look at it later. Alone, Willy."

"A blue film? The girls might like it."

"It's pornographic, Willy, but not in that way."

"All right."

"Not even a projectionist. You can project film, yes?"

"I have a set at my house in Wannsee."

"Wannsee, of course, the best. Do it there, do it here, but do it soon. When you see it, you'll know what to do. You always know what's the best thing."

"We usually have a movie. I'll run it after that."

"No waiters around, no projectionists, no girls. You and you alone! It's secret, Willy. Really, really secret."

"The staff here see many secret things."

"Unless you can run it when you're certain that you're absolutely alone, give it back."

"No, I can do it. And then after I've seen it, what shall I do? Is it for Hitler?"

He laughed a bit to himself, then smoked in silence for a while. "Now," he finally said, "the last cigarette, of course."

"Do you want another?"

"What I want is to go down those steps and stand by that tree. Such a lovely birch, decorated by Father Frost."

"Come, then."

"No, just alone. You have no idea how hard it is to be alone where I work." He whispered, then—a hiss. "It's madness. Complete madness."

He walked away down the steps and stood gazing out toward the mountains.

"Come back, the view's much better up here."

"Get away! Go inside!"

I thought, 'he's got that military roughness now.' I called to him, "We'll have our dinner in an hour. Stay. Stay the night."

He remained turned away, silent. Finally, I walked back to the house. The autumn air was sharp and I was in shirtsleeves, so I was just as glad to go back in.

I was putting my hand on the door when there was a terrific, echoing crack. I recognized it instantly as a shot. So did the SS. A moment later the alarm began whooping, its flat echo resounding back and forth.

Carlotta came rushing out. "Willy! Willy are you all right?"

I had already turned and was racing down the steps. Dieter's body was flat on the ground, a dark stain spreading through the leaves around him.

SS officers came charging up around the house with their guns in their hands.

"Shot himself," I called. "It's a suicide."

But it wasn't. He had put the gun in his mouth and pulled the trigger and—incredibly—missed. He'd shot out his left cheek and most of the teeth on that side, but he was very much alive, his eyes rolling around, wide with astonishment.

The guards carried him away at once and in a few minutes I heard the distant jangling of an ambulance bell. Later, the Officer of the Watch came in and explained that he had been doing some very difficult work, and sometimes it happened like this. He apologized to Eva.

She said, "Then he is a brave man."

I asked, "What will happen to him?"

"There's a hospital for such men. He'll go there. If he survives his wound, he'll stay until he's strong again."

Breakdowns and suicides were not unusual among the men who worked in those camps. I don't think I'll sound too callous when I comment that it's too bad that they didn't all kill themselves, the bastards. Most of them were happy in their work, though. They were doctors, remember, who had become convinced by their ideology that what they were doing was clearing up an infection. Gassing Jews was medical work. Just fulfilling the Hippocratic Oath, after all. "I will not give a lethal drug to anyone if I am asked, nor will I advise such a plan..." But what is the definition of "anyone?" In the National Socialist system, that was the *volk* in its entirety, but nobody else. There were no individuals, only the people as a whole. And the Jews were not part of the people. They were a burden on the body of the *volk*, like a boil or a rash, there to be cleared up by the social doctors of the SS.

If one accepts even a small part of an ideology, then the whole madness usually comes to seem completely reasonable. But not to poor Dieter. His moral compass was too strong.

When I went to see him in Dusseldorf a few years ago, he was quite well. As an SS, he'd spent some time in prison after the war, but his de-Nazification investigation had uncovered the record of his attempted suicide and he was there only a few months.

His face is lopsided and the cheek does not look wonderful, but he seemed healthy enough. We spoke a bit about our lives, his family with grandchildren and all. He asked after my children.

"My wife was injured," I told him. "We can't manage it."

"I'm sorry to hear that."

He didn't ask how and I wouldn't have told him. It was from her time in the Russian rape room, of course.

"You should see my bridge. It's architecture, not dentistry."

I said nothing.

"I was posted to Prinz Albrecht Strasse after my recovery. I worked in transport administration."

"With Eichmann?"

"No, he was different. That was the organization of schedules. I set up consists, first passenger cars, then later the infamous goods wagons. I would requisition them from the *Reichsbahn*, then move them into place for the transports. That was where Eichmann's unit took over."

It sounded very like he was confessing a war crime to me. If so, I was headed straight to Vienna and Simon Weisenthal.

He went on. "I did everything I could to slow that down. It was obvious that the Nazis were finished, so the slower I could go, the more would be saved. I sent cars onto the wrong sidings, put them onto lines that had been bombed and weren't yet repaired, that sort of thing. Nobody realized. Things were too chaotic. The closer we got to the end, the more of this I did."

"So you saved lives?"

"Willy, when you look at the numbers, it's not clear that I did anything more than clear my own conscience."

Slowly, tears filled his eyes. He made choked sounds.

That afternoon, I wrote a detailed letter to Weisenthal describing the meeting. A few days later, he telephoned me at the Adlon. He said, "We know of this man, but there's nothing there. No files. We've looked and so has the Special Prosecutor's Office. If you should get anything definite in the form of usable evidence, please forward it at once. We believe that Dieter Junger is responsible for at least a hundred thousand deportations from Germany and other countries in the west. He was one of the best administrators in the operation."

At first, I thought I would leave it there. Walk away from it. But then I didn't. I gave him and his wife a dinner. As he was a Catholic, I said, over cognac, "do you think confession absolves you of all those murders?"

Immediately, Grundl Junger burst into tears. Dieter sat frozen. Then he said, "And what of you, Willy? What did you do with the film? I counted on you, the great Willy, powerful, mysterious. Surely you could do something. But where is it? Did you burn it? I never heard of it again."

I'm not going to describe it in all its lurid detail, so if you're interested in the pornography of human suffering, please put this book away, it's not for you.

After our movie was done that night at the Berghof—you know, I think we watched something like *Das Grosse Speil*, which bored Carlotta silly, although she did enjoy watching the handsome footballers. Eva adored sports films and watched them whenever she could. Alf never wanted them.

Anyway, the girls went upstairs about one. I said that I was going to stay down for another cognac.

I sent the servants away, including the projectionist, and threaded up the film.

It was in Agfacolor, the very advanced German system. At first, it was quite dark. Shadowy figures. Then light came on, silver bright. I saw naked people, very many of them, a sea of bobbing heads in a low-ceilinged room. Billows of some sort of smoke began coming in from the far end.

I could not hear the screaming. There was no sound. But I could see it in the faces, the wide-eyed astonishment, the mouths open in silent horror. When my dreams return to that hellish vision, as happens still, I do hear it. I hear the voices of those poor people being suffocated.

None of that was a quick thing, the gassing. You didn't just go to sleep. It was nothing like the obliteration of a bullet. I saw a whole lifetime of agony unfolding in those fifteen minutes, I can assure you. The crowd surged, women trying to hold their children up to keep them from being crushed. One young woman in particular remains forever in my memory, her head bowed, her curls bouncing, her struggling baby held high over her head.

No, I thought. Impossible. No, there cannot be such a thing happening. I leaped to my feet. I thought, 'Satan is real. Satan has possessed the Germans.' And then, 'the tragedy of the Jews, the Germans, too, for this is not death only, it is the devourer of souls unleashed.' My mind, rendered stupid by panic, yammered to me, 'Hitler must be told! They've gone berserk. He'll want to stop this at once.'

They were dropping to their knees, jerking and shaking, shadows in the rapidly thickening fog. There were men going erect from air hunger. There flashed in my mind the recollection of how Alf used to like Carlotta to sit on his face and suffocate him, to get this effect. This caused me to realize that, of course, this was his doing. He did this, the man who had been gassed during the war and blamed the Jews for it, the man who understood the secret of the line between pain and pleasure, he did this, he designed it. I was looking at his work. He wasn't a distant figure to this, as history has recorded, no. Probably, under her and gulping for breath while she expertly tormented him, he was imagining this.

Toward the end, as the strongest sought for clear air near the ceiling, it became a pyramid of bodies, some jerking, some not.

After it ended, my immediate thought was that every human being is a sacred presence. Then I felt anger, followed at once by bitter, hopeless sorrow.

They were all dead, and yet there was something about them—I can't say that I saw it with my eyes—I think it was their goodness taking flight, at least in my imagination, the gold that is deep within even the most wretched of us getting free.

I know that doesn't make sense, but what about war does? That such a vast catastrophe could emerge from the mind of one dreadful little perverted man, for example, where is the sense there?

Ideology! The worst of all human errors.

The air cleared and the doors were opened. After a time men as thin as shades came in among them and began cutting their hair and dropping it into burlap sacks, and checking mouths and pulling out the gold with pliers. They were barefoot so that they wouldn't slip down in the piss and the shit and the vomit, and they read numbers on the bodies, too, and made lists.

Five months later, I was in Switzerland to meet Alan Dulles, who had just begun his mission there. I gave him the film. I said to him, "It's what happens to the Jews." I made sure he looked at it. As difficult for me as it was, I sat through it with him.

Afterward, he said, "Why are you showing me this?"

"This is what is happening to the Jews. All of them. Understand that."

"All right. I understand. But I can't see that this is actionable intelligence."

"Do you know how many Jews there are in Europe?"

"Quite a few. They do breed. Big families. The Jew wants more Jews."

I thought of grabbing that pipe of his right out of his mouth and ramming it down his throat. I said, "I believe that this is a process that will lead to the killing of many people. It's murder, you know."

"Ah, you're a Jew. I hadn't realized that. I am so sorry for the plight of your race."

"I am a human being, and so are these people. Put this on every film screen in the world."

"In color? Impossible. There isn't enough color stock on the planet for that."

"Then in black and white! What difference does it make?"

"We would have to know that this is real. That these aren't actors. Perhaps this is something created by the communists."

"Why would it be?"

"We know that Stalin intends to annihilate the German people. This would be justification for such a crime."

I could go on, but there's no point. He simply wasn't capable of seeing what was in front of him. He later told me that he sent the film on to Washington. I've had numerous archival searches conducted without result. Probably, he tossed it in the burn box. After all, it wasn't "actionable," was it?

After I had told Dieter all of this, he said, "Committing a crime that you don't want to commit is a terrible thing to bear, Willy."

Grundl said, "We go home, Dieter!" She jumped to her feet.

"Willy, if we didn't obey, we were put in prison or shot."

"But you were in that SS hospital."

He touched his cheek.

"I know that nobody got shot for being unable to bear the gassing of Jews."

Saying no more, he took his frantic wife's advice. They went off.

I don't think it's god who forgives. It's us. Only we can forgive ourselves, but there can be evil too great for that. I know this. I know it well. It is my life, also.

## 20

Late one freezing night in February of 1944, Adolf Hitler returned to the Berghof for what would prove to be the last time. He would not leave again until July, when something would happen that Churchill most certainly did not desire, which was the Stauffenberg bombing.

The Prime Minister had admonished both those of us who reported to him directly and the broader community of operatives that Hitler's life was to be preserved at all costs. The official decision to accept nothing less than unconditional surrender had been taken at Casablanca the previous January, and that depended on Hitler and his intransigent will. The last thing Roosevelt and Churchill wanted was a surrender offer from Germany.

For his part, Stalin's aim was simple: occupy the country, remove its factories to Russia and enslave the population. The west was talking in terms of partitioning it into a group of smaller states and making it into an agricultural zone. Later in the year, the details of this program would be reflected in what is known to history as the Morgenthau Plan.

Roosevelt never intended to implement the plan. The hidden

reason that it was publicized was to give Goebbels the means to terrify the population into fighting on at any cost.

The allied policy to bleed both dictatorships was at work here, a central reality of British and American policy that remains secret to this day.

I was glad that Hitler had stopped his restless movement from place to place, especially his visits to the front, and come back. He was safer here than anywhere else. We were, too, for that matter. The allies would not be bombing any place they knew Hitler to be resident.

Before his arrival, we were in a high state of excitement. All day the girls had been trying on dresses and fixing each other's hair, as a hairdresser could not be found. The Berghof had a barber shop, but not a hairdressing salon. For that, the girls would go to Berchtesgaden, where Frau Sauer would inevitably try to turn them into *hausfrauen*. In German, Sauer means grim, and grimness was exactly what she provided. Simple braids, plain cuts. *Kriegshaar,* it was called. War hair.

By ten, a dinner was ready in the kitchen, being kept hot. Constanze, Hitler's cook, had been here since yesterday evening. Three SS men had volunteered to do poison testing.

My one concern about his safety here involved Carlotta. She wouldn't kill him, of course, during their games. She was far too skilled for that. But I was now sure that she, also, was an agent, either British or Russian. She'd once threatened my life for trying to assassinate him, but where did she stand now?

If Stalin wanted him killed, as he might, and she was in the Red Choir, she was quite clever enough to get cyanide into his food right at the table, or into his mouth while they were at play.

I had been careful to keep any awareness of what he was doing to the Jews away from her, lest she act on her own. And, believe me, I have suffered through the moral complications of that decision. It is bad enough to be like Dieter, guilty of a crime you didn't want to commit. But to be guilty of one you couldn't help but commit—if you have any sort of a conscience at all, you are going to be working through that from then on.

In the months that I followed the secret 'preservation of life' order, over two million people were gassed.

On the nights when I sleep—when I can—they come. They always come.

And here he came up the steps from the driveway. The convoy was surprisingly short, just his car and two cars of bodyguards. Over the next months there would be many generals, but not tonight. Clearly as he was helped up the stairs, his eyes wide with fatigue and full of expectation, he was weaker than ever.

I'd been with him at the *Wolfschanze* at least once or twice a month, so I had observed the decline of the man, which was directly related, in my opinion, to the rise of Doctor Morrell. I had reported to Paul the possibility that Morrell was assassinating Hitler by means of slow poison. He had become an ominous, grim presence. He'd stopped laughing a long time ago, had Morrell. When we were together, he watched me as one might a prowling tiger. Clearly, he feared me. That made him dangerous, and I was careful to sleep only behind a locked door when he was around.

Dragging his left leg most noticeably, Hitler came in. His left hand was trembling slightly.

Eva, who had not seen him in at least six months, opened her arms and walked up to him and embraced him. But he was looking past her.

"What in hell is this," he said. He brushed her off and came into the room. He stopped before the table in the sitting area and stared at the enormous spray of flowers that stood on it in a lovely vase of the finest Dresden porcelain, an antique of the best quality. I know, because it was mine.

He picked my vase and hurled it to the floor, smashing it into a spray of exquisite fragments amid a confusion of flowers.

"Has everybody forgotten the fact that there's a goddamn war going on? What the hell do you mean by all this? It's an insult to the

German people. They have no flowers! There are no flowers at the front, are there? Of course not."

Carlotta said, "Wait, you." She walked over and began picking up stems of her beloved roses.

"Get away from there!" He pointed to Kempka, who had just come in. "You, call the servants, get this out of here, all of it."

"No! You need this. This is home, and you need it."

"You've talked back to me for the last time! Get out of my house!"

"I won't and you're going to shut up and listen. Look at you, dragging yourself along like a wet dog. Is that the leader the Germans need?"

He stared to speak.

"Shut up. You're here to rest and have a nice time and gain strength so that our genius can get us out of this mess and win the war! And I think that means flowers and good times and good food and the people who love you around you."

He was silent, swaying slightly. Would there be a final outburst? No way to tell, not at this juncture.

"Now, Eva opened her arms to you. Eva, come here."

She came quietly across to them.

"Go on."

She embraced him. For a moment, he was stiff, then he leaned in to her and there emerged from his throat a low, lost moan that rose and rose until it was a howl. It seemed to last forever, only gradually declining into long, racking sobs.

I said to Kempka, "Put them back."

As Kempka restored the flowers to a small part of the vase that hadn't broken, the three of us surrounded Alf and got him to sit down. Eva said to me, "Go put on some nice music, Willy, something he likes."

I chose Borodin's "Nocturne," to which he would often listen when he couldn't sleep. What he said politically and what he liked personally were two different things, and Borodin and Tchaikovsky were both favorites. He was partial to the Jewish pianist Artur Schnabel, for that matter.

He leaned back and closed his eyes. Eva unbuttoned his tunic. He said, "I had forgotten what it's like to be with people who aren't frightened of me."

"This is home," Carlotta said, "and nobody here is frightened of you."

His eyes went to her. Into them, there came a gleam.

Whore that she was, she saw at once what was behind it. "We'll get you straightened out," she said. She ruffled his hair. "Never fear."

Eva cuddled up to him.

"Mm. It's so nice to have you here. Nicer than the castle."

"That castle is haunted," Carlotta said.

He opened his eyes wide. "I've seen it, too! The shadow—the knight."

"But not here," I said. "Here, it's just us."

"Tomorrow there will be visitors."

"Which is why I've decided to do you now, Alf," Carlotta said. "I'm going up to the room. You're to come up naked and alone."

Eva crossed her legs and sighed.

"Sister," Carlotta said, "wait for him in his bed."

Hitler sat forward and put his face in his hands. "Why must I be like this?"

"Why not?," I said. "You're interesting and fun. We all enjoy you, so you should, too."

"Women have killed themselves over this."

Carlotta laughed. "I won't, obviously, nor will Eva. We've been looking forward to you." She stood. "Don't keep me waiting. You know what a mistake that is."

This sweet young woman, dripping false innocence, went upstairs to await the coming of the king of the world, naked and afraid.

Hitler said to Eva, "Will you be in my bed, then?"

"Oh, yes, certainly!"

"You do really want me, don't you? Even though I'm...crippled like I am."

She put her arms around his neck and gave him a kiss. He held her to him and kissed her long. It was not something I often saw. I waited. What I cared about was information he might drop that I could transmit to London. I was like the dog looking for scraps under the table.

"Well, Willy, here I go! Will you save me if I scream, Eva?"

"Just imagine me waiting in the bed for the moment you are let go."

He went off, moving into the shadows and up the stairs.

"Willy, he's weak, do you see?"

"I do, Eva."

"He's losing his war. He's going to be quite disappointed."

The understatement was so fantastic that I almost gagged. "Yes he is," I said. "Quite disappointed."

"What will he do without a country to run?"

It was unbelievable. I played along. "I don't know. Open a shop?"

"He couldn't do that, not after being so important. It would bore him. I think he should become a writer. That's what I've told him."

"What would he write?"

"Oh, I don't know. History? People love his writing. He'd gotten a wonderful sale for My Struggle. And it's quite good. Have you read it?"

"Indeed. Have you?"

"I had Fegelien explain it to me. I think I got it. It's the Jews. They started up the war. But I knew that already."

Do you see her tragedy? She was a simple kid plucked from an obscure life and plunged into Hitler's cockeyed fantasy world. But then again, she was hardly an exception. So were all the youth of Germany. To anyone in the country born after about 1925, National Socialism was literally the only thing they knew. Eva was from the previous generation, but she had started with Hitler so early that she also knew nothing else.

I often wondered if he really loved her. I know that he loved August Kubizek. Sometimes when he had been transported with passion by 'the solder's relief,' as he called it, he would gaze at me and whisper that he loved me. He would want to hold my hand against his cheek. He wept about Ernst Rohm. 'My love, my heart,' he would say. 'And Kubi—when we were boys, we were very bad.' He would want to whisper stories of his sexual games to me. I can only wonder that his parents didn't seek psychiatric help for him, but perhaps they never found out.

He worshiped Carlotta, but that wasn't love. Whatever it was, its intensity increased with his failures. The worse the war went, the more his guilt increased, and the more he demanded of her.

She was up for it, I'll say that. God knows.

That first night back, he hadn't seen her since the castle three months before. That was a long abstinence for him, and all the disasters of the fall of '43 and now into '44 had driven him into a frenzy of self-hate.

As a result, they were up there for several hours. Eva and I grew so worried that we finally went to the bottom of the stairs and called to them. All that came back was a sharp "*nein*" from Carlotta.

"She's got it in hand," I said to Eva.

"I hope he's not hurt. How can he be beaten for so long?"

"I think they're doing something else. There's no beating. I don't hear it."

"I just wish it was ordinary life! It's so hard to understand anything about him at all."

"He's a genius. We just have to follow along and keep him happy."

"Do I, Willy? Do you think?"

"He's in love with you. He just needs her to relieve his tension. She's only a whore, don't forget it."

"She rules over him up there. A whore and a Jew, but there it is."

We were still standing in the hall when there was finally movement on the stairs. When the door opened, he came out. He was naked, clean and scrubbed and not a mark on him that I could see. He came carefully down the stairs, hanging his head. He was sexually excited, his little business bouncing along.

They went away into his bedroom and I thought to myself, 'all is well.'

Carlotta hurried down then. She pulled me into Eva's suite and closed the door.

"Is everything all right?"

"Cigarette me!"

I lit her up. We were down to the last case of decent cigarettes, and so rationing them among ourselves. The best you could get in Germany now was no good at all. They tasted like burning hair, and may have been. I was working on getting mine sent just to the Swiss address with no transshipment bill, but shipping anything except war materials the originated in the U.S. was difficult, and no matter the destination.

"Shouldn't we go to our room?"

"Intercom." There was one in our room. Not here. She leaned against the door. "Willy, he wants me to kill him."

"That can't be true."

"He begged. *Begged*!"

"It's part of the game."

"I've been playing this game with him always, and that's not part of it, I'm sorry. And how he wants me to go about it—Willy, it's more mad than ever. It's psychosis. He's absolutely gone."

I held her. I did not ask her a thing. And, in fact, I wasn't even curious about the details. Whatever they were, they were awful and I didn't care to know.

Only one thing concerned me. "Would you do it?"

She looked at me, hooded, as she was clutching something in herself. Then the eyes changed a bit. "In the old *keitz* it was different. But this is not the *keitz*."

When she was a little whore running the streets, had she killed? I had wondered before, but had never asked, and again I didn't. She loved me and I her and that was that. My only interest in any murders of hers was that they not be discovered.

I decided to take a chance here. "What if you were ordered to?"

She went to the window and stared out into the darkness. "How long have you known?"

"I didn't. Now I do."

She was instantly in my face. "Fuck you, Willy Weber, just *fuck you*. You're a fucking British spy anyway. They all know it, the generals, Himmler, they all do. You and that Paul with his funny specs and his fake eyebrows. Amateur spies for king and country."

"And you're in the Red Choir."

"What of it? On the streets, what was I gonna be, a Nazi? Hell no, they'd've set me to work in a kitchen, take me outa the game. Peel potatoes instead of live like a goddamn princess? I don't think so."

"I communicate with London through Paul. How do you do it?"

"With the Russians? Their radios are dreadful. I use a tin can and a string that reaches all the way to Moscow. You have to shout."

I didn't press her. I suppose her contact was in the SS detail or maybe the kitchen. That wasn't important to me. "If you were ordered to kill him, would you do it?"

"Ha! Good question. To be honest with you, the Red Choir is full of shit and so is Stalin. He's Hitler with a different mustache. Anyway, I've been asked to do the opposite. Keep him alive, and report anybody I think might be planning to kill him."

I wondered if my analysis of the situation was wrong. But no, Stalin wanted to depopulate Germany, so he wouldn't want a capitulation, either.

After the fall of Stalingrad, life in the Reich had become even more frenetic. The bombings were simply fantastic.

She said, "He threatens suicide all the time."

At that moment, Eva came in. She was drowsy and happy and kissed Carlotta on the top of her head. "It's working always, Sister. It never fails. Our strange fellow!"

"We need to have a conference, the three of us," Carlotta said. "He's having a terrible time in the war."

"It's going to be a loss, he says. He just told me."

"We have to not think about that. No loss!"

"That's exactly what I told him. The Germans can't lose, not like last time. There are no Jews to throw the game."

"We need to keep his courage up, the three of us. Nobody else can do it."

"That's right," I said. "He'll never capitulate, but if the others get the job away from him—that pig, Goering, as one example—then there will be an immediate surrender. The Germans will end up slaves to the Jews."

Eva gave me a stern look. "Goering would do that? Give us away to them?"

"Certainly he would," Carlotta said. "I know him, remember. He's hated the war from the beginning."

"You're right, both of you. We have to give Alf the strength to go on and on until we win. As we will!"

"No sad faces, no defeatist talk with us. Let the generals do that."

It was nearly four and we were all beyond tired. Carlotta and I went to our room and got our clothes off and got under the covers. With the blanket over our heads we whispered together.

"Are we wicked or good, Willy?"

"Both."

"It's so strange, but you're right."

"We just have to keep him alive. That's all we need to think about."

"But what if he does start to win?"

"If that happens, then I'd love to kill him."

"Me, too!"

"Then we can do it together for king and country and politburo."

"But not the way he asks. Never. Some quick way like shoot him."

"Wax bullets?"

"Himmler and his fuckin' tricks. That's one I'd like to see cut into little pieces."

We slept in one another's arms, two scared kittens in the dark.

## 21

Throughout the winter and spring of 1944, Hitler kept up a continuous round of visits to Schloss Klessheim just across the border in Austria, where he saw various Axis heads of state, encouraging them, threatening them, doing whatever was necessary to keep them in the war.

Generally, he spent his nights with us. When he arose, Morrell would be there with a tray of injections. The only ones that mattered as far as I was concerned were Pervitin and Eudokal. Both were used at different times, and when he had them, he was in a terrific good mood. No thoughts of suicide then.

We had to watch him carefully when the uppers wore off, because he would fall right over a psychological cliff. The whole catastrophic business that was unfolding in the world beyond this gorgeous mountain retreat would come home to him, and that was when we worried. I wished he hadn't tossed Himmler's wax bullets away. I would have liked to have put them in his gun.

We made it all as nice for him as possible. I went on fake "spying trips" to Switzerland and came back with fictional news that the allies were bickering so much that Dulles wouldn't talk to the SIS boys. Paul would show up with pictures of crashed British "test" airplanes and such to encourage him. The Germans were working furiously on a fan-jet, so the pictures he brought of RAF "wonder planes" that had crashed and burned gave him great pleasure. A picture like that and a dose of Pervitin and he would be bouncing around the house for hours, telephoning generals with his usual brew of awful ideas, and so forth.

When Mussolini arrived at the Schloss Klessheim in a profoundly dejected condition, Morrell hopped Hitler up with Eudokal and he managed to talk him back into a much more favorable state of mind.

But the drives back and forth to the Schloss, which was about fifty kilometers, would make Hitler miserable. This was because he would inevitably see busses and such converted to charcoal burners puffing along.

This would upset him so much that he would put his hand over his eyes. Finally, I convinced Bormann to provide Berchtesgaden and the other towns along the route with petrol so he wouldn't encounter them.

In the months between February when he arrived and June 7 when he left for the western front, the great majority of days were quite orderly and even sedate. He would arise at about noon and have his breakfast, then at three we would walk up to the teahouse for apple cake and stories, his, Morrell's, even my fanciful tales of an anarchic, negro-packed, disputatious Jewmerica. He would shake his head at these fictions and say, "Listen to that! They can never win. Right, Willy, they can never win?"

"My rule of thumb, one German soldier equals twenty American, fifty if they're negroes."

He would slap his fist into his palm and say, "That's right! One for fifty!"

Carlotta would brush his cheek with her fingers and say, "The impossible is possible here. This is Germany!"

The hypocrisy may seem fantastic, I know, but he was turning into a child before our eyes, and responded best to being treated like one.

When he repeated the same story more than twice or so in the same sitting, Carlotta would wag her finger at him and say, "Now, Alf, not again. We need at least a day to pretend we've forgotten."

We would all laugh together. Keep him laughing, keep him hopeful. That was our job as given to us by our distant, invisible bosses.

More than ever, he dwelled on his boyhood days in Linz. He could wax rather poetic, really, speaking of his evenings in the opera house and of picnics in the forest, that sort of thing, his gruff voice dropping to a murmur when he mentioned his mother. Then he would gasp and glance guiltily from one of us to the next, remembering what he had told us about her. But was it true, or just a masochistic fantasy, of which he obviously had many? In any case, Eva would pat his hand and the tears would silently flow.

He smacked on his food now, relishing it in the grotesque manner of a old man greedy for life. This was especially true of the apple cake, which he enjoyed every afternoon with the relish of a last meal. In fact, he ate all of his food like a child or an old man, only sitting to a meal properly when we had company. I found his avidity particularly revolting. While he ate savory barley pudding, kohlrabi, asparagus and lovely cheeses, the average German was getting by on things like thin turnip soup and rotted cabbages, and those were the lucky ones. People drank acorn coffee and what meat was available was generally horse or something equally unpalatable. Rennet was a primary source of nutrition.

As long as no generals appeared to unfold their increasingly terrifying maps, the days could be rather pleasant, even. We would drive up into the mountains to the ski slopes, with Hitler bundled up like an invalid but enjoying it all hugely, especially Carlotta's ski lessons, which were memorable for the phenomenal eruptions of blue language involved.

She'd fall over after a few meters and you'd hear rising up from the heap, "Buttfuck! Shit! I hate this fucking, cocksucking snow! Fuck it!"

I would be in the car with him—we never left him entirely alone, never—and we would go into gales of laughter. She'd march over. "You fuckers, you're laughing!"

"No, no," he'd say, "at a joke! Willy told a joke!"

"What joke? Tell me, I like to fucking well laugh, too." She'd gather snow in her hands.

"No, no, I've forgotten! Willy, help me, roll up the windows!"

She'd smash snow in his face and he'd roar and brush it off, then I'd get out and grab her from behind and thrust her face in the window and say, "Apologize to the leader!"

She would say, very sweetly, "Fuck you, Alf. You ski. You come ski!"

The pleasure he took in all this—being just one of the crowd—was tormentingly pitiful. I hated him so much that the sound of his laughter made me want to smash in his face, but deeper within me there was also another feeling. I didn't want it to be there, but it was.

One evening when Eva was watching "Gone with the Wind," which she now did at least three times a week, and Carlotta was ostentatiously playing solitaire, he and I sat before the fire. We were both taking cognac, most unusual for him.

"Willy," he said, then stopped.

"Yes?"

"I want...you know what—again. Once. Just once."

"You make it sound very final."

He was silent.

"We have the rockets going over, Alf, and look at the British press, they're terrified. And the victory in Narva, don't forget that. The Hungarian occupation is going very well, too."

"You sound like Goebbels babbling nonsense on the radio."

"I'll give you a very pleasant time, Alf and enjoy myself doing it. But in return I want a promise that you will remain in this world. Without you, the people cannot succeed. The *volk*, Alf."

"Fuck the *volk*, Willy. But fuck me, too. Please."

We went upstairs together and, to my astonishment, he became prancingly effeminate. Just picture in your mind how that would have looked to me. And that is how it looked, but exactly. What I saw was far beyond Chaplin's Great Dictator dancing with his globe. All Hitler lacked was a cocktail dress.

He walked about waving his hips. He stopped, went to the big French doors that lined the balcony and pulled the drapes closed. Now he really let loose, walking toward me with exaggerated, mincing steps. He appeared more like an 18th Century French grandee than any woman I ever saw.

With a flip of his wrists, he said in a completely incompetent falsetto, "Am I surprising you?"

"Genius has that capacity."

"Only August has seen this. Dear August, so long ago. We were such a couple, we two, in our toppers and tailcoats and with our fine sticks."

"Do you want a dress?"

"Oh, Willy, dare I?" He fluttered his lids at me. "I'd simply adore it!"

"Carlotta's about your size. Her closet's full of fabulous dresses."

"She mustn't see."

"Why not? All she'll do is spank you. It'll be great fun."

"Oh, my. It's a new scenario."

"Let's go over to our room and I'll be your *femme de chambre*. We'll dress you in one of her sexiest numbers."

So we went downstairs and across. The girls were in the sitting area before the fire. *Negermusik* was blaring, freedom calling to their souls.

Jazz, you know, is deeply moral, and the blues are the most morally exquisite music mankind has ever created. As we crossed, "Don't Cry Baby" filled the trembling air, and I found myself wondering if Spiers had sold his Mefos in time.

This other Hitler, the true girl emerging from deep within, snapped his fingers as he pranced along.

Eva's eyes were closed, but not Carlotta's. They were never closed. She flicked her brows at me. I signaled with a hand to wait, then crooked my finger. She winked.

We boy-girls sashayed off upstairs.

"Lock the door," Hitler said as we entered our room.

"Why?"

"Willy, you can dress. You're beautiful, like Dieter. Oh, god, what have I done to my poor Dieter! I worry that he speaks of me, that he remembers."

"Dieter? He never said anything to me."

"No, he's good, I know. Still, there's the worry."

The man was not only not the ascetic history remembers, he was a damned satyr. I suspect that he killed a lot more of his partners than Geli. The ones who knew the truth were in danger, always. Carlotta never forgot this, but I didn't really believe it. He threw away lives like bits of soiled tissue.

"What can I do with this stupid snotbrake of mine? I look like a complete asshole when I dress now. Oh, Willy, my dear, it's so disappointing!"

"Cut it off."

"That would shake the world!"

"So let it shake. You can dress and make up both then. You'll be much more content."

"You're smirking, you devil." I was standing over him. He was at Carlotta's mirror.

"No I'm not. I'm not!"

"My allies would go crazy, the *volk*. I'd be an international laughing stock. Chaplin would shave his and make another film about me. I'd end up having to wear a false mustache for the rest of my life, a rat's nest glued to my lip."

"We'll both dress. Come on, it'll be fun. We'll do battle with our dicks like swords."

"You fuck, yours is too huge. I'm losing my war already, I don't want to lose to you."

I knelt. "Want me to blow you, Leader?"

He took my head in his arms and hugged me to him. "Willy, it's like being in heaven being with you."

"Oh, yeah, Alf. Oh, yeah."

I didn't have to blow him, thank God. I said, "Let's put you in one of her Sexschaparellis. Forget the fucking *rotzbremse*, I'll pretend it isn't there."

"Pretend now, but I must find a new life. When I lose the war, I'm going to Indonesia and becoming a doctor. It's all arranged."

I wondered if this was most precious piece of intelligence I had ever obtained, or bullshit? Hitler was a genius, so I knew better than to draw any sort of conclusion.

I got him into one Carlotta's more incredible numbers, sleek and black, gleaming like sharkskin. Of course, on him it looked like he was wrapped in some sort of flag. I got out her makeup and blackened and shaped his eyebrows. I powdered the mustache white.

"Open your mouth, honey."

He opened. "We used to do this to each other, the lips! Oh, such fond memory!"

"You and August?"

"Sure, before the fucking mustache. We'd step out and get ourselves fucked senseless any time. Factory boys, they know how to put it to you."

"Dieter?"

"I taught that poker everything he knows. What a fucking coward! But forget him. He's *volk*. Weak. They're going to be fucked to the wall and it's not my fault. I should've been born a goddamn Jew, they're the strong ones."

Understand that the dress on him, so exquisitely shaped for Carlotta, was nothing but a big silk bag. Nevertheless, he sailed around shaking his hips like a flapper. I stripped but I didn't put on one of her dresses. I would have ripped it to shreds.

Finally, he sashayed over to the bed and lay down. "Am I pretty?"

"Not very,"

"But play like I am. Please, Willy, you can play!"

I sat on the bedside and tweaked his big nose and called him a cutie. He giggled. Had he not been so very sinister, it would have been the funniest thing I'd ever seen.

Quite suddenly, and with perfect timing, Carlotta burst in. "You devil," she cried. She folded her arms. "This is going to be a very serious punishment for you, boy."

He leaped off the bed. "I'm so sorry!" He fell to his knees before her. "So sorry!" He began frantically kissing her hands. She caught my eye and nodded. I was to leave.

I realized that this was nothing new for them, just another of their scenarios. I had undoubtedly been playing a role pioneered by August. I would guess that it had started in childhood when he had been discovered in *vêtements pour femmes* and been treated to a thorough spanking as a result.

We make such a great fuss about sexual peccadilloes, even though they're really quite ordinary. They wouldn't be fun, though, if we didn't.

I walked downstairs into the dulcet tones of "My Own True Love" and joined Eva just as mammy upbraided Scarlett for leaving the house without a wrap. We spent the movie kissing and playing about and having a lovely time. When it ended, Eva, blushing with anticipation, went upstairs to wait.

I played jazz and smoked and drank, and wished I had some damn opium, just one nice pea. Or no, heroin. I would have liked a nice lid of very pure *etsch*.

Two lids, damnit.

Despite the fact that he was in healthy surroundings and being bothered surprisingly little with government and military business, I would say that, by the middle of April, Hitler's vitality had declined by half.

It was the reports that did it, the changing maps, and, I am convinced, Morrell.

I had become certain that he was utilizing small doses of strychnine, not to kill him but to weaken him and cause his decision making capacity to deteriorate. Did he work for Stalin or Churchill, then, or Canaris, or even some unknown player? Even himself. He must have despised Hitler.

To this day, I don't know and I never will. Morrell's deceptions have not entered history, and his personal notes are an incomprehensible muddle in an archive in Munich.

It was just at the break of spring—May in these parts—that I received an unexpected phone call. It was Paul. Due to the increasing anarchy within the Reich, he was now spending most of his time in Switzerland, entering Germany only as necessary. He carried both a Swiss diplomatic passport and one of the treasured "Hitler Passes," which consisted of a sheet of Leader stationary with a typed note on it: "The bearer of this document_____ shall be allowed to pass under all circumstances." The name was of the bearer was written in Hitler's hand, and his signature was at the bottom. Previously, that pass would get you anywhere in the Reich, even into its most secret places.

Not so certain now. The problem was that there were plenty of roving bands of Hitler Youth or just plain thugs who would beat somebody to death for five marks, and never mind their credentials. They were indifferent to things they knew nothing of, like personal passes from Hitler. They'd been more or less hungry now for a year or more, these kids. People can stand almost any privation but that, especially young people. If you teach boys violence and then starve them, they are going to use the tools you have given them to feed themselves—if necessary, with you.

I know that history doesn't record what was actually going on along the back roads of Germany by that time, but I remember all too well how dangerous it was becoming.

In any case, one morning early (before, as he knew, Hitler would be awake) the call came through from Paul. He was in Berchtesgaden and wanted an immediate meeting with me.

I told Carlotta that I was going into the town to look for a shipment of cigarettes and whiskey that I was hoping had arrived, and drove myself down in one of the 770s. That close to the house, it was still safe enough to do so.

Paul was in the *gasthaus* where we usually met. He was at that time being called "Claus Bausch," and was using the Swiss identity. Since he always had plenty of cash and little gifts such as Turkish cigarettes to spread around, he was most welcome wherever he went.

As there was coffee available, the *gasthaus* was crowded, which is probably why he had chosen it. Nevertheless, we spoke quietly, our heads close together. There was nothing unusual about this. It's how one conversed in Germany in those days.

First, he handed me two documents. They were Swiss diplomatic passports, one for me and one for Carlotta.

"What about Eva?"

"You've been in Europe too long to be so damned naive. Incidentally, Carlotta's listed as your wife. I hope that doesn't offend."

"Why would it?"

"Not everybody cares to be married to a whore. And a Jew."

I swallowed my outrage. "As soon as we're free of Hitler, we intend to have children. She dreams of them. Dreams of holding them. As do I."

He made a 'rockabye' motion with his arms. "Sweet, sweet, sweet."

"By what means are we to leave?"

"That BMW of yours."

"Lost it."

"Like my Delahaye. Requisitioned by Kurt Lischka, the devil. He paid me for it, I'll give him that. At least the Hispano is safe." He paused.

"There's a mission on for you," he said.

"All right."

"You'll receive a letter from Alan Dulles. It will request a meeting. You will tell Hitler, of course. When you get to Geneva, you'll be contacted at your hotel and given a document. You are to tell Hitler that you stole it from Dulles."

"Dulles has his office in Bern."

"That bastard knows nothing about this. He's more loyal to Ribbentrop than he is to Hull. This is strictly SIS business."

"Am I to know what the document is?"

"The plan for the allied invasion of Europe."

I have to admit, that nearly tossed me to the floor.

"My," he said, "you've gone pale."

"It's a fake, of course."

"It's the real plan."

"I—what?"

"You don't understand."

"Not at all."

"The landing is in the south, in Marseilles. The purpose is to cut off Kesselring, then invade Germany through Bavaria. Here, in fact, this region. He glanced around. This place could be full of tommies in a few months."

It seemed extraordinarily stupid to me. "Why not the north," I said weakly, "Calais or somewhere like that? The heart of Germany is up there."

"As are the defenses."

"I'm no strategist, but this sounds like a mistake. We could be tied up in these mountains for years."

"And he won't believe it, which is exactly the point. One must think as Hitler thinks, in terms of plots and conspiracies."

"He doesn't. He's quite straightforward."

"Be that as it may, our fellows think it'll lead him to reinforce Calais even further. Send a few divisions south, at most. We'll land virtually unopposed."

"If he does believe it?"

"Then he does. Let us know."

It was all very strange.

"How is he, incidentally?"

"A shadow. I think that quack of his is poisoning him."

"That's not good. Should we slice the quack?"

"In my opinion, he's trying a long game with some slow-acting poison. He's sickening him so that he'll perform poorly, not killing him."

"You're sure?"

"No. It's just that his health is deteriorating and Morrell is always hovering about with his injections at the ready."

"I'll take it back to HQ. If we need to get rid of Morrell, it might fall to you. Are you up to it?"

In this world of death, I had come to treasure life more and more, any life. "I've thought about that, and to be completely honest, I don't know."

"Damn you, you soft little shit! Try again."

I said, "I can. Yes." I felt sick.

"That flat you have in Munich—I've been staying in it. If I get arrested, you'll need to run."

"Why would you get arrested?"

"Because I'm a British spy working on German soil, you jackass."

"You're protected by Hitler."

"Who's in decline, as you say. If Himmler should get the upper hand, I'll be dead within hours."

"Incidentally, Hitler cross dresses."

"Ah, how amusing. With the mustache or without?"

"The mustache is real and he wishes it wasn't. It's an old scenario, apparently. He mentioned doing it with Kubizek. He dresses, flaps around, Carlotta appears, makes him strip and gives him a spanking."

"Memories of life with mama."

"Just thought you should know."

"I'll pass it on to the PM. He adores stories like that."

"Useful?"

He shrugged. "Who knows?"

We sipped at the coffee. Not up to Berghof standards, but pretty good.

"Anything else, Paul?"

"Just this. Carlotta Krause is the only one of you allowed to touch the gun. Never again, Willy!" His pleasant if narrow face now flushed. His eyes were tiny with rage.

So this was the real reason I had been asked down.

"I got that from her, too."

"The damnable thing is that you're too useful to kill, you stupid little man."

"She works for you, then?" She'd told me she was Stalin's creature. That's how I saw her, how I understood her.

"Keep asking questions like that and I'll accept the recommendation she has already given me."

I remember that I began to shake.

"If she has to kill you, you'll never see it coming and she won't get caught."

So she was an assassin as well as a spy, and not only that, she thought that I was so inept that I should be killed. And was willing to do it.

Or was he lying, and if so, why? For that matter, why tell me at all?

I was sickened. Was I just a little operative, here to do a job, to whom she was secretly entirely indifferent?

I had to get away from this subject. I could not bear it. "Nice to know my flat is still there, anyway."

"If it's bombed, it'll be by mistake."

"And Wannsee? I've wondered about that, too."

"Jews, bankers and Jewish bankers own those houses, and they will have them back. Plus, you're there."

"Safe, as always. My war disgusts me."

"It would me, too. I'm glad I'm not you. But never mind, it'll be over soon enough and you can become a pirate of another sort."

"I'm a pirate?"

"You steal essential materiel for Hitler using false licenses. That's fucking piracy and you know it very well, you little rich prick."

But of course he had come to loathe me. Knowing what he did, how could he not? I said nothing.

He went on. "The Brown House is being pulverized with high explosive tomorrow night. I'm leading in a crew of apparent *trummerfrau* to clean up afterward. Actually, disaffected aristos disguised in rags. We'll be keeping any files we find, of course. We need to know who the registered Nazis are. After the war, that information will be vital."

"There must be millions."

"Records are being destroyed already. The party is preparing to go underground. There's a plan to build a redoubt here in the Obersalzberg, to create an SS underground called *Werwolf*. Which reminds me. I'd also like from you any evidence of additional construction, especially underground construction, outside the Berghof perimeter or in."

"I'll do my best. Perhaps I can fuck the information out of Hitler."

He laughed breezily. "You haven't invited me to luncheon. I'm getting miffed."

"Couldn't that be dangerous for you?"

He shrugged. "I'm a soldier in a war. But I have something for him that will help both of us. If he's onto me and I get arrested, then too bad for me." He stood. "Let's find out."

As we drove up to the house, he spoke even more openly. "You have enemies, Willy. On this side, obviously."

I thought of Himmler and his wax bullets. "I should say so."

"On our side as well. Dulles, particularly. What did you do to make him into an enemy?"

"Showed him a film of Jews being gassed to death."

"What film?"

"It was given to me by an old friend in the SS. It shows a large number of people in some sort of sealed room that fills up with fumes. Horrific business. Somewhere in the east."

"Whatever possessed you to give it to that swine? He was probably delighted. He'd have burned it, of course."

I'd thought my getting it to Dulles quite the coup. "I don't know what he did with it."

"That's precisely the sort of propaganda we need. It's exactly the sort of thing that would turn the German people against Hitler at last." He all but bared his teeth. "If there's one thing about my job I detest, it's having to deal with amateurs like you. They always get themselves killed in the end anyway. Then you feel rotten."

"Thank you for the morale boost."

"I'm sorry, Willy. I can only plead stress. Slow down, there's another matter to discuss."

I did as he asked.

"You know Freddy and Lally Horstman, I believe."

"I've been in their salon."

"And you've met there perhaps Lorenmarie Schoenberg?"

"I'm not sure."

"Of course you don't keep a diary. Bollocks!"

"A diary could get me killed."

"Not if it's just innocent notes. No speculations or whatever. I want you to get to Berlin as soon as you can. Go to the Adlon in the lunch hour. The social set meets there. As soon as you see a familiar face, chat to them. We want to get to Fraulien Schoenberg or the Russian princess Missie Vassilchikov. There's a plot on to assassinate Hitler and these kids know all about it. We want it derailed."

"Why don't you meet with them yourself?"

"I've tried. I've offered to carry mail back and forth for them to Paris. We'd look at it, of course. But Missie is very clever. She ever so sweetly puts me off. You can ingratiate yourself, a wealthy American, they'll fall all over themselves to be in your good graces. Have a party for the whole circle at that wonderful house of yours. Feed them beautifully and they will become your friends."

"Does it bother you that those Jews are out there—what's happening to them?"

"Of course it does! Do you think me a moral idiot? You've just destroyed a real chance of embarrassing the regime into at least slowing down and you throw that in my face?"

"I agree with the conspirators. I'm not going to help you."

"Very well. Drive on. Let's go see Hitler, then. Enjoy luncheon with the devil." Then he murmured, "We'll see how much longer you last."

"You know, I can betray you, too, Paul. You need to pull yourself together. You're unstrung."

"No I'm not." He pulled out a flask and drank from it. "We absolutely must not end up with a situation where there are Germans to negotiate with. You've known that for a long time."

"Known it, but I don't agree and I never have. Anything that prolongs Hitler in power is monstrous."

"So why isn't he dead? You're right there fucking the man in the ass! Fuck him in half! Kill him!"

I knew the miserable truth was that the Casablanca decision was the right one. There must be no Germany left capable of negotiating with anybody. The Germans had to be re-introduced to civilization, and you couldn't do that while dealing with some rump government full of pigs who were pretending not to be Nazis.

"Fuck, oh FUCK, Paul!"

"I know, Willy."

We fell into silence. Around the next turning was the last of the SS posts. We'd just left the previous one and couldn't linger here long. I started the car.

"Will you go to the Adlon?"

"I'll do as you ask."

"I'll be in that little flat of Hitler's."

I was stunned. "The one where he keeps his sister?"

"The sisters are in the countryside. I'm borrowing it from him."

I had to hand it to Paul. He really was very good as his trade. The only person who had ever bested him was the man he was now so intricately and obsessively betraying.

As we arrived at the house, Hitler and Eva appeared at the foot of the steps, as they did for honored guests.

"Paul," he said, "I'm surprised. But you do have a tendency to just turn up. Welcome!"

"I've got something good."

"Excellent, excellent! Good news is most welcome around here."

We sat to a lunch at which the girls took the opportunity to insist on venison schnitzel being served in Paul's honor. "He does such difficult work, he needs solid food, look at him, how thin he's grown."

Hitler roared away about it, "The stench! How can anybody eat that? It's too much!" But he allowed it.

Carlotta, who was to his right (we were at the long table) chewed noisily. "Quit insulting my meat," she said, "or I'll smoke a cigarette at you."

Eva tore at the venison like somebody out of a cave. As she was skiing for hours every day, she was constantly hungry and starving for meat.

Afterward Paul said, "May we step into your study, Leader?"

"Most certainly, and with pleasure! Will it win me the war?"

"I think it could help a good deal."

"Do come with us, Willy. Good news is to be shared." He had been making doe-eyes at me across the table all during the meal. It was extremely disconcerting. The man was now gaga. He was absolutely the most horrifying excuse for a girlie-boy one could imagine. And absurd. Entirely. But I had achieved my objective. I was his most intimate confidante.

In the study, Paul pulled out a sheaf of British intelligence briefs with stamps on them indicating that they were restricted to the War Cabinet.

I had no idea what they were, of course, but I could see by the map that he unfolded that the information involved a huge land area, in fact the whole of the eastern front.

I know now that it was nothing less than an analysis of Operation Bagration, the massive Soviet offensive that would commence in June. There was only one thing wrong with it, although, at the time I couldn't tell this. As I have since discovered—and, in fact, was told by Paul after the war—the estimate of forces on the Soviet side was less than half of the actual total, while the estimates of *Wehrmacht* firepower were overstated.

As Paul and I translated for Hitler, he became increasingly agitated, then excited.

"Of course," he said as he listened. He was pacing up and down the room. "Now wait, listen to me! That estimate—how many tanks?"

"One thousand eight hundred."

"And where does this figure come from? Because I have a different figure."

"The British Army has a liaison officer attached to Zhukov's command."

He thought about that. "So it could be true."

"What estimate do you have?"

"Somewhat more. Around two thousand."

The truth, as I discovered after the war, was that the Russians had 5,200 tanks in the battle and the Germans hardly a thousand.

Paul continued, "It says here, 'the German system of fortified locations is expected to offer a significant obstacle to advancing Russian troops, possibly preventing the development of useful breakthroughs before the onset of winter.'"

"There, you see! You see! And how they have complained about my idea. Not one general supports me, not even Keitel! Ha! Excellent."

The *feste platze,* an idea of Hitler's, was a complete debacle and, in fact, the actual British assessment of Bagration places strong emphasis on the vulnerability of the Germans' rigid defense.

To my mind, the transmittal of this false document to Hitler ranks as one of the most successful deceptions of the war. By exposing Bagration to him when the Russians were trying so very hard to keep it a secret, the British created an air of authenticity that Hitler accepted uncritically. The fact that OKH revised its strength assessment when the documents were transmitted to General von Bock confirmed in Hitler's mind that Paul was his faithful supporter and gave them the status of holy writ.

He said, "If we win out here, I'm honoring you with an Eagle with oak leaf cluster and fifty thousand hectares in Byelorussia."

"I cannot express my gratitude, Leader."

Thus, the formerly clever Herr Hitler fell into yet another trap. Once the war started, his extraordinary insight into people seemed to leave him. The darkly clever manipulator of the '30s had been replaced by someone far less effective, and by '44 whatever insight he had possessed had left him completely.

At this point, he completely believed that the embarrassment he had visited on Paul back all those years ago had caused a permanent break between him and British Intelligence. Previously, he had understood that Paul was playing both sides and exploited that reality with subtlety and expertise. That was all gone now.

The false document caused him to make another fantastic error. In order to protect Army Group Center's flanks from what on the map looked like a planned encirclement attempt, he made the rash decision to strip it of its armor, which was sent south to counter the breakthrough attempt. But why not? The Russians' apparent lack of tanks meant that the center could be held by infantry.

What actually happened was that the full complement of Soviet forces struck the weakened middle of the line. The result was one of the greatest victories—and catastrophes—in the history of warfare.

Hitler lost 350,000 soldiers, most of them killed, including 31 of the 47 generals involved in the battle, and an almost unimaginable amount of supplies and materiel. The Soviets came out of it at the end of August with the Oder Line their next objective, and Berlin soon to be in artillery range.

And yet, in April of '44, the end still seemed far away.

Paul remained through the afternoon. After the hour in the study, we went up to the teahouse with an ebullient Hitler, laughing and joking as I had not seen him do in years. I found his happiness really very difficult to bear. In the tea house he even did a little dance, something he would do at moments of secret triumph.

I clapped and said, "Bravo!"

Wistfully, Eva said, "If only you could really dance."

"Himmler dances the Charleston," Carlotta said.

"After we win, I promise to learn."

So it went, the teahouse, the banal conversation, then back to the Berghof where Hitler went alone to his study and shouted excitedly into the telephone.

The hairdresser had come, and Eva and Carlotta had gone downstairs to the barber shop, which doubled as their hairdressing salon. As the sun set, I sat with Paul before the fireplace.

"You plan to stay the night?"

"Of course. The raid on Munich will come in at about 2100 hours," he added softly. "Two hundred and fifty bombers and a hundred fighters."

"My God."

"Day and night thousand plane raids will start hitting Berlin later this month. The Americans by day, us by night."

"How can they do that?"

"Come in at five hundred feet. That's under the flak. Now that escort fighters can stick all the way to target, round the clock bombing will become the order of the day."

We were silent then, for a time. I contemplated the enormity of it all, the vastness of the war, the unimaginable numbers of planes involved in the raids, the fact that the allies would soon be on the *Cote d'azur*, all of it.

Little did I know, then, that I was considered too amateurish and unreliable to be anything more than part of the deception. I suppose they assumed that if I was found out and tortured, I'd give in at once. As all I had were lies, it didn't matter much. In fact, it would even be helpful, as my frantically babbled confessions could only be the untruths I'd been told.

"I want you to go up to Berlin before it starts. We don't want you getting blown up down here." He stood. "Come on, let's go out on the terrace."

We stepped out into the sinking afternoon. The tang of the pines filled the air, the sun glowed on the Untersberg.

"I'm uneasy about microphones."

"There's only an intercom system. He's never mentioned any microphones."

"In any case, go spend a week in Wannsee. Go to the Adlon. I can't introduce you because I'm not trusted. But you'll run into Freddy Horstman or Lolly, I would think. They can make the introductions."

"To whom?"

"Gottfried and Melanie Bismarck. Loremarie, as I've mentioned. Missie Vassiltchikov, but be careful there. She's a sharp needle, that one. Adam Trott. He's particularly interesting. He and Missie and Loremarie are all in the *Auswärtiges Amt.* That's the hotbed of the plotters. They reach into the military through General Tresckow and others. Olbricht, Beck. The thing is, most of them are aristocrats. Georg Pappenheim."

To me a haunting name, obviously. This was the German bearer of the title, not the Jewish merchant.

"Willy, if people like Metternich and Bismarck end up in a new government, we'll have no choice to negotiate with it. That's what you must understand."

"I understand very well."

He stared up toward the Bormann's house. Lights were coming on. "Is he up there?"

"They'll be down for dinner. He came back with him from the *Wolfshanze*."

"He's usefully stupid. Maybe we'll get something good out of him. Any others coming?"

"Himmler could appear. One never knows. Morrell will be present."

"I'm going to recommend that one for liquidation."

I said nothing. I dreaded being asked to do the deed.

When we returned to the house, Hitler had emerged from his study and was in the great room looking through his phonograph records. He waved the sheaf of papers. "They're pleased. This will be going off to OKH in the morning. I spoke directly to Gehlen. He's optimistic about its authenticity."

"But not sure?"

"How can he be, Paul? He knows nothing of you. As far as he's concerned, it might have been dropped out of a plane right onto my head."

"Does the SD have anybody close to Menzies?"

"An operative, yes, but not at a very high level."

"They'll ask him to authenticate. I could turn up in such an investigation."

"I'll be alert for that."

Just like that, Paul had discovered that there was a German agent on the staff of the British intelligence chief. I wondered how long the operative had to live. A week? Less? Agents on both sides were vulnerable because of their need to use shortwave transmitters, which the radio direction finders of the day could locate fairly easily. The British shot spies promptly.

The Berghof staff had doubtless informed both Bormann and Himmler of Paul's appearance, and so we had a largish dinner party, with the two of them and their wives, Hitler, Eva, Carlotta and me and Paul.

It was shaping up as at least an endurable evening until the SS Officer of the Watch appeared and politely suggested that we go down into the shelter. A moment later the compound's siren started up and the fog machine began grinding away on the roof. The "fog" it produced was really smoke mixed with a very fine water mist, so it was sodden and stank of kerosene. Given that it generated what was generally the only fog bank for miles around, I often wondered why they used it.

"I hate that thing," Carlotta said. "The smoke makes me dream of cigarettes."

"Not tonight, not while I'm feeling so happy," Hitler said. He had congratulated Paul at least ten different times during dinner. By the time the meal ended, Himmler was almost unable to contain his glowering suspicion, or Bormann his furious jealousy at Paul's triumph.

Five minutes after the alert, the 'all clear' was sounded. The bombers had arrived over Munich and were not coming here.

Soon, a glow appeared in the sky. Hitler stepped out onto the terrace, with Bormann following. Paul nodded to me, and I went as well.

"I wonder about my flat," Hitler said. "That old place."

"My flat, too, Leader," I said. Not calling him Alf in Borman's hearing, God no. The wretch would go wild with jealousy.

"Himmler," Hitler said.

"I'll get him." There was music in the house, the Paganini Violin Concerto on a record. Terrific performance, too, consistent with Hitler's excellent musical taste.

As I asked Himmler to come out, Paul continued chatting to Eva and Carlotta. He was being rather voluble and they were attentive. I hoped that he wasn't trying to seduce Carlotta. He did a lot of casual seduction. He was proud of his skill.

Frankly, I was finding him more and more tiresome. The pressures of war, I suppose. He no longer showed me the elegant, witty gentleman who was presently on display for them.

Back outside, the glow had risen dramatically. Hitler said to Himmler, "What of the Six expedition?"

"The ambassadors wouldn't receive him."

Who was "Six," I wondered.

"Not at all? Not one?"

"Perhaps we should send someone of more stature."

"You, then, Heinrich?"

"I could take a concrete offer."

"Willy here got a marvelous document out of that spy in there. It's going to Gehlen for authentication. If it's the real thing, then we have an excellent chance regarding the offensive that's building up in the east."

"Why do you let a man like that even close to you?"

"My question, also," Bormann said.

"He's a double agent. They're very useful."

"Is he ours or theirs?"

"He was the victim of a small prank Willy and I played on him. When he reported it to SIS as fact, they were quite hard on him. Accused him of being a drunk and a traitor. So he gives me little presents."

I added, "He does it to take his revenge on them. He's very vindictive."

"Is he a National Socialist?"

"No," I said. "But he admires the leader."

"Well, let's hope Gehlen does some good with the authentication."

Eva called, "Wolfie, it's the telephone."

Hitler turned and went back to the house. He was stooped, his head down. Telephone calls were almost always bad news. Bormann dogged along behind him.

Himmler put a hand on my shoulder. "Willy, a moment."

"Yes, Heinrich?"

"None of this to that man."

"No."

"In your opinion, is he really on our side in any way at all?"

I had to be very careful here. Paul's life was the least of what was at stake. "I don't believe that he thinks he is. But that doesn't mean that what he gives us doesn't have its uses. That document, for example—it confirms the existence of a massive Soviet buildup. Obviously preparations for a summer offensive. There are probably inaccuracies intended to deceive us, but still, it's there, and now we know of the overall plan."

"That's a good answer."

"The only one."

"If you ever feel that he's become a real danger or has outlived his usefulness, telephone me."

"I will."

It seemed that Himmler had finally started to trust me a bit. I wondered if it would last.

He sighed. I followed his eyes.

The entire northern sky was shimmering red. I'd never seen anything like it.

"What happens to us, Willy?"

"We go on to victory."

"Don't bother with the charade. You know as well as I do. He does, too."

"Have you thought of getting out?"

"You do business in Argentina, yes?"

"We're having an easier time lately. Farrell is more friendly than Ramirez."

"And there's a real friend of ours just under him. Peron."

"Argentina is a big place."

"Exactly."

"How would you get there?"

"*Kriegsmarine*. U-Boat arm could do it."

"When would you leave?"

I could feel a bit of tension, then. He did not reply. So was this just another of his tests?

"I have a war case. 'The Collapse.' It analyzes the complete destruction of the Reich. In it, the Russians cross the Oder. That's when."

The *Wehrmacht,* the Foreign Office, the SS—all of them drew up these cases. "Does he know about it?"

"We need him to keep fighting. He's the only one who can keep spirits up. He shouldn't be told unless we have to leave."

More useful knowledge for Paul. "Let's go in," I said. "If we don't, he'll be back out and he doesn't need to see this."

But I was too late. When we turned around, there he was standing behind us, his mouth slack, his tired eyes deep. His entire form reflected the dull red horizon he was staring at, as if he was somehow absorbing the fire into his own flesh.

He said, "Do you feel it?"

"No," I said. Then, "Oh, yes." There was a very slight pumping of the air, as if little pops of wind were moving across the terrace. It was concussion from the immense bombs far away. I wondered if any of Paul's rubble women would be left alive to help him.

I approached Hitler and put my arm around his shoulders. "Come on," I said.

He shook me off, then ran ahead, stopping at the end of the terrace. His hand thrust into his pocket, then came out with something black in it.

It was happening so quickly, there was nothing to say. I ran to him. Himmler and Bormann followed, but slowly, I noticed. Very slowly.

I reached him and covered the gun with my hand.

He was calm. "Why not?"

"For your family and your people, Alf. Come on, let's go inside and be with the girls."

"The entire world would rejoice."

"Not your family and not the Germans, and what do the rest matter?"

Bormann and Himmler were now standing behind us. Vultures, waiting.

"Not us," Himmler said in a fuzzy voice. He sounded as if he was speaking over a bad telephone line. Bormann did not speak.

He let me take the gun. And now Eva reappeared. "There's another call, Wolf."

"Let me take it," I said. He nodded to that, and I conducted him back to the house. The gun was now in my pocket.

Paul and Carlotta were in the great room. Much to my annoyance, he was hanging over her, practically breathing her breath. He was allegedly teaching her English.

Hitler went on the call and said, "Please give your report to this man." He handed me the phone.

It was a Luftwaffe officer. He proceeded to report that the raid had consisted of 284 B-17 bombers, and that 50 had been shot down and another 8 severely damaged. I thanked him and rang off.

The room was silent. Hitler was watching me, his eyebrows raised over his sad, nearly empty eyes. I thought, 'that man's soul has left him.' I said, "Extraordinary news. We brought down fifty bombers tonight."

Hitler barked out something between a laugh and a cry of agony. "Goering must have accidentally done something right! Bravo!"

Eva called from the great room, "Does this mean we shall win?"

Nobody responded. Coffee was brought. The music played on.

## 22

The next morning just at dawn, I drove Paul down to Munich with the idea of continuing on to Berlin and carrying out the extraordinarily disturbing mission he had give me. I knew very well that SIS would turn over the names I gave them to the Gestapo. Every person on that list would die, and horribly.

It sickened me, the whole business, you cannot imagine.

Carlotta insisted on accompanying me to Berlin. “Willy,” she had said, “I couldn’t stand the waiting. I simply could not. If you go, then I want to go, too.” I wondered if by ‘go,’ she meant simply travel to the city or be killed? I didn’t press the matter, but by the way she clutched my hand in the car, it was clear that she expected death at any moment.

Nobody was innocent about strafing anymore, and certainly not us. Life could end in an instant, or we could be maimed and left to die a lingering death.

Over the years, she had become steadily more sophisticated, more elegant and more beautiful and, above all, more deeply committed to the two of us. Even so, I had recently found myself gazing at her when she slept, and wondering if she could follow an order to kill me. Or, for that matter, could I follow one to do the same to her?

I never dreamed it at the time, but these were the best years of our love affair, when it was full of the passion and endless mutual fascination that characterizes young love. I cared about the significance of every flicker of her eyes and was interested in every mole hidden on her skin, in the line of her lips, the tone of her voice, what she read, even how fast she turned her pages, what she liked to eat and didn't, how she smoked and what she preferred to drink, her fashion sense, all of it. I was fixated on her and she on me.

I suppose you might disdain her, saying 'a whore living a filthy life, who could care about such a creature?' My response is that lovers continually astonish one another.

My love for her was making me a much more other-directed human being. I was beginning to taste something of the unconditionality of true love, which extends from the smitten couple outward. 'Everybody loves a lover' works both ways. As Carlotta and I fell in love with each other, we were also falling in love with the awful, equivocal and agonized world in which we lived.

Sitting beside me now was a splendid young woman, glowing from within. Certainly she was a whore, but she didn't allow her personal and professional lives to overlap. For example, she was no dominatrix, just an efficient sex worker. When I took her in my arms, she was supple and giving. She liked to melt into the embrace of her man and be lifted by him into our private cloud of love.

As we passed the road to the airfield where the Hitler Flight waited, she said, "Surely we're not taking the train."

Paul said, "They've got long range fighters now, Mustangs and Spits."

"The trains are hell. Anyway, they hit trains, too."

"Carlotta, we're going to stay with the car. The Autobahn isn't often bombed."

I would have preferred some innocuous little saloon, but 770s were the only cars available to me at the Berghof. I'd had four jerrycans of fuel put into the boot, but I didn't mention that. If we were strafed, we'd burn, and Carlotta didn't need to think about that.

As we drove down through the mountains, I said to Paul, "there was talk last night of a peace mission to Stockholm. The number six was mentioned."

"Six? In what context?"

"It had something to do with visits to allied embassies."

"Ah, that would be a name. Doctor Franz Six. Foreign Office. Well, those peace feelers are useless. They won't get anywhere."

"They discussed the idea of Himmler going personally. Even Hitler himself."

"Hat in hand to the British Embassy in Stockholm? No."

"He's known for years that things weren't going to end well. Don't assume that it couldn't happen."

"It won't matter but it would be an irritant and we don't want it to happen, so if you have any indication that either of them might turn up there, I want notice. Dr. Six, I don't care."

As we drove into the suburbs of Munich, we fell silent. Until you have seen it for yourself—and I hope you never do—you cannot know the emotions that seeing a city on fire elicit. Woe, fear, that's what to call them.

First, there is a stench, and in this case it was chiefly of escaping gas. Also cordite and burning buildings. The air was hazed with yellow-gray smoke through which crept trams clanging their bells and strange, humped figures, darkly wandering.

I would have skirted the city as much as possible, but we had to go in through Ramersdorf in order to deposit Paul reasonably close to the Brown House, which was in Brienner Strasse. This meant driving straight in along the Tegenernseer Landstrasser. As it was a main thoroughfare, it was being rapidly cleared of debris, at least, but I was still concerned about a puncture. The car was equipped for repairs, but I didn't want any delay. It would be dangerous to still be on the road at night. One had to drive with covered lights and crashes were a constant problem, not to mention highwaymen. As soon as they saw a big car like this that wasn't in convoy, they were liable to be on it at once. In fact, I thought that at least one carload of them had followed us for a time in the forests on the way down. Colonel Ruffner, the

Officer of the Day, had suggested that we convoy, but I didn't care to have the SS making notations about our route and stops.

I was able to get Paul only as far as the Palace of Justice. The streets beyond that led toward the Brown House were complete heaps of rubble, but it wasn't far as long as one didn't mind climbing a few hills of smoking ruins.

He got out and went silently off into the haze.

It took three more hours to pick our way out of the devastated city. More than once, we saw the twisted remains of a bomber, looking very sad indeed. In fact, everything looked sad. Terribly, terribly sad.

Carlotta said, "We do not have to visit a madhouse to find disordered minds. Our planet is the mental institution of the universe."

"Is that from...Schopenhauer?"

"Of course not. He never wrote a sentence that clear in his life. It's Goethe. From Faust."

Once we were on the road again, the sumptuous beauty of a spring afternoon in Bavaria unfolded around us. Across the rolling farmland there was a mist of green, new growth of wheat and barley and cabbages and carrots coming up, all of it undoubtedly destined for the troops, out there on the frontiers of the war attempting to fulfill Hitler's idiotic ideological fantasies. Tangles of flowers were appearing here and there along the road, blue cornflowers for the most part, as I recall. There was much mud still and even frost in the high places. But it offered a promise that the beauty of new growth would soon overspread the land.

"I wonder if Dachau got hit?"

"I doubt it. They stay away from the camps."

"Why do that?"

"So as not to kill the inmates."

She laughed bitterly, got a cigarette from her case and drew in a long drag. "Did Paul tell you to kill Alf?"

"The exact opposite."

"My orders, too. Keep him alive. He fantasizes about me killing him. He wants a slow death, he says." She turned her voice to gravel.

"'I want to die gazing into your eyes,' he says. Isn't that amazingly sick?"

"He is amazingly sick."

She smoked reflectively, gazing out the window. "'April is the cruelest month, breeding lilacs out of the dead land.'"

"'Mixing memory and desire, stirring dull roots with spring rain.' That was good English, Carlie!"

"Paul taught me."

Instantly, I was annoyed. Sophisticated, handsome older man. "Ah. Nice of him."

"Willy, I want us to make love in a very leisurely way, in a house where there is no intercom. That shit listens, I know he does."

"Probably."

She leaned far back and blew smoke at the ceiling. "I'm remembering the last time we were in Wannsee, bathing together in your huge tub. Then taking advantage of the blackout to go down to the lake naked. Dear heaven, it was so cold, I thought you'd get frostbite you know where."

"I did."

"You're lying!"

"I am."

In the event we could not make Berlin before dark, and so had to stop in a *gasthaus*. The proprietress was sullen, obviously angered by our big car. In her world, the only automobiles left were jalopies running on charcoal burners.

She wanted our internal passports. "Two rooms," she said. As the Reich encouraged babies, unmarried cohabitation wasn't illegal, but we were deep in Catholic Germany, so we didn't complain.

Outside of the Hitler Bubble, life was very different. We had to give ration coupons for our supper and she was very pleased to bring us a single anorexic sausage to split between us, and two modest helpings of sauerkraut. No mustard or seasoning on anything. There was beer, though, dark and richly hoppy. Afterward, a couple of mouthfuls of strudel that consisted of three thin slices of apple in a soggy crust. This was followed by generous mugs of acorn *mukefuck*.

Absurdly, I called for cognac. Equally absurdly, she had some apple brandy that her husband had made, she said, "before he went away." It was sharp and coarse, as would be expected, but gloriously aromatic, filling one's head with the very soul of the apple. I still remember that simple stuff as one of the finest drinks I have ever tasted.

As we were retiring, she drew up her lean form and said pointedly, "It rocks the whole house."

"What does?"

Her lips became a narrow line. She said, "You know very well, Herr Weber."

We went up to my room, which is the one we would stay in, and buried our faces in the big down-filled pillows and laughed.

One can come from the south through Potsdam to Wannsee. There is no need to go anywhere near central Berlin, so the roads were clean and quiet, empty of all except official traffic, and very little of that.

We were just approaching Potsdam when there came the distinct sound of an engine overhead. I saw nothing, and it soon faded. But I remembered the horror of the strafing on the road in France and sped up.

Now the sound returned. This time it was screaming, as if the engine had gone haywire. But it hadn't. The pilot had. The hunter had found some prey.

"Willy?"

A terrific booming, nothing like the movies, I can assure you. Sounds to crack open the head, then a roaring flash of silver so low the prop wash nearly blew our canvas top right off.

A sharp curve rushed toward us.

"Look out!"

I swerved, managing—just—to go wallowing through it in the big, ungainly vehicle.

Then he was back, coming straight at us. He was virtually on the ground. He couldn't miss.

"Head down!"

I slammed on the brakes—and the road behind us erupted into a spray of flying tarmac. Now I jammed the accelerator to the floor and the car leaped ahead. I was aiming for a copse of trees that I could see overhanging the road about half a kilometer on.

We had become a matter of principle for the young knight in the plane, I knew that. He had to get us now.

"Where's the Luftwaffe?"

"In Goering's garage."

We reached the copse. I pulled the car off onto the berm, up next to the trees that crowded it. "Get out."

We ran deeper into the copse.

The plane was so low that I thought he was actually trying to see under the trees.

I grabbed Carlotta and we threw ourselves to the ground amid the tree trunks. Again, the cannon sounded, thundering like Satan's cough.

The plane pulled almost straight up, corkscrewed and flew away.

We waited. A breeze rustled the trees above. Something peeped, some early creature of the spring.

The car was perfectly intact, or so we imagined as we approached it. But there was a large rip in the canvas of the top and a great hole in the wind screen.

Carlotta grabbed me and pressed against me in silence. From the position of the damage, it was clear that the bullet would have blown my head to pieces.

'So it would be hard for you,' I thought. 'Hard to kill me.'

We kissed carefully, each of us, I am sure, tasting the miracle of the other.

I had seen the face of the boy in the plane, fierce, intent eyes above an oxygen mask. We would have been another target hit, hardly mentioned, just a trivial vehicle, doubtless singled out because of the fact that it was the type that carried officials.

When we finally got to the house, Fritz and Maria were overjoyed to see us. As the door opened into that lovely, welcoming space, I found myself almost moved to tears. The elegant flow of the staircase was invariably pleasing to my eye, and on the table there was a spray of hothouse flowers. A faint scent of something good came from the kitchen. Beyond the arch under the staircase, the sunny room that Carlotta so loved was open to the view down to the lake.

I said to Fritz, "Put the car out of sight in the garage."

As he went out, I noticed men in our garden, no fewer than four of them.

"Maria?"

She was flushed from the hot kitchen, her gray bun tight, her forehead beaded. "Yes, Master Willy?"

"Who's that out there?"

"*Ostarbeiter*. They came up all together, saying they were sent here by a lady in the mountains. They had a paper. Fritzl hired them right away. They're farmers, good with the garden. They're putting in beets, turnips, runners, all sorts of things. And the flowers, of course, not to forget them. There's a rabbit hutch and a henhouse has been constructed." She lowered her voice." "They will go out and steal chickens for us."

"You are to buy chickens, Maria."

"They're very dear!"

"Do it anyway. No stealing."

"But they're Russians. They prefer to steal. It's their honor."

"Then let them steal, but find out who they stole from and pay them later."

"Very well, Master Willy."

Eastworkers were Russians and Poles. The ones in my garden were not forced laborers, but men who had answered the call for workers that had gone out among the captive nations in 1940 and '41. Unlike their leader, the practical Germans did not see the sense in starving perfectly good people to death when they could be made use of, and Russians who hated Soviet life saw opportunity in the Reich. The first round of foreign workers from both east and west, for the most part volunteers, were not ill treated, not like the eastern front POWs who would come later. Those men were housed in urban camps and the long brown barracks that seemed to fill every inch of free space in German cities. Workers such as the ones I had were paid a regular wage and lived with their employers or in ordinary apartments.

Much is made of the horror of slave labor in wartime Germany, and the SS controlled plenty of that. Free foreign workers farmed, sewed, built planes, made bullets, drove trams, you name it, they were everywhere. They had to report to the local police station once a week. That was the extent of their confinement.

At Yalta in 1945, the allies agreed on forced repatriation for all of these people, with the result that most of the Russians ended up either dead on the road home, shot on arrival or sent to the Gulag. I don't think many survived, but any records are locked up in the vaults of Moscow.

At night we would hear our fellows in the cellar where they lived, singing and playing a *balalaika* they had probably stolen. One of them had been a Red Army doctor. The other two were his orderlies. They had been captured together in the first days of the war. "Fritz officer say, you come. We think, why die in cage for Stalin? Fuck him. We come."

I am happy to say that two of them survived the war, both in improbable ways. But then again, in a conflict so lethal, all survival was improbable.

The next forenoon we set out for Berlin, going in on the train rather than taking the bullet-holed Mercedes.

"What're they like, aristocrats," Carlotta asked as the train clattered along.

"You must've seen a few in your time."

"We didn't get many at Madame Kitty's. Mostly just Jews and Nazis. The odd clergyman. Damned odd, usually."

"Well then, you shall see."

"I don't want them looking down their long noses at me. They'll get a big 'fuck you.'"

"You're a lovely, sophisticated young woman now. Nobody's going to be looking down their noses at you. You can even spout poetry—and in English, no less!"

"That's the only English I know. I told him I wanted to learn your absolute favorite, and he said that's what it was."

One did not kiss in German trams, so I leaned close to her and said, "I am kissing you." Whereupon she took my chin and kissed me hard and long, to a rising chorus of *tsks*.

In that moment, I recall that I found myself imagining the children we would have together. I still dream of them all the time, and have for years. At first, they were babies, my imaginary twins, Willy and Albert.

My mother used to say, 'Willy, never forget how good it feels to hold a baby in your arms.' It was a rather awful thing for a little boy to hear, but having done it once or twice now, I do know that I have missed yet another of the worthwhile experiences of life.

My imaginary children have grown up. Over the years, I bought them marvelous imaginary toys like the real ones *Vati* used to buy me, wonderful fire engines and bicycles and such.

We got off the tram in front of the Adlon and went into the lobby. It was quite crowded and for a moment all seemed normal, almost pre-war normal. But then I noticed a furtive glance here, another there, and soon felt the familiar atmosphere of threat that lingered over all social gatherings in the dictatorship.

Most of the people in the lobby were busy getting luncheon sandwiches, but some of them were in close conversation. Intriguers. In among that lot I spotted Lally, then Freddy Horstmann.

"Come on. Now be nice, remember we're on a mission. You're a sophisticated, elegant spy. Mata Hari, but shorter."

She proceeded to goose me. I wasn't expecting it and shouted. All faces turned toward us. I called out, "Ah, there you are! Freddy!"

"Yes...oh, the American, yes!" We walked up to him. He kissed Carlotta's hand and I kissed Lolly's. "How can it be that you're here? Our countries are at war, or are you too rich for that to matter to you?"

"We go where we please, my dear," I said. "Allow me to introduce my fiancée, Carlotta Krause. Carlotta, Herr and Frau Horstmann."

"Yes, you've mentioned them. I'm absolutely fried with envy. The next time this oaf goes to your salon, I hope he'll remember that I don't just cook and iron."

There was a brief silence. I could see that they had been thrown off by the personal nature of her first words to them, not to mention the self-invitation. Also, she had lifted her accent above the *kietz*, causing her to sound like a charwoman putting on airs.

To cover her rough talk, I said, "My Bavarian."

"Ah, yes. What brings you in? I recall that you're in Wannsee."

"The Foreign Office. My business arrangements."

A woman whose back had been to us now turned around. "The Foreign Office," she said. "That's where I am. Perhaps I can help."

Freddy said, "May I introduce the Princess Marie Vassiltchikov. This is Herr William Weber and his fiancée Fraulein Krause."

I kissed her hand. Before she had said another word, we were joined by a second woman who proved to be Loremarie Schonburg, the Princess Eleanor-Marie Schonburg-Hartenstein. "Did you say you're Americans? How extraordinary, no, nostalgic. Yes, having an American here is nostalgic."

I said, "Our countries have been at war before. In the end, we had the pleasure of rediscovering our friendship, and I think it will happen that way again."

The princess Marie said, "I must step away," turned, and disappeared into the small crowd. I saw her speak to somebody and a moment later a man came over. This was Adam Trott.

Loremarie said, "So, how do you find us?"

"National Socialists?"

Her face turned to granite. "I am a princess of the German realm."

"Airs," Carlotta muttered.

I said quickly, "I am the son of Freethinkers who migrated to America in 1848 to get away from the Hohenzollerns."

"So that's why your accent is so measured. German isn't native to you."

"I've been told that I sound more like a book that can talk."

"Why are you here? And how?"

"He can go anywhere," Carlotta said. "He is a very powerful

young man."

That brought another silence. "Yes," Loremarie said, "all the power has slipped out of our fingers."

"If the Kaiser hadn't been such an idiot, we'd still have a decent Germany," Carlotta said.

Loremarie's eyes went back to her, rested on her face for a moment, then returned to me. Lally and Freddy drifted away. Adam Trott said something in her ear. "Nonsense," she snapped, "let me do it."

I saw him squeeze her arm hard enough to make her wince. Then she threw off a blazing smile. "Since he's so powerful, Dearie, he must know the president personally."

"He's Herr Weber. He knows more than just the president personally. He does business with him. And with Churchill. Winnie. They all do business together."

They stared at her in wooden silence. 'Treating with the enemy' was a crime punishable by death.

She's a catastrophe, I thought. But what else could I have expected?

"I do have some political acquaintances, yes," I said quickly. "My shipping company, you see."

"Oh, don't ship anything here. We're the Nazis, remember."

Adam Trott said, "Really, Lore." (The contraction Nazi was an insulting term in Germany in those days. One did not use it openly. One said 'National Socialist.')

"I'm only being frank. What if Hitler was gone? What would you ship here then?"

"I'm afraid my shipping is very dull. Minerals and such. Heaps of stuff brought up from mines in South America."

"Oh, a world traveler! I could not be more jealous. But not to us, surely."

"My ores come from neutral countries and are shipped under neutral flags to the highest bidder. My company is Swiss and so cannot trade with the enemy. Switzerland has none."

She thought about that. "But if Hitler was gone, would you then ship automobile parts, say? I have a wonderful Cadillac that won't go because some part is deficient and needs replacement. Or foodstuffs, American turkey and that delicious bacon you have. Would you ship that?"

"Hitler is not gone."

The two of them stared at us. I stared back. Carlotta took out a cigarette and Adam Trott lit it. He said to me, "How long have you been in Berlin?"

"Not long."

"Perhaps then you would like to be shown around a bit. There's a party at the Italian ambassador's house tomorrow night. Do you play Bridge?"

"Bridge? My goodness, yes! But one doesn't see much Bridge in Germany."

"What do you know? We have Bridge clubs all over the country."

"It's Eva," Carlotta hissed, "she's the one who plays *Skat*. She can't understand the simplest thing."

"A friend? Here in Germany?"

My heart had dropped into my stomach, but she realized her mistake.

"No, in America. A German who lives in New York."

"We cannot emigrate, we aristocrats. Our lives are tied to our lands. Would that we could, I would have been gone from here the moment the paperhanger appeared beside that old fool Bismarck."

Trott stared straight ahead, as if he had not heard.

"Will we receive an invitation, then, or shall we just arrive, and if so at what hour?"

"It depends on the bombs, doesn't it? You'll be on the list, and if your invitation has met up with you, all the better. His parties normally start at eight, but if there's a raid going on, then an hour after it ends is the normal rule."

"And we simply take away the place-cards of the dead. Have you been under a raid yet?"

"No," I said.

"Yes," Carlotta said.

Finally, Adam Trott became more animated. To be specific, he laughed. "What an interesting couple you are. Side by side and in different places at the same time."

Loremarie grabbed my arm and pulled me aside. "You are not a German and therefore you don't see what we see. But that young woman is obviously no fiancée. She is a girl of the street, if you want to know. A Lily of the Lamplight."

"Gosh, I had no idea."

"Bring her to the ambassador's. He'll be elated." And then, in the next instant, the two of us were back in the conversation. Some social skills have not only to do with grace. Speed is often important as well. I don't think Carlotta even realized that the exchange had taken place. Adam Trott's face, however, was bursting with contained mirth.

That afternoon at home, Carlotta read and looked out at the few boats on the lake. She said little. I don't remember the evening.

Dinner the next night proceeded along predictable lines. It was an informal affair among friends, not an official dinner. In other words, there were no Foreign Office officials present, no Ribbentrop, no Dr. Six. Missy Vassiltchikov and her sister were there, the Trotts, the Shonburgs, Gottfried and Melanie Bismarck and some others, and me and Carlotta. As Bridge was to be played, I had taught her the game in the afternoon, assuming that, with her intelligence, an hour's lesson would enable her to at least manage a credible failure at the table.

Little did I know.

I had also taught her how to converse at dinner, and as she was seated between Ambassador Anfuso and Adam Trott, she did quite well. She was obviously being offered to the ambassador as nice piece of strudel. As this was immediately clear to her, also, she played the two men like a couple of trombones, with the emphasis very definitely on the 'bone. Had they known that she was actually Hitler's very personal mistress, they would probably have had coronaries, but her professional skill was such that they were treated to the illusion that she had simply never known any men quite as interesting or charming as the two of them.

I listened carefully to the chatter, but nothing was said about Hitler, and the seating did not allow me to converse with Loremarie without committing the gaucherie of crossing the table. As I was already there with my "Lily Marlene" in tow, I thought I'd better be on my best behavior.

Afterward, we went into a very nicely appointed card room, the twelve of us sitting to four tables, with the intention of rotating across the course of the evening.

In a Bridge evening, one soon gets to know the flow of play, and you can hear by the communications who knows what they're doing and who's a "conversational player." I soon became distracted by a series of sharpish exchanges at Carlotta's table. After barely half an hour, she and her partner, Gottfried Bismarck, had completed the contract.

To make a long story short, from that first game until the end of her life, Carlotta was a marvelous Bridge player. The few times she came to San Antonio, she cleaned right up at the country club, and it's not as if there aren't some good players there. Had she cared to play seriously, I have no doubt that she could have become a master.

In any case, the only partner on that evening at Anfuso's with whom she did poorly was me, and this was because I was so flustered that I kept making tyro mistakes, and here she was the tyro. By the end of the evening, she was blazing with anger, and I was afraid that she might make me submit to some of her Hitler tricks when we got home.

After Bridge, Adam Trott, the ambassador and Karl Schonburg became engaged in a long conversation about the financial health of various Italian grandees (never good) and Carlotta and I were left to Loremarie.

We stepped out into the back garden, which was entirely dark. The embassies, of course, followed the blackout regulations. It wasn't a deep garden, and one could hear lapping from the lake. A breeze was setting up busy little waves that one could not see, but could imagine in the dark.

"If this country were suddenly to be in the hands of good Germans, what would happen?"

My heart gave a little twist in my chest. "If?"

"If, yes. Poof, like that?"

"I can't say."

"But you know Roosevelt? Can you say if he would negotiate?"

"He originated the idea of unconditional surrender."

"Nonsense," Carlotta said. "I know him, too. He's a negotiator by nature. He even negotiates his smoking rights with his wife. She's got him down to ten cigarettes a day."

I was flabbergasted. What could she be thinking? Neither one of us knew a damn thing about Roosevelt's personal habits, let alone had any idea if he even thought there was such a thing as a good German. I knew that Churchill most certainly did not.

"Oh, you do know him, then. I was afraid it was just talk."

"Not at all. Say Hitler's dead. The Nazis are on the run. Names like Bismarck and Metternich come to the surface. I think you could expect something. But why do you ask?"

"I must leave that question unanswered, but with an obvious silence."

Carlotta barked out a laugh. "I must tell you that Anfuso's certainly not in your *putsch*. He spent the evening trying to convince me to go to Italy and meet Musso. Singing the praises of that old satyr. Ha!"

Even though I could not see Loremarie in the dark, I could assume that she'd gone pale. There can be no more plain spoken a person than Carlotta.

"Don't worry about your 'obvious silence' either," she continued. "Your secret's safe enough with us, and Americans haven't got the slightest idea how to intrigue, so don't worry about this one." She tapped me on the chest. "Right, Willy?"

"If I have followed the conversation—"

"You haven't, so squeeze your bunghole shut for once in your life."

I heard Loremarie's gasp. I said, "It's been a lovely evening."

"Yeah, I've got six thousand marks in my purse I didn't come in with. So take me back to New York where I can spend them."

"Marks aren't good in New York. There's no exchange."

She laughed. "He might be a dumbass when it comes to *coups* and shit, but he can turn dirt into money, so you'll find a way for me to spend my marks, am I right?"

"How do you get to New York?" Loremarie said faintly.

"Take the diplomatic flight to Lisbon, then the flying boat. He does it all the time. For men like my Willy, the war hardly exists." She gave me a tug down below that I hope Loremarie didn't see, but I've never known.

I will say this, after the war we had no invitations in Germany. But then again, there were damned few anywhere, at least for me. Carlotta played a lot of Bridge and in all sorts of places.

We had not gone to the ambassador's in the Mercedes. It was just a short drive and it was after dark, but we couldn't very well arrive in a shot-up car.

Instead, I had an Olympia which I'd had Fritz buy for me. I'd said to him, "I want to buy a little saloon. It was the Merc that drew the fire."

"Yes, I understand perfectly, Herr Weber. There are plenty on the lots."

Of course there were. Nobody had gasoline. But as we could draw from the Chancellery's supply, I hadn't any concerns about that.

"If you can find a good one, buy it for me. There's jerrycans of petrol in the boot of the Merc. Take one with you so you can drive off."

"A jerrycan? I'm not about to travel on the U-Ban with a jerrycan of gasoline to explain. I'll put a liter in a jar."

He brought back an appropriately nondescript machine, the sort of thing that not even an extremely bored allied pilot would waste bullets on, then have to explain to his intelligence officer why his gun camera footage showed him shooting up a jalopy.

We drove home. We had succeeded in our mission. And now came the first great battle in the war of love that was to become our life.

# 23

As we were pulling into the garage, she snapped, "why are we riding around in this heap?"

"Because the fancy heap attracts unwanted attention."

"At night?"

"It also has no windshield. And a hole in the roof."

She got out and stalked into the cellar room where the Russians were sleeping. There were snorts in the dark.

She stomped upstairs. "Fuckin' gorillas..."

"They're good gardeners."

I followed her up through the *rez-de-chaussée* to the upper floor. With exaggerated care, she closed our bedroom door behind us and twisted the lock.

"Ah," I said, "promising!"

The next thing I knew, a *chaussure* had whizzed past my head and bounced against the wall, springing it's slender heel right off. I turned to see her ripping off her splendid Maggie Rouf evening gown and hurling pieces of glowing blue fabric to the floor in the form of rags.

"Bitches! Bitches and shits! Fuckin' stuck up garbage! May they goddamn well rot in hell! Those fucks—they're gettin' a dose of the Gestapo, every one of them." Her eyes blazed. She laughed and it was ugly. "You can smell 'em, those filthy cunts, smell 'em from a mile away. Filthy aristos, nobody teaches 'em how to douche."

Naked now but for her bra, she lit a cigarette and stalked to the window. She threw open the blackout shade. "Hello, Germany, look at me! Look at the cheap, tacky little *beinl*. Oh, yes, they know."

"Carlotta?"

"Fuck you! Stare at your million mark dress, you fucking capitalist roader!" She grabbed a scrap of the cloth and spat on it. "I don't give a shit!"

"Darling—"

She clutched her breasts and screwed her eyes shut. "They know a whore, yes. You see, they want to feel superior. They have a need, so you can't fucking hide from *them*!" She threw herself down on the bed. "You know something? I knew one of them. One of the men. How do you like that?"

"Did he know you?"

"What do you think, asshole?"

"Did he?"

She leaped up and at me. She was right in my face, breathing like the most beautiful damn dragon on God's good earth. "Fuck yes. Fuck. YES!"

"Which one?"

"You think I'm gonna ever tell one john one damn thing about another john? Stay outa my business, shitkicker."

"You know, if you were fighting for the *Wehrmacht,* they'd win."

"What? Oh, I see, a joke. It's an attempt to 'lighten the mood.' But of course, you're an American. Everybody's smiling in foolish America! But this is not America, this is Germany. *Civilization*, you stupid ape, and your wife has been repeatedly insulted! Repeatedly! By those weasels in their tattered finery. A fucking nest of traitors. Alf's gonna love to hear all about them! Those pigs! Bastards and bitches, they'll end up under the damn axe, you wait and see!"

I had made a decision. I was finally going to defy my orders. I was not say one thing about this conspiracy, not to Paul or to anybody else. Not one word. Hitler needed killing, and if these people were the ones to accomplish it, then fine.

But she had orders, too, same as mine. Give up the conspirators to our handlers.

I took her in my arms. Her hands became claws. The cigarette was somewhere on the floor. She was about to rip into my chest when instead she leaned against me, put her arms around me and cried the bitter, bitter tears of a woman in a trap from which there could be no escape. I understood that her anger really came from the fact that she hated the idea of getting these poor people killed as much as I did. She wanted to hate them so betraying them wouldn't be so very damn hard.

As I stroked her hair, it gave me great pleasure to feel her leaning against me. Her man. Proud of it, too.

I lifted her onto the bed.

"Do we have any opium, Willy? I want a nice fuck and a nice pipe."

"I have eleven peas left. After that, no more. The trade up from Morocco is over."

"I just want my knob, my pretty lamp and one delicious pea." She opened her arms. "But first, get in here."

As I undressed, I said, "You should think about one thing. You completely fucked them over at Bridge."

"Our rabbit hutch is full of geniuses compared to those morons. Idiots, should've been gassed at birth."

There was a silence. Everybody in Germany knew about the gassing of the mentally incompetent.

She burst into tears. "I hate this place! I hate Germany! Germany is a crazy house!"

I lay down beside her, then slid across to her and took her the way she liked to be taken, held so tightly that she could hardly move, so that she could struggle and not win, and then sink into my strength and be overwhelmed by my passion for her and my total devotion.

I kissed her and loved her and kissed her and loved her, and the hour grew late. On the distance, there were thuds, a sound like a giant walking in the far night. Somewhere, bombs were falling. But in Germany in 1944, bombs were always falling somewhere, day or night, it did not matter.

We lay still. I whispered again and again in her ear, "I love you, I love you, I love you."

She said, "What's that smell?"

"You. You smell wonderful."

"Get off." I rolled away and she sat up. "Holy shit, the rug's on fire!"

I leaped out of bed to find a spreading black scorch in the carpet and dancing with blue flames. She shot off the end of the bed like a gazelle and in a moment was back from the bathroom with a glass of water.

I soaked a towel and between us we got the fire under control. Then we laughed together, two shapes in the smoke. We turned out all the lights and opened the windows to let it out, then went downstairs naked and ate head cheese and drank cider.

All across Europe at that moment there were people hungering, children, mothers, fathers, the old and the young, Russian and German boys at the front, Jews in long, dark dormitories, so very many.

It was a fine head cheese that Maria had bought, and the cider was as crisp as the apples from which it had been made.

Back upstairs, Carlotta smoked her pill and slept in my arms like a cuddly molly cat. I did not do any opium. I didn't want to fall asleep with my own lamp still going and end up with another fire.

I held her at once tightly and gently, as if she was a fragile saint in my arms. My impossible jewel, by a miracle sent to me from the desperate archipelago of her childhood.

Sometime later, perhaps around four, I was awakened by the distant ringing of the telephone. This house had been wired for telephony when it was normal for there to be just a single instrument set on a small table in the foyer. I threw off the covers and hurried down, thinking that a call at this hour was never good news. But it was nine hours earlier in New York, twelve in L.A.

"Hello."

"Willy?" A tiny voice, very old.

"Vati?"

"Yes, the very same! Come home, I miss you." My heart, which had soared with joyous surprise, now sank. It was Hitler, not my lost father.

"Of course, we're setting out in the morning."

"Why did you go and leave us? We're both pining away."

"Carlotta wanted a social evening."

"You go all the way to Berlin for that?"

"We dined with Ambassador Anfuso and some friends of his. She has a marvelous new gown and she wanted to show it off."

"He's close to you in Wannsee. That's good. Safe. Eva's very jealous."

"We don't want another catfight."

"I don't know. They can be quite entertaining. They're both very good at it."

"They send you letters denouncing each other."

"Those letters have given me a chance to laugh, so maybe they'll start in again. I want you home. I'm uneasy about the roads and you daren't fly."

"I bought a little Olympia. No self-respecting allied pirate would bother with such a machine."

"You never know, Willy. Just be careful and hurry back." He said more, but it was a murmur.

"What's that?"

"There's love here for you," he repeated in a sharper tone, then immediately rang off.

During the conversation I had smelled coffee and so went into the kitchen where I found the Russians boiling up a huge pot of it. As soon as I appeared they all went to their feet and bowed, placing their fists on their foreheads.

They had a little German, I had a little Russian. So we more-or-less talked. I discovered that there would be carrots and small onions soon, so we could make rabbit stew. Runner beans would come in

June, and lettuces and tomatoes. I astonished myself by unexpectedly remembering the BLTs I used to get at the Busy Bee when I was a boy, the tomatoes, the crisp bacon, the slather of mayonnaise. With my sandwich, I'd have a Coke served in one of those funnel cups. Then afterward a big slice of cherry pie.

In another instant the recollection was gone, but it left behind a strong sense of home—as if my American past was fighting to retain its place in memory, so that I would not forget all I loved best.

I drank some coffee with the gardeners, then returned to bed and slept a bit. I was uneasy in my heart. The reason was that disagreements which in peacetime might be purely theoretical can in wartime become extremely serious points of difference between friends and lovers. For example, there are many stories of brothers on opposite sides in the Civil War, and I very much feared that Carlotta might be about to end up in the same position.

In peacetime, we could have simply argued. But if she insisted on following our orders and giving up the conspirators, we might have to act against each other, and how far might that go? I was certain of one thing: the plotting of Loremarie and her friends was not going to be revealed to Paul Dukes or to whomever was handling Carlotta, let alone directly to Hitler. I was determined that he would face these assassins.

If Carlotta remained intent on following her orders, what was I to do? Must I kill the woman I loved? The lives of a great many people might depend on it. I felt sure that these aristocrats as normal, civilized people, would stop the killing in the camps and eventually empty them. They would negotiate a peace that the allies would in some way have to accept. At the time, I imagined that I might save a hundred thousand Jews. Even thought I had graduated from the ten thousand I had imagined some years before, even with all that I knew, I was still incapable of seeing the scale of the thing.

Should my loyalty be to the love of my life, or to the lives of others?

I returned to the haunting image of the woman who had held her baby high in the gas room. She had brown curls. I never saw her face.

She may have been pretty or plain. But I would never forget the writhing little body in her hands, or her bowed head, or the gas swirling lazily in the air.

Carlotta, who usually awoke around noon, was up and dressing by ten.

"We have to go back to the Adlon, Willy. We only really have the one name. We need to know the rest of the plot, the ringleaders, who is to carry it out and when and where. We need to know all of these things."

"Alf called in the night. He wants us home. He sounded pretty miserable."

"Good. When I know he's miserable is when I enjoy life the most."

"I told him we'd get on the road this morning."

She turned from her dressing table. "Well, guess what? We won't. That old shit's misery doesn't matter at all."

"He's also the most powerful man in Germany. We ignore that at our peril."

"Then call him and tell him something! Any damn thing! I've got catarrh. The car's on the fritz. Anything!" She whirled around and faced me. Her face glowed in its frame of brown ringlets, so haunting to me. The Louise Brooks look was now *passé*. Her beauty was like a sweet breeze blowing over you, reminding you that the world, for all its pain, has also this to offer. "Do it! Now!"

I went downstairs and telephoned the Berghof. Thwarting Hitler always made me uneasy, and I was glad to find that he was in conference and could not be disturbed. I then asked for Julius Schaub and was put through to the adjutant. I told him that we would be arriving in the evening as the car had gone wrong and was now being attended to by a mechanic. He took this matter-of-factly, which Hitler would not have done. He might well have sent a car out from the Chancellery to drive us, a complication I did not want to deal with.

At eleven, we set out for Berlin in the Olympia. Our plan was to lunch again at the Adlon, then drive on south, going as far as we could manage before nightfall.

Driving up through the Grunewald to Charlottenberger Chaussee, one would not have known that there was a war on. The trees were stark, having just started leafing out, but it was a fine day and the strips of snow here and there on the ground reminded one that winter was finally becoming a thing of the past.

"The one I won't be chatting to is the dumpy fellow with the big bald head."

"Herr Puckler?"

"If that's the little troll with the big bald head, then yes. Obviously."

I had noticed him gazing after her during the dinner, and how she maneuvered to avoid him during the Bridge session. I assumed that he must be the former customer.

All along Unter den Linden one saw bombed out buildings. There was a general impression of tattered decline everywhere.

The Adlon still stood in a state of regal, unbombed majesty. It wouldn't last, but in the Berlin of 1944, little would. Nowadays, it's half vibrant city, half bombed-out ruin. The Brandenberg Gate now has that wretched wall going right through it. I often wonder if it will last. If Hadrian's Wall and the Great Wall of China are any example, the last thing they do is what is expected of them. But the Soviet Empire is so monolithic and vast, it seems impossible that it could ever end.

Almost as soon as we walked in, I saw Loremarie Shonberg and she saw me. She came hurrying over. "There you are, Herr Weber and that sweet, elegant fiancée again! You two are always together, then. Charming! I'm here with Adam Trott whom I believe you trounced at Bridge, Carlotta dear, so you can expect him to pout, and a few other conspirators—but I shouldn't say that! In this country now, even an innocent jest can turn out to be fatal."

As she uttered the last sentence, her face became entirely serious. It was an ominous and effective display, conveying everything while admitting nothing.

The last thing I wanted was for Carlotta to find out any more names. But I couldn't very well try to take her away, say, into the restaurant.

She said, "Oh, a conspiracy! What fun. What's it about, counterfeit ration coupons? Stolen petrol?"

"That's Missie Vassiltchikov's department. She's in the A.A. They have a petrol store in the ministry's garage. If you need it, she might get some for you, but she's not here today. She's out in Potsdam with another friend, Marie Gellsdorf."

"Ah, the conspiracy grows deeper," Carlotta said.

Loremarie glanced to one side, then back again. Across the lobby there were two men reading newspapers. They couldn't have been more obvious if they'd had "Gestapo" signs hung around their necks.

"It's all very serious, my friends." Then, to me, "You're an American. How can an American stand this place? It's unbearable for us Germans."

At that moment, a distant, mournful wail arose. Carlotta went as white as paste. "Bombers!"

"They've been coming a lot lately," Loremarie said, her voice betraying only the mildest concern. Then a handbell began ringing, the porter calling us to the cellar. "Ah well, let's go down."

"Down? Where is down?"

"The cellars, my dear. Come, there's no time to waste. The whole hotel could fall in on us."

Carlotta looked up toward the tall, beamed ceiling. Her mouth dropped open. "The whole hotel? We'd be buried alive."

"It's a regular luncheon ritual here, and people get buried alive all the time."

The ground was beginning to shake as the great mass of bombers came plunging closer. I later discovered that there were 682 of them on that day, and that 63 were shot down.

Without another word, Carlotta turned and ran for the front door, tripping along on her heels. For an instant, I couldn't believe it. Then I was just simply terrified for her and ran after her.

"They'll arrest you if you go out," Loremarie called, her voice lilting with amusement.

It was a fine and even possibly a night in prison if one was found in the streets during a raid. But what did we care? We wouldn't be spending a moment in any prison. The Hitler passes we carried would be respected by the Berlin constabulary.

As it was a daylight raid, the planes were coming in almost on the ground. Nevertheless, the nearby Zoo flak tower in the Tiergarten was gushing fire. Its roaring combined with the howl of engines to set up an ungodly echo in the streets.

Carlotta ran right out into Unter Den Linden, stopped in the divider and looked up into the bellies of the passing bombers. You could see right into the bomb bays where there were stacks of bombs with red-painted noses.

An instant later, the government buildings beside Parisier Platz exploded like Vesuvius. They were only a few meters away, so the detonations were completely overwhelming, a soul-shattering deluge of sound accompanied by hot, blasting shockwaves that came like blows from giant fists, hammering us again and again as we stood screaming, our cries swallowed in that noise.

The objective of the raid was to wreck official Berlin, and the Adlon was right in among the government buildings. Now smoke began pouring up from the direction of Voss Strasse and the New Chancellery and the *Propagandaministerium* of the ratlike Goebbels.

I saw too late that Carlotta had broken away from me. By the time I realized she had gone, she was already getting into our car, which had been parked on the curb in front of the hotel. She started it and went shooting out into the street.

"Carlotta!"

An enormous bomb struck so close that there was nothing but a silver flash. When you didn't hear the sound, that was often the last thing you didn't hear. The car ran up on the opposite sidewalk and began moving along it. I could see her behind the wheel screaming and crying, lost entirely to the world. As she passed the Arts Academy, part of its facade went tumbling into the street, ending up as a heap of rubble that blocked her way. Had any more come down, it would have crushed the car and her in it.

I reached her. She was sitting frozen, her mouth agape. As I watched, a long line of drool slid out. I opened the door.

"Darling, come quickly, we've got to get inside."

She did nothing, said nothing.

I opened the door. "Carlotta!"

"What is this here? What's this woman doing?"

Another wave of planes swept over, their roar drowning out my attempt to answer the policeman, who had come up out of a hatch in the sidewalk.

If you imagine that raids only took a short time, think again. A big one like this could last for hours as formation after formation came over, one after another, like a storm that refused to clear.

"She's panicked. Help me get her out."

Together we lifted her out of the vehicle.

"What's she doing here? This is a fine she's getting."

"It's her first raid, forgive her."

"Oh, fuck!"

"What's that? What's she saying?"

"A fuckin' bull, aw *shit*!"

The awful whistling you hear in the movies started, immediately getting louder. The policeman pushed her down and threw himself on top of her. I followed his lead, hitting the sidewalk just as a thunder loud enough to shatter one's teeth erupted. The shock waves kept sucking the air right out of my lungs. I couldn't even scream. Then a shrieking whir started up as a twin-engine *Luftwaffe* fighter appeared in among the bomber formation. For an instant cannon crashed, then the plane were gone, disappeared over the roofs.

I looked toward the Adlon which, to my amazement, was standing. It was wreathed in smoke, but appeared undamaged. We listened for a moment, but no all-clear sounded.

"Come quickly, the hornets are still buzzing!"The policeman hustled us down a ladder into what appeared to be some sort of access space for U-Bahn maintenance workers. There we found ourselves surrounded by a group of *Jungmadel* in their black skirts and tan jackets, each one with her hair neatly braided in pigtails.

"It's against the law to be out there like that," the squad leader announced, her child's voice sharp with recrimination.

"Has anyone got a drink? How about a cigarette, at least." Carlotta turned to me, her eyes still glassy. "Willy, for Chrissakes, cigarette me." The children's breath in this confined space was extremely sour. Nobody had toothpaste anymore.

On the wall there was a sign, "*Rauchen Verboten!*" No Smoking. But when I glanced up at it, the policeman merely shrugged.

I drew out my cigarette case, and as more bombs exploded above us, causing the space to fill with dust and paint chips, solemnly handed them around. All the children took one, ten and twelve years old though they were. In an air raid, everybody drank what they could and smoked what they could. The feeling that death is coming at any moment causes you to seek for whatever comfort you can find. Many a baby was conceived in an air-raid shelter. Nice people did not peer into corners.

One of the girls looked at her cigarette and said, "This is lovely. What brand?"

Carlotta announced, "This man is very wealthy and important. He has everything. Perfect cigarettes, of course, that's natural with him."

Everyone smoked solemnly as the little shelter quaked and shuddered and the trap door overhead clanged open and shut with the shockwaves.

Another girl said, "I fear the leader is in danger. They are bombing our government buildings. What horrible people to do a thing like that."

"He's fine, he's in the Berghof, we just saw him yesterday. Isn't that right, Willy?"

Absolute silence. Wide eyes. The policeman's jaw between his knees.

"The leader is not in Berlin," I said.

"Yes, I knew, and so should Grendl," one of the girls responded primly. "His standard was not on the Chancellery flagpole this morning. We were on our way across the city when the raid came in. We're not supposed to be in the center at all, but the U-Bahn stopped."

Shortly after, the all-clear at last sounded, the policeman

conducted the girls through a metal door and back into the U-Bahn station, and Carlotta and I climbed out into the street.

Water was spraying up from a broken main, adding a mist of rain to the choking mix of smoke and dust in the air. Incredibly, we heard a tenor. He was singing in a strong and practiced voice, "*Vesti la giubba*" from Pagliacci, his voice echoing in the sudden silence like thunder departing with a storm.

"Put on your costume, powder your face.

The people pay, and they want to laugh..."

I took Carlotta's arm in mine and together we went back to the hotel. As we approached, the doorman opened the door smartly for us. We went through into a cavern just now being lit by candles. Apparitions were coming up from the depths, chatting amiably, some of them carrying sandwiches or bottle-beer, which staff would give out during raids.

"See there, we could have had a sandwich."

"Those children were too young to smoke, Willy. You should never have given them cigarettes."

"It's my nature to corrupt the innocent."

"For which you should be ashamed."

"But I'm not."

"I was innocent until you corrupted me."

"You were never innocent."

"I was never a drug addict, either. Oh, look, there's dear Herr Puckler! Herr Puckler, hello! Have you had a pleasant raid?"

"I wouldn't say..." He trailed off. They stared at one another. The next moment, his eyes filled with tears and he turned away.

She flew away from him, the grace of her movement like an ascension, as if she had risen from some grave. As a waiter passed, she grabbed a beer and drank deep. It was being served out in bottles, not in steins, cold pilsner. I got a Radebecker and to this day I don't remember any beer that tasted so rich and delicious, nor had a head like that, perfumed with the scent of life itself. When I am in Berlin I make a point to have a Radebecker, and I always raise my stein to my Carlotta.

She was off, waving a hand toward Loremarie, who, to my horror, was conversing with a grave and resplendent *Wehrmacht* general. Now, foreign office personnel like Adam Trott were all well and good as conspirators, but if somebody in this country was going to overthrow Hitler and his cronies, they had to be in the *Wehrmacht*. I had never seen this man in any of the conferences at the Berghof, so he wasn't a war general, but I could tell by the intensity of their conversation that he must matter a great deal in some way.

Carlotta could, too, and the next thing I knew, she was standing with them, laughing and pushing Loremarie on the shoulder. When they'd partnered last night, they had made an absolute killing. Had their stations in life not been so different, those two would have become fast friends.

I hurried over, only to have Carlotta introduce me to General Falkenhausen. He was a compact, very precise sort of a gentleman but he was also grinning with sheepish avidity at my dear sexual genius, my raw angel, whose look had captured him at once. I thought to myself, 'what happens when a Gestapo interrogator sticks a fishhook in his penis and starts tugging at it?' 'Angling,' they called it, an infamous torture.

I could predict the outcome: on about the third tug, he would be telling them everything he knew. By the fifth, he would be adding things that he didn't know he knew. By the tenth, when the flesh was ripping open and the hook dislodging, they would know the secrets of his soul.

Moments later, Carlotta whispered to me, "We've got everything we need. Let's get out of this stinkhole."

As we left, I found some newspaper in the rubble and a piece of a broom, and used this to wipe the dust off the car's windshield and windows.

"How did it get here?"

"Where?"

"It's on the goddamn sidewalk! What the fuck?"

I couldn't think of a reply. After maneuvering it back into the street, we headed off along Unter Den Linden. Driving through the potholes and around the new craters, we picked our way slowly out of the city.

Once beyond Charlottenberg, there was no damage left to see, but below Potsdam, a new phenomenon appeared. Those little villages that are down there, that look like something out of a fairy tale, had been set alight. Had not the autobahn bypassed them, we would never have gotten through.

"Willy, they're burning everything now."

"They will burn the country. Every village, every town. As long as Hitler stays."

As if she was feeling cold, she crossed her arms over her chest.

"Do you want your jacket?"

"Is there any opium there?"

"At the Berghof? Alf and Eva got into it. If we're lucky, maybe a pill or two."

"How is it that you let them find it?"

"They scoured the house, obviously. It was in an improbable place, or so I imagined." In fact, the peas I had left at the Berghof had been in our closet in a little bag, hidden under one of her clothes heaps.

"She's not going to find anything, not that silly. It was him."

"Probably." I contemplated the idea of Hitler pawing through our things in search of narcotics. It was completely believable.

The car was unusual in one respect, which was that it had a radio. This was not what you would see today, a couple of knobs mounted in the dashboard, but a large box affixed to the floor. There was a remote control wired to it and screwed onto the dash, from which one could turn it on and off and slide through the stations. It must have been mounted by a previous owner. They did not come so equipped.

Once the sun went down, it was possible to get *Soldatensender Calais*, the new British propaganda station, which offered both hilariously cockeyed news that wouldn't fool a fool, and marvelous music. The presenter, "Vicky," would say "*Und jetzi fur mehr von diesem bosen neger music,*" and out would come Cab Calloway or Billy Strayhorn.

Carlotta so loved to dance that she would do it right in the car seat beside me, snapping her fingers and bobbing her head, her whole body moving to the rhythm.

She and Eva and I would often dance together. As always, Alf would say, 'after the war, I promise to fox-trot.' Anyway, when he did try, he ruined the fun, he was so awful. We weren't allowed except when only the four of us were there. Officially, no partying in the leader's house while the war was on. Except when nobody was looking.

Sometimes, we'd purloin his jazz records and sneak down to the SS barracks and have a real dance. The kitchen girls would come with sweethearts from the town. Every window had to be kept closed. If he was out walking and heard the music, he'd be furious. Once, the ever vigilant Bormann came come upon us and put all the SS on report.

It cost me fifty packs of cigarettes to get that one wiped off the books. Bormann never knew. He was sent a report detailing punishments that had never actually been meted out, which he showed to Hitler with great pride. Hitler said simply, "Rubbish. Take it away."

After dark, we found a horizon marked by glows, the light of more burning villages. This type of terror bombing, which involved firebomb attacks on little, innocuous places, is at best indirectly mentioned in the historical literature. I suppose the records have been lost. War is full of unimportant cruelties.

"We need to stop for the night. Munich's still hours away."

"Sure, I'm hungry anyway."

"We'll have to use ration coupons, but hopefully something can be managed."

"My Willy—he'll get his girl fed beautifully. I know it."

I pulled off the highway and began driving along one of the narrow farm-to-market roads. I was intentionally going toward one of the bombed towns. Let her see.

After a half hour we found ourselves in a community about thirty kilometers north of the city. I don't recall the name. Signposts were removed at that time.

We drove slowly along what looked like the main street of hell.

"There's no *gasthaus* here, get out."

There was a heap of burned bodies, though, being added to as we watched, by three bedraggled firemen in leather rags.

I drove on. "If only he was dead, no more of this."

"Cigarette me."

She smoked in silence.

# 24

On the evening of June 5, 1944, I sat in the darkened Great Room at the Berghof with Eva. She was preparing to have "Gone with the Wind" projected, as she did now almost every night. By this time, Carlotta found it so maddening that she would go upstairs and close our door so she couldn't even hear the music. Alf wouldn't come close.

Albert Speer had been up for a few days, and he and Hitler were playing with the model of central Berlin that Speer had built, which had been set up on the big map table in front of Hitler's magnificent window. They had the lights out so that Hitler could peer along the streets using a penlight. He like to imagine how it would be to drive down them at night.

Eva said to me, "How are the men I sent you doing?"

How strange that she would bring that up. It seemed a small enough matter, and I had thanked her. "Very well. Very well indeed."

"Ah. In America is it not also true that a note of thanks is sent?"

"But I did, I—oh, Lord, I must have forgotten the code. The censors have opened it." There was a code for letters among the inner circle. Its presence meant that they were delivered just as letters had been before National Socialism.

She said nothing, and I knew why. She was wondering what I might have said. I could so easily have compromised her.

I thought back. "It simply thanked you for the gift. There was only that."

"Ah, well, perhaps it'll turn up."

I reached over and took her hand. "I must thank you again, right now. They're a real treasure and a lovely gift."

"We Germans are privileged to be able to make gifts like that, just as your people could in antebellum days." She squeezed my hand. "So much has been lost." Then, more loudly, "Begin!"

The film started. She had the projectionist keep the volume low in order not to disturb Speer and Hitler. If he heard too much of it, he would complain that it would put him into an irrecoverable coma.

Should he decide that he wanted to look at another film, Eva's favorite would be turned off at once. Lately, he had been watching the Heinz Rhumann comedy, "*Quax, der bruchpilot*." Also from time to time, his own favorite to repeat, "*the Blue Light*." We listened often to "*Heimat, deine Sterne*," which had been premiered in Quax' "The Stars of the Homeland." Whenever he heard it, there would be silent tears. Then he would want to go out on the terrace and look up at the blazing sky, the two of us. Once he said, "We must be absolutely unsentimental. Sentiment is weakness." Then he took my hand, and we stood there while I enumerated the constellations for him and pointed out the different major stars and planets, a process that he always enjoyed. Another time, he said, "I haven't time to think about stars, but I enjoy them. Do you suppose there are wars up there?"

"Hopefully not too many."

"Having a war is like cleaning a house. When it's done, everything is fresh again."

Except for the corpses and the ruins, but I didn't say that.

He continued, "You contemplate the constellations, but you know what I do? I design pillboxes and portable ack-ack. Only you are under the stars of peace now, Willy. The rest of us Germans must fight."

"I fight."

"You direct ships at sea that you never float in, waiting for the British torpedo." (I had lost a number of ships lately, but to whom I could not be sure.)

When GWTW got to the part where Scarlett is attacked by the destitute blacks on the road out of Atlanta, Eva, on that night, asked for it to be stopped.

"I have some questions, Willy."

"Of course."

"Why did the Yankees hate the negroes?"

"Did they?"

"They sent an army down to the south to throw them off the plantations so they would starve. But why? What had the negroes ever done to the Yankees?"

Of course, "Gone with the Wind" is a deeply fallacious story, a pure piece of Confederate propaganda.

"They were freeing them from slavery."

"But why? They were so happy as slaves. In fact, I used to tell Alf that we should make the Jews slaves. They're just the same as negroes, natural servants. It's only when they become powerful that they go wrong. They can't handle responsibility, just like the negroes. We could have made the Jews happy and gotten good work out of them into the bargain. Instead, we've had to spend a fortune locking them up."

Let's finish," I said. She laid her head on my shoulder, and as she liked to do, began touching me through my trousers. She would lay her fingers there and press it gently, then when it was really big, giggle and thump it.

"You feel so good in me," she would whisper. She had confided that Alf's small size made it difficult to tell that he was even there. "I'm afraid I'm like a zeppelin hangar for him, but you, you're a fine big zeppelin."

Often when Carlotta and Alf were upstairs, she would invite me into her bed. I banged her softly, banged her hard, slowly, quickly, dancing about, going deep. She was easy to enjoy, that woman, very much the animal.

About two, Hitler tired of his game and went to bed, Eva following. They would lie together like two children. In recent months, the elaborate upstairs rituals with Carlotta had dwindled. Now, she would go in with them and play about with his privates while he lay on Eva. That worked sometimes.

The vampire doctor was still at the house, asleep in one of the easy chairs in the Great Room, there to juice Hitler or sedate him, whatever was required. In fact, he was ever present now, forever dosing him with those crazy fluids. I had been stealing from his kit and mailing samples to Paul in Geneva. With a frank from this house on them, the Gestapo didn't touch them.

I did not know until after the war that the results of the tests had appalled the British doctors. Hitler was being injected with things like hog semen and liquefied bull testicles, and cellular material from animal immune systems. They wouldn't even test the stuff on prisoners, on the theory that this would be contrary to the Geneva Convention.

The mad doctor might have been killing him, but nothing overt like strychnine was found in his potions. Just as well. Had it been, I would certainly have been the one designated to assassinate him. Hitler was now so dependent on Morrell that SIS worried that he would give up and commit suicide if the doctor was dead.

It seemed to me that the worse the war went, the filthier Morrell became. He lived down in the Platterhof and thank god, because he smelled like a hog himself.

Just after dawn, I became aware of voices downstairs. For a moment, I hoped that he had died in his sleep. That was something I thought increasingly might happen, the way his health was deteriorating. His hands, especially the left, trembled more or less constantly. He shuffled rather than walked. He could no longer make it up to the tea house.

The doctor was trying his various cures, but you're not going to relieve St. Vitus' Dance with bull testicles. In fact, to this day it's completely incurable and just gets worse and worse. If I ever come down with it, I'll shoot myself while I can still take aim.

The voices I was hearing didn't sound alarmed, but they went on long enough to draw me out of bed. I threw on my robe and went to the top of the stairs. Officially, I was still supposed to keep myself away from the generals and their staffs. Fine by me. I found contact with them ever more humiliating. With Speer, also. He had a face exquisitely capable of registering contempt, with those hooded eyes and cruel lips. A nasty face.

It was Hitler's adjutant, Heinrich Borgmann, a quite serious and competent man. He was talking on the telephone in the impromptu situation room in the salon.

He was among those who lived in the Berghof, which was full of little bedrooms. Hitler disliked being alone and he liked people near him who showed deference and did not argue. Borgmann was among those who could take his late night drivel without falling asleep.

I listened from the top of the steps to this call.

"Yes," he said, "yes. Very well." Then I heard what I thought was the phrase 'west wall.' Then he became silent.

I went down. "What is it?"

"For the leader."

"Should we wake him?"

"That's nothing to do with you."

"What about the west wall? Is it the invasion?"

"Some British and American troops have appeared on a beach in Normandy. That's all."

"Have you heard this from Rommel?"

He looked at me disdainfully. "Rommel is attending his wife's birthday, as if it was any business of yours. That was General Keitel. He was informed by General Rundstedt."

Speer, who had been breakfasting, came in. "Is this the invasion, then?"

"Troops on a beach in Normandy. That is all I have been told, Herr *Reichsminister*."

"No details? Not how many? Which beach?"

"General Keitel stated that it was a preliminary report."

He turned and went toward the kitchen.

"You're not going to wake him up?" Speer asked.

"He receives news after breakfast." With that, he went off.

Speer and I were left staring at one another. Defying protocol, he pulled out a cigarette. He was trembling so badly that I had to steady his hand as he lit it.

"This is it, we're finished."

"Where in Normandy?"

"What business is it of yours, you—" He shook his head. "What are you doing down here anyway, listening in on official business? Get upstairs." He lowered his voice. "I'm sure if he wants a kiss, he'll call."

My face burned, I couldn't help it. "You're a stupid ass, Speer."

"Get away from me, you reptile. And never touch me again. Now I've got to find some lye soap to clean my hand."

I stomped up the stairs. I'm embarrassed to say that the humiliation was so acute that it evoked tears. For a time, I stood in the corridor, too ashamed to let Carlotta see them and ask me what was wrong.

When I did go back in, I found her sitting on the bedside fumbling with her own cigarettes.

"Has it started?"

"You overheard the call?"

"Of course. I was on the stairs."

"I think it has."

She lit up and blew out a dragon's stream of smoke through her nose. "And he isn't to be told, did I hear that?"

"Borgmann thinks it's trivial."

"Just as well." She threw herself back on the bed. "Incidentally—" She stopped, then tossed a pillow over the intercom. "I'm putting in my list."

We hadn't spoken of this directly in a month. I'd thought that she'd quietly come to agree with me, but now here I was up against the fact that I could not allow her to do this. But how to stop her except by killing her?

That is what war is. It makes killing essential. You're advancing.

You find that cannot get down the road unless a man blocking it is killed. So, despite all of his complexity and richness, this being essential to himself and considered precious by those who love him meets a fragment of lead that destroys him.

"He could kill a hundred thousand Jews. Your people."

"I'm an Aryan now, remember. Clean and pure. No more insect blood oozing through these veins."

"You don't believe that rubbish."

"I believe we have orders, both of us, and I've waited long enough hoping you'd come to see sense."

"I can't do it. My conscience won't let me."

"I have to, for the same reason."

"If Paul finds out you did and I didn't, I'll be killed."

"So go down the hall and do the bastard yourself. Choke him. Suffocation fascinates him, he'll love it."

The intercom buzzed faintly from under the pillow. We both turned toward it. Was the pillow not enough?

I reached over, pushed it aside, and pressed the talk lever. "Yes, Alf?"

"Come to me."

"Yes."

She threw her arms around me. She whispered, "God, Willy!"

What had he heard?

"I love you," I said.

"I would never hurt you, my darling."

"I would never hurt you."

I hurried through the silent house, across the cold downstairs where the Germania model glowed in the early sun, and then up to his study.

Borgmann was there, Bormann and Speer as well.

"There has been a troop landing near the town of Caen in Normandy," Hitler said. "I want you to repeat what you told me before."

"The main invasion would come in Marseilles."

"And what did I say?"

"Calais."

"So this is a feint and Marseilles will be one, too. But Rundstedt is advising that I release 15th Army to move south at once. But no. The allies have landed in the bocage in hopes of tying up our armor in that tangle. So I won't send them. No. The divisions stand where they are." He looked to me.

"I can only repeat what I was told."

"Which may or may not be true."

I nodded.

He thought for a moment, staring down at the top of his desk. "No, what you got is a deception. Who would go in down there? I once thought it made sense, but the position is ridiculous. No, it's an absurd idea."

Speer was glaring at me like a lizard gone wary. He had just heard something that he had not suspected. Hitler's lover boy was also involved in secret affairs of which he knew nothing. It wouldn't change his hate, I knew that, but it might increase my stature in his eyes just a bit.

"It could be Normandy, then. Let's contact—" I glanced around the room. "—the other one. Maybe he has some sort of a signal."

Hitler nodded. "That's good, yes." He went and stared out into the rising morning. "Yes," he said at last, "that's essential." He looked from one to the other of the three men present. "If we may have some privacy."

Borgmann clicked his heels, bowed, turned and left. Speer, now almost goggling at me, strode out. As always, Bormann lingered.

"You, too, Martin, thank you."

"There need to be notes taken, surely. At least for the file."

"That is exactly what is not needed. Good morning."

He left, flashing me a lurid smile as he drew the door closed.

Hitler waited for a moment. His face was fixed, rigid almost to the point of being a death mask.

"Willy, are you a double agent?"

What had he heard? All? None? "Yes, of course, Alf. But I'm your double agent."

"Hah, you and Paul! I understand his skill at dissembling, he's English. But you're mostly German and we're terrible spies! Look at the Abwher, look at the Foreign Office. Absurd. Willy, a number of things have happened between us that have led me astray."

"What, Alf, tell me?"

He waved a hand. "No, no. Nothing is certain. But this Marseilles business—let's just say that it is following a pattern."

"It was what I got, but I never advocated it. In fact, I remember saying that I thought it was unlikely to be true. We both agreed on that."

"Willy, this is the invasion. Maybe Normandy won't be the axis of it. Maybe that will be Calais. That's what I think now, anyway."

"Alf—"

"Listen, please! Those others must see me only as decisive. Between us, I can be as I really feel, unsure and afraid. You know that I've known we would lose this war from the days of Todt."

"So you have said."

"It is time to begin thinking of the future—the time after the war is lost."

"I hate that idea so terribly much."

"Ah ha, not as much as I! They'll hang me, Willy, no doubt in a public square in London."

"They don't have public hangings."

"They'll make an exception, and if it's Stalin who gets the trophy, he certainly will. But you see, what we're doing is a beautiful thing. Extraordinary! Raising an entire race to its destined place at the pinnacle of evolution." He shook his head. "Just extraordinary..."

As his tension rose, his left hand began to shake so much that he hid it.

"You needn't do that."

"Of course." He laid it on the desk and stared at it. "Off on another journey of its own, it seems. How strange the body is." He met my eyes. It felt like looking into a cave. "Do you know how my generals get at the *Wolfschanze*? You've heard that, in the toilet?"

"Yes, the vomiting."

"So come with me and help me!" He leaped up and sprinted the length of the room, then rushed into the bathroom. He draped himself over the commode and retched. I took a cloth and dampened it, and held it against his forehead. He coughed, retched again, tried to steady himself with his weak hand and toppled against me.

I lifted him back onto his haunches, then got him a glass of water. He rinsed with it, then spat it into the bowl. Next, I gave him some mouthwash, and he did the same again. He groaned and sat back against the wall. "I can see them," he murmured, "see them in the night...my god, how could I...but no." His eyes opened wide. "Willy, NO!" He smiled and began struggling to his feet. I flushed the commode and drew him up.

"There, Alf, better?"

"Of course not. Come, let me show you something."

I followed him back into the study. He picked up a large black photograph case that was lying on the coffee table in the sitting area. He sat down on the couch that was there, then patted the seat beside him.

"Come, sit, look."

He opened it onto a large photograph of a macabre little machine. It was some sort of aircraft mounted on a ramp that angled toward the sky.

"Where does the pilot sit?"

"This is a rocket aero. It flies itself and keeps going all the way to London. It then falls and detonates an 850 kilogram bomb."

I was horrified. The rumored *wu-wa*—wonder weapons—were real. Everybody speculated about them but nobody really believed the rumors.

"Does it—how does it know where to go?"

"We're Germans, Willy. This is the nation of brilliance." He turned the page and there was the thing taking off in a cloud of smoke and flame, then again and it was high in the sky. A final shot showed it striking the ground with a terrific blast.

"I can put up thousands! True wonder weapon! Shock weapon!

This and the German soldier, that's what we have on our side! Todt had to be eliminated. He was infected with Jewish defeatist ideas."

"I thought he died in a plane crash."

"He had to." He said it with a finality that told me it had been an assassination. That has not entered history, but I believe it to be true. Hitler couldn't have functioned with a minister for armaments who believed that the war was lost. Or, in Todt's case, knew it to a mathematical certainty.

"And now I want to talk to you about something just once. Once only. If even the wonder weapons don't enable us to prevail, what shall we do with ourselves?"

"The Germans?"

"Never mind them, the future belongs to the strong. If they prove to be weak, then—" He spread his hands, an eloquent way of expressing something that was perhaps beyond words. Then he smiled reflectively. "But it's a big world and we'll still be alive."

"Will we want to be?"

"Here's what I think. We could go to the east. There are submarines that could get us there. If I shave this—" He touched the *rotzbremse*. "—and use some of those techniques of Paul's, I could be seen as just another person. On some quiet island, I might regain my health, even."

I already had the information about this horrible weapon, a major *coup* for me, information that had to be gotten to London at once, and now here came his escape route. A productive morning.

"What sort of an island?"

"The Dutch East Indies is an archipelago full of unexplored islands. We could live native, hunt pigs together, you and me."

"You're a vegetarian."

"Never mind that crap. That's all for show. I thought you knew that."

"It used to be."

"Well, it still is. The girls could gather vegetables and fruits. We'd live in a grass house."

But this was fantasy, of course. Or was it? His entire life had been devoted to breathing unexpected life into absurd fantasies.

"That sounds terribly wonderful, Alf, and terribly sad at the same time."

"Underwater travel is completely steady. No waves to knock you around. Reassure the girls about that."

It sounded as if he had already planned this. Was Himmler involved, or were the rats organizing separate departures from the ship? "Are we leaving soon?"

"Absolutely not. Not until it's definitely lost. Let's see what those flying bombs can do, and if we bottle up these two advances."

"Has Stalin stopped in Byelorussia, then?"

"Not yet. We'll snip off the head of his attack. Then we'll see how they bleat over the radio at us." The British *soldatensender* made an attempt to sound like actual German armed services radio stations, but the Russians contented themselves with fake news delivered in atrocious accents.

He leaned back and closed his eyes. "Go now. Send in Morrell if you will. I will have inevitably the calls from Keitel and Rundstedt and Rommel. They will start soon, 'Fifteenth Army, down from Calais! Do it, do it, emergency!' Do you think I should do it?"

"I hesitate to say, but I'd think that reconnaissance might decide the matter."

"In what sense?"

"I'm no expert but if it's the real invasion, there's going to be an enormous amount of shipping in the water off Normandy. Transports, protective naval vessels, thousands of them. I'm sure observers in the coastal fortifications already have photographs."

He said nothing, but only sat staring ahead. Then he got up and went to the doors that opened onto his balcony. "The beauty of the morning. Why not take the girls for a swim? A day at the lake, they'd be delighted."

"Will you come?"

"You might be what they all say you are, a clever bastard of a spy who ought to be shot. But you have a sense of humor, I'll grant that."

As I left him, I felt as if I might be sick myself. Had he overheard us or not? I couldn't tell. Maybe he was trying to get me to run, flush me like a pheasant. Take the girls swimming—*now*? If I slipped away from them at the lake, got in the car and made for Switzerland, what would happen?

I'd been given some truly extraordinary information just now, also. But that could be part of the trap, another temptation to get me to reveal myself.

These robot planes were the real thing, and that was incredibly important. Bombers and fighters took weeks to build, but a small robot plane fitted with a thousand pounds of explosive was another matter. Despite its damaged condition, I had no doubt that German industry could turn such things out in great numbers.

And the business about escaping! What if he was planning to simply disappear, leaving Germany to fend for itself? This would leave behind a complete confusion, neither a clear break like the assassination I'd been hoping for or the continuation of his 'never surrender' policy that the allies wanted. It would be the worst possible outcome.

To get back to our room, I had to once again cross downstairs, damnably enough. The salon was now filled with military men, all poring over a map of France that had been spread out on the table.

I could feel my cheeks growing hot as they all watched me pass.

I assume, by the way, that it's clear why I do not appear in Speer's memoirs. He repudiated Hitler in public, but not in his heart. Thus his true weakness, which disgusted Speer, was never referred to, not even obliquely.

"What?" she said as I came in.

I shut the door, walked over to her and gestured for her to stand up from the desk where she'd been sitting.

I drew so close to her that my mouth was against her ear. "There is suspicion. I don't know of you, but certainly of me. If I run, will you come?"

She pulled away, then turned to face me. She held my cheeks in her hands. With tears brimming at the edges of her eyes, she solemnly shook her head 'no.'

I nodded. I understood, of course. Until she was herself compromised, her duty was here, just as mine would have been if the situation had been reversed.

Again I went close. "In case I'm unable to pass this in my direction, you must pass it in yours. First, there are robot flying bombs being prepared to strike London. Maybe Moscow, too, I don't know. Also, he has some sort of escape plan that involves the Dutch East Indies."

She looked at me, mouthed 'what?'

"I know. It's incredible. But he might just be planning to disappear from the face of the Earth."

"It's a lie," she whispered.

I turned the intercom on its face and covered it with a heap of pillows.

"Probably. I suspect that he's waiting to see if the story comes back from some source he must still have in Whitehall. Then he'll know I'm not straight. The flying bombs, too, but that sounds more likely to be true. If I get either one to Churchill, my guess is that I'm dead."

"Maybe and maybe not. Remember, he's in love with you. I know these men who stifle their desire for other men. When they finally break through, if they ever do, it becomes the most exciting thing in their life, the most precious thing. I see him making rabbit eyes at you. Every move you make, he watches. Everything. He's completely infatuated."

I remembered him prancing around that night like a real temperamental. It was the funniest and most horrifying thing I'd ever seen. He had all the femininity and grace of a box. And with that infamous mustache over the simpering lips—good God.

I pulled the pillows off the intercom. "Alf suggests we go swimming."

"Today? Now?"

"Not him, he's a bit busy. You and me and Eva. Maybe the

Fegeleins if they care to." Eva's sister Gretl had married Hermann Fegelein a few days before. Eva had been in love with him for a time.

So I sent Carlotta off to get Eva and telephoned the motor pool for my car to be brought out.

Eva had only now finished her breakfast and had been in the kitchen organizing the various meals of the day, as the house was filling with guests.

I had understood some time ago that her imperious style derived from a ludicrous attempt to imitate Scarlett O'Hara. The servants called this her "Tara fiddle-de-de" attitude. They really loathed her, this simple person who was of no higher rank than they but who acted as if she was some sort of princess of the blood. Hers was very different from Hitler's egalitarian style and easy humor even in the face of kitchen disasters like the collapsed soufflé that had greeted General Oshima a few days before. The disaster had happened at one of those dinners that Eva so hated, where she was left upstairs to eat off a tray with us and listen to the radio instead of look at a film.

We picked Gretl and Hermann up at the Platterhof. This made it a very gay party, but it did nothing to lighten my mood. The usual discreet SS protective squad in plainclothes followed us. They made no secret of it. On the contrary, we shared lunch as usual. Was there somebody else though, who we would never see?

We went to the Konigssee where we swam a bit, then sunned ourselves, sheltering against green wooden windbreaks from the rather sharp breeze that came up in the early afternoon.

I gazed into the dark, deep waters, watching fish lazing about in the weeds, and wondered if the human species would ever come to any peace at all, let alone one so profound as that of these calm and ancient beings.

# 25

As disaster followed disaster for the Germans over the next few weeks and the end of the war raced ever closer, I vacillated again. It now seemed that Carlotta was right. The *coup* had to be stopped. At this point, Hitler's death would only cause a complication for the allies and probably not reduce the loss of life much at all.

In any case, strychnine or no strychnine, I was sure now that he would soon die from Morrell's injections. One amphetamine would lead to a sudden explosion of energy and optimism, only to be followed by an equally sudden collapse. If he was having a nervous attack, another type would transform him from a frantic, terrified maniac into a stupefied cadaver.

Those were the narcotics. Then there were the bull and pig injections. As they increased, his odor, always strange, took on an animalistic quality. You could literally smell in his sweat the cells of the cattle and pigs that flowed in his veins.

At night late, he would call for me to meet him in his study. I would sit with him while he went over and over the casualty figures. On the eastern front, he would not allow the Germans to retreat, especially now that his ideas had received support from British Intelligence. (He was actually right about "perfidious Albion." The British are true masters of deception.)

He would say 'we must not retreat an inch, because then it's going to become a rout.' That might have been true, as well, I don't know. Certainly, I did nothing to argue against it and did everything to encourage him in his stand fast rules. Stalin's orders were to kill rather than capture. In fact, if a Red Army unit showed up in the rear with prisoners in tow, the soldiers would be made to shoot their balls off and watch them die, then themselves would be sent to a punishment battalion.

Goebbels had finally gotten Hitler to agree to his "total war" plan. Everybody would fight. Hundreds of thousands more would be sent to face the ocean of gunfire pouring in from east and west.

"Total war" sounds an awesome business. It's not. It's filthy and grubby and miserable. Banal. The corpse of a little boy on the roadside, his rifle longer than his body, the corpse of the old man hanging from the tree—when you see such things up close, it seems all very stupid and pointless.

Hitler's generals were increasingly at odds with him over the stand fast strategy. The daily briefings in the salon became terrifying affairs, in the sense that they predicted ever more serious disasters, which promptly unfolded.

I will say that the reports of him shrieking and going on at these meetings are exaggerated. While I was not at the table, I was in the same house, and he maintained a calm in the face of adversity and communicated a sense of confidence that was quite amazing. The Russians continued to make shocking progress against Army Group Center, which by the end of June had collapsed into disorganized remnants. Not only were the soldiers killed and the equipment lost, the command infrastructure was irretrievably damaged by the capture of so many general officers. There was nobody left at the front to carry out orders from OKH. Nobody knew how.

The idea that the Russians might turn south and come here to Bavaria wasn't completely out of my mind. Who knew what they might do? Hitler discounted the possibility, but he became obsessed with the fear that the western allies might send in a parachute unit to capture him, using the same techniques that Otto Skorzeny had used to pluck Mussolini out of the alpine hotel where the Badoglio government had imprisoned him. He fantasized about being hanged in front of Buckingham Palace while millions celebrated.

During the day, he was confident and cheerful, kept that way by Morrell, but when night fell his fears would come out to haunt him.

"Willy," he would say, "if parachutists come, kill me, don't let them take me."

"The SS will kill them all."

"Five thousand? Ten? I think not. You must promise me, the moment they start dropping onto the terrace, knock me cold then smother me, cut my throat, anything." I'd briefly had his gun in my pocket, but it was now kept in Eva's closet, well away from anybody.

The days passed peacefully in that quiet place, with summer rising, the bees humming in the meadows, and the sky as blue as the virgin's veil. The cars would come and go, the generals come and go, the communications center down the road hum with reports, and the position markers on the great map be moved, and in the night Hitler would retch and tremble, often in my arms.

Whatever form the conspiracy took, I doubted that it was going to unfold while he was in residence here. There was simply no opportunity.

I had convinced Carlotta of this, and we had agreed to wait until and if he was in a more vulnerable situation before we gave up the names of those good people.

But I knew that Hitler's growing paranoia was going to cause him to leave the Berghof, and once he was in a more public setting, even if it was the *Wolfschanze* where army officers came and went constantly, they would strike.

I admitted to Carlotta that I had again changed my mind about the conspiracy. Given that the Reich had only months to live, not that many lives would be saved by his death, and unconditional surrender was the best policy.

On July 13, Hitler decided that he could no longer sleep at the

Berghof for worrying about kidnap. The next day, he moved to the *Wolfschanze*.

I thought that the conspirators would waste no time,

That same evening, Carlotta took a short walk on her own, and when she returned told me that she had transmitted the names to Moscow. Later that night, I did the same, reaching Paul at my flat in Munich, which was, like Eva's house, still undamaged.

"Why so long, Willy?"

"We had to be sure."

"You've been sitting in the Berghof for weeks. I view this delay as a betrayal."

"So have me shot. At this point what do I care?"

"About your own life?"

"I'm past caring, Paul."

"That's a lie. You care too much about it. That's always been a problem with you."

It was true enough. I suffered from a very unmilitary desire to live.

On the afternoon of July 20, Eva and Carlotta and I were alone in the Berghof. We were planning a vacation, and debating between Paris and Geneva. The French capital was still appealing. I knew that Hitler would never allow us to go, not with the allies closing in, but also that he didn't need to find out. Travel in that direction was now restricted to the military, but we thought we could probably get space in an officer car.

The three of us were in Hitler's study. I had just telephoned G.I. Gurdjieff to learn about conditions in the French capital. He had urged us to come. "Very quiet. Easy. Plenty coffee, plenty wine. I make you dinner." I had put the receiver down when the phone rang again.

Carlotta and I never answered calls there, so even though I thought it might be Gurdjieff ringing back, I let Eva take it. She listened for a moment, then gripped the instrument and gasped. She hurled it aside.

"Eva?"

She screamed.

Carlotta, who had been reading on the couch, threw her book in the air and leaped up. "What in hell?"

She kept on screaming.

I rushed to her. "Eva!" I tried to hold her but she shook me off. She ran out onto the balcony. An instant later, I saw that she was climbing over. "Oh, God!"

As she started to topple away into the air, I grabbed the back of her dress. It was a flimsy summer frock and began to tear. Worse, she started kicking against the outside of the railing, attempting to shake me off.

"Carlotta, help us!"

She came and reached out, but couldn't get purchase. I could feel the dress giving way. There was nothing left for me to but heave at her and hope I could pull her back.

One of the guards had seen from the driveway and now ran up under the balcony. "What's happening?" he called.

"I don't know! I can't hold on!"

"Let me die! Let me die!"

"What is it, Eva?"

"He's dead!"

I almost let go, I was so shocked, but as she spoke she stopped struggling and I got her partway back. Now Carlotta could grab her under her right arm and between us we pulled her to safety.

"What has happened?"

"They said dead!"

"Who?"

She hesitated. She stared at me. Her mouth fell open. "I don't know."

I leaned down to the guard, who was still staring up at us. "Go to communications. Inform the duty officer that somebody has telephoned here and told the fraulein that the leader is dead. Send the duty officer back at once with whatever news we have."

He ran off. Carlotta and I got the collapsing, hysterical Eva back inside and put her on the couch. Carlotta sat with her arm around her.

"Did he say a name at all?"

"I don't remember. Only, "*der Fuhrer ist todt.*" I heard no more. Oh, god, Willy! God!"

A moment later, *Standartenfuhrer* Studnitz came running up the stairs. I knew him chiefly as a terrific dancer and a good social companion, but his long, chiseled face was grim now.

"Communications with Rastenberg are closed off. At Zossen, they're waiting for orders but have no contact with high command. Some tanks are moving in the capital. That is all that is known."

He threw himself down behind Hitler's desk.

"No," Eva cried, "not there!"

"Of course, forgive me!" He jumped up and saluted the empty chair. Then he bent forward, covered his face with his hands and uttered a long, ragged moan.

Our world was flying to pieces around us, and here we were alone in its silent center.

I looked at Carlotta and she looked at me. There was a rosy flush in her cheeks. Her lips sagging, she shook her head slowly from side to side.

What had happened? Had the allies not used the lists? Had their policy changed?

I went to the desk to telephone Paul. Eva said, "Who are you trying?"

"Paul."

"Oh, yes, yes!"

Wagner said, "Perhaps best to wait."

I had no intention of waiting. With Hitler dead, the three of us were in jeopardy. If Himmler was in power now, orders were going to reach the SS barracks at any time calling at least for me and Carlotta to be shot. If it was the aristocrats and the generals, all three of us would eventually be arrested and probably hanged.

"No," I said, "we need information immediately."

"Who is this, then?" Studnitz asked.

Eva said, "A friend of the leader. Very knowledgeable and very loyal."

I asked for my flat in Munich. To my surprise, the telephone was answered—by a female voice.

"Herr Dukes," I said. And there he was. "Do you know anything?"

"I know a lot of things."

"About what has happened at the *Wolfschanze*?"

"Should I? Is something unusual going on there?"

"You should try to find out. If you do, please let me know." I rang off. "He knows nothing. Apparently."

"Who in Berlin?" Eva asked. "Herr Goebbels? He's always well informed."

"Goering," Carlotta said. "I can try him."

He might know, but he wouldn't take a call from Eva or me. She was a different story. They despised each other, but he also wanted her.

"Try."

"She knows the *Reichminister*?" Studnitz asked.

"Intimately."

He smiled slightly. "Ah, good!"

She made the call. "The *Reichminister* please. This is Fraulein Krause at the Berghof." She listened to somebody speaking, but said nothing. After a few moments, she hung up. "He is very busy. He will call back as soon as possible. He told the secretary, 'tell them to sit tight.'"

My immediate impulse on hearing that was to jump up, get in the car and race for the border. But the SS would prevent me, I had no doubt of that. It would put me under suspicion, too, and with no Hitler to protect me I was likely to end up under arrest, followed by torture and death.

Without Hitler, I that I was even more vulnerable than the women. The inner circle absolutely loathed me. I was living proof of Hitler's most unattractive weakness. If the Nazis stayed in control of Germany, they would raise him to the level of a god and I would end up in an unmarked grave.

I was not then a person who knew much about helplessness. My experience of the Third Reich had been one of singular privilege. I split my time between beautiful villas. At a time when most people had barely enough to eat, when the atmosphere in crowded cities stank from their halitosis and body odor, I used luxurious soaps from the Florentine *profumiere* Santa Maria Novella and could sink into the huge bathtub in my unbombed villa whenever I pleased. In winter, they scrounged for lumps of coal. I had an endless supply. And here, in this exquisite retreat, I was not only housed and fed beautifully, I was guarded by elite and deferential troops.

A din of vehicles outside drew us onto the balcony. It looked out toward Bormann's house, but to the left one could see into the driveway. In it stood two *kuebelwagens* and a transport truck. Fully armed and helmeted SS were everywhere. They were surrounding the house.

Carlotta made a low sound, then slid her hand over mine. She wasn't under any illusions, either.

"I so feared it," Eva said, "I have feared it every day. That beautiful man and all he has done!"

Neither of us responded. What was there to say? Carlotta took her hand. Studnitz paced. I handed out cigarettes.

"If he comes home and smells that in here—" Eva stopped abruptly. She covered her face with her hands.

I felt like a trapped rat, frankly. I was surprised at myself for not having thought this out more clearly. But I'd assumed that the allies would use double agents to leak the names of the conspirators to the Gestapo, and that would be that.

I thought to myself, 'what can we do? Nothing.' At the same time, anything could happen at any moment. We could be thrown in cells. We could end up on a desperate run for the border.

All I could think to do was to keep up our strength.

"Let's have luncheon," I said.

Eva looked at me like I was mad. "I can't think of it."

The telephone rang. "Willy," she said.

"I'd best not."

"Answer it!"

I jumped up and grabbed for it. It had now rung about five times. Studnitz watched but made no move.

"Hello?"

"What, are you still sleeping down there?"

"Alf!"

Eva rushed across to me and grabbed the instrument. "Oh! I'm fainting!"

She was, too. I literally had to hold her up.

"Yes," she said. She listened. "Yes! Yes!" She listened more. "Oh, yes, I'm coming my *schnuki*, I'm coming!"

She put down the phone and slumped into one of the chairs before the desk. "He has survived," she whispered. "A bomb. He is unhurt."

I thought to myself that he might have survived, but I doubted that he was telling her the truth about any injuries. And indeed, despite the propaganda to the contrary, he was damaged by the bomb. He'd already been in failing health, but now the decline would escalate dramatically.

"Studnitz," she said, "I'm going at once to the castle. Inform the flight that we will be leaving within the hour." She turned to us. "Pack up. Fine things, everybody! We'll be at our best, to cheer him and give him strength."

I'd never before seen her take command of any situation so forcefully, but she certainly did it today.

I can't find anything in the historical record about our trip to Rastenburg, but it certainly happened. In fact, the castle is only mentioned as housing for visiting dignitaries. There was a guest house in the Wolf's Lair complex, but it was no place for anybody, let alone a guest. In fact, the whole Wolf's Lair was awful, a pestilential hellhole. Summer had come and there were so many midges that you had to wear netting hats. The flies would form buzzing clumps against the ceilings of kitchens, if you took off the netting not only would the mosquitoes eat at you, the flies would try to propel themselves up your nose.

If you spend any time in that region, you will soon understand why the Prussians were so dour.

When Hitler found flies in his food, which did happen, even he could not make light of it. He'd send it back with an order that the cooks had to eat it.

I was really very nervous about long-range allied fighters waylaying us, but we flew in what was supposed to be a "safe" air corridor too far east for the Mustangs and too far west for the Sturmoviks.

I didn't believe any of it. Surviving a flight of any kind in the Reich in those days was just a lucky accident.

As we passed Munich to the west of us, Eva peered out, trying to see if she could find her house. Later, it would be badly damaged, but at this point it was still intact. She used to stay in it when she went down to work in Hoffmann's art press. They made postcards and prints and so forth, and she counted on that work, I think, to prevent her from going completely mad.

She was always inviting Carlotta to take on a job there, but she delighted in not working at all. "I've done enough work. Now that I've got two rich men wrapped around my fingers, screw the time clock."

Some time clock she'd had in her life. Her only time clock had been how fast she could turn a trick.

On the flight Eva said, "Willy, I've been meaning to tell you that he doesn't want you back in the *Wolfschanze* again. I've been putting off telling you, hoping I wouldn't have to."

I knew why, of course. My presence there had embarrassed him, too.

"Then why am I on the plane?"

"You'll stay at the castle with us. Look on the bright side. You can stroll around in the swamp with us and listen to the frogs croak."

She could certainly charm me when she wanted to, and I laughed.

As soon as we landed, she telephoned him from the airfield. "He says to wait for him. He sounds in a wonderful mood! He's coming when he can."

A wonderful mood? Morrell was hard at work.

When he did come, late in the night, he brought a macabre souvenir—the uniform he had been wearing when the bomb exploded. You might have seen it in photographs. But seeing it up close, holding it in one's hands, it was completely impossible to believe that he had survived.

The trousers were in shreds and covered with scorch marks. They had been torn to pieces by shrapnel, and yet his legs were not scratched. The tunic had most of the back ripped out of it. But here he was, smiling and confident.

To this day, I wonder if what appeared to happen and what really happened were two different things. He had a body double, but he was intended just to be seen at a distance. No double could have been handling the briefing he had been attending. Gustav Weler was a completely unremarkable man with a soft voice and a retiring manner. He could double for Hitler, yes, but never for an instant replace him.

Could there have been another one? If so, perhaps he was in the briefing and wearing these trousers, because the man before us now was certainly Adolf Hitler, and frankly, he seemed even less injured than the reports were claiming.

We had been told to wait in the suite at the top of the castle. We'd smoked plenty on the plane, and had busied ourselves cleaning up and getting into fresh clothes as soon as we arrived, so the three of us were running around in various states of undress when the door opened and he came striding in.

"Oh, what's this, a harem? Willy, two at once, I'm impressed!"

"Oh, Alf," Eva said and ran to him, a svelte, bronze goddess wearing only slippers. She threw her arms around him and covered him with kisses.

"Now, now, I'm fine! Fine!" He took her by the shoulders and leaned her away from him. "Get dressed, really!"

"Why should I? It's just us. You get undressed!" She tugged at his necktie.

"No, oh no. None of this deviltry. We're having a dinner here and

I'm going to sleep here. I mean, *sleep*! Well away from that mad tangle." He threw himself into a chair. "You'll be happy to know that they're shooting themselves already."

"Who were they?" Carlotta asked.

"We'll get to that, believe me. Swine! Kill me, will they? *Me*! Devils! We'll root them out, every one of them. *Schweinhuntz!* Monsters!"

"But who?"

For a moment, he stared straight ahead. Then he turned his gaze to her. In that instant, his face had filled with suspicion. "Do you have any ideas?"

"Not really. I don't know many people. As you know."

"Willy? You have social connections in Berlin, I believe. Do you have any ideas?"

"He knows that Horstmann couple," Carlotta said.

Damned fool! She was playing it too close.

"I do, and some of their friends. We had a Bridge evening at Ambassador Anfuso's recently."

"Who was there?"

"What do you want, Alf, a list?"

"Who in hell's name was there! Tell me that!"

"Ah, well—the Bismarcks, yes. The Schonbergs. I need to think back."

"What was said?"

"I beat their blue-blooded asses at Bridge," Carlotta said. "I've got six thousand marks to prove it. We were going to go to Paris and spend it."

"No going to Paris!"

"If I can remember anything that might help us, I'll tell you, Alf. There were a number of people there from the aristocracy, but I don't recall a thing being said that suggested that they knew of anything like this. I would have told you instantly."

He leaned his head back against the chair and closed his eyes. "You're the clever one, Willy. You never let me down."

In the context of the conversation we were having, it was an enigmatic statement, and you do not want a man who holds your life in his hands to become enigmatic, believe me.

I went around behind him and began massaging his shoulders. "You're as stiff as a board, Alf. Do you have a headache?"

"Certainly I have a headache."

We drew him a bath and made him as comfortable as we could. The three of us bathed him. I saw some bruises coming up on his body, but they looked to me like contusions from a truncheoning. Again, no broken skin.

There was no sex. The man was drained. Whether he was actually in the bombing or not, I don't know, but he was just simply hollowed out. The effect was of a walking corpse and it was profoundly disquieting.

Secular to my core though I am, I have at moments in my life wondered if there might not be some aspect of existence that we simply don't understand—not that ghosts, demons, gods and such are supernatural, but rather that they do have some sort of existence, but one that is not accessible to us, or beyond our comprehension.

On that night, bathing this naked, emaciated, trembling creature, such a thought entered my mind. He still spoke, recognized people, ate, offered opinions and all the rest, but it simply did not seem to me that he was alive.

We got him cleaned up and I valeted him as best I could, the end result being more or less adequate. Then we all dressed our absolute best, me in my old monkey suit and the girls in the terrific dresses they had brought for the occasion.

When we came into the salon, he clapped and smiled. At first, fine, but he kept on. He clapped, smiled, nodded, looking from one to the other with his dead eyes. For all the world, he looked like a gigantic wind-up Hitler doll.

A fine dinner was then served, all vegetables and grains. We didn't torment him with meat and nobody smoked to tease him. That doesn't mean we didn't want to smoke. We were sweating it out, let me tell you.

There were asparagus spears, carrots, little cabbages roasted in breading, a seasoned porridge of groats and a bean-and-greens salad, followed by a chocolate *bombe*. We had wine, he had a bottle of pop.

The next day for the plotters, for their families and friends, in fact, for anybody who had so much as crossed their paths, a terror of exceptional brutality began. Justice meant nothing. Any fantasy that suggested guilt resulted in conviction. By law, even the families of conspirators were in danger of death.

And for once, I was not immune. I fell, also, into its vortex.

# 26

Hitler disappeared into his Wolf's Lair, into the fiery rage of the narcissist under threat and the increasing catastrophe unfolding on all fronts. We received no further visits at the castle, no calls to go to the *Wolfschanze*. Finally, I sent him a message through his adjutant that we were leaving. Receiving no reply, we went with Himmler back to Berlin aboard *Sonderzug Heinrich,* racing through the night under blackout. A plane had disappeared on the run to Munich, and the Luftwaffe was re-evaluating the safe zone. The wreckage had not been located.

Supposing that we might at any moment be called back to Rastenberg, the three of us stayed in the Wannsee House rather than making our way to the Berghof.

I listened to the BBC every night and was appalled that they were broadcasting more and more names as being connected to the bomb plot. It was an attempt, I thought, to get Hitler to execute some of his own loyalists.

Then, one night about three weeks after the event, I received the greatest surprise of my life. I heard my own name.

"Eva, Carlotta, come!"

They rushed into my study where we kept the radio. "I've just been named as one of the plotters."

They both stared at me. I stared back.

"But it's impossible," Eva said.

Carlotta went running off downstairs.

"What are you doing?"

She shouted back, "Calling Alf."

It was eleven in the evening, the usual time of his final briefing of the day, and indeed, he was in conference and couldn't be disturbed. She said to the switchboard operator, "Give him the message that the call is from Herr Weber at his home in Wannsee and it's urgent."

Half an hour later, the telephone rang. We were downstairs in the sun room and I ran for it.

It was Paul Dukes.

"Paul, let me ring you back tomorrow. This has to be kept clear."

"The Gestapo is on their way to pick you up. Better get out of there."

"Get out? Run?"

"Of course run. You're liable to be shot!"

"You did this."

"Willy, just get out. Get out of Germany by any way you can." He rang off.

"That was Dukes. The Gestapo's coming to arrest me." I ran upstairs to grab my razor and some fresh collars, with both Eva and Carlotta following close behind. I planned to get in the car and make a run for the border.

"Don't try to escape, Willy," Carlotta said. "That tells them that you're afraid and that you were warned that they were coming. That's what a guilty man does."

Eva came along behind. "What's happening?" she asked in a shrill voice.

"Eva, when Alf calls back, it's going to be up to us to save Willy's life. Somebody has tricked the Gestapo into arresting him."

"What's that? What sort of trick?"

"Eva, when Alf calls back, you must tell him that the British are broadcasting the names of people who weren't in the conspiracy, people he needs at his side, so that he'll have them executed. Can you remember that?"

"I have to tell Alf that you're not guilty. But of course you aren't, you're our dear Willy!"

"We'll do it together," Carlotta said.

The balalaika was thrumming away in the cellar. As had become the habit in the neighborhood, there was a party of former POWs going on down there. I said to Carlotta, "Go quiet them down." She was the only one who could control the Russians when they were drunk, which was essentially all the time, vodka being the Russian vitamin.

As she barked down the cellar stairs at them, the lights of many cars appeared in the street. Four men in plainclothes and another in an SS uniform came striding up to the door. Immediately, pounding began.

When I opened it, they grabbed me and started manhandling me down the front walk. Others pushed past into the house.

As I was being hurried along, Carlotta came running up with something in her hands. Before they could stop her, she had draped it around my neck. It was my Eagle.

"This man is a friend of Adolf Hitler and of Germany. You've come here because you've heard the British spout out his name on their lying radio. They did it to harm the Reich. Without the materials this man's company brings in, we can't build planes."

I was shoved roughly into the car.

"You fucking morons! You'll hear from the leader about this, believe me!"

One of them men grabbed her arm and shook her. "It's a fuhrer order! That's why we're here! We know he's got a damned Eagle. You think we'd be here if Hitler hadn't personally ordered it?"

She said quite evenly and calmly, "You will find that you have been deceived." She turned toward the house, where men could be seen moving past the windows with Eva rushing about among them.

"If anything is damaged or stolen, the *Seicherheideinst* will receive a bill."

"We don't pay bills for damage caused by searches."

She came forward and leaned into the car. "You will."

With that, she walked back into the house, the car started and off we went.

I was terrified, but also impressed. With Carlotta on my side, I might have reason to hope. But had Hitler really ordered this personally? Given the suspicions I thought that I'd been detecting, it seemed possible. If not, then had Paul engineered it, or had he sincerely tried to warn me?

Whatever arcane reason he might have for turning against me I could not imagine. But at a time like this with chaos all around and in a dictatorship with no fixed laws, things might not be what they seemed.

The Berlin Gestapo and SS HQ in *Prinze Albrecht Strasse* was the most feared building in the city, and as I was led in and up the staircase to the great, arched corridor into which so many had been taken, never to return, my stomach gave a heave, but I managed to keep the contents back. It was probably illegal for me to have dined on *foie gras* and orange duckling anyway, given that they weren't exactly on the approved ration list.

With my Eagle still dangling around my neck I was led into another corridor in which there were dozens of people coming and going, some of the in plainclothes, some of them uniformed SS.

"Is the *Reichsfuhrer SS* present in the building?"

"What's that to you?"

"He is my friend and I'd like him to know I'm here."

Someone behind me cuffed the back of my head. "Don't try that stupid stuff. It's so boring."

The next moment, a man came along in manacles. One of his eyes was swollen closed, but I recognized Adam Trott from the Adlon and the Anfuso Bridge evening.

We went into an even narrower corridor, this one lined by low doors. The next thing I knew, I was pushed into a completely windowless cell. I had time to see a bucket in the corner and what looked like an old wooden door on the floor, then the light went out.

Darkness absolute, and I mean *absolute*. The terror was just amazing. A scream burst out of me before I could stop it, before I even realized that it was coming. In a dictatorship, the distance from the top to the bottom can be very short.

The dark brought with it an illusion that the room had become huge. But as I flailed about, the closeness of the walls told me that it was little more than a closet. Claustrophobia set in. But if I squatted on the door and didn't touch anything, that awful sense of the limitless returned, soon bringing on an attack of agoraphobia.

Fear had dried my mouth. I was terribly thirsty. At the same time, I needed to urinate. I'd seen the bucket, but when I felt for it, I turned it over and was immediately oppressed by the stench of its contents spreading through the space. Finally I did the only thing I could, which was to stand on the door and piss onto the floor. I remained standing there, leaning against the wall. If I straightened up, my head scraped the ceiling.

I'd never been confined before and I never want to be again. It is an agony beyond belief. To this day, I can't even think about prisons, and when I read of these new "super-maximum" jails, I get physically ill. What devil ever got that idea, and where did it come from? I'll tell you where: this place, that's where.

I don't know how long I was in there. Hours. I do know this: every fifteen minutes or so, I panicked and went somewhat mad. I screamed, I pounded on the door, I even "heiled" away, I am embarrassed to say.

To make matters worse, there came the distant sound of "Meier's Bugle," the air-raid siren. Here I was in this trap and a raid was going on. If the building was hit, I'd be buried alive or cooked to death in here, boiled in a ghastly stew of piss and shit.

I covered my ears to shut out the thudding shock of exploding bombs and that hideous whistling. The racket made by the flak towers was such a relief that I cried. I actually cried in hope that the allied planes overhead might be knocked down. That's what having all of your security ripped away in a moment can do. Your loyalties disappear, your dignity evaporates and your only remaining moral is the raw hunger to live.

Add to that a thumb screw or a hot poker burning away the rectum and your oppressors will get results every time. This is why people under Gestapo and SS torture talked. Everybody talked. Not that they told the truth. Torture may or may not get that. Torture gets whatever will stop the pain. It also causes confusion. Half the time, victims can't remember their own names, let alone who they might have seen or what they'd done.

Again without warning and I don't know how much later, the light went on and the door opened. Contrary to the movies, there was no politely aristocratic officer with a monocle asking me questions at first, then regretfully turning me over to the torturers.

I was manhandled out of the cell, kicked for knocking over the bucket, then put in manacles that must have weighed thirty pounds. I was then pushed and dragged along to another room. Inside was a wooden bench, a couple of chairs and, on the wall, a photograph of Hitler. It was, in fact, the same one that hung in Eva's foyer in the Berghof. Carlotta used to scoff at it. 'He thinks it's military. It's psychopathic. It's the photograph of a crazy man.' She knew.

My shirt was ripped right off my back, my collar springing and my studs flying all over the place. I was pushed down onto the bench and they commenced rubber hosing me. I'd seen a few George Raft pictures. I knew that the rubber hose was being used because it didn't bruise.

It hurt like the very devil, though. Even as I'm writing this down all these years later, I can still feel the flaming agony of it, like having hot irons laid against my skin.

From other rooms, I could hear wailing and begging, desperate screams, snapping sounds, crunching sounds, the crack of whips.

"Who did you see in the corridor?"

"A lot of people. I don't know."

"One man in manacles. Who was that man?"

"Adam Trott."

"Ah, surprise! This one is as weak as a baby, and an Eagle on him, too."

There came another rain of blows to my back.

"When did you join?"

"I joined nothing!"

"Don't feed me that shit! Adam Trott is your *friend*, Herr Weber."

"I played Bridge with him at the Italian ambassador's house."

"Work on his feet and work on his dick. Call me in half an hour."

They pulled off my evening pumps. I was still lying face down and could see nobody. "Silk stockings, look at this!"

"Where's my Eagle? You've taken my Eagle!"

"That filth is in the garbage. Nobody wants to touch it anymore. It's been around the neck of a traitor."

"You hear something the *British* put in a broadcast, and that lands me here? I import chromium, bauxite, rare earths. The Reich can't build aircraft without them."

"The Reich will get along without your crap."

"Actually no, it won't."

When they beat the bottoms of my feet, the wave of pain was so intense that the world simply ceased. Turned black. Was gone.

The next thing I knew, my eyes flew open. How long I'd been out, I've no idea. My heart was racing and a nurse who looked like Frankenstein in a little white cap was drawing a syringe out of my arm.

I had been turned over and there was a man sitting beside the bench looking down at me. Half of his face was a melted ruin, the eye sewed shut, the cheek a sunken mass of scars, the lips red ropes with teeth grinning behind them. The other half was gentle, green eyes, a soft mouth. He was a young man, very sad.

"Thank you, nurse." He heaved a sigh. "All right, Herr Weber, here it is. A complaint of high treason has been lodged against you. You can be in court tomorrow and get it over with or you can hold out and we can keep on until you either tell us all you know, or you die in this room. Come clean with me right now and you'll be shot. Honorable death. Hold out one more second and your chance is lost. We go all the way. No turning back."

What should I say? I didn't know anything.

"I am going to read a list of names. You will say 'yes,' 'no,' or 'unknown to me' after each name."

One after another, he read off about twenty names. Whenever he came to one who had been at Anfuso's, I would say "Bridge party."

Afterward, he was silent for a time. Then he said to someone at my head whom I could not see, "Get acid, please."

This was the acid bath, then. They sprayed you with nitric acid, flaying you alive. My bowels let go. Nobody spoke. When I saw a fellow in a cheap suit come in with a bucket, a scream burst out of me. Again, it wasn't something I did, it was simply something that happened.

Ritual adds terror to torture, and I had to watch as they carefully funneled the sour, reeking fluid into a sort of insect sprayer.

"Start with the feet, please. Just a bit to get it going."

When you are tortured for answers you don't have, it is the worst thing imaginable. I couldn't save myself even if I wanted to.

I became aware of a woman's voice outside rising and falling. Then the door burst open and an SS officer in an elaborate uniform entered.

The woman roared, "That's him, there he is!"

"Fraulein, stay away!"

"*Frau*, Asshole! Get him out of there!"

Carlotta had come, somehow. She barged in waving papers. "Get him off of that! How dare you! And what's that shit in that thing?" She kicked the sprayer right out of the torturer's hand. It flew against the wall and burst, instantly spreading noxious fumes through the room.

With everybody coughing, we vacated at once. They had to carry me. One does not walk after the truncheoning of the feet, I can assure you.

"You!" She pointed to the man with the ruined face. "Get his Eagle! You scum, throwing a German Eagle in that wastebasket! Who do you work for, Stalin or Churchill?"

He ran in and came back with it.

I recognized the SS officer with her. It was Paul. He said, "This outrage will be punished." He gestured. "All of you." Then, to the one with the face, "You can expect a concentration camp. Without what this man provides, we cannot fly. We cannot build cannon. You heard an enemy radio broadcast and brought him here."

"We received an order—"

Paul slapped him across the face. "I don't speak to filth! Traitor!" He said, "Carry him out. NOW!"

The entire corridor, which had been bustling with prisoners and guards, had fallen silent. As I was carried along, the faces peering down at me looked like death masks, as gray and empty as Hitler's had been in the castle.

I knew that this couldn't be legitimate, not when the only people actually involved were a foul-mouthed whore shouting her head off and a heavily disguised British agent. But this was National Socialist Germany, land of chaos and confusion. A government built around Darwinian principles functions like a cage full of apes. Put them under pressure and chaos ensues.

When we got to the street, there was Paul's wonderful old Hispano sitting in front of the building. I was bundled into the back with Carlotta and he took the wheel from the "chauffeur," who was the Russian doctor from my gardening team, swallowed by one of my own tuxedo jackets and wearing a pince-nez with no glass in the frames.

"We've got to get you to Switzerland," Paul said. "Why in hell didn't you run?"

"I didn't have time. And I thought it might make me appear guilty."

"*Appear*? You've been at the Adlon with the conspirators, at the now infamous Anfuso meeting, all of it!"

"That was a meeting of the conspirators? Anfuso's a big fascist."

"Which is why it was held there. While you were busily playing Bridge, they were creeping off into the shadows and laying plans."

"How did my name end up on that broadcast?"

"It wasn't from me. That's all I can say for certain."

If that was a lie, he wouldn't have been in Gestapo headquarters risking his life. There was only one other person on the planet who could have known to do it. For whatever reason, Churchill must have turned against me.

"Winston?"

"Unlikely. More likely some MI6 idiot."

I wondered. I had delayed and delayed giving Paul that list, as a result of which the conspirators had almost succeeded. So perhaps a warning had gone to Churchill, 'Weber isn't reliable.' Effectively a death sentence.

"Car following," Carlotta said sharply.

"Just keep on track back to the house. Willy, I'm sorry to say this, but if you get arrested again—" He handed a small silver capsule to Carlotta.

She said, "This is cyanide. You bite down on it. Takes ten seconds." She slid a finger across her throat. "I've seen it done, they don't feel a thing. Keep it in your cheek. If they try to search your *klugschleisser*, bite." She held it out. "Open up." She stuck it into my cheek. "Don't make a mistake, my love." She pulled one out of her own cheek. "We're all wearing them tonight. Not Eva. She has no idea what's going on. She's running along behind the goons hitting them with her slipper when they try to sneak your silverware into their pockets."

When we arrived back in Wannsee the doctor got his assistants to carry me up to my bedroom.

As we ascended, I heard the telephone ring. I thought, 'good god, they're calling ahead to see if we're back.' Not thinking straight, of course.

We were on the landing when Eva shouted up, "Come quickly, Willy."

It was him.

"What is it, Willy?" he asked. His voice was faint with exhaustion.

"The British put out my name on the BBC as a conspirator."

"And?"

"The Gestapo came and got me. I only just got away from them."

He did not respond.

"Alf?"

"Nobody could be that stupid."

"The British are trying to use the situation to get you to kill your friends."

He grunted, then rang off without another word.

"What did he say?" Carlotta asked.

"He grunted."

"What?"

"'Uh.' He went, 'uh.'"

Eva frowned. "If they show up here again, I shall tell them to go away."

"Now take me to the bath. I need a soak and I need morphine, I'm in bloody *agony*!"

As they manhandled me back up the stairs I heard Eva ask Carlotta, "Why can't he walk?"

"Eva, stay innocent, dear love. You're the last child in Germany."

The Russian doctor proved to actually be a doctor. He injected me with morphine from my dope kit and began attending to my feet, which is the last thing I remembered until I opened my eyes to the light of morning and Carlotta sitting beside the bed reading.

"Good afternoon, sleeper. Alf called and said it was finished."

"What did he mean?"

"That."

"Whatever is 'that?'"

She shrugged.

Paul later said that he had some indication that a "cell" of some sort in the Gestapo had been uncovered and its participants shot. Nothing more ever came to light.

Carlotta was reading intently. She would soak up anything she could, this woman whose only education was in exotic sex.

"What's the book?"

"Musil."

"Ah. Banned, of course."

"I only read banned books. The others aren't worth a *ficking pfennig*."

The Kreislers had left behind a house was full of excellent literature, that is to say, banned literature. Fortunately, the Gestapo types who'd ransacked the silver, the pantry and my study were not readers or they'd have ripped them all to shreds, and some of them were very fine.

"I think I'm better."

"Alf's better, too. He breathed down the phone at me for five minutes. 'I can imagine it...I can imagine it.' Fucking asshole."

"You're alive because of that fucking asshole."

"I'm alive because I'm a clever little *fickstuck*."

I got out of the bed, but when my feet hit the floor it felt as if they had burst into flame. I lurched back, missed the bed, hit the floor and let fly with every curse word I knew.

"I am reading, Dear."

"Jesus Christ! Those fucking guys!"

"As I said, I am reading."

"Help me!"

"Go froth at the mouth in another room."

"Come on, Carlotta, do the bitch act tomorrow."

She slammed the book shut. "Eva! Get the Ivans in here, Prince Willy needs transport."

"What's with you today?"

"I hate this hell country and I want out. If we went to Switzerland we could get married and make our way to America. We could be in the high buildings instead of sitting here in this dump waiting to have hot irons rammed up our asses by crazy men! This is why I'm doing the bitch act, and I think it's perfectly reasonable."

The Russians appeared, sweaty and dropping clods of earth off their boots as they tromped in.

"Where go now?"

They put me on a chaise in the sun room. That room remains one of the loveliest I know, with its tall windows overlooking the sweep of garden down to the lake. In those days, what one saw was essentially a sort of pocket farm, with chicken coops and rabbit hutches against one wall and a vegetable garden covering half of the ground. The other half was planted in flowers, all manner of them, and I remember them on that morning dancing.

Beyond that spread the lake. Even in this last summer of Hitler, when his madness was in the process of being cut out of the soul of Germany by the allies, boats nevertheless raced on the late summer water.

One I recall with a blue striped sail that was there almost every day scudded along heeled well over, its bright prow cutting the perfect surface of the water, a happy blade.

I was served a *ragout* of rabbit and a crisp green wine, one of the bottles of *vinho verde* I'd had brought up from Portugal when the Germans held France. The Americans had liberated Paris on August 25 and were now closing in on Aachen.

They were coming, my countrymen, and bringing the future with them, tired soldiers, just kids most of them, afraid all the time and so far from home.

# 27

As the months passed, I grew more and more afraid for more and more reasons. Chaos kills, and chaos ruled. Clearly, the war was ending, and with every day that passed I became more determined that Carlotta and I must survive, and less sure that we would. Love wants to live, though. More and more often now, our talk turned to the children we would have, their names, their looks, their dispositions. We imagined them asleep, at play, at their lessons. There were three of them. She had a boy and two girls. I had a girl and two boys.

When the wind was right in Wannsee, the stench of Berlin came like a reeking ghost, rotting garbage and remembered fire.

Over the autumn and into the new year, there was a tremendous decline in everything. Electricity became sporadic. The water didn't run properly, and when it did the servants had to filter it through chamois before it could be used. We began carrying water up from the lake.

The endless air raids were breaking Germany like a mechanical toy being shaken by an irritated child. The Red Army was on the Oder. As "*festung Berlin*" was largely a fiction, it wasn't clear to me why Zukhov didn't simply march into the city, and this concerned me very much. I could imagine Russian soldiers appearing without warning some night.

Life in the city was hell, even for the leader. As a result, Hitler was often with us in Wannsee. Fear had become the center of his being. Like many old people, the approach of death had caused him to become obsessed with life. Contrary to the assumption that he committed suicide in an atmosphere of dark acceptance, he strove for life, he fought every inch for it. The avidity of his hunger for personal survival disgusted me. But that's the narcissist. As far as he was concerned, he was the world. The rest of us were only actors on his stage, our fates of little concern.

My house was a haven of order in a lunatic wilderness. Berlin itself was a mad symphony of stenches and improbabilities. Given no toothpaste, halitosis drifted in the streets like a gas. The sweet rot of the dead seeped out from the rubble amid the sound of ringing telephones. People called the ruins constantly, 'is my love all right, my wife, my husband, my child?' The love of one for another was being raped by the bombs. And yet, as the BBC reported what the Russians were finding in the east at Sobibor, Treblinka, Auschwitz and so many other places, I could not help but see justice being done.

Never imagine that the Germans didn't still love Hitler in '44. After the July 20 plot had failed, rallies were held all over the Reich to celebrate his survival. Millions filled theaters, stadia, all the meeting places. They didn't have to come. Nobody forced them. The fact that the Hitler madness had infected my beloved Germans forced me to harden my heart toward them and to look with equanimity on their fantastic suffering. But I hated doing it. They were so damn pitiful, scrabbling about in the rubble of their lives, their dusty faces trenched with tears, their hearts corrupt.

Once a demagogue's ideas capture a mind, that person's moral life ends. He hungers to submit, and by so doing to forget the uncertainty of conscience that dogs human life.

Hitler came and went at my house, arriving and departing unexpectedly and without notice. His convoy would draw up and here he would come along the front walk assisted on both sides by SS officers, his jaw working faster and faster as he approached the house. He was eager to be here in this little corner that remained alive. His excitement would cause his left arm to pump furiously.

When he entered, he would say "Willy, hello, how are things in heaven?"

I would reply, "Now that you're here, all is well."

For whatever reason, he enjoyed wearing my things and padded about the house in my sheepskin slippers and red velvet smoking jacket. The slippers were too large by a size and flapped on the floor, and the jacket descended past his knees. He had one of his father's pipes which he often held in his mouth, usually without lighting it. But not always. Earlier, he would smoke while signing death warrants and murder orders. Now, he did it for some deeper reason. He seemed at times to take on the gruff, sullen spirit of his father, and one would see a malignant stranger lurking in his eyes, the demon father.

He wanted opium but I was clean out. Even Goering was out, well and truly. I know this for certain because I offered him gold for it.

Hitler slept in the bunker only if caught at the Chancellery during an air-raid.

We listened constantly to the BBC, which was now a more reliable source of news even than *Wehrmacht* position reports. Also, Hitler had come up with another, rather clever idea. We would pick towns east of the Oder and telephone from their books, which he would bring with him from the Chancellery. If a Russian answered, then we would know that they were there, and he would mark it on the big map which was now spread on a table in the wonderful oval ballroom that was the architectural centerpiece of the house. If a German voice answered, he would hang up, and we would mark that town as still in our hands.

He worried more and more about the Jews. "I do not wish to fall into the hands of enemies and end up the center of a spectacle arranged by Jews." He had begun to worry not only that he would be hung in public, but that he would be stripped naked and his insufficiency put on display for all to see. He feared dying amid gales of laughter. Or again, "They'll suffocate me in a glass gas chamber for the pleasure of the mob."

I was beginning to understand what had actually happened in the east, that it had not been ten thousand or a hundred thousand but millions upon millions. I am told that it had been too fantastic to imagine, but that I did not remains the core of the shame that now dominates my life.

In Wannsee, life had continued on tolerably well. Strange things were going missing. Not only was there no toothpaste, washing soap was a rarity, sometimes difficult to acquire even on the black market. We had an off-the-books hairdresser to the house to attend Eva and Carlotta. For the most part, I could not get decent cigarettes anymore, although after the Allied disaster in Holland that is known in history as Market Garden, Kensittas, Senior Service and Luckies appeared on the black market. I remember that our "grocer" once showed up with a remarkable acquisition on his wagon. He brought it out as if it was the bust of Nefertiti or Priam's gold.

It was so beautiful and yet so heartbreaking that I almost wept. I paid two hundred and fifty marks for that six pack of Coca-Cola. Maria made rennet ice and we sat around the dinner table, all of us, including our Russians, who were now simply part of the family and went anywhere in the house. I was as inept then at keeping servants in their place as I am now. I'm a democratic snob, I guess.

Anyway, I served out Coke floats. Hitler wasn't there and I'm glad. He didn't deserve a Coke float.

Thanks to our Russian gardeners and Maria's expertise at putting food by, we were able to present a decent enough table three times a day all through the winter.

There was a sameness—the meat was either rabbit or chicken, but she must have evolved twenty different ways of cooking each of them. She could schnitzel a rabbit so that it seemed uncannily like veal. I taught her to fry chicken "southern style" by simply describing what it had looked and tasted like when I was a boy in St. Louis.

Hitler called this the "Love House." He was happy here and I hated that. But I also hated the fact that another man's happiness angered me.

He no longer made annoying remarks when he saw meat come to the table. Unless the secretaries were about, the endless rants were also much less frequent. Carlotta would walk out or, as before, ostentatiously sleep in his face. I would listen for a bit, then go to reading. Eva would smile and nod, but it was obvious that she understood little. The moment he started, Gretl would announce that her baby was making her tired and retire.

He was now a profound drug addict. Any real doctor had been cashiered. Only Morrell remained. I no longer suspect that he was intentionally poisoning him. Unintentionally, though, yes. He was a crank and an idiot. For example, Koster's Antigas pills, which he gave him at the rate of four to a meal, contained strychnine. They didn't work worth a damn, either. Vitamultin, which was not a vitamin preparation but just more amphetamine, went in by injection, and there was always a bowl of Pervitin capsules near to hand. Eukodal he popped as a candied pill. At night, there would be a heavy dose of Nervacit for sleep, and Heroin was in use, too.

One night when the two of us were alone together, he began talking about the future. "Do you know of *Werwolf?*"

I lied automatically. "I do not."

"We're fortifying the *Obersalzberg*. You wouldn't even know the Berghof. There's construction everywhere. We're building immense underground galleries where the SS can stay, coming out at night to remind the German people that National Socialism is still their only future."

I remembered my orders. I had to tell Paul immediately.

"That's a real inspiration."

We were sitting side by side on the couch in the sun room. He laid his hand on mine. "I knew that would be your reaction. Would you join them?"

"Certainly."

"Well, I have another mission for you. A higher mission. There is a submarine in the base at Hamburg, U-234, that can reach the far east. It has been loaded with some of your uranium for the Japanese, who are well on to making an immense bomb that will be dropped on San Francisco by zeppelin. You and I can be on that u-boat, Willy. It's big. Our women can be with us."

Extraordinary intelligence. "We would go to Japan?"

"Not at all. The destruction of one American city won't be sufficient. The Japanese are going to lose their war, too. No, we'll be let off in the East Indies. Indonesia. By the time we arrive, the Dutch will have returned. There will be people among them who will help us. This is already arranged."

To cover my shock, I smiled. "Wonderful, Alf!"

"An idea I had. It's all worked out."

My only thought was that this must not happen. Hitler had to be publicly tried in a fair trial and afforded a proper defense. When found guilty—as he would be, for his crimes were too public to be denied—he had to be executed. Above all, he must not disappear into the whispers of the world. From a hidden vantage point like an obscure island, who knew how much influence he could wield?

"You've spoken of this before," I said. "It sounded hopeful but not practical. Is it?"

"All we have to do is drive up to Hamburg and get in the boat."

"U-234 can travel that far without refueling?"

"Not only that, it can make the dangerous parts of the voyage entirely under water. If we can get to Hamburg, we can get to the East Indies."

I forced eagerness into my voice. "When do we start?"

"A few days. A week at most. There are still unfinished arrangements."

"How can it go so far under water?"

"There's a device that allows it to breathe from below."

This was the *schnorkel*, which had been much touted in the press as another wonder weapon.

But how would I communicate all this to Paul? All through the war, getting in touch with him had been maddeningly difficult. The reason, of course, was security. If I knew his whereabouts and was arrested and tortured without his knowledge, the Gestapo might show up unexpectedly at his door.

Since my arrest, our security was tighter than ever. Had Himmler guessed the truth about us, or been told by somebody? Or had the American OSS operation in Switzerland been the reason I had been named on the BBC? Given the inept codes that it was using and Allan Dulles' habit of transmitting brags about his achievements to Washington, it might have been. I was, as an American, one of those achievements.

The central reality of an operative's life is that you never know where you stand. In field work like ours, one lives always in the night and fog. Any sense of certainty is an illusion, and a dangerous one.

I couldn't wait for Paul to show up or telephone. I couldn't go poking through the ruins looking for him. In any case, he was probably in Switzerland. I had no safe way to contact the SIS Swiss bureau from here.

I considered using Carlotta. Being in the Red Choir, as I was now fairly sure was the case, she had no worries about compromised codes. Russian codes do not break any more than Russian masters lose at chess. But her only means of transmitting her reports was through her contact in the Berghof guard unit.

I decided that we had to go south. But how to do it? Not only would the trip be dangerous, the fact that we had no compelling reason to make it would raise suspicions, and those suspicions would fester in Hitler's mind while we were gone. After all, he himself might well have been the one who turned me in to the Gestapo. He loved me but I was also his enemy, which I think he hid from himself, but also understood very well.

I told Carlotta the story.

"That shit. His life is so important? *His* life!"

As Hitler had taken over the master, we were now living in one of our own guest rooms, but at least the house had no intercom system.

Then she said, "Idea: Eva's best dresses are in the Berghof. I know she wants them. We could offer to get them."

"He won't let you go and I can't transmit information through your contact, there's no arrangement for that."

He wouldn't allow her to travel the roads—either her or Eva, for that matter. When he'd looked at the car that had been strafed, he had been so shaken that he had hugged me warmly, this man whose most affectionate moments were usually stilted to the point of being comical.

"I'll say that a man can't possibly manage to make the right selection. She has hundreds of dresses, remember. "

"Long shot," she said.

"When we arrive, you make your report and we keep going straight on to Switzerland."

The idea flooded me like a fresh breeze on a stifling day. Why not? Our war could be over. A new life would unfold.

But then fate intervened, and it was a terrible intervention. On the morning of March 28 as we were preparing to make our journey, Albert Speer telephoned with an invitation and a request. The five of us, me, Carlotta, Alf, Gretl and Eva, had just sat to lunch when the call came through.

"Speer here, are you hearing me?"

"Yes, the connection is good."

"Come to the Philharmonic tonight. Bring your wife. It's the final concert of the war. Your friend Dukes will be there. I thought we could box together."

Extraordinary. Did Paul somehow suspect that I had urgent information, or was this coincidence? "Yes, absolutely, we'd love to come." Carlotta had become my "wife" in the eyes of everybody but us. We were determined to have a fine wedding, but we already lived as a couple.

Had Paul somehow arranged that this meeting take place? If so, why would he, and why would he use Speer, that snake?

It was possible that Speer had become disloyal. Hitler had discharged him for defeatism, replacing him with Karl-Otto Sauer. Since then, he had become decidedly more friendly to me. As one of the few survivors of the July 20 Plot roundup, I was considered to be in Hitler's special favor. Frightened that he might have one of his fits over some logistical problem or other, decide that Speer was to blame and sentence him to death, the slave-driving cur had slithered his way into my orbit.

Like most of the inner circle, he knew that Hitler was spending time with us in Wannsee, and therefore that I had his ear and might be able to "fix" things from time to time.

The record shows, rather incredibly, that Hitler and Eva were living during this period in Hitler's rooms on the top floor of the still intact part of the Chancellery. But it was a target and a death trap, and he only went in it when it was necessary to do official business, or if he wanted to go into the basement and look at the Germania models, which had been moved back from the Berghof. When an air raid came in, he would hurry to the bunker.

Soon, he would be living in it, true, but understand that it was no luxurious suite, which is why he avoided it as long as he could. The lower bunker where he stayed was only about 2500 square feet and yet fitted out with 15 rooms, all of them necessarily cramped, wretched little affairs. The ventilation system droned incessantly, and he was terrified that somebody would fill it up with poison gas. This was despite the huge air filters meant to prevent that. It was also below the water table and so damp that it felt like a swamp. The walls were always wet. Furniture brought down from the Chancellery warped and a gray haze of mildew grew on the cushions. It also invaded clothing. The lighting cast everything into morbid shadows. He would say of it, "I feel like I'm already buried when I'm in there." And that was another fear. A direct hit would bury everybody in it alive.

One of the greatest of all German fears during the war was being buried alive and then slow-cooked in a fire. This had happened during the Hamburg raid of '44, when thousands had been trapped in the above-ground shelters there and cooked when the city was blanketed with incendiaries. When it was entered, the discovery was made that people had torn their own melting skin right off their bodies.

Many shelters were huge concrete affairs built above ground. To prevent crowd-effect panic, they were divided like the bunker into a warren of little rooms connected by long, narrow corridors. They were ill-ventilated, stifling nightmares, and Hitler's bunker was little better.

So here he was. He was like a horse-stomped snake, already dead but still dangerous if one got too close. And he was much too close.

When he was with us, the SS occupied the downstairs and filled the surrounding neighborhood. I'd talked him out of bringing mobile flak. The last thing we needed was for allied reconnaissance to detect guns like that sprouting up in Wannsee.

Regardless, we attempted to keep life moving along. We lived a regular existence, arising at a normal hour, breakfasting, taking luncheon in the typical semi-formal manner and dressing for a proper dinner each evening. During the day, I worked on my business, which was requiring more and more attention. Back in '42 when the Union Commerce Bank in New York had been closed by Congress for trading with the enemy, I had moved my financial focus to Geneva, which entailed elaborate procedures to properly fund drafts being drawn to do things like pay salaries in the United States and Mexico without causing suspicion in the Treasury Department and triggering an FBI investigation.

They wouldn't have found anything amiss, though, because my ability to fulfill my contracts with the Reich had ended with the collapse of the German position in France. Since the occupation, all of my shipments had been coming in on the safest route, which was through Lisbon, across Spain and France and into Germany.

There was no way now that they could be shifted back to the Port of Hamburg, as the allied blockade was absolute. All shipping entering the blockade zone would be sunk, neutral or not.

So all my product now went to England, which was not only entirely legal but also pleased me very much. However, the British Exchequer was not like the Reich Treasury. They paid but slowly, meaning that lines of credit had to be used in order to maintain cash flows.

It was a complex business and now that it was being handled out of Switzerland, Fred Miles could no longer manage the financial end, just the mining and shipping. I had a factor working for me in Switzerland, but he required constant approvals for payments and signatures on various legal documents, bills and loans.

I should have travelled there more often, but after what had happened to us when we came up here, I was loathe to do it. I was doing everything possible by telephone and post, but this was dangerous because, after all, the entire business now involved shipping supplies to England.

Despite our pleasant life, we could hear the bombs in Berlin and sometimes in Potsdam, but we'd ceased even to think about it and never bothered to go to the cellar during raids.

Hitler had taken over not only our bedroom, but also my upstairs study. He would spend hours in there with Carlotta. Whatever they did, it was silent. I didn't inquire. Eventually, she would come get Eva and it would be the three of them. I was no longer invited, thank God.

I try not to remember the times I was intimate with him. The touch of his cold, dough-like fingers was like the slithering of worms along one's skin. I have waked up many times in the night thinking that I was covered with maggots.

Getting back to the luncheon and the invitation, I returned to the table and announced it.

"If there's a raid..." Gretl said.

"The hall hasn't been hit yet."

"Which means that its roof is an inviting target," Hitler said. "It's like that fool to extend such an invitation."

Carlotta said, "I want to go." She brought a tearful shudder to her voice, my clever little actor. "It means so much to me."

"Then go! I won't forbid it. I just think it's foolish." Hitler stared off into the cloud of rococo *putti* that danced up the wallpaper in this gay room. "Just like Speer! He's a fool. He lacks judgment!" He seemed to sink into himself. "We can all go. We'll spend the night in the bunker. It's perfectly all right."

"It's awful," Eva said.

He went white. "Well, all right, it's awful! So is everything else in Germany except places like this—the mysterious, magic house of Herr William Weber. I don't know why it's untouched. Nobody does. Wannsee, the Jew hole...untouched!"

"We all know why," I said, "so we take advantage. We're safe here."

"I've cleaned them out! Cleaned them out!" He struggled to his feet. "It's a miracle! One of the greatest human achievements and look how I'm vilified on the Jew radio! But of course, I did what was necessary and I almost succeeded." He went to the window, which overlooked our pocket farm and beyond it the lake, on which a lone boat sailed along. "Look at them. Nothing stops the Germans."

"That boat with the blue sail is there every day."

He turned to me. "When there's no wind?"

"Not then."

"No..." On the distance, a Mosquito was circling on some reconnaissance patrol. "The hell with that Goering, telling me I could defeat Britain from the air. So tempting, so easy!" He threw himself back down in the chair. "Never be tempted by the easy way, Willy. There is never an easy way. And now that *plan*! My God, that plan! To make this a nation of farmers, to take everything, all of our genius and give it to the Jew states, those corrupt hellholes where the people are crucified on the cross of capitalism! Jew hellholes..." He leaned forward and hid his face in his hands. Eva stared. I did the same. Carlotta went to him and laid her hand on his head. After a moment, he took it and kissed it. "Look at us, you and me. Two Jews." He laughed, which declined into a painful sounding cough. "My own blood did it! I destroyed myself from within!" He grabbed his own throat. "From within! Me! ME! The Jew blood in me creeps into my brain and whispers lies."

He sank down. Morrell was now standing in the doorway. I nodded to him and he came forward and injected him. "We shall have a rest now, Leader," he said.

"Yes, very well. I need it."

The concert was at five and it was already half three, so we had to dress and leave. Fortunately, Morrell had given him a real knockout dose of whatever it may have been, and his SS boys carried him up to the bedroom. There was no need to undress him. At the Wannsee house he shuffled around in the slippers and robe, wearing under it either a nightshirt or nothing.

The journey in to the city was ghastly, a voyage through a glowering skeleton lit by the starved light of a waning moon. Along Unter Den Linden there was nothing left standing, just the dark, staring eyes of windows and in the center divider piles and piles of bricks left by the rubble women.

Here and there, a figure picked its way carefully along the cluttered sidewalk.

The traffic apparatus was finished, so driving through the blackout was especially hazardous. Phosphorus lines had been painted at intersections where one was expected to stop. Then you peered left and right to try to spot the faint downward glow of shaded headlamps.

At last we came to the Philharmonic Hall in Tiergarten. My plan was to get us to the Leader Bunker if there was an air-raid.

Eva and Gretl, who were staunch Catholics, had said that they would be praying for us from the moment we left until our return.

A surprisingly large crowd was assembling. Contrary to what we had believed, bombing had left the hall with very little roof. The doors were also gone. In the next month it would be completely destroyed, as Beethoven Hall had recently been. There was actually another concert on May 26 in the Titania Palace, but this was the last one during which the Third Reich was still governing.

We found Albert Speer and Paul Dukes in one of the boxes. On the way in, we had discussed the matter and come to the conclusion that Speer knew perfectly well what Dukes was, and was actively helping him with an eye toward life after the Third Reich.

Speer, who was and remained until his death a convinced Nazi, deserved to be hanged with the rest of the rodents who met their ends at Nuremberg. But he wasn't. The tribunal appeared to accept his faithless and half-hearted admission of guilt and let him off with a jail sentence. There must have been more to it than that, but I have never been privy to that information.

The concert began with the finale of *Gotterdammerung*, appropriately symbolic and played, I thought, with intentional and ironic bathos. Then Tashchner played a personal favorite of mine, the Beethoven Violin Concerto, during which the crowd of at least a thousand people began to stir eagerly, as the hall was filling with a rare aroma, the scent of real coffee.

Speer, who could arrange almost anything, must have done it. Had Paul asked him to create a distraction? I've always thought so. In any case, the moment poor Taschner, who could see that he had lost his audience, brought the concerto to its final bars, everyone leaped to their feet and crowded toward the lobby and its coffee bar. Speer did the same, leaving me and Paul and Carlotta alone in the box and, in fact, alone in the entire hall.

I conveyed to him the information about the tunnels being dug in Berchtesgaden for the *Werwolf* program, and then the escape plan.

He said after a considerable silence, "You've finally earned your pay packet."

"Don't ride me anymore. I'm loyal and I live in hell because of it and I'm sick of your veiled fucking threats, Paul."

"Oh my, Mister Mild Manners gets his back up."

"You're a shit, Paul," Carlotta said. "Just a natural shit."

"Yes I am, and that's why I'm good at what I do. Speaking of which, invite me to dinner. In Berlin, one eats like a rat in a freezing cellar. I'm sure the Wannsee House is very pleasant indeed."

"Not wise. When Hitler sees us together, it feeds his paranoia. One evening with the Gestapo is quite enough for me."

"That was Himmler, by the way. He's sending out peace feelers in all sorts of directions and trying to settle scores. He knows you're bent. He just can't reach you, not directly."

"I'll never know the truth. It could've been him, you, even Churchill."

"You've been in espionage long enough to know that there's no such thing as truth in our work. Our truth is the lie that sells."

Happily, Speer returned. "I would have brought coffee but one could only take the one cup."

"A shame," Paul said and I could hear in his voice that he meant it.

It pleased me to know that he had to live like an ordinary Berliner. Now that Hitler had finally let Goebbels have his "total war" declaration, all the restaurants were closed, even Horcher's, which had been serving extraordinary delicacies like roast beef right up until the final night.

We had plenty of coffee at home.

After the concert, there was a macabre display put on in the foyer, much to Speer's dismay. As one went out, there stood a line of children dressed in Hitler Youth uniforms, all carrying cigarette trays. But there were no cigarettes in them. Instead, they contained silver cyanide capsules.

"Be sure and take one, Paul," I said.

"You take one. Take two."

"I don't need any more," I said dryly.

He started to pass them by, then hesitated. He picked one up. The little girl he got it from smiled up at him, her gray teeth gleaming. "Heil Hitler," she cried happily.

"Wise," I said. "You could be next."

"Don't send anything more to Dulles, will you?"

"So that's what you're angry about. I have my factor in Switzerland feeding him innocuous bits."

"It's irritating SIS. And it's dangerous for you. Your name keeps appearing in decoded messages. He rattles on and on about his wonderful source who lives right in Hitler's lap. If we're decoding them, you can be sure that Himmler's doing the same."

I made a mental note never, ever to drop Dulles so much as another crumb. I said, "I'm trying to build a case that'll enable me to survive my inevitable trial."

"For what?"

"Trading with the enemy. I've made a bit off the Third Reich, as you know." In point of fact, there was an inquiry after the war but no trial. I could fill my fleet with food for starving Europe, which I did, and at my own personal expense. My operations in '46 and '47 cost me five millions, and also got me appointed Food For Europe administrator.

The crowd was thinning and Carlotta was shivering in her ermine. We stepped out into the forecourt.

Paul continued the conversation. "A bit? A bundle, from what we hear."

"We've got to get back. He wakes in the night. If we're not nearby, he's frantic."

"Between the two of you, you've got the most incredible confidence trick going in history. You do know that, don't you?"

"Watch out, Darling, he's about to hit you for money."

"Is she right, Paul? Do you need money?"

"They can't get it to me from Switzerland anymore. Impossible. But not for you, of course. You have a way."

"How much?"

"Five thousand. Ten if possible."

Carlotta laughed. "See who's the confidence trickster here? Give him nothing."

I pulled out my book and drew him a check on my German account for twenty. It was the same amount I had given long ago to Hitler.

"Very generous, thank you." He folded it and put it in his pocket.

I draped my overcoat across Carlotta's trembling shoulders. One would think that ermine would be warm, but such wraps are not really designed to be proof against weather. They are meant to be admired under chandeliers.

It was still a quiet night, no sign of any bombers. The war seemed to have taken a brief recess. But as we returned along Unter Den Linden, beneath the high moon, we saw a heap in the road, cloth fluttering around it.

"Don't stop, Willy."

"No."

"Oh, he's moving! Stop!"

I pulled up and got the torch out of the glove box. Holding my hand so that the light would shine just on the figure in the road, I looked down at what proved to be a young man in a threadbare private's uniform.

Pop eyes stared up at me. Carlotta gobbled back a scream. He looked like a goggling, frog-eyed parody of a human being.

I knew why. "No eyelids," I said. Many a soldier had come back from the front like that, with their eyelids frozen off. Then the eyeballs would swell and dry out. Blind, pop-eyed, they would struggle on, staggering westward toward home.

I gazed down at him in the light of my torch. Although he had not been moving and was quite dead, he gazed back, his bulging eyes making him seem avid. The frozen do not acquire the sheen of death until they thaw. His expression—the lips parted as if in amazement, those glaring eyes—was that of a man crazed with wonder.

I wondered how many he had killed, Jews, Russians out there on the floating plain. I reached under his collar, but his tags were gone. There was no poignant wallet of photographs. And yet he had come all this way blind. Only home draws a man so far.

Carlotta took off my coat, then threw her own over him. It drifted down like a cloud dropping from the fingers of a deity. I said "he's dead" and reached to pick it up.

"Don't. I'll never touch it again."

The pale ethereal fur swayed in the fitful wind. The man's eyes glittered. Fumbling about in the corpse of Berlin, he had never come to the end of his journey.

I laid my arm around Carlotta's shoulders, protected now only by her silvery evening gown.

We left him there covered in her fur, in the cold night on Unter den Linden. He will remain there forever, a small incident on that night of music, a lost detail in the awful grandeur of wartime memory.

# 28

Roosevelt died on April 12. We cried, we both did, we hid and we cried. Hitler, was now spending more of his time in the garden bunker at the Chancellery. He worried that communications to Wannsee might fail or the enemy might appear unexpectedly. On this day, however, he appeared at the house, shambling up the walk, supported as always by SS. He came in beaming.

"I shall dance! On this day, I shall!" He did a couple of little hops in the foyer.

By this time I was so sick of him and so horrified by the news of the camps in the east that I couldn't think how even to address him in a civil manner.

Eva, who would no longer leave his side, had come with him. Grinning and twirling, she rushed in shouting, "It's all over, we've won! We've won after all!" She was glazed with gaiety, only her eyes betraying the fear that was now her truth.

The Russian doctor, who was now doubling as my butler and—thank god—valet, had answered the door. He wore an ill-fitting tailcoat we had brought down from the attic and, as always, the glassless pince-nez. (I never mention his name because he is alive and thriving in the USSR. If they knew of this episode in his life, they would send him to the gulag at once.)

"Heil," he blared, throwing a terrific Hitler salute. Fortunately, the irony of all this was too subtle for the excited Hitler to notice.

Eva called for champagne, which was brought by a red-eyed Fritz. He and Maria had been weeping also. There was no further pretense among the household that they were anything but mortal foes of the dictator. We had to be careful, though, about the Russian gardeners. Their memory of the *Wehrmacht* was that it was an invincible force, magnificent and terrible, so they were still afraid of its power and nor to be entirely trusted.

Eva put a record on—some gay, featureless German popular tune of the sort that was cranked out, it seemed, daily in the Third Reich. This music was relentlessly lively, inoffensive, unoriginal and entirely forgettable. But anyway, it made fox-trotting possible, so I joined her in the sun room.

"No dancing for me, I lied," Hitler said with a laugh. "Later!" Then, more seriously, "Stop and listen, Willy."

I did as ordered.

"It'll be another week before we make peace with the western powers. Then I've got to move fifty divisions to the Oder. Make no mistake, it'll be a near thing still."

Stamping her foot at him, Eva shouted, "Oh, it won't, it won't! We've *won*!" She threw her arms open. "We were dancing, Willy."

I took her in hand again, bobbing along amid the chaises and the chairs while Hitler stood watching out of those filmed, dead eyes of his. The pumping left arm kept up a macabre rhythm.

Carlotta drank champagne. She was keeping an excessively bright grin plastered to her face.

Maria served cheese canapés she had made from of some of the monumentally uninteresting German cheese that was now the only thing one could get, even on the black market. We no longer went into Berlin to the NSDAP commissary, so I don't know what they had there. Herr Grimmer's little wagon was stocked with less and less every week.

To our distress, Eva and Hitler proceeded to settle in again, so here came all those SS and the fussy valet and the appalling cook invading Maria's kitchen and Morrell, who now smelt at least as bad as Hitler, and the glum parade of generals with their unending litany of bad news.

If Hitler ever even tried, in these final days, to negotiate with the western allies, I heard nothing of it. He may have. I'm not writing a history here. This is my document, what I experienced and remember.

He returned to the self-caricature in my robe and slippers, and began carrying that dreadful pipe with him in the pocket, or hanging it out of his mouth unsmoked. God only know what sort of relationship he'd had with his father, but I don't think it's right to blame all the horror on him or, for that matter, on the sainted mother who, as he had confessed to us, was really a sadistic monster. No, he created the Third Reich. It was his idea and all of its cruelties and excesses—and I mean *all of them*—were his inventions.

He once said that the method of killing Jews with gas was "humane." But he knew the truth. He knew that it was a dreadful thing to do or why would he have spent so much time screaming down telephones to the camps and browbeating Himmler about concealing the evidence? He knew that the gas was an awful, agonizing death, too. He saw the films. The one I saw—the dreadful, dreadful one that has become the center of my memory of that whole time—is never far from my thoughts.

I dislike the historians who shield knowledge of Hitler's twisted nature almost as much as I do the Nazis who try to spread rumors that the Holocaust never happened, or the ones who say "not only the Jews suffered. You have to look at it in context."

Others did indeed suffer, but the devastation of the Jewish race was completely beyond imagination. And he was the one responsible. Directly. There were many documents that revealed this, too. I can only think that they must have been burned by people attempting to preserve some shred of credibility for him, the swine, or perhaps they have ended up hidden away in one of too many U.S.

Government archives along with, I suspect, film of the gas chamber actions.

There was more than just that one roll of film. They used to watch them in Himmler's *sonderzug* on its siding in Rastenburg, or in the small theatre in the *Wolfschanze.* The minutes of agony that those people endured at the end of their long, hideous journeys were a source of satisfaction to them all.

I want to know the fate of those films. By February of '45, Hitler was absolutely obsessed with hiding evidence of the killings, and especially evidence of his involvement. It is this void that enables the extraordinary evil of Holocaust denial. And this business of evil being "relative"—forget it, it's not. Evil is evil. There are no excuses.

On the 15th of April, a flotilla of generals arrived at *Haus Hitlerficker*. Attacks were expected on Berlin from north, south and east. They could commence at any time, probably at dawn on the 16th. The Red Army would field at least three million soldiers and too much armor and artillery to be counted, in view of the lack of air reconnaissance. Opposing them would be a rag-tag collection of *volksturm,* mostly consisting of boys and old men with single-shot *panzerfausts* on which they were untrained and a few exhausted and poorly equipped regular troops, perhaps two hundred thousand.

He listened to all this very carefully, nodding and saying *"ja, ja"* as the details were outlined.

Then he exploded. Completely. Right in the middle of my foyer where they had unrolled their maps.

"It's a betrayal! Traitors everywhere! They have never been with me, not one of them, not from the beginning, not at all! They have wanted only to betray me and betray the German people and our ideals! Now, shoot them! Shoot them all, every one!" He glared around the room. "Who has done this? Who? Tell me! Tell me at once!"

General Heinrici said carefully, "General Schorner will attack from the south, General Steiner from the north."

"A pincers, then?"

"Yes." Heinrici clicked his heels.

"I return to the Chancellery now." He headed for the door.

I said, "Leader, you need to change."

He looked down at himself. He was in my robe. "Ah, of course, Willy. Linge, we're going! Dress me! Where is Linge? LINGE!"

The valet came hurrying downstairs with Hitler's clothing in his arms, and changed him right there in the foyer. When the robe was pulled off, I heard more than one gasp. Hitler naked looked like a spider, narrow and emaciated, his skin like vellum. The stench coming off of his body filled the room. His crack was dirty brown.

"Alf," Eva shouted, "what is this? Look, they're here!" She tried to shield him from view by holding up the robe as a screen. Carlotta stood with folded arms in the entrance to the sun room. Her expression was quizzical. It seemed to say, 'how could this become any more absurd?'

Linge got him dressed and off they all went, Eva strutting along behind him in the heels she had decided to wear that day. The convoy must have been ten vehicles.

We had come to dread the ringing of the telephone in that house as much as the sound of an automobile stopping at the curb. It was on the 20th that Fritz answered the call that led to the ruin of my precious Carlotta, and of our life.

It was his young adjutant Gunsche, who used to spend most of his time plotting to get combat postings, but who was now sticking close to Hitler and staying far from the front. Wise boy. He survives to this day.

He said, "Herr Weber, the leader wishes to warn you that the Russians have cut the roads to the south and are likely to be in Wannsee tomorrow. He offers an invitation to come into the bunker with us."

I gripped the phone; my breath left me. There had been no sign of fighting here, not even much sound of it in the distance. "Where?" I managed to say. Carlotta, Fritz, Maria and the Russian doctor all gathered around me.

"Fifteen kilometers," he said. "They are likely to turn you out and take the house. There are executions, Herr Weber. Rape, a lot of it.

You know, you are rich. They will not treat the rich as they are used to being treated by us."

"How possible is the journey?"

"At this time, still possible."

He rang off. Slowly, I replaced the receiver in the instrument. "The Russians," I said. "They're coming."

Without a word, the doctor went off.

"What shall we do, Herr Willy?" said Fritz.

"I think you two should stay right here. They'll billet a general in this house. He'll want your service."

"They won't kill us?" He nodded toward Maria, who was weeping, but not only with fear. There was in eyes a light I had never before seen in them. It was a lovely and terrifying thing to witness.

"I don't know, Fritz."

He went to her and took her hand. They stood together, taking in their fear an oddly formal pose.

"Carlotta, we can either dare the roads south or go into Berlin."

"Not Berlin!"

"The risk to the south is death."

"The risk in Berlin is death."

We embraced.

I went into the garage to check the condition of the car, which I had not used recently. It had half a tank of petrol. After that, there would be no more. So how far would it get us? My best guess was about eighty kilometers.

I thought it possible that we could make it through the Russian lines on our Swiss passports, but where were those lines, and where did the western lines start? I couldn't answer either question.

Back upstairs, I found Carlotta packing. "I've changed my mind. I think we should go to Berlin. It's just too dangerous the other way. There are too many unknowns. In the field, we might be taken as Swiss diplomats and we might not. In Berlin we'll be able to count on the passports." She paused. "Where is Paul?"

"As usual, no idea." The last we'd seen of him was at the concert.

Our Russians had instantly evaporated. Wise men. One of them,

Georg Antonov, reappeared months later in Paris and became a wrestling champion, of all things, for the US First Army. The last I heard of him, he had been granted American citizenship and was living in Pittsburgh. The doctor is in Leningrad, practicing at the neurological institute there. The others, who knows?

In the garage after the car was loaded up, Fritz and Maria and Carlotta and I held one another tightly. Fritz demanded to go with us. "You can hardly tie your tie, Herr Willy. You've no idea how to be without service."

"Fritz, you'll be drafted into the *volksturm* the moment they see you."

"Not as servant to a diplomat, surely."

"We don't know." Goebbels' idiotic 'total war' directive called up every man and boy who could move. "Anyway, you need to keep the house as best you can. They mustn't steal the Kreislers' paintings, the Watteaus and Ruisdales, and that Klimt in the attic—that must be guarded carefully. It's very fine."

"Herr Willy," Maria said, "if the Kreislers are no more, then what?"

"The paintings are alive, even if their owners are not. They must be treated as living treasures."

They kept the house without incident through the brief Russian occupation, and later it developed that the paintings were still there, and even most of the silverware.

Old Fritz died in that house in '55. A stroke. Maria passed away in hospital in Berlin in '60. Her heart.

I enjoy going and seeing the Kreisler family now, I have to say it. I wouldn't have let myself be known to them, no more than to the others whom I accidentally saved or whose property I by chance preserved. But there was no choice. I could not hide from the deed or the formalities of the transfer.

Now it runs with children, you know, that house. A third generation of Kreislers and they live without the least fear. In Germany! They show me reverence. I find it dreadful, but I go anyway. They invite me and I go.

So it was in the evening of April 15, 1945, under the light of a new moon, that Carlotta and I set out for Berlin. It didn't seem safe to tempt the Grunewald again, so we went up the west side of the lake along the Kladower Damm into the ruins of Spandau, then worked our way slowly to Pariser Platz and the Chancellery, arriving there around midnight.

There were guards on the ruined Chancellery entrance, not *volkssturumers* or exhausted *Wehrmacht* soldiers but regular SS who proved to be *Liebstandarte*, and who were extremely nervous. I didn't think it wise to drive past them and turn into the underground car park, not in my old Olympia, so I stopped and went up the steps to where they stood in a disorderly group, smoking nervously and eyeing me as they might a hind in the forest.

There was, however, a list. We were on it. So we took the car into the basement garage, which turned out to be filled with state cars, great, gleaming limousines. I saw Hitler's old 770 there, its top down, its worn leather seating testament to many years of use. He had ridden in triumph in that car, his arm raised, his face composed in his dictator's scowl. Many times, I'd ridden in the back while he slept in his leather driving helmet and Kempka drove us through the mountains to the Berghof. When I was first coming to know him, he had ridden in the back with me.

After parking and arranging for the car to be filled, we were helped to the bunker itself, which was in the garden. As you approached, you first saw a tall round tower with a peaked roof. This was the ventilation system, and it made a loud droning noise. It also had a sinister cast to it, especially in the wan light of the new moon, as if it marked the lair of a black magician or a sinister troll—which it did, both things.

You know, I still cannot get through Disney's *Fantasia*. When I see that little mouse figure attempting to contend with the runaway brooms, I can't stand it. I have to leave.

We were taken to a room in the upper bunker, the *vorbunker*. It was a concrete cell that contained an iron bunk bed fitted with canvas straps for mattresses.

"Nice," Carlotta said. "Every expense has been spared."

Hitler and Eva had two rooms in the lower bunker. They weren't much better, but at least there was a proper bedstead. It was also a lot quieter down there, but almost impossibly claustrophobic.

I could imagine no worse death than being buried alive in the company of Adolf Hitler.

We were in our room on April 22 when orderlies arrived with more bunk beds. Goebbels was bringing his family and they were to be installed in this room. We were then shifted into the tiny space into which the secretaries were jammed in sleeping shifts.

Wannsee had indeed been occupied, so there was no getting back there. I'd been on the telephone to Fritz when a Russian staff car had stopped out front.

It probably seems incredible that such a thought would even cross our minds, but we decided to try the hotels. The Adlon had been bombed to rubble, but some of the others were still going.

But we delayed. We spent time between raids in the garden and slept some in Hitler's Chancellery flat, which was then still intact.

I told Carlotta, "Our rule must be to stay out of the bunker as much as we can." For once, she agreed with me.

The morning after our second night in the Chancellery, I awoke to find an SS guard watching over us, standing right there in the sitting room, blocking the door. He had a radio and in a bowl on the table beside the door there were two cyanide capsules. "In case we get word," he said. He wasn't unfriendly about it. He just assumed that we would want to commit suicide with our beloved leader.

Like hell. I had a pistol now, and real bullets. The second that guy said "*der Fuhrer is todt*," I intended to pull it on him. If I had to, I would shoot our way out.

I understood why Hitler intended for us to die with him. He absolutely did not want anything about his inner life to reach history. We were his most secret dreams turned into living, breathing people. Our mere existence, let alone the tales we would tell, would drag his legacy in the gutter. (He considered himself a hero and a saint, remember.)

On the 29th, artillery started coming in very heavily, and now we had no choice but to move into the bunker. Bad news, because I had to go unarmed. Nobody carried weapons around Hitler.

For most of the past two weeks, I had been making calls to friends in Switzerland, trying to find a way out. I'd hoped that something could be arranged, but with Berlin cut off, we were trapped.

One afternoon when it was quiet, Eva came with us to the garden. "Oh, look at all the butts," she said. "This is where you smoke."

"We did," I said. "No more cigarettes."

"No, I suppose not." We sat on the little bench together, the three of us. "It's time, you know," she said quietly.

"Time?"

"For us." She opened a hand. In it lay two cyanide capsules. "We're married, you know," she said. "Since yesterday."

"Congratulations," Carlotta said dully.

"Do you have cyanide?"

"We do."

"Because none of us may survive him. They could get all sorts of things about him out of us and ruin his place in history."

Carlotta sucked in breath, fighting to stifle the burst of derisive laughter that was clamoring in her throat. She turned quite red.

"The Goebbels' will do it also. Their children, too. It's necessary. They would all be raped."

"Better that than death," Carlotta said. Unwanted sex had been part of her life all of her life, so it sounded not so bad to her.

"Raped until dead. It's the usual way with the Russians. I would be. You, too, Carlotta."

"Willy, the greatest failure of your life is that you have, at this moment, no cigarettes."

"I agree completely, Love."

The wail of Stalin's Organs began echoing in the sky. These horrifying rockets sound like banshees the size of whales. Any time now, they might start dropping right in this garden.

Eva took Carlotta's hand. "Before we go down, I want to say this just privately. I hated you so much. Then I loved you so much. I love you now."

"Thank you, Eva." They kissed, Eva with trembling love, Carlotta with professional skill.

There was nothing to do but go back down those steps. We couldn't run. There were guards all around.

I will never forget the walk down into that soggy concrete hell-hole. As we entered, I could hear him screaming—wailing, actually, like an animal in a trap.

As Eva descended, Carlotta stopped me. "We can't. We'll never come out alive. Now is the time, right now."

It was true. I knew it.

But then I saw a shadow at the top of the steps. SS. I whispered, "they have orders."

Looking up to the glow of the day was like raising one's head from the bottom of a drowning pool.

We did the only thing we could, which was to go down. I thought that the war had gotten us after all, and right at the last moment.

We were taken, virtually under guard, to the lower bunker. I knew the SS guarding us. It was Franz Richter from the Berghof with whom we'd danced and played many a game of cards.

Franz knocked on the door of Hitler's apartment.

Silence. We waited. One did not knock a second time, not unless you were a *Reichsminister* or commanded an army.

"I wonder if the boar are rutting," I said. We'd also hunted in the mountains, boar, deer, meat for the carnivores in the vegetarian trap.

"The land is the land, Willy. It'll still be there. We'll hunt." He lowered his voice. "You know...after. We'll get a party up with old Dieter."

I couldn't believe I was hearing that name again. "And where is he?"

"He was at Beelitz."

"Nice!" Carlotta said. It was the hospital that Hitler had used when he was ill.

"They moved them west last month."

"So he's—"

"Captive, and I'm sure he's delighted."

Eva opened the door. We went in to find Hitler seated on the couch where he was, a few hours later, to die.

The change, in just the few days since we'd seen him, was a real shock. He trembled like a trapped rodent. His eyes were watchful, filled with suspicion and, above all, sadness.

There then came out of me a statement that I was not expecting to make, and had never dreamed that I would make.

"You've lost everything, Alf. It's finished."

He nodded. Eva pleaded with her eyes.

Carlotta giggled. "Want a final shit storm?"

"Ah! Shut your mouth!"

She laughed aloud.

"Willy—" He patted the couch beside him. I sat. With difficulty he laid his trembling left arm around my shoulder. I felt it there, heaving. "It's finally your oath. Do you remember?"

"I do."

"Then we do it together."

"What?" Carlotta asked sharply.

"After dinner. A nice dinner, a toast to me, the—"

"Holy fuck, Willy, what's this?"

Hitler said, "We lived as a family and we die as a family."

"Fuck that! I'm not your family, I'm a whore."

"I have loved you for years!"

"I love you, too, Carlie," Eva said. "This is us. This is the family. It's noble and it's right."

Carlotta stood and threw the door open. And there was Franz. He smiled. "May I help?"

"Go fuck yourself!" She slammed it.

On the surface, I was quite calm, my usual benign self when in Alf's company. Inside I was seething. I didn't want to die, but I also wanted to protect Carlotta's life, which, in the everlasting way of lovers, was more precious to me than my own.

Our dream of a life together might die, but hers to have children must not be destroyed. Even if I didn't make it, she must have the opportunity to find another man and make the family she dreamed of.

I saw a chance—long, probably too long, but there, and the only one.

"We are not family," I said firmly.

"But you—you're my son."

"Oh, come on! No son fucks his father! You're sick, old man, but not that sick, not even you. Carlie's right. I'm a whore, too. Just like her."

"Then you die because of what you know! And as what they believe you to be, family. In the honor of the family."

Here it was, the moment of the last throw. "Honor? What a joke. We have no honor Alf. We're spies, both of us. As for that oath of mine, that was just another trick."

He chuckled. "No, no."

"From the beginning, I had only one thought, to destroy you."

"But why? How could you hate such a genius as me?"

Carlotta burst out laughing. "He worked for the Brits. I was in the Red Choir. You know who my contact was? He was one of your SS."

"You two should be ashamed," Eva said.

"Ashamed? Fuck your face, you prime bitch! We're proud! Your royally fucked up little boyfriend here is the most awful human being who ever walked on this poor tired goddamn planet. I did a terrifying, hard job and a disgusting job and so did Willy, and I'm proud of us. Proud!" She folded her arms. "We lost you the war, you know that? We fucked you to the fucking wall!"

"Obscenity! Stupidity! Betrayal!" He wobbled to his feet. "But a joke? You two? You're just a couple of perverts like me, unlike me very pretty. Unintelligent, though. Unlike me."

"Not so stupid, Alf. Remember Dunkirk? You held back because I convinced you Churchill might sue for peace if you did. Complete lie. I was in touch with Churchill. We invented it together. I got the BEF out and where are they now? In Hamburg guarding those subs so you can't carry out your escape plan. I engineered that, too."

Now his face was more serious.

"It's the whole war, Alf," Carlotta said.

His color was changing. He was turning pale. A sheen of sweat appeared on his brow.

"You know the most important thing? It was the heavy water? Remember that?"

His eyes glittered now. They were inhuman. I can't explain it more than that. It was no longer a human face, that's all.

"I remember."

"You know all about the uranium bomb."

"Yes."

"I made a fortune selling you uranium I knew you could never use, because I helped Paul get that heavy water out of France. And in the Battle of Britain, remember how I couldn't get you enough rare earths? I was selling it to Churchill, of course. You, the big genius. You created Nazism because you're a sick man and actually rather a stupid one, and you lost the war for the same reasons."

"Guards! Get in here!"

The door flew open. Was it going to work? I allowed myself to hope.

Fritz rushed in, gun drawn.

"Take this garbage out! Get it out! Take these two pigs up into the garden and gut them! Disembowel them and leave them to die. And when they are dead, you come and get me because I want to see it. I want to see it with my own eyes!"

"Yes, my Leader!"

Nobody moved.

"Go! Get on with it!"

Fritz took us out. As we ascended through the stunned silence of everybody in the bunker, I hoped only for one thing, which was another artillery barrage. Only that would give us any chance at all of escaping, and a damn slim one at that.

In the event, it was quiet.

I was now desperate, fearing not only death, but a particularly horrible one. "Fritzl," I said, "he'll be dead by morning. Then where are you? There's been no trial. You have no order. The Russians will be in here and you'll be a murderer."

He laughed.

And then, to my astonishment, so did Carlotta.

He holstered his gun and produced cigarettes. "Tell him, Carlie, before he soils his trousers."

"Fritzl is my contact. He ran the Red Choir at the Berghof."

I must have swayed because he said, "Don't collapse, Willy. Just get the shit out of here. And don't worry about Hitler. Some of the other SS in the bunker are Stalin's men, too. We intend to keep the old bastard alive to hang in Red Square."

Two other SS appeared. One of them had a gutting knife, curved to a point and gleaming.

"Shit," Fritz hissed, "run!"

With no further signal, with no word, we turned and ran across the garden to the shambles of the Chancellery. As we did so, there was a barrage of shots. I don't know who was firing, probably Fritz, because they didn't seem to come very close.

From here we could go down into the car park, which we found empty and completely dark. I got out my torch, which itself could barely emit enough light from its dying batteries to see three feet. I cast it about.

The big cars were all gone, every one of them. But then I saw our Olympia in a far corner.

We ran to it. The key was there, so I turned it and pressed the starter. It turned over, then began to run.

"Thank God," I said.

It stopped. I saw why. The gas gauge was pinned on empty and we had just used up the last ounce or so in the fuel line.

"Shit, shit, fuck! Carlotta, I'm so sorry."

"Stay calm! Let's just go out the front on foot."

"The Kaiserhof is ruined, the Adlon, the Excelsior."

"The *kietz* is not ruined, dear."

So out we went, but not into a place that was even recognizable as a city. Complete chaos was now the rule. Here and there old men and boys dashed about, some lugging the heavy, ungainly *panzerfausts*, others carrying shotguns or rifles.

As we left the Chancellery, the SS guard, recognizing us, saluted smartly. Thank god not everybody carried a radio.

As we hurried toward the Wilhelmplatz U-Bahn entrance, we found ourselves stopped not by SS or *Wehrmacht* or even *volksturm*, but by a gang of boys in bits and pieces of uniforms. A short distance along the road, there was a man hanging from a lamp-post, his legs still kicking.

The leader of the boys, a child of no more than fifteen, shouted at me, "Where are you going? Where is your weapon?"

"I'm a Swiss diplomat," I said. "I've just come from delivering important information to the leader."

"Papers!"

Carlotta drew her Swiss diplomatic passport, which in those days was a board-covered letter that had to be unfolded. It contained in French and German a statement to the effect that the bearer of such-and-such a name was a diplomatic officer of Switzerland, and offered the individual's title and a brief description.

The boy grabbed it and read, his lips moving. As he pored over it, he said to the others, "go and fetch the rope." He handed the paper back to Carlotta.

In the meantime, I had searched all of my pockets and found not just no Swiss Diplomatic Passport, no American passport, not even my *Reichspass* or my priceless Hitler pass.

Somebody else had become me. In a time in which photographs could easily be switched on the few official papers that bore them, this was an easy thing to do. Anybody in the bunker would have wanted my superb credentials.

"I'm sorry, my document is misplaced."

Beside me, I felt Carlotta's entire body tighten, a palpable sense of urgency coming off her.

I was terrified, too. More, I am sure. After all, I was the one who was about to die stupidly in this stupid war.

Ahead of us, the body on the lamp post dropped to the ground with a cracking thud. Artillery shells burst over the Chancellery, setting up a terrific racket. Had we still been in the garden, the shrapnel would undoubtedly have killed us.

In the humming, uneasy silence that followed, Carlotta spoke in Russian, which we had both learned a little from the doctor. "I'll go left, you go right. Meet in the zoo."

The boy had a small pistol. "What do you say!" he screamed. "What's that?"

She said, again in Russian, "No bullets in the cylinder. Maybe one in the chamber." With that, she took off running like a fox. She was wearing a pair of "secretarial shoes" she had gotten from Traudl Junge in exchange for some exquisite heels. 'I hated to give them up,' she had told me, 'but let her totter off to her death. I might need to run.' As Traudl survives to this day, I assume she had two pair of secretarials.

"No, not you," the boy screeched as he thrust the pistol right into my face. "You hang, you! Now!"

The others had disentangled their rope from their last victim and now came up to put it around my neck. The noose was soaked with blood, I'll never forget it. Most of the children were crying.

They were too short to lift it around my neck and bade me kneel. Once again, I found myself facing death. So, did the pistol have a bullet or not?

But then I thought, 'why worry? If you don't take the chance, you die by the rope.'

I turned and went dashing along Wilhelmstrasse in the direction of Leipzigerstrasse. The boys came running along, shouting and hurling stones at me, but no bullets were fired. At that time I was far stronger than the average German as I was much better fed. Soon, the boys were well behind me. As I passed through Potsdamer Platz, I shifted into Bellevue Strasse and approached the Tiergarten at a lope. The boys were now gone.

The zoo in normal times had been wonderful, full of children with balloons and ices, the glorious collection of animals on display in commodious cages, ponds and runs. Now it stank of death, cordite and burnt hair. There were people butchering the body of an ape. As I approached, a woman threatened me with a knife. The remains of Giraffe, their necks bowed backward from rigor mortis, lay rotting in their enclosure. The only living animals were rats, and they scurried everywhere, unbothered by the human presence. They had probably already discovered that they were too fast for the exhausted, starving Berliners to catch.

I had been there for about fifteen minutes when I began to feel fear—not that any harm would come to me, but that something had happened to my Carlotta.

I went round and round, up and down the paths, to the entrance, even over to the looming zoo flak tower, now silent, which proved to be jammed to the gills with humanity. It stank like a gigantic sewer.

I could not find her and I did not find her.

So it is that I now must tell the hardest part of my story.

She had gone not to the zoo but to the Zoo Station, where she had been captured by a Russian patrol. Here, suddenly, was this exquisite woman in cashmere and silk and fur, dashing through the ruins. As she told me later, the passport almost worked. But they could not stand to let her go, probably the most beautiful human being any of them had ever seen in their lives.

Now I am sitting in my study in Manhattan. It's the afternoon of November 8, 1980. I know that it's a jolt to go so abruptly from the streets of dying Berlin to this safe and settled place, but I am doing it for a reason. It is time to give over the narrative to my love. She wrote it all out, everything that she endured. Whenever I read it, it breaks my heart. But war breaks hearts. That's what it does. When lives are lost it breaks them, but also sometimes when they are not, and sometimes especially then.

So follows, in the next pages, the testament of the bravest and best human being I ever knew.

## 29

# MY TESTAMENT

BY CARLOTTA WEBER

In my beautiful girlhood, remembered with the sweet honey of pure sentiment, I was a filthy little whore. Superb start!

A joke, you see.

I write in English because I no longer care to write or speak Deutsch. So don't expect anything fancy here. Except it would probably be just as shitty in German. Let me be frank.

I love to read and learn. I like to read a book and just think. It's not like I don't have a temper, though, and they can piss me off royally. For example, you want to learn about ancient Rome and in comes Gibbon. He tells you everything. Wonderful! Then everything else. And more, then more. Then he retells it. You realize that you will only finish this if you should die of advanced old age.

After about sixty pounds of Gibbon, I give up and had Willy explain Rome to me. It took three hours and I know all the best stuff. For us Deutsch, it's the battle of the Teutoberger Forest. That convinced Augustus to not extend the empire into our lands. As a result, as old Hitler used to say, "we have no past." In my opinion, we were left without civilization for too long. We are in our blood still wild. (And I'm only part Jew. That's the good part. The rest is a wild German. Fucking wild.)

I have no past, either. Or if I can manage to quit lying, the truth is that I have no past that I want to remember.

It was my typical ratshit luck to end up with Alf. It was good luck because his cash put food on my table and he saved me from the typical fate of the Jew. It was bad—really shitty—because, I mean, he was Adolf Fucking Hitler.

I met him about a month post my eleventh birthday.

He was not a man who had normality in any way, shape or form. First off, all men who come for sex to a kid are going to be odd. He was odder even than that. When he first showed up, he was shy. He wanted me to think he was ok. The fuckhead. What kind of a moron would think that, Herr Hitler, since I'm eleven and you're a grownup and I can see your trousers have a log in them? Like, he wants a little girl, so why bother to pretend anything is ok, because nothing is fucking well ok.

He would have me sit in a chair in the hotel room and lick a lolly while he knelt at my feet. For that, twenty marks. Not at all bad!

You have to understand that all the weird stuff that these guys want is really boring. It's not sex. You know something? The only man who ever really had sex with me is Willy. I know, I'm bad, I fool around. I fell in love with Eva. I fell in love with Angie. There's some kind of a man deep inside me, I think. I like to love the softness of the woman but I also need to be loved by the hardness of the man.

I love Willy but mostly I'm damn mad at him and don't know why.

Anyway, back to lovely Alf. He wrote to me little notes about what he wanted. "Order me to drop my trousers and to lie on the foot of the bed and you beat me with my belt." So I did. It was yet more money, so I began to think about what else he might like. In later years, when I got bigger, he would like to take it lying in my lap. It was like having a big carp or something laid out over me. Ok, it was fine. This is how his mummy had done it.

He would carry a dog whip when he went about with his friends, but this was only to make him look strong and disguise that he was really a toe-sucker, as we used to call such men. Those guys were all mothered by man haters, in my opinion. No affection, only punishment. Men aren't as durable as us. That kind of shit in childhood fucks them up more than it does us. Or maybe not. What do I know?

Over the years, I saw him quite a lot. In fact, whenever he was in Berlin, he would stop in the Excelsior because I was a medicine-girl working out of the pharmacy there. He would send for me. Once or twice a month at least, through the years. As I got older, I made efforts to still appear as a little girl. We all did that. Our money depended on it and if we didn't and tried to grow up, soon enough our alphonse would come and we'd be the one taking the whipping. I'm not at all that way, so I was sure to be a good girl all the time.

My alphonse, or whore-master, was called Kurt Saperstein. He was a Jew, naturally. Jew whore, Jew alphonse, of course.

When Alf got the chancellor gig, I didn't see so much of him at first. I thought 'sure, I'm a Jew. The great man can't fuck around with a Jew.' Too bad, he was useful to me.

Soon things got hot for the alphonse. There began to be roundups in the Berlin underworld, and he was apparently taken in one of them. I don't know. One day he was gone. That was him. He's gone. The gas, most likely.

After Alf got the power he starts making all kinds of shitty laws. People who used to be crooks of all kinds, people I had known in the neighborhood all my life, were suddenly marching around in Hitler uniforms. Pickpockets were now SA. Rent boys and fancies were now SS. Really scary. Your pocket gets picked by a Brownshirt, what the fuck are you gonna do about it? Keep smilin', *ein kleines Mädchen*.

People who used to be real civilized like some of my clientele turned into other people. What a time! Alf would stand up there and spout out the stupidest goddamn crap you ever heard, but his voice was like some kind of a drug. To them. Never to me. When he started in ranting at me, I fucking well slept in his face. Asshole.

It was now very much illegal for medicines to work out of hotel pharmacies, so I had to stop with that. I had only about a week's money usually, so how am I gonna eat? It was also illegal to streetwalk and I was still too young to be licensed as a *kontroll* girl. Anyway, that was soon gone, too. There were still lots of whores, of course. We are not so easily defeated by mere governments. If your cunt is your cash, you will find a way to fill it.

So I needed cash and now had no customers anymore. Hitler, I figured, was long gone. I mean, a Jew whore and a medicine? No way.

There were a few sororities that were still considered ok because the NSDAP bigwigs went there. Super exclusive. So I put on lipstick, my best dress which was a blue satin evening number I had stolen right out of some dress shop and a cloche hat that framed my face very nicely, and went looking for inside work. My best grown-up look. I was Louise Brooks to a T.

I went to the best first, Kitty Schmidt, who had Salon Kitty in Geisebrechtstrasse 11. That is in Charlottenburg, *tres* exclusive.

She really got me, wow. She was a lesbian and I was in her bed in ten minutes. Never mind the job. I had that. I mean, the *chonte* just fucking flips over me. So I am sleeping in her bed and doing customers, but no longer as a medicine. I'm so sophisticated that I take my ciggys in a long black holder.

One night, special guests! She spends two hours on my hair and makeup. Then I go in the parlor with her and there is a tall English, with him a short *Deutsch* who I recognize instantly. Even though he's got on a fake mustache and a hairpiece, it is ever-loving Alf!

His mouth drops open. Tears appear. He stands. He takes my hand. We go up into a room. He throws himself down on his knees, he lays his head in my lap and he says, 'I thought I lost you, I thought I lost you forever!"

That night he is miraculously weird. He needs more humiliation than he ever did. We are at it for hours. I'm working up a fucking sweat, I am heaving and hauling and spanking and whipping and smothering and all kinds of stuff that, oh, shit, was just unique.

When he finally gives out, after maybe ten climaxes over the course of the session he says, I want to be at your feet forever. I never want to be away again.

He knows I'm a damn kike. We both know it.

He smelled in my toilet. He would put his tongue in the water, I think. I don't know, I never looked. Anyway, it was strange to see this politician giving a big speech and know that he had knelt before me an hour before and tongued my bunghole.

Gloria Steinem would say I was exploited. Fucking right! And that's why I'm here. It's why I lived.

He and the English were fast friends. Later, the lord turned out to be a very clever spy, although he kept nearly getting my poor husband Willy killed. Willy is extremely rich and nowadays so am I. He's a very nice fellow. He just wants a woman, nothing more. I very much like that. I am mean to him. I don't want to be, but it just happens. I blame him for trouble I get myself into. I know it's wrong and it's stupid but I can't help it. I'm from the gutter. That makes me damaged goods and he loves me anyway. To me, it feels like he's just pretending so he can get in my pants, and it makes me mad. I tell myself, 'why would he pretend?' I'm a nothing. He could throw me away with the other trash. He gives me everything but I'm still just mean. You know what real love is? A guy who puts up with the kind of shit I dish out.

I did good surviving the war. I'm proud. I was a spy, too, just like Willy. Although I got no medals. Why? Because I was a communist then. If Stalin could see how I live now, he'd throw up, and good! That prick. If he'd ever have caught up with me, I'd have gotten a lead medal right in my heart. A lot of German communists who were in the Red Choir got shot. I was in the Red Choir. Anyway, who wants to live in the east? Talk about a complete shithole.

I used to sit and read and smoke cigarettes while he kneeled. It could last an hour, until he got up the nerve to ask for what he wanted.

His desires were always embarrassing to him, and the more powerful he got, the more unpleasant they became. I think that some of the women who committed suicide over him did it because they thought he was a god, and then he asked for them to do these strange things. He was a pig to ask nice girls for that kind of shit. That's whore stuff. Our business. I gave him some very serious whippings for asking those nice women shit like that. I'm a pro, I have no emotions for him. They were fucking worshiping him, and look what they found, a creep who liked to gargle sewer water. I mean, that fucked up. Worse.

This man needed professional attention and not just from sex workers. He needed a psychiatrist.

Ordinary women think in terms of love and being kissed and admired and all that. If somebody asks them to shit in his face, they are not going to take that well. Or the man that just wants a beating like momma used to administer, no they don't get that. A lot of guys with exotic kinks are very smart. They can make people do anything they want. It makes them feel guilty. That was my Alf all the way. Kinks them right up.

It's fortunate for the sex professional because they have to pay plenty for all the crazy stuff they want.

Anyway, when he figured out that I came under his own Jew laws, he simply became completely wild. Not that he now hated me. The opposite. He wanted even more being fucked with. Now he wanted tying up. He would have me sit on his face until he passed out, then he would wake up and ask to go again. During these sessions, he would shoot off three or four or five times without even being touched.

When I found out he'd killed all the Jews, I tried to kill myself. That was afterward, though. He was dead then. We were living in America when I saw the newsreels in a show on television. Not the film Willy saw. I never saw that and I never want to. I'm pissed off he even told me about it.

Is there a Satan? Fuck if I know, but if there is one, he sure as hell got in Alf's head.

Willy tried to keep the Holocaust from me. He knew it would make me feel guilty because it makes him feel guilty and we are very much alike. Both whores in our souls. But we have souls. Oh, yes.

He had known how much the truth would make me suffer. I knew it had been bad. Alf was crazy on the subject of Jews. But what he did was not something that was easy to figure out at the time. They just sort of seemed to melt away. One did not know that they really were melting in ovens. I mean, who would believe such a thing?

Anyway, after I knew, I was feeling sad all the time and being so mean to Willy when he lived with me in Malibu that he found a doctor for me to see. This was Dr. Brandt, the famous psychiatrist. All he did for me was throw my ass right out of his office.

The first day, it went ok. But then I told him I was the Jew whore who used to shit in Hitler's face. Naturally, he thought it was a neurotic fantasy and so we went on talking it out. Then he decides he wants to see my husband, too. He asks him, 'do you know about your wife's Hitler fantasy?'

Willy laughs. Unfortunately. He says, 'no, that's no fantasy. That's exactly what she was. She was his mistress from age eleven to age 26.' Well, naturally, he threw me right out of there, which pissed me off big time and made me even madder at Willy.

I didn't get cured, and I'm sure as hell not planning on trying that again. My past is too horrible for people, even doctors. So I am left still wondering why I am so mean to my poor guy. It's like, from beating up men all through my young years, I sort of can't figure out how to deal with them except by being mean.

I know he loves me so much. He sits in his car on the PCH watching the garage. I could always drive well, by the way. Anything he says to the contrary is his own pure fantasy. My car I had back then was poorly constructed. Also, it could not go backwards because that had not been invented yet, if you want to know. Very fucking inconvenient, those old cars back then.

I watch him from the kitchen window, but I never let him in. I want to but I can't. Oh, goddamnit! I want to! Oh, shit! I have these fucking gigolos in here. I'm such a shit! Oh, Christ.

Willy sits out there, poor guy. All I have to do is just gesture from the kitchen window—move my hand a little bit—and our whole world would change.

Aw, poor guy. I hide on the floor and I cry. The door to my heart is open but some other door down deeper in the cave is closed. I can't open it. I love him but I can't get rid of the meanness. I just can't. It feels so fucking awful and so fucking good at the same time.

Oh, life goes on and we're not here forever and I just cannot—fucking, fucking *cannot*—give my man what he needs.

He will not even think about going to another woman. Instead, he lives like I'm already dead. Alone in his apartment in New York. Riding his ships sometimes, god knows where. Going to London and trying to get people to play Bridge with him but they always cut him. Then he goes back, aw fuck! I got hundreds of friends. I play with the cream all over the world. I am cream, actually. They don't care if I cuss. They love it. I have, like, an unbelievable rep. The kike who foxed Hitler in his own den. Too bad it fucks me as far as movies are concerned. But I don't really care. Acting's a bore. I've been on too many sets not to know that.

Every so often I see a man who looks at you with the sheep's eye. I give a few whippings. Studio execs, mostly. It makes me feel a little homesick, really.

Willy has these private dicks pretend to be beachcombers when I'm having parties and so forth. When I see them I think, 'there's my Willy, he's loving me from afar.'

I don't want him near me because I end up screaming at him every time and I hate to scream at him but I can't stop. I can't have kids, I'm just like our friend Eva who I used to look down my nose at because she had one royally fucked up vagina and couldn't have kids. Then the Russians got hold of me, oh my god, they got me good. I can't even have any kids now either, so I thought I would do something else with my life. Act. Any whore is a naturally good actress. That's why I understood Hollywood—it's all whores, practically. I mean, that's how they start out. Starlets are whores. That's the job.

Anyway, I wanted to do this and Willy would help me, so he said. He got me Sam Diamond, my useless drek agent. I know he pays Sam to take my calls. But you see, there's the dirty rumor that I'm Hitler's Jew whore. If I get an acting role they figure it'll come out, my past. It's a real bad past, no question there. I wonder if Dr. Brandt clued them all in. Somebody did. I used to suspect it was Willy and dream about putting a knife in him.

Willy could buy me a goddamn fucking studio! He's richer that Croesus, actually. But he got it from being the Hitler fucker, if anything more tainted than me. You watch what happens when *he* tries to socialize. He wants so little out of life, he just wants to play Bridge. Unfortunately, everybody who plays socially knows who he is except those beanheads in Texas he pals around with.

He goes out on their ranches and rides on horses. You won't find me on one of those things, no thank you.

As I said, I got ruined for the bearing of children by the Russians. Right at the end of the war, just when you're thinking maybe now it will be ok, we were trying to get away from Hitler so he wouldn't force us to eat cyanide like he did Eva. We got separated. Willy went to the zoo. I said 'zoo station,' I remember that perfectly. "Zoo Station, Willy." Who in the world would say zoo, there was nothing left there but a bunch of burned down apes and so forth? People cutting off rhinoceros meat.

I waited in the Zoo Station for him until the goddamn fuck-all Russians show up, basically. You know, I've got a fair mouth on me and I gave them that mouth. Boy, I gave it to those lugs. They weren't bad kids and, you know, they hadn't had a woman in a long time and not only that, there was a Stalin Order to rape the German female at any age or state of health, and I was young and pretty and clean as a whistle, nothing to worry about there.

They set up these rooms in, like, busted up chemists or milliners or whatever kind of burned out shop they could find. They were right on the street so others coming past wouldn't miss them. Here and there, they'd find a mattress and drag it in.

Now the girls they threw in the rape rooms mostly had just either had only the one husband or maybe a lover here and there or were still virgins. These women had no idea how to survive a serious fuck storm. A woman can get her insides torn out. So I became kind of a nurse to them in the one I was in. Mostly, it was more casual, just they see this girl on the street and do her or go in a basement where the

Berliners lived (no houses left standing) and rape one or two. The average girl, she might take one or two or three rapes, rarely more.

But if you were pretty, oh, fuck.

Russian women are your basic human trucks, so to these boys we were really something. They were scared kids with huge dicks, peasant boys who were used to being rough on their own broads. Their officers told them, 'be tough, be hard, hit 'em!' Sometimes as they fucked they cried. You want them to enjoy it. That softens them. It's when they're not getting what they want out of it that men fuck too hard.

To get through gang rape, you have to be open inside yourself. Open like a soul before god, you before the red chorus of pulsating dicks. This kind of inner opening is the Zen of fucking. You have to be a rug. They are lying on a rug and they are fucking a rug.

I would say, 'you relax your cunt, you let the muscles go flat.' I'd finger fuck them to show them how it was done, 'let your cunt relax around my hand, just do it, sister, unless you want to come out of here with the damn thing in a sack around your neck.'

But you know, you get fucked fifty times in a day and your poor self just kind of sinks. When they'd start really bleeding, we'd just haul them into the back, into another room, so you couldn't see them. Leave them there. They lived or they didn't, end of story.

There's bones under every street in Berlin. Plenty of them are girl bones.

The next thing I know, I hear English. American talk like Willy could do. That accent that still sounds so strange. You'd think the American could talk exclusively through his nose if he wanted to.

So we are released. No doctor, no hospital, of course not. Nothing like that for the damn Germans. I mean the Germans, they were hated then. They had been so cruel themselves that I think even saints would have been moved to be cruel in return.

I got taken up by a major, Charlie Wallace. He had chocolate and *schnapps* and, most important of all, cigarettes. Luckies, almost as good as Willy's exclusive ones.

I had given up hope for ever finding Willy. He was like that Eva film, gone with the wind. I loved him so and missed him so. I used to pray when they were screwing me and screwing me that he would all of a sudden appear in the doorway with a great big pistol and just blow their brains right out of their stupid heads.

Never happened, nope. I guess that's another reason I'm mean to him. My heart says, 'you're my man, you should've saved me.' My mind says, 'but Carlie, it's a big world, give the guy a break.'

Guess who wins. The furious heart, every time.

Anyway, Charlie got me to his billet and let me take the first bath I'd had since we ditched the *Fuhrerbunker*, and this was now late 1945. So much dirt flowed off me that I almost clogged up the tub. When I come up out of the water, he said, "You are the most beautiful woman I have ever seen." I thought, 'good, this guy I can make use of.'

Which I proceeded to do. I got him to take me around in his Jeep instead of having to walk everywhere to queue for a chunk of salt fish or whatever. Understand that when the war ended, the mess didn't. In fact, it got worse. In Berlin, there were no lights, no water, no electrics, no phone, no trams and the U-Bahn was, like, fucking iffy. If that. Plus, there were people walking everywhere. Germans coming home from the East, Poles and Russians returning east, French and Italians going west. Everybody filthy, miserable and hungry.

Sometimes it hits me how amazing it is that this whole incredible mess started with just one man and was caused on a daily basis by him and him alone for years, and it just makes me crazy.

Alf tricked people into hating things they had no reason to hate and fearing things that weren't dangerous and despising things like democracy that were good for them.

So there they went storming across half the planet to fight for crazy fantasies with real guns and kill all the Jews for absolutely no good reason whatsoever. Not to mention the Gypsies, they got it, too.

I want to be the best lover there is for Willy. Except I am the one who has ended up with nothing to give. No kids out of me. As I cannot be an actress due to the bad pr fear, I thought I'd be a writer but I send my stories to, like, *the Atlantic* and *the New Yorker* and they always come back.

No kids, no Hollywood, no write, can't love one unless it hurts another, I'm, like, FUCKED UP!

Anyway, Major Wallace got rolled in an alley and his throat slashed. Typical whore job, and what do they find living with him in his billet but a whore.

So off I go to jail. Military prison, American. A few guards looked pretty eager but I am happy to say that nobody came on. Mostly they were matrons anyway. Some girls in there were pretty cute. Also some of the matrons.

I fall in love with women but prefer to make love to men. To be honest, there is nothing like a dick, not in this woman's book. Not all men are crazy, I have found. Most, but not all. When I was a kid I just assumed that was how they all were. I mean, I actually thought Alf was normal. Willy told me that this one girl who was his cousin told Alf that he was psycho and needed to go to the doctor. He killed her. So yep, he was psycho.

Charlie was nice to me. He liked to kiss and hug, but he never tried me on. He knew I was a complete mess inside me. I hurt all the time, I bled when I shouldn't, I was no house for a guest. You see what a good man can be? I need to remind myself of that more.

Anyway, I am in jail when this kid eventually comes along. He speaks English only. I gather after piecing together what he is saying that I am to be tried for the murder of Major Wallace. My English was then still very limited, so I say my best thing even though I have no real idea what it means. "April is the cruelest month, breeding lilacs out of the dead land."

We stare at each other. He leaves, then comes back a few days later and reads documents to me and the next thing I know, I am being tried in some office. There's not even a judge's bench. No robes. Just a few officers smoking and chatting to each other and I understand not a word.

Every time they stop talking and start writing, I say my English, "April is the cruelest month, breeding lilacs out of the dead land." I know this English to be very fine and I hope it tells them that I matter in some way.

I don't get hit for murder thank God. They decide on manslaughter with extenuating circumstances. And why? Not because I took a life. I did not take a life. They hit me with the charges not because they thought I was guilty but to clear the case. Less work for them.

So it's six months in women's prison. To me, this means Mauthausen and I am terrified. But that's not it. Instead, it's one of the Berlin jails, not actually terrible. A lot of the women are in not because of real crimes. People used to do things back then to get put in jail so they can eat. So it's sharp thinking girls and nice old ladies who smack over the potatoes, their eyes crazy with excitement.

Potatoes were for them a miracle, but I had been eating fine with the major, god rest. I often wonder what really befell poor guy. I never have known.

Then one of these war miracle kind of things happens. I am saying all along that I am Frau Wilhelm Weber and he is an American. Trouble is, the only paper I have that says anything like that is the Swiss Diplomatic Passport and they soon found out that was fake.

Still, as my term is up they are looking for what to do with me. If I'm dumped on the streets, they know I'll trick again immediately. They are trying to restore order and releasing whores into the street is not how to do that. Somebody decides to actually look for Herr Wilhelm Weber.

A man comes to the prison in a beautiful suit. He's tall and he shimmers like a god. Every jaw drops to the floor when he comes striding into the social room.

I know him instantly. It's Willy, my Willy and oh he is more beautiful than ever I remember. But I am not beautiful and he does not even see me. I stand up, a woman stooped from gut pain and in a gray rag and I try not to cry but I do. My stupid stupid stupid tears, I have always hated them!

As he looks from face to face, I see something the others cannot see, which is the shadow in his powerful, fine eyes. I know so much of this god and his terrible secrets. He looks untouched, as if he has been in heaven the whole time and not dealing with Hitler.

Untouched by the war. Except for his eyes. Oh my God, *Willy's eyes*! They are still like that. Always, always! You cannot look into those things, it's dangerous. He smiles so gently and he's so elegant and he has these real gentleman manners, but *he is in hell* which only I, his wife and lover, can see.

I want to take him in cradle arms and sing *wiegenlied* for him. I sing very gently. I used to put my hand on Alf's head and sing him to sleep, and I want to do the same for Willy right now, to deliver him.

You need me, Willy, hey! Recognize me! Hello! FUCKIN' HELLO!

Shaking his head, he turns away. He picks up the leather case he has brought with him, his business case full of unimaginable valuables, we are all sure.

That I must tell him my name hurts more than anything I have ever known. But if he leaves here, my life leaves with him.

I say it, "Willy, it's me. This is me. Oh, Willy, this is me. It me! Me, Willy!" My heart fails, my gut swoops like a terrible ocean. I want to be beautiful so badly. I fight my way to a smile. I say, "Ha, I need a bit of lipstick."

He looks upon me as if from a cloud. An angel in a fine suit of clothes, hell in his eyes. He comes across, coming through the assembled jury of dirty women in dirty gray. He takes my shoulders and his hands seem huge.

From the other side of the barred door, the higher universe, a female voice lilts, "Mr. Weber, the embassy in twenty."

"Yes, Jenny."

She looks like she's made of palest fruit, young and fine, her blond hair braided across her brow, her eyes full of smiles. I know everything in an instant. She wants him and she's nearly got him.

I'm as thin as death and I stink but we have had so much together, having endured such terrible trials and dangers, and all of it arm in arm. I belong to him, to us. Is there still an us?

I say, "April is the cruelest month," but can say no more. Those stupid tears again, preventing me from expressing my fucking self!

I feel then the most wonderful sensation I have until that moment in my life ever known. It is his arms coming around me. They are strong and I, who have had to trick all my life, need this so badly. I sink into him. I hide my face in his jacket. Anyway, it's too ugly for him to look at any more than necessary.

"Oh my darling, darling" he says, "you're alive. I thought they got you, baby. I sure did."

I think I hear in there a false note. So is he really glad? Maybe. Because he's got another life now, a fine American life. I fear that I can never be part of it. I think this at once and completely with all my soul.

The idea upsets me so much that I have to gobble in my throat to make enough spit to talk again. Then I do the stupidest possible thing, the meanest possible thing. I've got so much anger in me, it's like my soul is riding in a runaway train. Instead of words of love, words of gratitude or happiness—all of which I feel—I I whisper in his ear, "*Hitlerficker*."

He blows air out through his mouth, then leans back and looks down at me. Then his eyes close. They're tight. His lips spread back from his teeth.

"I've got a meeting," he says carefully. "But I'm going to get you out of here, Carlotta. I will take you to Paris and dress you again and you will come back." He winks at me. He is so perfectly spotless and smooth that it looks like a doll winking.

I hold him as tight as I can. I know that I feel to him like a clinging leaf. I say, "Willy, I hurt. My cunt hurts. It hurts all the time."

"What is this? What are you saying?"

"The Russians did it. They took me and took me for weeks and I hurt, Willy. I bleed all the time and I hurt all the time. I need doctor. I need doctor."

He stands up. "Matron! This woman is injured. What's being done?"

Sergeant Gertrude, as she is known, marches up in her splendid American uniform. "She has been examined and passed." This German bitch was a guard at Mauthausen, we all know it.

"Examine her again! Today! I want a report on my desk at the embassy before five."

"You can't order me."

"No, but I can order your boss, and I'll order him broken to private if I don't see that report. And no lies, do you understand?"

So now she'll hose me down tonight. Did we invent that business of the beating that doesn't bruise? Probably. Anyway, I'm for it now.

The doctor did come and I was fixed with a run of penicillin into my veins. I don't like things going in my veins. I saw too much of that with Alf. I find it disgusting.

Sergeant Gertrude didn't hose me down at all. Instead, she did something much meaner, much more vicious. Sometimes to this day I think about finding her and giving her a piece of my mind that she will never forget. But you cannot reach the cruel. If they had hearts to hurt, they wouldn't be as they are.

Willy did not come back. I waited all the next day, then went to sleep crying, then waited again all the next day, and the day after, on and on through the dragging months, waiting and crying, waiting and crying. I was in there and I was ugly and I couldn't get out and get a perm or anything and I was losing my Willy who was the finest man any woman could hope to have. I used to imagine him and Jenny strolling along Ku'Damm her getting dresses and hats and shoes and them having ices somewhere. I completely forgot the Ku'Damm was dead.

Then one day they called me to the front office. That meant one of two things, you were going to solitary or you were getting out. When I saw my bundle, I thought it was solitary and now Willy wouldn't be able to see me even if he did come. But it wasn't. I had done my time for the crime I did not commit.

The only street clothes I had was the dress I'd been wearing in the Leaderbunker. It lay before me, a navy blue memory from hell. It had been washed and stitched but you couldn't wear ruined finery like that, it was going to come apart right out on the street.

They gave me a military coverall that made me look like a rubble woman. In that and with ten marks in my pocketbook, I went out the door. I had in my hand the address of a sewing factory where I could go to work.

On the street there was a tan car, much prettier than any of Hitler's buggies. As I turned to make my way down the sidewalk, the door opened and out came Willy.

"Carlotta, where are you going?"

I stopped. I turned.

"Haven't you read my letters?"

"I got no letters."

He stared toward the prison. "Come on, let's go before I kill somebody."

They had seen that I had a rich American. The only thing they could do in their bitterness and meanness was to not let me see those letters that would have delivered me from the hell of my own heart.

I got into the car and it was beautiful, rich leather and glowing wood, far more beautiful than the Hitler cars.

"What is this wonderful machine?"

"This? It's an old LaSalle I've had for years. I had it shipped over. You don't want to drive around Europe in a German car just now."

And guess where we were living? In the Wannsee House, of course! There was General Spiers from Texas billeted with us. His wife Alicia was kind. She was kind to *me*, can you imagine? She's the reason for my funny German-Southern accent. She worked with me on my English every day. "You will be a fine lady in America, Honey. You must be able to speak properly."

Willy had already sold the house back to the Kreislers who had successfully escaped and were living in London. The US Army was renting it until the end of the year. This was the year '47 now. Sir Paul Dukes would come in the evenings and we would get up a Bridge game. They would draw straws as to who would be my partner. I always win at Bridge unless I'm partnered with some fucking idiot. I oughta go pro. Maybe that's my place in life, like Willy says, Bridge master.

Willy got me an elegant, old fashioned German wedding dress of the finest lace and we got married in that house. Yes, I did! I had wine red roses at my waist and there was a photographer and Alicia and Paul and the new man, Reinhard Gehlen, who was working with him, and also Fritz and Maria. The registrar had on a morning suit that was partly burned.

So now I was me, officially. Me, the American! Little piece of shit from the shitkicker *keitz*, now the American.

Me, I'm an American. I'm writing this years later but it's still just —oh my God! I have my Statue of Liberty on the mantle here. I know it's nothing much and people laugh at it but they don't what a thing like that can mean. I put it right in front of that wonderful Klimt of the garden that Willy bought from the Kreislers to help them get their fortune back in order. He paid 'em a million dollars, can you imagine, a Klimt? It's worth about two hundred today. Back then, maybe fifty. But I love it.

My American masterpiece and my German masterpiece are together.

I remember when we came home. The US Army Air Force flew us in a plane that had a living room and a dining room. Better even than Hitler's plane and General Spiers was only a general. Except maybe he and Willy paid for it all. He's rich, too.

When we came in from Gander it was afternoon and there was New York! You can't imagine what that is like, seeing New York for the first time in your life. There were orange ferries in the harbor and ships everywhere and nothing bombed out or anything, and there, standing there on that island was Lady Liberty with her torch just like in a picture. And here I was, just this little person who had started with less than nothing and been plenty bad in my time but I was part of the tired and the poor and the weary of the world too, and here I come!

I am here. Me. I am an American. I turned it all around here. I was such a shit in Germany it's just unbelievable to think that was ever me. Now I have my charities, I work with troubled girls, I work with hurt girls who have nothing and not even hope. But I show them they can turn their lives any way they want to go. I am good at this because I did it myself.

After my wedding, he took me back to Paris. Willy, as head of the Food For Europe program, had business in all the capitals. He had even put his own ships to work moving grain. He did not charge a thing for this.

"My little fleet hardly matters, but we all need to do as much as we can." That's my Willy, so sweet and mild. If he wasn't like he is, he would have shot Hitler the bird early on and gone back to America.

I guess we should all be grateful, because he not only was the *Hitlerficker,* he fucked with the old bastard's head, but good.

We went to England and Willy got the George Medal from King George. But the medal is named after another King George. It's such a strange place. In my opinion the English have more customs than any other people in the world. There are even customs about how to hold a teacup. Pinkie out means you are one class, pinkie in another. I am obviously the pinkie in class. I am welcome there in the Bridge world even though I cuss. You know who played a goddamn good game of Contract Bridge was Ike. He was such a fine Bridge player that his officers wouldn't play with him. This was an interesting man. He smoked all the time, lighting one off the last. He had a dirtier mouth than me. The grin made him look like a kind of easygoing dope. Very deceiving! He as smart as God and as tough as shoe leather. Later, he drove his wife to drink and she used to wander off and end up in the bushes around the White House. He had two wives, actually, Mamie and Kay. I met Kay. She looked like she was about to turn into a horse.

We went to the White House. Before Ike, though. It was Truman who was president. He was a little sharpie, that one. He pinned the Intelligence Medal on Willy. That stupid Allan Dulles decides to tell Albert Weber the story of how brave his son had been because he gained Hitler's trust by fucking him.

That did it. The old man put a gun in his mouth and *blam.*

Boy, Willy cried. Did he, did he! That Dulles is one of those men who is smart and dumb at the same time.

Willy threw the medals in the Rhine. He said, "they belong to the Jews who are my responsibility." Well, hell, I could have killed Hitler, too. He used to give himself hard-ons by getting me to smother him, the freak. He's the best argument there is for there being no god. No god could make a man like that. Once Willy said he thought maybe he was a real demon. But then later he claimed he never said it. He did though, one evening on the beach at Malibu. The servants would have a fire and drink themselves silly on Saturday night. We were standing down by the water, the surf was pale and strong, the tide striving toward us. He said, "Hitler was a demon. That's what a demon is. Anything it touches, it corrupts. That's why it couldn't be killed. It only left this world when it was sure it had done all the damage it could."

He was probably drunk I guess, that's why he doesn't remember.

I want to say this in closing: I love you, Willy and thank you for loving me. You gave me everything I have and every moment of happiness I have ever known. I am sorry I am so mean.

# 30

It was two years ago on the Literary Walk when my life truly ended. Our life. I was deep in this memoir, actually just then writing about Carlotta's ruination of my little sportster on her way to France when something drew me back from the depths of memory, all the way to the present moment. Someone had sat down beside me.

"Scribble, scribble, scribble," she said. "Don't you ever stop even for a cigarette?"

It was Carlotta.

I said at once, "It has been much too long since I have seen such beauty."

She smiled and I was instantly captured again by the sweet pain her eyes convey, especially to one who knows of all that hides in them. You simply cannot imagine a smile like that until you have witnessed it.

The old woman, as always on her bench across from me, smiled, too, leaning forward as if in anticipation of a treasured scene in a play, the Macbeths sitting down to dinner, perhaps.

Carlotta's smile always reminds me of the expression on the face of the figure of Flora in Botticelli's *Primavera*, that same combination of sensuality, mystery and, if you will, danger.

I took her hand and kissed it, her still exquisite hand. She still appears so young, or perhaps it is my eyes.

"My old fashioned Willy," she said. "I have to tell you something that will make you laugh and something that will make you cry. That's why I have come here and found you."

"How did you?"

"Simple enough. You are only going to be in a few places and you weren't anywhere else."

"First, I want to know what will make me laugh. I'm always hoping to laugh."

"Angie and I built that house?"

They had employed my architect for the Malibu house, John Lautner, to build them one in Palm Springs. "Yes?"

"She threw me out on my ass."

The old woman gasped and leaned closer. She had begun chewing her gums. I thought that she would have done it at a hanging, too.

"I'm not laughing, Darling. I'm sorry for you."

"OK, now here it comes. You're still in love with me, I know it, I accept it."

"Thank you."

"So get ready."

I was sure that she'd gotten married, but this time to a boyfriend in a "legal" ceremony, and she was going to ask me not to press charges. "Carlotta—"

"Shut up! Don't you say a word. It's not what you think. She threw me out because I have cancer and she does not like cancer."

That hit so hard, it was incredible. Then I thought, this is Carlotta, maybe it's some small thing that she's come to believe is the end of the world.

"My darling, how dreadful."

"Willy, it's all over me. It's in my breasts, in my chest, it's all over me!"

She covered her face with her hands.

The old woman stood and came slowly across to us.

I shook my head, but she gave me that same smile, like Primavera, but in her toothless memory of a face. Then she laid a finger on her lips. She sat down beside Carlotta.

My mind rushed down white hospital corridors, Sloane-Kettering, the Cleveland Clinic, the Mayo.

"I have had radiation and it has made it stop hurting. There are these drugs but they're really godawful and they don't help much. I'd rather be eaten by the cancer than puke my fucking life away, Willy."

She closed her eyes and went suddenly quiet, as people do when their next sound will be a sob and they do not wish that to happen.

I put my hand on her leg.

"Don't touch me! Not now!"

"Ok!"

"No, no—oh, God. I keep thinking it's contagious."

"It's not."

"So they say. Still, I just—" She looked up into the green and glowing trees. "OK, prognosis, terminally shitty. Time—six months, three good, three bad. That's UCLA." She regarded me. "I'm going to Sloane in the morning. Doctor Timothy Winter. The best oncologist on the planet, as they all are said to be. I have never seen so many extraordinary reputations. And yet all the patients get fucked in the end. All of us."

I never left her again, not for moment, not until it happened. Six months? That was sadly optimistic. Of course, she'd been putting off going to the doctor for years. Growing up as she had in the dog-eat-dog hell of the Berlin underworld *keitz*, her instinct was to conceal anything that might reveal weakness. To a whore in that time, sickness and death were pretty much the same thing.

She had been in town for a couple of days, staying at the Sherry. I said to her to come home and she said "Yeah, it's time."

She laid her head against my shoulder.

This was so very pleasant, feeling the presence of my beloved, her warmth, inhaling her faint, sweet scent. "It's been a long time," I said.

"I'm sorry."

"Sh."

"No, I'm ashamed. I was not a good wife."

"No, no, darling, we did our best."

"I'm so mean to you and it's because you love me and I know that and I can't help it and it just--" She wept, then, bitterly and it broke me inside and I did too, and the old woman watched us bawl, and laid her hands on our heads.

Into my weeping, Carlotta said, "If there's nobody to grieve for me, what did my life matter?"

Her words were like fire in me, beautiful, painful fire. "We gave what we had, both of us, all we had."

She took my chin in her hand and turned my face to hers and kissed me.

The fires of the past immediately reignited. It will never end, that kiss. Never. I had my girl back. After all this time, I had my girl back. She had finally come home, and I was just so very glad.

The old woman watched us as we left the park. I walked slowly because Carlotta was struggling, I could see it.

Once at the apartment, we went then along the hall to my bedroom where I had been always alone. She had not come with me here since we first came to the states, in those brief months before her anger captured her soul away.

I undressed her like a boy would, gently and uneasily, and I looked upon her as a boy might all in wonder, as if she was the first woman on the first day of the world. She was so thin that I could see the bones in her hips but I decided that I will not see that, and saw instead the glowing body of her youth.

I carried her to my bed and laid her down, and she lay like all the Venuses in all the paintings of Venus that have ever been, and I chose not to see what was scarred and what was gone. I undressed and she laughed with delight when she saw what was there.

"Oh, you're still so fucky for your Carlie!" She clapped her hands. "I'm glad I have so much left. I've loved being beautiful. It saved my life. I was too pretty to gas."

That was always her story, but at this moment, it was also to feel the old delight and we did, in kisses and the old sacred pneumatics.

As I finished I said, "Carlie, Carlie, Carlie" in the old way, gasping it from my joy and my body. I sank down on her but she was too weak and I slid beside her instead.

"Oh, Willy, that was so very fucking nice. I had forgotten how nice it is with us."

"It is. It's all we have. It's all we've ever had."

"I've screwed you over a million times. I've fucked other guys just because they weren't you and I don't know why and I'm so damn sorry."

"Darling I forgive you and you forgive me."

"For what? You didn't do anything."

"Nineteen forty six."

"Oh, Love, no, we were unlucky, that's all."

"You were. I was dining on roast goose."

"Don't go down that path. I can't follow you and stay nice."

I held her and her arms came up around me and the gratitude flowed through me like water from God. She sank against me and I felt her dancing inside to the music that we never hear, not really, not with the ear, because it is the secret music of the soul. We fell silent in the hidden song of the married way, and joined the flow of the night.

She fell asleep so suddenly that it was as if she had died.

I took a pillow and covered my face so that I could weep without disturbing her. After I had controlled myself, I lay beside her and her hand came into mine, and we lay like that side by side. The sounds of the city in the deep night drifted up from below, the occasional horn, the lonely wail of a siren, the voice of our night doorman Gino raised in song, "*Funiculi, funicula.*" My mind drifted back to the Berlin apocalypse, and the voice singing Pagliacci in the ruins. When I am going to see Pag and Cav at the Met, I start crying the day before, for all the voices lost.

Unwanted thoughts came, as they always do in my life, of Hitler who had saved her life and made me rich. He created us both and destroyed us both, all at the same time. He was a ghost in that room, standing over us and between us, always, the hook of his evil set deep in us.

I kissed her many times in that night, and in the morning when she awoke, she sang a song from her earliest days, before the starving time, when she was maybe six or seven and the light of the sun meant a good day to come.

"*Brüderlein, komm tanz mit mir, Hände reich ich dir,*
*Einmal hin, einmal her, das ist nicht schwer.*"

"Little brother, come dance with me, take both my hands, first this way, then that way, round and round, it's not hard."

While we breakfasted, I sent the servants down to the Sherry for her things. She said, "I think I've still got something. I think I do!"

"Are you kidding? You're a goddess. *The* goddess, as far as I'm concerned."

"A hard goddess for you."

"Did you ever meet Pamela Travers at the Foundation?" I was referring to the Gurdjieff Foundation in New York. Pamela was something of a teacher there—a brilliant, inlooking woman, deceptively flawed, as every good teacher must to be.

She shook her head.

"She says, 'to lie in the lap of the goddess means to be unsure.' That's what it feels like to love you."

"That's Willy, still spouting the good old philosophical bull crap."

"Ah." I stood up from the table. I took my girl of bones in my arms, then carried her down the hallway to our bedroom where we did it again. She said, "Willy, oh God it hurts, but it feels good at the same time." Then, "Do you enjoy me? Do you enjoy my cunt?"

"It's my home."

"I love having you in me. I've missed it so much."

From my dresser, my old bedroom clock softly tolled the hour of nine. Like most of what I have except for my pictures, it came with us from Germany. After the war, Gerdy Troost asked me if she could do some work for me. I let her do my Munich flat. I have never been in it since. I've never seen it and I never will.

"If we're to get down there, we need to go."

"Is there a maid who can dress?"

"My servants aren't servants. I wish they were."

"Ask her."

Lauren came in looking confused and quite put out, but managed to help Carlotta pretty efficiently. For my own part, I still remember the era of the valet fondly, but try finding one nowadays. It seems to me that men of the type who used to brush suits and hair for a living now want more. They wear gold chains, deal drugs and play in rock and roll orchestras. My experience of valets was that they were all opportunists. They sold stock tips and such on the side, that sort of thing. No more. Who would dream of being a valet? Nobody is your answer.

With Carlotta in a blue frock with a starched front and looking not a day over thirty, we set out for Sloan-Kettering. On the way down I did something I have done only rarely in my life—I prayed. I said the Jesus Prayer from *Franny and Zooey*, which was the only one I could remember, having learned it from the book back when it appeared in the New Yorker.

As we rode down in silence, I remembered her first days here and her amazed whispering, "*Ich ben in Amerika, ich! Ich ben es, ich ben es.*" She cried hard while outside the Empire State Building slid past and a newsboy cried, "Seven convicted, one goes free," again and again. "*Frei,*" she said, "*eir sagt frei.*"

In the doctor's office, she flipped through *Vogue* while we waited. Ten minutes maybe. It was quick.

Doctor Augustus Winter burst with a bonhomie that I found incredibly tiresome, but which seemed to lift Carlotta's spirits somewhat. He had her MRI up on a light box, and proceeded to explain her cancer to us. It was a truly dismal recitation, made more malignant, in my view, by his fallacious smiles.

There was nothing to smile about, it was terminal cancer. She hung on his words, my poor dear love, which made me despise him even more.

Afterward, we lunched at Lutece. She called Jack and Charlie's "Snot City," by which I assume she meant "Snob City." I suppose that's there for someone who comes strolling in for the first time wearing sneakers and a sweatshirt, but I've never felt any sense of it.

There were a good couple of weeks. We shopped, we dined, we sat in the park going over old times. Of course, one had to be careful, given that so many of our old times are not exactly drenched in the glow of fond memory.

Every time I made love to her, it was as if I had reached some corner of heaven. In the middle of the second week, though, she would screw her eyes shut and grimace and the tears would flow when we did it, but then she would say, "Oh, Willy, that was lovely. It was so lovely!"

No, Darling, you were in agony and I know it. It was then that I made a decision of marriage that comes to some of us. One night late, when I was bounding along and she was crying and laughing at the same time, I thought to myself, 'this must be the last.'

After I stopped, I kissed her all over. I kissed her from the top of her head to the tip of her toes, and with each kiss committed that part of her to memory.

Lucky marriages conclude with a last time, and so ours, for all its troubles, was such a one.

I never thought that I would know the grace of that, and I am so grateful to her that she managed to overcome the hurt in her long enough to return to me.

Within just a couple of weeks, she was thinner and obviously weaker. She would groan in her sleep. She was gobbling pills. We returned to Dr. Happyface, went through another clanking, buzzing MRI and received the verdict that, "I'm really rather surprised." He pointed to the film, which was on a viewer in his office, a room dominated by a sixteenth century Spanish desk carved with serpents, of all the odd things for a doctor to sit behind. He continued, "We're seeing it now here and here, you see. Do you see?"

"That's my brain you're pointing at? Is that right?"

"It is, Mrs. Weber. I'm so very sorry."

Was my Carlotta's mind going to disappear into her cancer? "What should we expect?" I asked.

"We can try another round of radiation, and we have something called the CMF Program which we can try."

"Drugs?"

"Yes, Mrs. Weber, CMF is a combination of three drugs that sometimes achieve remission, and it can be impressive."

"The side-effects?"

"Mrs. Weber, in your situation, given the metabolic picture, there will be aggressive side effects and we'll need to monitor carefully because they could be very serious."

"In other words, the cure could kill me."

He nodded.

I said, "Doctor, we're people who've been through a lot. You be frank. Tell us where we are, here. I think we both want that, is that right, Darling?"

"The fuck I want that! I want to go to Paris! Let's go to Paris right now!"

So that is exactly what we did. We got up from our chairs and walked out and got in the car and I telephoned my pilot and asked him how soon he could be in the air. (I'd gone from a little Lear Jet to a big Grumman, so we could make the journey with only a refueling stop in Gander.)

We went to the Crillon, of course, straight to the old suite. It's much redecorated, but still recognizable.

She stood in the middle of the living room and turned slowly around. "Can you imagine," she said, "what we did in here? Who we were with?"

"Oh, let's not go over all of that."

"Why not, it's something to remember! Oh, goddamnit, Willy, I'm dying. Fuck, fuck, fuck!"

She fainted. She just turned into a rag and dropped. I almost caught her but not quite. I heard her head hit, a sound like an egg cracking, but ten times the volume.

I went down to her and cradled her in my arms. "Carlotta!"

One eye opened. "Did you do that on purpose?"

"You did it, you fainted."

"My head hurts! Nothing makes me madder than hitting my goddamn head!" She sat up. "Remember doing opium?" She pointed to a rather prissy loveseat. "There was a big couch right there. We did opium on that couch. And the bath! Oh, that huge tub, we fucked in that tub and I—" She stopped. "Do you think we're sinners, Willy?"

"God would never abandon you, Carlotta. You're just his kind of gal."

"I'd better be, because otherwise I can't explain a hell of a lot of shit I got up to."

"You fought for your life. And thank god. If I had not met you, I would not have had a life."

"Don't be an idiot. For a man like you there's a woman every three feet."

"There is only one Carlotta. Only one such soul."

"You go all poetic. That's nice. I'm delighted. But have you noticed I'm fucking still sitting on the floor?"

I helped her to her feet, then to the loveseat.

I had planned dinner at Taillevent, but she said, "All that food, please. It's an impossible thought."

We dined in the room. She had a consommé and a bit of salad, which she picked at indifferently. Then to my amazement, she said, "Let's go to the Berghof."

"I've been there. It's a ruin."

"I know, I've been there, too."

Her eyes met mine. Then, as was always true now, she fell without warning into a deep sleep. I carried her to bed and tucked her in and went in beside her and slept with my face in her hair and my arm across her breast. She smelled so good and even though she was bony now she was warm and being beside my woman again at long last was very good.

She finally woke up around eleven in the morning. Fortified with coffee and painkillers, she returned to the extremely unpleasant idea of going back to Hitler's mountain court. I couldn't say no to her. How could I? So we went out to Le Bourget and flew to Munich. I didn't want any drivers to ask questions about why we were going where we were going, so I rented a car and we drove down to Berchtesgaden on our own.

The town is really not much changed, so little, in fact, that one can easily imagine that convoy of Mercedes rumbling through with Hitler in the first car slumped beside Kempka and sound asleep.

"Remember my car, Willy, my wonderful little Beamer? I had such fun in that car! I drove all the way to Paris in that thing."

"Leaving the bumpers behind along the way yes."

"Don't say it, it's so embarrassing! I wonder what became of it?"

"God only knows. Maybe it's still parked in the Crillon. That's where I left it. I think."

"You're always leaving valuables around. You're awful."

As we passed up along the familiar roads, the way grew narrow and rutted, but there was nothing to stop us. There was a sign for the Eagle's Nest, which is still intact, but nothing to indicate the location of the Berghof.

What a forest of memories, though.

We had booked for the night in the Zum Turken, which has been returned to its former state and ownership. No more SS, no more Nazi bustle, just ordinary people in ordinary lives, come up for the air and the views.

From the hotel, one can see the Untersberg far better than in the Hitler days, because the Berghof is no longer there.

It was about four when we arrived, and she wanted me to sit her in a chair situated so that she could watch the sunset across the mountains. She closed her eyes, though. She was very tired.

"Do you remember our little room?"

"Certainly."

"That was the first real home I ever had, that little room. I used to lie in our bed and watch you sleeping and think, I have a man. I do. Me. A wonderful man, and he's mine. Little shit medicine from the old *keitz*, nobody cares whether junk like that lives or dies, but I have a man, and it's this man and guess what, you shit-faces of the world, he *does* care. Then I'd give you a hard-on in your sleep and in a few seconds you'd be on me. Real sex, and really good. Oh, boy!"

She fell asleep right there. I had to carry her to our room. She was so light, it felt as if I was carrying sticks. But nobody's young anymore, and I was winded by the time I got her in bed.

Fortunately, the bellman was there to help, and a maid. "Madam is feeling ill?"

"Madam is."

They probably thought she was drunk.

I knew her comment about sex was an invitation, but I also knew that it was for me, not her. She was ready to endure her pain for my pleasure. I lay beside her and whispered to her in her sleep, "How beautiful you are, how beautiful you are," and she smiled and sighed and her hand found mine. It was cold and trembled like a little bird.

She slept and slept, the sun awakening her as it crawled across the room, only in the afternoon lighting up the bed where she lay.

"What time is it?"

"Three."

"Let's go, Willy, we need to go to the *keitz*. We need to do it now."

We never went closer to the Berghof than the Zum Turken. Fine by me. The path to hell is under there, I'm convinced, somewhere in the tunnels that still honeycomb the hill.

I got her back to Munich and we took the plane on to Berlin. I'd booked us into the Adlon. She awoke briefly in the car, then more fully in the hotel itself. I'd ordered up a wheelchair and was grateful for it. She could no longer walk at all. Crossing the Zum Turken to the car was to be her last journey on foot.

She had a proper German meal and actually ate a bit of it, some sausage and a few mouthfuls of kraut. "My food," she said, "it's good. Only in Germany does it taste like this." She paused. "Willy, if only none of it had ever happened, the world would be so much better."

"But it did and here we are, and the past belongs to the past."

"No it doesn't. It belongs to us."

In all of these years, I had never seen the place where she grew up. It turned out to be in a little street called Drehenstrasse. Turning Street. It is a sort of elbow street, dark. One side is the back of a new office tower, but the other still contains a modest little row of houses.

"There." She pointed to one of the old structures.

"That's a big house."

"Down in the basement, you idiot. There!"

It was just that, a cellar. There was a metal door, beside it a barred window. "I used to put flowers in that window. I got paddled for spending a mark on petunias once." I wheeled her across to the building, then worked the chair down the few steps into the space under the front stairs. "Here, I came in and out of this door a thousand times. Right here, the same." She sat before it. "Willy, I think I am needing morphine. Can you get me some morphine now, please."

"Do you want the hospital?"

"Oh, go fuck yourself, hell no. I have a suite in the Adlon. Fabulous! Of course I don't want to go to the hospital."

I remembered *Muti's* dying then, in that sunny hotel room in Nice, and now I was taking Carlotta to another hotel to die, but in the dark of a German autumn.

It has been my fate to outlive all of my women. *Muti* in one hotel, forty-seven years later, Carlotta in another. And Maddy, god only knows what happened to her in the sea.

The hotel had a doctor on call of course. He strongly recommended hospitalization and for a time I feared that he would not provide morphine in the hotel, but it turned out that there was no legal restriction and he did.

Oxygen was brought, not to prolong her life, but to make her dying more comfortable.

All the next day I sat beside her listening to that machine go *whoo-poom, whoo-poom* as she slept with her mouth hanging open and her eyes sunken so deep they looked like caves.

Toward evening, she said, "*Schnapps*! *Sigaretten*!" She tried to dance in the bed, waving her arms and snapping her fingers. Then quiet came again, but for the stupefying rhythm of the machine. There was a nurse who sat at the foot of the bed watching over us, who would give her more morphine when she complained.

Then she said, "*Meine muti, wo bist do genagen?*" 'My mother, where have you gone?'

She had been left in that room when her mother was killed, just left there. "I went to the Excelsior and started being a medicine so I could get money to eat, is that so wrong? I raised myself. Nobody else was gonna do it."

Albert telephoned in the night. He said, "I'm coming, Uncle Willy, I'm going to be there in the afternoon."

"You cannot be in my presence. Remember the trust."

"It's Aunt Carlotta! How dare you try to stop me! Anyway, nobody cares now. Nobody will know."

"I will know. Your honor will know."

"Your wife is dying and you're all alone with her in some hotel room. You need your family now, damnit, and I'm coming."

"Honor trumps sentiment, Albert."

"God help us." He hung up.

Sometime toward dawn, I woke suddenly, aroused by a movement. The room was dim, the nurse was nodding in her chair.

Carlotta had pulled off the oxygen mask and was sitting up and staring at me. She looked completely astonished. She said, "Who in the world are you?"

"I'm Willy. I'm your husband, Honey."

"Yes, of course, how stupid of me. And shall I play the wife or the daughter, or a schoolgirl? Do you wish that?"

"Oh, no, I said, you're the wife. My wife."

"And a stern wife I shall be, yes, is that it?"

Death came then. That was all there was. The wonder of it enveloped me as I felt her leave, a shadow full of memories sweeping backward into the past, leaving behind the most impossible thing I have ever seen, my goddess stopped.

I felt a hand on my shoulder. It was the nurse.

"Is it done, Nurse?"

"It is, Herr Weber." She reached past me and turned off the oxygen. Then she lifted the sheet over Carlotta's face.

The dead crowd the memories of the living. When I walk the streets now and see the complex, extraordinarily rich faces of the human race, I also see the shadows that follow them in memory.

There is a secret bond among the living, and that bond is loss. I speak now and again to *Muti* and *Vati* and Maddy, but it is my conversation with Carlotta that continues on. She is the only friend I have, the only one I can count on to be there when I am lonely. I say 'Let's talk' and she says, 'later, I'm busy, I have work to do.' Then I say, 'No, all you have is to be loved.'

A great soul passed through my life. She had absolutely nothing on her side and nobody to help her, but she made it anyway. She was born in a cellar and died in a suite.

Carlotta Krause Weber it says on her coffin in our old tomb in St. Louis. The space immediately at its feet is mine.

When I remember her, I try to remember, in a certain way, around Alf. By that I mean that I remember the way we discovered each other in our room in the Berghof, two kids falling in love. I choose not to remember why we were there or what we had to do, or who we were with. Above all, not that.

Once a long time ago, Eva asked me, "Am I stupid, Willy?"

"You're a lovely person, but not intellectual."

"I know it, I love to ski and swim and all that. I can't keep my mind on a book. I ask Carlotta to tell me what they say, but it makes very little sense." She paused. "Willy, is Alf losing?"

"He is, Eva."

"Oh, I'm so sorry for him. Poor man! Why did they attack us? Everybody seems to hate the Germans. I don't understand it at all."

"It's your job to love, Eva, not understand."

"We're two wives and two husbands! Aren't we something? A new kind of marriage."

"We're not married."

"Oh, yes we are. Alf and I are married in whispers, and you and Carlotta are married in your eyes. I'm dumb as a post, I know it, but that doesn't mean I don't see things. I do."

Oh, darling Carlie, 'married in your eyes' is married forever. Beyond death, married. That registrar in the Wannsee house in '46 was only a footnote in our marriage.

After the rape room, you said to me, "Willy, I'm broken in my soul.

I'm Germany, broken. I can't love, I can't feel a thing. You need to get rid of me. Back to the gutter. That's where Carlotta started and where she ends. That's home for her."

I felt you then in your vulnerability and your dear fragility, and I took you in my arms and nursed you back to love. You came out of jail enraged at me. Yes indeed. But I didn't care. You had always needed your temper to make you a person. Nobody was going to listen to you unless you were furious. So I just let you yell and scream and slap me and spit at me and curse me and all of it, knowing that it was your life that had made you furious, the life of somebody who was casually stepped on, because she mattered so little.

I regarded your willingness to be my wife as an act of compassion. The fact that we fought for most of our lives is no tragedy. That was the only way you could love. You knew no other way. When you would scream at me and call me every name in the book, I would hear you inside yourself saying, 'I love you, I love you, I love you.' Or maybe it's just my fantasy. What I need to believe. I'll never know now. Any chance that I might lies in your tomb.

Carlotta, I belong to you. My consolation as I walk this long road is that every moment that passes means that I am a moment closer to you. That is all the happiness I now possess, and it is a great happiness. I was the consort of a goddess who rose out of a cellar instead of a sea shell. If there is any there there, then you will receive me, I trust. I'm sure you'll be furious at me for taking so long, but if you weren't furious at me, how would I know you?

After you died, I filled the apartment with five hundred roses. I felt like I was living in a parade float. Nobody could understand it and I didn't tell them a damn thing.

I have replaced the Seurat in my office with the portrait of you that Alice Neel painted, the one you thought so fantastically hideous. But we always think our truth ugly when we see it, do we not? In it I see your anger, your sorrow, your sensuality and your beauty, even a flicker of the wonderful false innocence that was your professional mask.

The sun rises, a day passes, the sun falls, night comes. I remain on this strange journey, hoping that I will not last, god forbid, until some fragile age.

I want to be with you. That's all I want. I haven't been cursed or yelled at or shouted down in too long. I know you need to be heard and need to be held, I can feel it.

When we finally moved to the United States in '47, Carlotta took up English and American literature, reading much of it long before she knew the language sufficiently well. But that sort of thing never stopped her.

She said some delightful things, and I noted them down. "Carlottaisms" I call them. I've thought about having them crocheted, and hanging them here and there in the flat. Here are some of them, so that you can remember that wonderfully improbable mind:

On Joyce's Ulysses: "Stephen Dedalus peers into his navel and there's Molly Bloom peering out."

After reading Walt Whitman's "Song of Myself:" "A poem longer than the Mississippi. Let a woman go on like that, claiming she's the whole fucking universe, see what happens. Men!"

On Longfellow's epic "The Song of Hiawatha:" "'Gitchee gumee.' That about sums it up."

On E. L. Doctorow' Ragtime: "Coalhouse Walker is a ripoff of Michael Kolhass. But that's ok, Kleist was just a German."

On *The Decline of the West*: "Spengler conceals the fact that he doesn't know what he's talking about by doing too much of it."

She hated the *volkish* movement. "Holderlin makes Germans weep for a Germany that doesn't exist and never did. That's why he's so dangerous."

She would float along in the swimming pool at the Malibu house reading Fitzgerald aloud and crying her eyes out. "One way or another, every character in Fitzgerald is Zelda. They're all Zelda, trying to see in the window at the Ritz."

She read Freud carefully, in both German and English. Her verdict: "Freud understood men. That made him a scientist. He thought he understood women. That made him a fool."

She thought a lot about Hitler, but said very little. This is one thing she said: "Dictators are lost souls. They climb to the top trying to find themselves. Then they fall off."

Gibbon made her furious. She wanted to learn about the Roman Empire, but as she ploughed along, she'd curse him continuously. This is why: "Gibbon never confined himself to just one sentence when ten would do."

She was enraptured by the Schliemann treasures, but when he came under criticism recently, she decided that he was no scientist: "Schliemann just assumed that he found Troy. Who knows what the fuck he found?"

She had read Mien Kampf. She said, "It was too dull to be read, and Hitler knew it. He just wanted it to be bought so he could pretend that everybody agreed with him."

Henry James made her even more furious than Gibbon. She would throw one of his novels against the wall and stand there cursing at it so furiously that her cats hissed at it, too. "By the time Henry James gets to the end of a sentence, he's forgotten what in shit's name it was about when he started it."

None of that would have been remembered, in fact she wouldn't have happened at all, if she hadn't been beautiful beyond compare. Without the softness and the spunk, she could never have been a medicine or much of a whore at all. If by some chance she had survived into the Nazi era, it would have been a miracle. But with a mind like hers, maybe she could somehow do it. I think, though, that she would have been gassed along with most of the intellectual cream of Europe.

I saw a documentary made by the Russians showing them cutting open bales and bales of hair, blond braids, brown braids, mats of it, tangles of it, pigtails. Her hair would have ended up in a bale like that. It would have been one more shimmering cloud of brown among the many.

One thing you learn, living a life like mine: there is no such thing as an unimportant person.

As her struggle to find her own true path grew more subtle and informed, she turned more and more to the poets, especially the great sagas of loss and redemption. Dante and Milton were her poets, living in dignity in her soul.

When she discovered Milton, she said, "There, that's the voice. That's mankind. We are falling." She used to read from "Paradise Lost" most wonderfully. One would think to declaim it, but she read it in an intimate, domestic voice, warm and shuddered with tears. Eliot was Willy's favorite poet, but she found in Milton what she described as "solace." She said, "If there is any such thing as proof of God's mercy, it is 'Samson Agonistes.'"

I have made therefore its final lines her epitaph:

"His servants he, with new acquist
Of true experience from this great event
With peace and consolation hath dismissed
And calm of mind, all passion spent."

# 31

So there you have her, my beloved Carlotta. She was not mean, she was hurt, the most hurt person I ever knew. I told her I didn't remember the conversation about the demon, but I do. When I have felt particularly mystified about Hitler, I have sometimes considered a supernatural explanation. But I don't think such belief is the strongest part of anybody who seeks to explain away the sins of man in this way. What's that Flip Wilson used to say on Laugh-In, "the devil made me do it?"

As she does to me, I belong to Carlotta. That we did not die together feels like a mistake of some sort, as if the order of the world has been violated.

This whole memoir has been my own book of conscience. I know that, had I been a more aggressive man, I would have been able to help Carlotta overcome her own demons and settle into the warm marriage she so badly wanted. I know that I would have handled the Hitler situation differently. In the depths of me there is a passivity that should not be there. Ironically, it is a defiance, an establishment of self in the face of my father's power. My interest in Hitler started as youthful rebellion. But he was demonic in his cleverness and he used my desire to be a man separate from my own father to capture me.

This memoir was originally called *My Hitler* because he is mine, in me. And every person who raised his arm or even now would like to, he is in you. He is in our hate, in our prejudice, in the lies we tell ourselves, that the other man is somehow less. In our willingness to believe lies because they feed our hate. Our Hitler is what is weak and small and ugly about us.

I am thinking about my life, and I am thinking now that this is concluded. I lived a life that led to many deaths and was made rich by it and got medals for it. I changed the title to *In Hitler's House* because it is the story of the people who lived and loved there, him included. For yes, we loved. In that secret house of peace hidden in hell, there was love.

My medals embarrassed me terribly, but I regret throwing them in the river. It was not my right. When you are honored you need to respect that and be humble before it. What I did was an act of arrogance.

What I did was also an egoistic attempt to acknowledge my personal responsibility. I could have killed Hitler. I didn't. There you have it. Or if only I hadn't given him money in the early days maybe none of it would have happened. But I'm not alone. If Ford hadn't given him cash or Thyssen, maybe he would never have gotten off the ground. And what of Watson? What dreadful guilt that man must have felt. If Hitler hadn't had the IBM sorting machines, he would never have been able to do such a thorough job on the Jews.

Watson wouldn't have wanted what happened, nor Ford. Thyssen certainly didn't. He spent time in a concentration camp for his belated resistance to Hitler and wrote a book of conscience, too.

I think that yesterday afternoon was my last time on the Literary Walk. I had a funny thing happen. My old lady across-the-walk wife has been gone for a while. But that's New York. You don't chase after your anonymous friends, it's not the done thing.

A shadow came and there was a woman standing in front of me. She was heavy, in her forties and sweetly inelegant in appearance. She thrust a pair of knitted socks into my face. Green knitted socks.

I said, "No thank you."

"No, is yours. From my mother."

I was mystified.

"She sit there many years."

"Oh my gosh, of course! Well thank her for me. Has she moved away?"

"Oh yes, very far, very good."

"We are good friends."

"Ah, yes, she say this."

"I don't want to intrude, but we never actually spoke. May I know if she's coming back?"

"No, no."

"May I know her name?"

"Is Ivanka. From Russia long ago. You know us Jews, we like to travel around. Her son, you knew him."

"Her son?"

"He made turnips and green beans for you."

I was surprised, to say the least. "He was a doctor?"

"Oh, no, not my brother. Oh, no. Stalin— " She drew a finger across her neck.

So he had been the third one, the one who disappeared after the war. Shot, then.

"How ever did you find me?"

"Certain Russians, we know. You are known to many, Willy Weber. You save."

Tears came, damned things. "But not your brother," I managed to croak.

She leaned over and kissed my forehead, then turned and quickly walked off.

I sat there looking at my socks which I am now wearing and may never take off. By the time I realized that I had just been told that Ivanka had joined her son, the woman was out of sight. So she slipped away like that, leaving a pair of green knit socks in her wake.

I'm feeling better today. I've been at low ebb. The doctor's solution is to give me Vitamin B shots. But I'm like Carlotta, I detest shots.

Did Morrell turn him into an animal? Is that what happened?

No, for when Helene Bechstein told him he was "a shabby sort of a chancellor," in 1933, he was already vile and Morrell was not on the scene.

I live now in silence. I no longer read. I no longer listen to music. I have devoted myself to the art of silence.

As it happens, it's Friday again. I'll go down to Jack and Charlie's. What if I didn't show up on a Friday, would they celebrate or close? Every time I sit to table there, they feed me exactly the same meal. I've been eating it for more than a few years now, and I'm afraid to ask for a change. Or has it been an eternity? I wouldn't want them to think I haven't liked it. But you know, now that I think about it, I haven't seen Jack and Charlie in years, either. People die. They do that.

The place has changed, especially the bar. When I was a boy they used to be able to pull a lever and the whole thing would disappear into the wall. Raids were wonderful fun. We all tipped the policemen and toasted the precinct. They were most frequent around Christmas time. In anticipation, the club would be so jammed then that you had to call ahead. Reserving a table at a speak—*Vati* always found that hilarious. Golly but in the old days, before I brought the curtain between us down, *Vati* and I used to laugh so much together.

This condition I am in, and that Carlotta was in, is called depression. There are pills these days that you can take for it. Carlotta had some, but she never took them. I have some, but I never take them.

In my dreams lately, I see the sun. Isn't that strange? Who sees the sun in their dreams? I've never heard of this from anybody else. Sometimes I think it's Carlotta so bright all I can see of her is light.

This is the light that is

# AFTERWORD BY ALBERT WILLIAM MARTIN

JUNE, 2016

That's where it ends. "This is the light that is" What, we will never be told, but do we need to be? I think we know, all of us, in one way or another.

He was coming back to the text in the afternoon. As was his habit on Fridays, he drove down to the 21 Club, which he always called Jack and Charlie's, for lunch. But when they reached the restaurant and his chauffeur opened the door to let him out, nothing happened.

He had died so quietly that Mr. Johnson had not noticed. When he had gotten into the car, he had seemed entirely normal. But sometime during the drive down to 47th Street, his life came its close.

That was on November 3, 1980. Aunt Carlotta had then been dead for two years. During that time, his struggle with grief was very profound. He blamed himself for the deaths of my mother and my grandfather. He blamed himself not for Carlotta's death but for her life. Not her early life. She had saved herself with cleverness and determination. It was during her life in America that he felt he had failed her.

Because his death had come unexpectedly, the State of New York required an autopsy, which I'm sure that my fastidious uncle would have been most unhappy about. He was very proper and formal. In the city, he wore a business suit or what he would have called a "lounge suit" during the day. Even in the '70s when he went to dinner in the evenings he dressed formally. This was true even if he sat alone. He must have looked a sight dressed like that in the humble little Zoe Chase Restaurant that he so loved, and even more so when spending a late evening in Therese's ultimately bohemian and super-fashionable Little Secret, both now long gone.

From time to time in my teens I used to go to the Zoe Chase restaurant in hopes of running into him, but he always eluded me. Her husband, "the Count," dressed formally also. So perhaps they dined together, to make it look more ordinary. Once as I walked down the steps, I thought I saw two men in tuxedos going to the back.

The autopsy showed that he had something called aortic valve stenosis as a result of a congenital defect. This often goes undiagnosed, as it did in his case. The coroner reported that there seemed to be no clear reason for his heart to stop, but as this was the only problem discovered, on his death certificate it states that he died of cardiac arrest.

I don't think that's why. I think it was Carlotta. That light he saw was no dream. It was Aunt Carlotta, come to collect her husband and take him to the final land.

In all the years of my life, I don't think that I encountered my uncle ten times, not until after Aunt Carlotta died. Then he was a little more forthcoming. He would telephone and ask after the boys, always very polite and distant, but at least he was there.

I telephoned him, also, but he was always extremely brief, even brusque.

The only period of his life when he was not true to his formalities was when he set himself up as an "old hippie" in the Haight during the summer of love. Aunt Carlotta said that he was searching for the youth he had been denied. They may have been fighting then, I don't know, I didn't keep track. If so, perhaps he was trying to make her jealous enough to come back to him.

In any case, he adored and revered women, and some part of the romantic in him must have drawn him to that place in that time, where all the women were dancing.

I found his manuscript on his desk. He claims in it somewhere that it was being typed by his secretary. This would have been Linda Forbes, but she says that she never saw this material. And yet, she is mentioned in his acknowledgements. The whole document was in 114 handwritten notebooks. Just like the rest of him, his handwriting is very regular and precise.

When I read it, frankly, I was just appalled. The lurid horror of the thing really threw me. The sexuality of the monster Hitler and the depraved ways in which Uncle Willy and Aunt Carlotta engaged with him was, to say the least, deeply shocking.

I wondered if any of it could really be true? Could this actually be a novel? One cannot find Willy and Carlotta in history. God knows, I've tried. Many more of the Third Reich's documents have been destroyed than is realized, I think.

I did find the photograph of him and Eva that he mentions. It's in the Library of Congress, in a photograph album of Eva's. There they are in top hats with cigarettes in their jaws, just as he described. He looks a raffish devil of a fellow, I must say. As, indeed, he was.

Aunt Carlotta's testament is definitely in her own hand, and she was so completely plainspoken, I cannot imagine that she was somehow abetting a fiction.

No, I think that this is a true memoir.

My wife and I agreed that there could be no question of publication. I paid back Grosset and Dunlap's on the contract.

My sons were then fourteen and seventeen. We owed it to them to keep it out of sight.

In discussing its accuracy with experts on the demagogic personality, I did discover that sexual perversity is the norm among such men. It's quite ordinary for them to want all sorts of peculiar things, and male masochism does often arise from childhood maternal domination, especially if the child is otherwise unloved. Then its only contact with the mother comes during chastisement. The pain is dreadful, but with it comes also the pleasure of touch.

There follows the very sort of sexual dysfunction that Hitler displays here, where pleasure cannot be "allowed" without first experiencing pain.

Our decision to withhold the manuscript was made in 1980. But it's now 2016 and times have changed. Now we are an elderly couple and the boys are middle aged men with families of their own.

In the world of 2016, humanity finds itself living under stresses that are causing the specter of fascism to re-emerge. There must be no mistake about the fact that what is politely called populism in a number of western countries is really a new birth of the old idea of rule by the club.

It's understandable where it comes from: the disenfranchisement of labor and the restless cultural pressures attendant on mass immigration sparked by war and climate change. But where it might go, and how easily, is not clearly understood, and this is why we have undertaken to publish Willy's memoir now.

I have been made particularly uneasy by the rumors of sexual peculiarities that dog some of our current leaders. This sort of thing fits the profile of the demagogue, and suggest to me the possibility that a dictator awaits within more than one of the current crop of so-called populists. Guilt and rage inherited from childhood drove Adolf Hitler to the point of complete indifference toward—even hatred of—the lives of others. I see that now in too many powerful people.

The western invention called democracy, arguably the best thing that has ever happened to mankind, is once again in danger. It is important to remember that the journey from the rantings of a man most Germans in 1930 thought was crazy to the start of his dictatorship was just a matter of months.

Hitler gained power because he knew how to exploit fear. That is happening again in the United States and some European countries as well. Maybe demagogues won't win any current round of elections, but they are there, and that's the danger. The Nazis attained power even though they had a minority of the vote and were a minority party.

It does not take a majority to win power in a democracy. It takes a committed minority.

We do not understand the power of our fears to steal us away from what is best in ourselves and awaken the monster that sleeps within us all. But the demagogue does understand.

Once an evil regime starts up, it quickly becomes a relentless mechanism. As long as it is prepared to perpetuate itself by destroying its opponents, it cannot be stopped.

I have wept over this manuscript, exulted over the acts of courage and heroism that Uncle Willy so diffidently narrates. I have worried that perhaps my own moral courage was failing me in my unwillingness to publish it. But twenty years ago or ten, it would have been nothing but a curiosity.

Now it is what I and my wife and sons regard as an essential warning. This is the time for Uncle Willy and Aunt Carlotta to tell their stories.

I'm glad of this, because it gives them a shadow of life, and we miss them so. Although we saw all too little of Uncle Willy, Aunt Carlotta often visited us in Connecticut and the boys spent time with her in Malibu. It was such fun to listen to her trying not to cuss around the children. "Fuck, I'm saying fuck in front of the kids. Oh, fuck! Shit! I'll shut up, fuck me."

We finally just taught them everything. Cunt, fuck, shit, cocksucker, the whole litany without which she could not speak in any of the four languages she had so proudly attained.

She was a wonder with the boys. I remember when my Willy was seven and Albert five we had them believing implicitly in Santa Claus. Given that we're a German family, Christmas is a famous celebration in our lives.

Albert said something like, 'Santa is coming tonight, Aunt Carlie,' some innocent thing like that. Her response was "Who? Oh, god, don't you believe that shit. Who could be telling you those silly lies? What do you think he's gonna do, ride around in a sleigh heaped with ten million presents? How is that gonna work?"

They both burst into tears, of course. She was horrified. She gathered them in her arms and said, "I'm your Santa Claus now. I will give you the best presents." Which she did. Although giving a ten year old a Ferrari was rather a failure. He has it still, though. He drives it now, certainly. The matched Palominos that arrived on Fifth Avenue one Christmas morning were another notable complication. Also, you do not give teenage boys growing up in Manhattan an apartment of their own, especially without mentioning its existence to their parents.

We sometimes cuss at each other around the dinner table, just to honor her. You know, they weren't little people in a big situation at all, neither one of them. They were big souls and lived big lives, which they fit very nicely, thank you.

Look at the things they did. The information they got to the allies was priceless. If you read his manuscript carefully, you see that Willy tricked Hitler in many crucial ways. He played what may have been an instrumental part in keeping him from overrunning the Dunkirk evacuation. He helped get that heavy water out of France in 1940. Had it remained there, Hitler might have gotten an a-bomb by '42 or '43. There was the *Wehrmacht* order of battle he got to Churchill, the D-Day deception that helped keep the panzers away from the allied landings, the Operation Bagration deception pulled off with Paul Dukes, and probably more that he never mentioned.

I so regret his throwing his medals away. I understand the emotions behind the act, but I wish they were part of the family, with us to honor his courage.

He did some of the most repulsive things I can imagine anyone doing—they both did—on behalf of humanity, so that Hitler would take them into his deepest confidence and love them, and therefore fall into the traps they set for him.

There is one thing that is very strange indeed that remains unresolved in the manuscript. This is what Willy reports as Hitler's plan to escape by submarine. He says that the allies reacted to it by hammering Hamburg with bombs during the last days of the war, but this is wrong. What did happen was that British troops entered the city, their assault beginning on April 28. So it might have been possible before that to reach it from Berlin. Difficult, but possible.

As near as we can tell from analyzing the manuscript, Willy and Carlotta escaped from the bunker on the 29th. At that time, Hitler was still there. It's possible, though, that it was earlier, even as early as the 25th. Willy simply is not clear.

Aunt Carlotta never mentioned a thing about any submarine escape. I never managed to speak about Hitler with Uncle Willy at all.

With her, when the name Hitler came up, she would grow sullen. She could not talk about him and look you in the eye at the same time.

"He was deranged," she would say. Or, "your uncle was very brave with him." She would say, "leave it alone, the past is the past." But as the boys grew up, their curiosity grew with them and the questions became more persistent.

One summer weekend when they were with her in Malibu, she got a little drunk. They both look in varying degrees enough like their uncle when he was young to cause her longing and uneasiness. They reported later that she began, very inappropriately, to flirt.

Willy, the oldest, attempted to turn this into a session of reminiscence about life in the Berghof. He had a little recording device in his pocket which he had shamelessly turned on. Not a nice thing to do, but it had a valuable result.

This is a transcript:

"Aunt Carlie, was the Berghof air conditioned?"

"All right, shut up, shut up! You and your questions, you fancy little pricks! Hitler was a demon so fucking awful that the devil kicked him out of hell. You think he killed himself? You think he's dead, even now? There are secrets so terrible that nobody's even gonna breathe. Evil so deep doesn't die easily. It's fungus, it's cancer.

"As for us, we were whores. Do you know what that means, you stupid fuckface? Clean up those pimples, Albert, you're gonna make the girls toss their cookies in your mouth when you kiss them.

"Well, a whore could kiss you and no matter all that facial festering. I could. Whores are people who are not considered people, not even by them. They're things. Understand this. Nothing more than things. Your dear revered uncle was called the Hitler fucker. And he did it. Sure, it was true. But is that so bad? He could do it and the old man was begging for it all the damn time. Willy could make love to a damn knothole in those days. He was unstoppable. He didn't care. He didn't care about morals either, no more than me.

"Do you even begin to understand? Look at your little faces. At least put your jaws in your pockets, don't leave them on my nice clean floor. Whores don't care. Understand that. So fine, he did it. Sure. As for me, what did I do? I did shit so bad you can't imagine it, you little pink American piggies. Sure I did, I was keeping myself alive. I was a fucking Jew in Hitler's house. So was he, for that matter. Don't stare at me like I'm in a goddamn zoo! This world is not what it seems. Nothing is what it seems. You rich kids, you wade in blood and walk on bones and you don't even know it. Such pitiful fucking little shits, you make me sick. (Laughs)

"We were whores and spies, using our beauty—and we were both goddamn beautiful—to get secrets for the allies. Whores and spies. Fuck us in the face, goddamnit! If war doesn't kill you, it turns you into a whore. That's what happened to exclusive-club silk suit Willy. As for me, I was gutter born and raised and I belonged in that Berghof, which was the gutter with polished knobs." (She falls silent. There is a crash. She has thrown her precious Statue of Liberty at Albert.) "Don't you ever make me go back there again, never, never, never! That is hell and it lives in me. It's in me, in me! Oh, boys, I'm sorry. Goddamnit Al, did I hurt you?"

She cries then, a howling agony. When you hear her do this, it's as if hell's door has opened and this is the sound that comes from within.

A few weeks later she was dining in Paris with me and Grace when she asked us, "What happens if I slap your kids completely senseless one of these days?"

Grace replied, "My children have never been struck."

"Well aren't they lucky, then."

I warned them that she was likely to become even more violent if they ever brought Hitler up with her again.

Now notice in the transcript where she seems to cast doubt on the suicide. "You think he killed himself? You think he's dead, even now? There are secrets so terrible that nobody's even gonna breathe."

At the time, the words went past me. They seemed figurative, no more. But when combined with Willy's comments about Hamburg and submarines, and now the new information that is coming to light, I found myself wondering what really did happen back then.

Willy's papers contain copies of *Kriegsmarine* mission orders for a number of submarines, including U-234, which he mentions specifically. At Yalta, Stalin told Truman and Churchill that Hitler had not died in the bunker, which eventually led to a MI-5 staff investigation and Hugh Trevor-Roper's book, *the Last Days of Hitler*.

Stalin's motive was apparently to keep the ghost of Hitler alive as a kind of bogeyman to frighten his various unruly subject nations into a sense of need for Soviet protection. His claims were, in other words, disinformation.

Subsequently, there have been numerous books about Hitler's possible survival. I have read a number of them and they don't really carry much conviction for me. For one thing, they have this desperately ill man traveling across half the world, ending up in places as diverse as the Andes and Indonesia. As Trevor-Roper says, "the desire to invent legends and fairy-tales...is greater than the love of truth."

In this era when even the President of the United States believes and repeats "fake news," that statement is worth calling to mind, and frequently.

There is a cottage industry of Hitler hunters writing books and making documentaries. One of them offers the opinion that Hitler died in 1980, at the age of 88! A more pessimistic author has the date as 1964. In truth, if the Hitler that Uncle Willy describes as he was in '45 had even lived another two years, it would have been a medical miracle.

An FBI document that was declassified in 2009 asserts that Hitler escaped to the Argentine. Its former secret status dignifies it with a sense of validation, but it reads strikingly like the stories that were being spread in 1945 and 1946 by the Soviets. Also in 2009, a skull fragment found in the garden of the *Fuhrerbunker* and long thought to be from Hitler's skull was discovered to be that of a woman. My guess is that it's from the skull of that simple, tragic figure, Eva Braun.

U-234 is interesting for another reason, and, I think, a more important one. It was carrying uranium—probably from the mine in New Mexico, in fact, shipped to Germany by Weber Sea Transport. While there has recently been a book published about the destruction of the heavy water plant at Vermok in Norway, nothing has as yet been explored about why the Germans would be trying at that late hour to send uranium to the Japanese. The full story of Axis attempts to build an atomic bomb is not known, and probably a worthy area of study.

As to Hitler's escape, he probably discussed it with Willy for the same reason that he encouraged Eva Braun to believe it. He wanted them to be compliant until it was too late and death could be forced on them. He would not have wanted any of the three of them to survive him, not a bit of it.

What did happen, though, is that many middle and some high ranking Nazis did escape. No question of that, and I fear that we may be just beginning to see their generations-long efforts to undermine western democracy bearing fruit. In recent years, the Nazi salute has appeared more and more in political rallies in more than one western country, including the United States.

I have so much less memory of Willy than I wish I did. Fleeting glimpses, only. His was an elegant face framed in my memory by white hair. There was an immediate impression of great gentleness.

I so wish that, at some point in his life, he had known inner peace. Both of them.

How ironic that Adolf Hitler gave them both everything they had and took it all away at the same time. I have hoped, actually, that there is an afterlife, so that Willy and Carlotta could be free at last of their regrets, and Hitler suffer his truth. I don't really believe in that sort of thing, though. Just wish. Hope, I suppose.

Typical of Uncle Willy, he left more than one instruction regarding the disposition of his remains. One scrawled note says, "Even though it gets worse every day, they can't find out what's wrong with me. I guess it's death I'm dying of. No diagnosis for that. Burn the corpse and scatter the ashes. That's where I belong, in the wind."

Another one says, "Put me in the mausoleum in the space just below Carlotta. Bury me with *Judea Capta* in my hand and my Eagle on my chest. I want both things to go into my grave with me, my honor and my dishonor."

Honor was central to Willy's inner meaning. He had been taught at his father's knee a version of it that seems to me to have been too rigid. On that night in '32 when his father found about the oath he had made to Hitler, he should have said to his son, "An oath made to a false man or an evil man does not carry any weight. Forget it." Instead, he insisted that the oath was unbreakable and that it had destroyed Willy. He disowned his poor boy.

So Albert Weber bears part of this burden, too. Such inflexibility can only come from an exaggerated sense of self-importance. To him and also to his son breaking an oath—any oath—was unthinkable, and that is wrong. Eventually, though, Uncle Willy saw beyond this, and thank god.

He has tried to make up for what he regarded as his fundamental failure. His foundation makes twelve million dollars in grants every year. He gives to Jewish causes small and large. The World Hunger Foundation, education, the list is long. After the war, he even gave to a charity that helped the survivors of German soldiers and another that did the same for British families who were left without a breadwinner. You can see in the record that he tried to find a way to help Russians and Poles but came up empty. All of this has been done in such a way that the actual man behind the charity cannot be seen, and we intend to continue to respect his diffidence.

We buried him as he instructed the second time, in the old mausoleum in St. Louis in the niche below Carlotta's. I laid his Nazi eagle on his chest and closed *Judea Capta* between his stiffening fingers. I felt then the last touch of his hand, cool, rigid, no longer really human. I imagine *Judea Capta* there now and always, and the eagle gathering mildew, its weight causing it to sink into him.

It's winter here in Stamford. It's been hot, now it's freezing in this era of deranged weather. But it's cold today and I'm enjoying that. The sun has set and there's a half moon hanging on the horizon.

Uncle Willy in his writings often mentions moonlight, so I went out, thinking to commune with his memory. I've just come in from a walk down our long road and back. Everything was palely shining with frozen dew. It was really quite magically beautiful.

Willy would have liked it, everything jeweled and shimmering in the quiet. He was a sacred being, a creature of light. They both were. That's the truth of it.

If there is something of us that lingers, then I wonder if they have found the same sort of peace with which my own heart surrounds their memory?

It's time at last to leave them behind in my mind, if not my heart. Never there, no.

I think that it is most appropriate to conclude their story with the closing lines of the poem that was so dear to both of them, Eliot's "Waste Land," which they considered the defining poem of our age.

From my youngest years, Aunt Carlotta could recite every line of it, and hearing her do that was an experience never to be forgotten. She was frustrated in her acting career, but she would have been an absolute genius. The words in her voice became what they were meant to be, living things concerned with the measure of our time in all its terrors and with the promise of peace beyond.

"These fragments I have shored against my ruins
Why then Ile fit you. Hieronymo's mad againe.
*Datta. Dayadhvam. Damyata.*
*Shantih shantih shantih*"

To that peace, *shantih*, the peace beyond understanding, I commend the memory and the souls of my beloved aunt and uncle, William and Carlotta Weber.

**The End**

CPSIA information can be obtained
at www.ICGtesting.com
Printed in the USA
LVHW051603300623
751030LV00009B/254

9 780985 813178